The Gorgon, a monstrous figure, thrashed against the icy grip that held it captive. Its serpentine body writhed and contorted, but the first clone, a cold, emotionless replica of Felix, held firm. With a sickening crunch of ice, the second clone lunged forward, its blades glinting in the dim light. It drove the blades deep into the Gorgon's chest, a grotesque sound echoing through the frigid air. The Gorgon's blood, a thick, dark liquid, splattered across the ice, staining it a sinister crimson. Its body slumped forward, a lifeless heap.

the Weavers

Ian Hart

Cover designed by Steve Bermundo
Published by Sphinx Publishing
.

ISBN-13: 979-8-9917303-1-0 (paperback)
ISBN: 979-8-9917303-0-3 (ebook)

DEDICATION

This book is dedicated to: Carla Web, Natasha Giles, Ric Parish, and Mark. W. Smith.

TABLE OF CONTENTS

Chapter 1

A Chrysalis

In a barren stone courtyard, a woman's figure could be made out in the moonlight. The moon was full, and not a single cloud blemished the night sky. She gazed up as the stone statues that stood guard peering down on her in all her finery. These statues, relics of her forebears, watched her with an eternal, stoic silence, as if poised to divulge their secrets should she dare to ask.

A chilling gust of wind stirred the last remnants of autumn leaves, sending them swirling into the air like ghostly fragments. The woman remained statuesque, her robes billowing outward with an almost otherworldly grace, and loose strands of her hair fluttered across her face in a tangled dance. Her gaze was fixed on the moon, which hung like a crystalline shard in the abyss of the night sky, ensnaring her in its hypnotic brilliance.

Her trance was abruptly broken by the sound of heavy, leathery footsteps echoing through the dimly lit corridor that snaked through the shadows. Her head tilted slightly, a movement that seemed both deliberate and instinctive, as if her very being were tethered to the stone beneath her. The footsteps grew louder, echoing through the cold air, and then suddenly ceased just inches from where she stood.

Emerging from the darkness was a man cloaked in a long, black hooded robe. The barren branches of a nearby leafless tree cast grim, skeletal shadows over them.

"Pray, do tell me, are you quite well?" she asked, her voice laced with an edge of unease.

The cloaked figure, his breath coming in ragged gasps, labored to regain his posture. "Yes, milady," he managed, though his voice betrayed his exhaustion.

"What did it impart to you?" Her eyes, dark pools of intensity, fixed on him with an unwavering, almost predatory focus.

"Milady, a portent has been bestowed," he replied, his breath still uneven as he struggled to regain composure.

Her eyes widened, then narrowed with impatience. "What did the leaves reveal to you?" she pressed, her tone sharp with urgency.

He inhaled deeply, steadying himself. "When the celestial spheres align amidst profound loss, curious and portentous events will surely follow! The leaves have prophesied of entities destined to face unimaginable grief: two formidable conflicts, four perilous trials, the interment of the desecrated, and a family fractured. A raven then descended, cawing its dire forewarning. I tarried not."

"Do we possess knowledge of those who shall bear these burdens?" she asked, her breath catching in her throat as she awaited his response.

The man lifted his head, his hood falling back to reveal a gaunt, hollowed face etched with lines of fear and despair. His ears, pointed and stark against the moonlit sky, lent him an almost otherworldly appearance. "Milady, this omen is a grievous curse upon the bearer—or bearers—whomever they may be. The foreboding I experienced whilst interpreting the leaves was most overwhelming."

As his words trailed off, their heads snapped toward the dimly lit corridor. The unmistakable sound of armored guards, their footsteps echoing like a relentless stampede, approached with alarming speed.

"You imbecile! We've been discovered!" she exclaimed, her eyes wide with dread. "We must make our departure at once! You shall take the northern route over the hills toward the Forest of Metus. I will follow the river to the west. It is imperative that we do not appear together."

With one last hurried glance, they slipped through the ajar gate and vanished into the darkness, their figures swallowed by the night.

"Time is a fleeting thing, never pausing for anyone. It barrels forward, regardless of what it encounters," Miss Hughes, an elderly woman with a gentle demeanor, explained.

In the foyer, Miss Hughes addressed a group of about thirty small, wide-eyed children, around seven and eight years old, who were visiting on a field trip with their teacher. The children's eyes wandered over the room, soaking in the many sights. They stood before the two enormous iron doors they had just passed through.

Noticing they were ready for her teachings, she continued warmly, "The only things we have to remind us of the past are these relics. We have preserved and cared for them for hundreds, even thousands of years. It is our duty—

which includes each of you—to cherish and pass down the stories of these precious pieces. These items are reminders of our diverse existence. Taking care of these moments in time will help those who come after us to understand who and what came before them. Such efforts will shape the world they live in."

From a young age, Miss Hughes felt a deep calling to educate future leaders and nurture the bright minds of this country.

She smiled at the chubby-cheeked children before her. "Come along, dear ones," she said, guiding them to the next exhibit.

They followed her down the long, dark marble hallway, where many more wondrous sights awaited. Long glass cases, stretching endlessly, lined the corridor. These cases ended at a grand stained-glass window depicting a meadow of rolling hills and flowers, with autumn leaves casting vibrant shadows through the multicolored glass.

Inside the cases were gem-encrusted necklaces, rings, tiaras, and other valuable trinkets. Each item was meticulously displayed with a small, cream-colored card detailing what the item was, what it was made of, and the origins of its design.

Further down the display, past the crowns, pendants, and oversized loose jewels, lay an egg the size of an over-inflated rugby ball. Upon closer inspection, the egg wasn't crafted from precious metals or gemstones like a Fabergé Egg. Instead, it was made of some kind of resin or crystal. Despite the lack of traditional precious materials, it was a wonder to behold. Peering into the egg gave the impression of gazing over a galaxy, with countless stars suspended in a milky-white cloud.

No card was placed next to the egg.

The class continued their tour, learning more about the museum's vault of knowledge until it was time to leave.

Every morning at 9:45 a.m., come rain or shine, the beloved tour guide, Miss Hughes, opened the museum doors to the public like clockwork. She had never missed a day. Even when she had her wisdom teeth removed, she showed up to work, though in pain and with her mouth full of cotton balls.

The museum was established in 1926, and it had only ever had two tour guides. Miss Hughes was the second. She began working at the museum in 1952, at seventeen, when she was a rosy-cheeked girl with long brown hair, always tied back in a ponytail. The locket she wore held a picture of her parents, Martha and Douglas Hughes—a sweet but plain-looking, hardworking couple.

Her favorite times were spent listening to the stories her father told while she sat on his knee. These stories were not fictional or mystical but gritty, factual accounts of war and great unrest, and they continued until his passing. His tales inspired her to work tirelessly at her job, day after day, year after year, without a single complaint. Miss Hughes never married or had children of her own. To her, life's work was learning and teaching anyone willing to listen.

One item that never moved or received much attention was the egg at the far end of the cases. It lay untouched except for the occasional polishing. No one knew where the egg came from or what it was made of. The only information available was that it had been purchased at an auction in England about eighty-five years ago by Marshall Grimsley for £215. The egg had been gifted to the museum after Mr. Grimsley, an art collector, passed away a few years prior. He had donated several valuable pieces of art and jewelry to the museum.

Lord Fedrick, a new arrival to town, arrived from South Africa a few decades ago. He was a short, stout man with a well-manicured mustache and normally dressed in a three-piece suit. His serious demeanor was complemented by a mane of white hair, and his face, etched with deep wrinkles, resembling a map of a river diverging into countless smaller streams.

Lord Fedrick quickly fell in love with the town's charm. Each week, he climbed the mountainside to gaze upon the town from above. He reveled in the sunrise as it bathed the city in its golden light. In his letters, he described the town as a town that got too big for its britches but decided not to get out of them. He invested a considerable fortune in the town, focusing his efforts on enhancing the school, the library, and his cherished sanctuary, the museum.

Lord Fedrick visited the museum daily, immersing himself in its history as though discovering it anew. Through his interactions with Miss Hughes and the groups of small children, he gained a deep affection for her. An eager student, as she fondly referred to him, he constantly sought more information about each exhibit they explored. Miss Hughes always responded with a warm smile.

Their bond grew into a treasured friendship, and they frequently spent lunchtime together in the park next to the museum. On a bench, they would discuss history and the world as they knew it. Miss Hughes confided in him her dream of visiting the Great Pyramids of Giza, the River Nile, and the treasures of the Far East. Yet, her commitment to the museum and the young minds she taught kept her firmly anchored to the town. She admitted that the stories Lord Fedrick enacted made her heart race, but she would never abandon her dedication to educating the eager students she encountered.

Miss Hughes was more popular than even the mayor. Everyone knew her, and it was likely that she had known most people since they were children. Well-respected and beloved by all, she was always smiling, even in the midst of a storm, knowing she would get wet walking home.

On December 29, she was making her usual four-block stroll to the museum. Snow had fallen overnight, blanketing the ground in white fluff. The falling snowflakes brushed gently against her cheeks as she briskly walked down the sidewalk.

To Miss Hughes's surprise, Greg Turner, a local store owner, bounded out of his car toward her. He was out of breath, his cheeks and nose flushed red.

"Good heavens, Gregory, what seems to be the matter?"

"Miss Hughes, you must come quickly," he replied. "Lord Fedrick is in the hospital. He's had a heart attack, and it looks bad!"

Gregory helped Miss Hughes, who was well into her eighties, across the icy street to his car. They rushed to the hospital in his old Cadillac, which sped off as a green blur, fishtailing in the slush on the road.

The hospital was about a mile away, on the other side of town. A few nurses on a break saw Miss Hughes outside and guided them through the swinging ER doors. The nurses didn't ask why Miss Hughes was there; they all knew about her friendship with the patient. They had even been voted the cutest couple in town for the past two years, despite never having been on a date. This news had made them both blush with innocence when they discovered they had been nominated and won.

The nurses led her to Lord Fedrick's room. When Miss Hughes entered, she gasped. No longer a man full of vigor, he now looked fragile and depleted. Before raising his hand, he turned his head slightly and gave her a longing gaze. As he did, his heart stopped beating, and his arm fell to his side. His once vibrant eyes, so full of life, darkened, as if he had become a withered puppet discarded to the side. Prior to seeing Miss Hughes, Lord Fedrick had requested not to be revived if his heart failed again as long as he had seen her. He wished to die with his last image being of her.

Miss Hughes lunged toward the bed, collapsing onto it as her hand clasped his lifeless body, pressing her cheek against the gown draped over him. Her unspoken love was gone. No more adventures, no more stories, no more Richard the Conqueror, and no more Lord Richard Daniel Fedrick— her unrequited love. Her knight in smooth, three-piece wool suits. The man who had made her days more joyous and special had left her.

Miss Hughes's well-worn face, lined with smile lines and crow's feet, now seemed to reflect a world stripped of its joy. Only death, misery, and sadness remained for her.

She got to her feet and lowered the side railing of the bed. Sliding off her shoes, she lay next to him. A genuine gentleman, a man she'd never kissed, a man she respected and cherished—her idol, her storyteller.

She closed his eyes with her fingers and kissed him on the lips and forehead, whispering in the softest voice, "There was no one before you, and there will be none after. My heart will forever be stitched to yours, Richard."

As she placed his hand on her chest, she closed her eyes and slipped away peacefully.

The doctor and three nurses initially didn't notice Miss Hughes's passing, focusing instead on the gentle and heart-wrenching gestures of a lady mourning her loved one.

The nurses were inconsolable, deeply feeling Miss Hughes's pain. They exited the room after the doctor gently asked them to give Miss Hughes some time to say her goodbyes.

About an hour later, Kellyanne, one of the nurses, went to check on Miss Hughes. When she received no response, she placed her hand on Miss Hughes and gasped at the cold flesh.

Kellyanne had known Miss Hughes since she was old enough to grasp the hands that tickled her belly as a baby. She had affectionately called Miss Hughes "Grandma." Raised by her single father after her mother died during childbirth, Kellyanne was the spitting image of her late mother, a fact that her father, Arthur Meyers, a hardworking mechanic, cherished. Arthur had always dressed Kellyanne like a doll and treated her like a princess, hoping she would become an educated lady—something he felt he could not provide for her.

Kellyanne, a redhead with porcelain-white skin, wore her hair in a ponytail just like Miss Hughes. She let out a heart-wrenching scream and slumped to her knees on the floor, tears streaming down her cheeks. The doctor and nurses who heard her distress rushed in to find her face contorted with sadness, her mouth silently mouthing the word "Why?" as saliva ran down her sides and snot oozed freely. They tried to console her, holding her tightly, unsure of what to do or say. They noticed Miss Hughes's lifeless body still clasping Lord Fedrick.

Miss Hughes had regularly checked on Kellyanne and Arthur, always ensuring they had everything they needed. When Kellyanne grew old enough to enjoy story time, Arthur would drop her off at the museum to listen to Miss Hughes's tales and assist her. As a child, Kellyanne would cling to Miss Hughes's skirt and follow her on guided tours. The exceptional stories Miss Hughes shared inspired Kellyanne to become a nurse, particularly the tales of wartime and how women played crucial roles in caring for the injured.

No one in town loved Miss Hughes more than Kellyanne. She never missed an opportunity to send a gift or a card, letting "Grandma" know how much she was loved and missed. In return, Miss Hughes would send lengthy handwritten letters detailing the joy Kellyanne brought her, often mentioning a fresh batch of caramel and marshmallow cookies waiting for her on the kitchen counter. Kellyanne knew her adopted grandma appreciated the small gifts, even though they saw each other daily and lived next door to each other.

This dreadful day made the entire town come to a halt, mourning as if their collective heart had been wrenched from its chest. Never before had the town wept so deeply, and it continued to grieve for two weeks following their profound loss.

No happiness, joy, or laughter was heard. Even when new life entered the world, the town showed little emotion. New mothers and fathers welcomed their babies, but the town remained somber. To them, Miss Hughes was a mother, a sister, an aunt, a grandma, and, most importantly, a steadfast friend. She was the one who always had the answers. The town's unshakable pillar had been taken from them. Miss Hughes was now like sand, scattered by the wind, never to be seen again. The town was crippled at its core.

A storm erupted that night, with freezing sleet and chaotic winds whipping about with no rhyme or reason. The storm violently stripped the last dead leaves from the trees, leaving them bare and exposed. Power lines swung wildly back and forth, and the streetlamps shuddered against the storm's fury.

Inside the museum, large lights resembling dandelion puffballs pulsated with a steady glow. They were suspended from the ceiling by long bronze stems adorned with intricately scrolled leaves, casting their light along the long corridor lined with glass cases.

Outside, Neptune, which was normally invisible to the naked eye at night, glowed like a tiny blue bead. It was as though the storm mirrored the town's collective emotions—confused, burdened, angry, and saddened. The moon, making its way across the sky, was about to eclipse Neptune's light as if to hide it from the world. When the moon obscured the tiny light, something inexplicable occurred: the moon glowed a soft blue, amplifying Neptune's light. This beam of light filtered through one of the green panes of glass and focused on the solitary egg. As the light touched the egg, its shell began to shift, as if it were a larva in a cocoon. The shimmering specks of color inside pulsated, and within moments, the shell transformed into a soft ivory blanket adorned with small crystals and pieces of mother-of-pearl.

The blanket revealed a precious item at its center—a sleeping baby.

The baby had chubby cheeks, black hair, and skin as pale as alabaster. The pillow within the case provided a comfortable bed for the sleeping infant, completing the egg's transformation and revealing its secret.

As the storm subsided, the clouds reclaimed their rightful place. The moon continued its path across the night sky, and the once-visible blue bead of Neptune faded from view behind the cloud cover. The town was quiet and still, with only a few streetlamps casting their light. The harsh wintry night gave way to the brilliant morning sun, which began its work of melting the snow deposited the night before.

The next morning, red-eyed and heartbroken, Kellyanne took the day off work and visited the one place she knew better than anyone else in town now—the museum. She wanted to relive the times she had spent there as a child, recalling the tales of bravery and heroism that Miss Hughes had shared with her.

Kellyanne climbed the icy steps of the museum. As she reached the top, she grabbed for the door but found it locked. Grandma wasn't there to greet her inside as she had in the past. Overwhelmed by deep sadness, Kellyanne wiped away the tears that had started to flow.

She reached into her coat pocket and fumbled around for her keys until she found the one Miss Hughes had given her when Kellyanne was studying for college classes. The large, old key, still surprisingly shiny for its age, fit into the lock. Kellyanne turned it and pushed the bar down to open the door. The sound of the hinges echoed through the great hall. The only other sound was Kellyanne's soft footsteps.

The emptiness of the museum was unsettling. Her somber stroll down the hall, taking in all the familiar sights, was tinged with melancholy. She ran her hands over every glass case she passed, peering into them. Her long gaze allowed her to remember everything Grandma had told her, and her eyes welled up with tears that wouldn't stop.

When she reached the far end of the hall, where the stained-glass window depicted flowers swaying gently, memories flooded her mind. But suddenly, her head spun, and her eyes widened in horror. She staggered backward into the potted ferns, then pulled herself up and peered into the case, tapping the glass. The arm of a sleeping baby shifted inside. Kellyanne frantically tried to lift the lid, but it wouldn't budge.

She dashed down the hall and out the front door, almost slipping on the steps. Sprinting the four blocks to Grandma's house, she ran up the front porch and plunged her hand into her pocket, fumbling through the keys until she found the right one. She opened the door and rushed to the roll-top desk where the museum keys were kept. She grabbed them quickly, glancing at a small, oval-shaped picture frame of her and Miss Hughes taken on her high school graduation day. Without a second thought, she placed the picture into the interior pocket of her long gray coat.

Kellyanne hopped into her 1981 dark blue Camaro and sped off to the museum. The streets were quiet; children were in school, and the cold kept most people indoors.

Arriving at the museum, she raced inside to the information desk, grabbed the phone behind one of the placards, and dialed the police to report the situation. Then she hurried back through the long corridor, trying each key on the case imprisoning the baby. After about fourteen tries, the lock finally popped open.

As she lifted the lid, she heard muffled sirens approaching outside. Reaching in for the now-awake baby, she heard several heavy footsteps heading toward her.

"Kellyanne, what's going on?" an officer shouted.

She unbuttoned her coat and tried to explain what she had seen. Carefully wrapping the baby in the blanket she found with him, she placed the baby into her warm coat.

The officers had all known Kellyanne since childhood. They remembered her as the little girl with a light-red ponytail and well-defined freckles. She was the same girl who had helped them study in school. Will, Berk, Seth, and Darrin were all good friends of Kellyanne.

She had been there for each of them and their wives, welcoming their children into the world—except for Berk, since he and his partner had no children.

Will and Darrin went to check the museum's cameras to see how the child got locked in the case and if anything had been stolen.

Once outside, Kellyanne grabbed the railing to keep from slipping while holding the baby. Berk opened the door to one of the two police cars, and Kellyanne slid across the back seat with him. Seth then escorted the group to the hospital through the slush.

As they drove toward the hospital, the baby tugged on the small picture frame in Kellyanne's pocket, glancing at it before putting it into his mouth. Berk smirked, noticing the baby gnawing at the frame, and said, "He must be hungry."

Kellyanne tried to focus on what Berk pointed out, but her grief still consumed her, and a smile would not grace her face for some time. After multiple stints in the labor ward, she realized something was not normal about this baby. The motor skills the baby was displaying were not typical for his age. With a gentle tug, she pulled the picture frame out of the baby's mouth and placed it into her side pocket.

They soon reached the hospital and were greeted by several nurses who were taking a break outside.

"Could you page the doctor?" Kellyanne asked. "We need to have this baby checked out."

"Is he yours?" one of the new nurses asked.

"Well, no, we have no clue. We don't know who he belongs to. The police are investigating."

"Where did you find the baby?" another nurse asked.

"Kellyanne discovered this little stowaway in the museum, locked in one of the cases," Berk answered.

The nurse was dumbfounded and in shock. "Locked in a case? Oh, dear Lord," she gasped.

Without hesitation, the nurse brought them to an examination room.

A few minutes later, a doctor arrived. "What's the matter?"

Kellyanne placed the baby on the exam table.

Dr. Lance Clark leaned forward and examined the baby. "Nothing seems to be wrong with him," he said. "I would like to run some tests, which shouldn't take more than a few hours, to make sure he's as healthy as he seems."

Berk and Seth headed to the police station to write their report. Berk filled out the paperwork while Seth reviewed open reports online, searching for any missing persons cases or baby abductions filed in the past few weeks, even though the baby appeared to be just born. Seth found nothing.

Will and Darrin then returned to the department to report that nothing was missing except for the egg. The police department issued an announcement to local radio stations that a baby boy had been found and they were trying to locate his parents. They also called surrounding hospitals to check if there were any recent births that were not yet accounted for.

"So, who's going to be monitoring this little one?" Dr. Clark asked as he spooned pudding he'd purchased from the hospital cafeteria out of a cup.

Kellyanne, still holding the child, glanced at Dr. Clark.

Several hours later, tests confirmed the baby's clean bill of health.

Chapter 2
A Home

The news ran a story about the child. Almost a week had passed, but no one had come forward. The police department's efforts had led them nowhere, and no one responded to the radio announcements.

Kellyanne's father, Arthur, stopped by frequently during that week to check on her and the baby. Now retired from the garage he had owned and operated for years, he had plenty of time on his hands.

"Don't you think you should name my new grandson?" he joked.

Arthur had been bugging her about marrying her long-time boyfriend and having children he could spoil. She'd always responded with, "I have no time for kids," but this time she cried. "They wouldn't be able to meet Grandma."

"You're exhausted," Arthur said, getting up from his chair. He embraced his crying daughter and kissed her on the forehead. "You'll be all right. Grandma would want you to be happy and live a full and exciting life. She's still with you. She'll always be in your heart and on your mind. She'll guide you and your actions without you ever knowing, because she taught you how to be a smart and kind person."

"It's getting late. I should start heading home," he added.

Kellyanne stood up, placing her free arm around Arthur's waist while resting her head on his shoulder as they walked to the front door. "I'll think about it, Papa, but no promises."

She kissed him on the cheek, and in return, he gave her a tight bear hug. Arthur leaned in and, as softly as he could, tickled the baby's belly. The two then exchanged "I love yous" and parted ways.

Kellyanne headed upstairs and got both herself and the baby ready for bed. She pulled open the top dresser drawer and placed a soft blanket inside. She laid the baby down to rest, and he was soon out like a light.

Unlike the baby, Kellyanne was a light sleeper.

A week later, Kellyanne decided that the Kennedy House, the once state-run orphanage now operating as a foster home one county over, should take the child. She wasn't ready to commit to raising him.

After breakfast and a bottle of formula, she wrapped the child in the blanket she had found him in, then grabbed the hospital documents and a few bottles of formula from the kitchen counter. Kellyanne placed a small knit cap on his head.

Securing the baby in the car seat, the pair headed to the Kennedy House, seventeen miles away.

The roads were icy, and navigating the bends and hills was daunting. Stepping out of the car in her winter boots onto the shoveled pathway sprinkled with rock salt, Kellyanne reached for the baby and the few items she'd brought with her.

At the front door, she rang the doorbell.

A tall, thin man with broad shoulders answered. He wore a wide grin and a goofy Christmas sweater, even though it was past Christmas. Attached to his legs were a set of twins covered in moles, holding each other's hands. A tall boy peeked his head around the door, while a moody younger boy stood behind them with his arms crossed in the hallway.

"You must be Kellyanne. And that's the little one?" he asked.

"Correct on both," Kellyanne replied quickly, handing over the baby, the legal paperwork, and her notes. "I'm sorry, but I must rush off. I'm due at work in an hour."

The handful of children ran around his feet, all trying to get a glance at the bundle she had just placed in his arms.

As Kellyanne hurried back to her running car and pulled out of the driveway, the tall man watched with a look of befuddlement, wondering why she seemed to be fleeing.

Chapter 3

Family

Henry Pines and his wife, Laura, ran the house, a couple dealing with personal tragedies. Their unhappy marriage was not the result of anything they had done but was rooted in a profound loss. Despite this tragedy, the couple remained committed to their goal of raising a large family. Laura Pines had suffered a devastating miscarriage a year and a half into their marriage. Further complications meant Laura could no longer have children, prompting Henry to quit his job as an electrician and take the position as head of the Kennedy House. Since her miscarriage, Laura had been in a deep depression, often resorting to self-harm as a means of coping. Taking on the position allowed Henry to be near his beloved wife so he could monitor her and ensure she didn't do anything drastic.

Laura Pines was a small, pale woman with pale yellow hair and eyes filled with eternal sadness. After the loss of their unborn baby boy, she flinched when Henry touched her, except during rare moments of consolation. She felt like a failure and believed she was the ruin of their hopes and dreams. Now, she focused on the children at the Kennedy House to distract herself from her pain and to keep the dark thoughts at bay.

Henry, with sandy-blond hair, deep blue eyes, and a scruffy face, tried to bring joy into their lives. He was always striving to put a smile on Laura's face and make the children laugh. Together, they were sweet and loving.

Henry brought the baby into the parlor and, with a silly expression, interrupted the reruns of old black-and-white cartoons playing on the TV. "Is everyone ready to see what's for dinner?" he asked. His comment made Laura snort with laughter and the children giggle.

There were twelve children, not including the newcomer: Bobby, Chance, Emma, French, Jackson, Matthew, Milly, Mitch, Orchid, Rose, Sabrina, Theodore, and Trisha. Their ages ranged from two to twelve years old.

The group had its variety of characters, including Mitch, the loner; French, the book nerd; Sabrina, the hippy; Jackson, the problem child; and Theodore, the glutton. Navigating such a gamut of personalities was a task for anyone, but they worked together like a well-oiled machine. The reasons for the children coming to the home were varied, but with compassion, guidance, and discipline, they were growing up happy and healthy. Each child had their own take on the new arrival—some were excited, while others were not so pleased.

The Kennedy House had two pets: a cat and a dog. Betty was an orange tabby who silently roamed the halls and would try to lie on the children's faces, almost smothering them. Then there was Grumpy, a fawn-colored pug who, crotchety and old, only showed affection to Laura.

Henry placed the baby on Laura's lap. As he did so,

Grumpy woofed in irritation, displeased with the new addition to the house.

Betty the cat sat perched on top of a bookcase, surveying the activities in the room.

"Why do we have to eat him? I thought you said it was tomato soup and grilled cheese night," Chance said.

Laura patted Chance on the head and laughed. "No, of course not. We must fatten him up before we can eat him!"

French spoke up. "Isn't that the baby they were talking about on the radio for the past week or two?"

Henry and Laura nodded.

Chance frowned. "Does he have a name, and does he need a big brother?"

"I think he does need a big brother," Henry said. "Do you think you can handle the task? And why don't we name him now, since the paperwork that came with him is pretty much blank?" This was a way to help all the children connect with the new arrival.

Names came spilling out: Spike, Barney, Batman, Charmander, Superman, Jacob, Teddy, Pants, and Socks.

Sabrina commented, "Pants and Socks isn't a name! Jasper is a good name."

Henry noticed that Chance, the youngest, hadn't said a word. He was lost in thought. "Hey, Chance, what do you think?"

Chance, speechless for the first time in his life, thought for a few seconds before the name Felix slipped from his mouth.

"Why Felix, Chance?" the Pines asked.

Chance responded, "Well, everyone here likes Felix the Cat. He makes us all giggle!"

The rest of the children chimed in, "Yeah!"

Laura's eyes brightened. "Felix it is!" she replied, gazing

down into Felix's big gray eyes.

Henry began sorting through the paperwork. "Well, we've got his first name, so we just need to fill out the rest. Any ideas for the last name?"

Before any of the children could speak, Laura, still looking into the baby's eyes, said, "Grey! Felix Grey. Welcome, Felix, to your new home," she whispered.

"Felix Grey it is," Henry said, searching the cabinet drawers for a pen.

With the initial excitement over, the children snuggled up at the feet of the Pines on the big shaggy rug and watched morning cartoons.

Chance put his head next to Felix's, staring into his eyes, and said in a tender tone, "I'm going to be the best big brother you ever had."

Chapter 4
A Partnership

A few years passed, and a brotherhood formed between Chance and Felix since neither of the boys had been adopted. The Pines would have loved to adopt the pair, but Laura did not pass the social worker's interviews. Since the two boys were not old enough to attend school—Chance was four and Felix was two—they spent much of their time watching old movies, potting plants, and preparing seedlings for the garden in the hothouse with Henry. Strangely, everything Felix helped plant grew bigger and healthier than anything Henry could produce alone.

When the boys were not with Henry, they were doing arts and crafts with Laura. Felix, still a toddler, often made a mess with the paint and glue. However messy he made it, his creations always ended up looking better than anything Chance could produce on paper.

As winter turned to spring, the snow melted to reveal bright green grass, and the estate transformed from a winter wonderland into a bloom-filled paradise. The front lawn was overgrown with lilac bushes bearing purple and white flowers. Even the Italian cypresses that grew between the windows soared toward the sky. The flowerbeds that curved and shaped the front yard were planted with white and purple flowers.

Henry took the boys out to the backyard to work on the veggie patch. On the first day of spring, they started working. Henry tilled the hard ground to soften it and prepare it for planting. The freshly overturned soil provided fun for the two boys as they went to each mound to collect worms for Henry. Chance had a tough time grabbing the worms and pulling them out of the soil, but Felix, with his nimble fingers, never tore one in half. The worms slid out easily, as if the tunnels had been buttered. Henry would either use them for fishing or put them in the hothouse for the flowerpots. Next to the tilled earth was a large hothouse where Henry grew some of the most beautiful flowers for Laura. Every day, Henry cut only the most spectacular specimens for her. In the middle of the hothouse was a small stone pond with water lilies and koi fish.

Chance and Felix liked to play near a large maple tree at the back of the property. Located a few hundred feet from the woods, it gave the boys privacy from the rest of the household. An old tire swing hung from the maple tree, and they would pretend to be pirates.

Chance always did the talking while Felix just listened. Oddly, at age two, Felix still hadn't uttered a single word. He only communicated through smiles or frowns. Felix had been seen by a case worker and Dr. Clark. Everything appeared fine—no abnormalities or developmental disorders. He was developing into a healthy young boy with a most amicable demeanor. Felix grinned more than he frowned, and most of his time was spent playing with Chance. The

majority of the household thought his way of communicating was quite unusual.

After a few hours of playing, Henry called the two boys
into the house. He had been sitting on the porch for a little
more than an hour, watching them run around and con-
quering the grass "seas" of the backyard. They headed back
to the house.

Henry asked, "Find any treasure in them thar seas?"

"No," Chance replied before launching into a tale of how
at least twenty cutthroat turncoats had surrounded them.
The story continued: "All was lost until quick thinking and
cannon fire by Felix saved the SS Winnie the Pooh and her
crew."

Henry lifted both boys into his arms with a huge grin.
"Well, you must be some starving sailors then?"

Felix, with energy to spare, nodded, while Chance replied, "Yes, we must regain our strength to be ready for the
return of the mighty pirate king."

"Who's that?" asked Henry.

"Oh, we don't dare speak his name too loudly. Legend
has it that calling out his name will summon him and his
pirate horde." He then whispered into Henry's ear, "Bad
Bones Magruen."

Chance then switched back to speaking in his normal
voice. "He's the captain of the Canned Spinach."

When Felix heard the words "canned spinach," he jerked
back violently as a reaction. When he saw or smelled canned
spinach, he would heave. Even now, hearing the words made
him grimace and cringe, recalling how he had convulsed
when they first attempted to feed it to him. Canned spinach
had never been seen in the house since.

"Oh, no! The crew of the Canned Spinach must never
return!" Henry exclaimed. He thought all the reading he and

French had been doing was paying off, as Chance's vocabulary was becoming quite extensive.

The boys made it into the kitchen, and before Laura could mention it, they slipped off their shoes and hugged her legs as she scrubbed some pots and pans from earlier in the day. Her mood softened, and the corners of her lips began to curl. "Why don't you boys go watch some TV?"

Chance helped Felix onto the burnt-orange couch in front of the TV in the parlor. Felix passed out on Chance's stomach as he crawled up onto him like a lap dog, and Chance soon followed suit.

A little while later, noticing there was no noise from the TV or the two boys, Laura went to check on them. She found them sound asleep, like a picture from an adorable postcard.

She tiptoed over, took an afghan off the back of the couch that she had crocheted a few years earlier, and laid it over them.

Laura had already placed dinner in the oven, slow-cooking it for that night. On the menu was baked spaghetti with extra veggies and breadsticks, and for dessert, chocolate mousse with fresh blueberries. This was the last meal before the school year ended, so she made sure it was something the whole household would enjoy.

All the children were off for the summer, and no summer jobs or trips were planned. As tradition dictated, they would pitch a few tents out back near the koi pond, and Henry would teach them life skills he had learned as an Eagle Scout. The children loved this time of year. They got to play all day, except for two hours of mandatory study, because education was important to the Pines, even when school wasn't in session.

In the evenings, when things were winding down, the

boys would collect wood for the fire while the girls went inside to help make and deliver thermoses of hot chocolate to the bonfire. Henry read aloud to the whole group. During the day, sometimes French didn't want to play games, so he would read adventure stories like *Robinson Crusoe* aloud to Orchid, Milly, and Trisha. On occasion, when Chance and Felix weren't saving everyone from the cutthroat pirates, they would sit and listen in. The rest of the children played hide and seek and tag.

This was Theodore's least favorite time of year because the kitchen was off-limits. It was also the time of year he lost the most weight.

Henry took this time to let Laura relax and focus on things she wanted to get done. The only two major tasks Laura had daily during the summer months were making the food and doing the laundry. These limited tasks freed her time up to paint or knit. She had been painting since she was a young girl and was quite accomplished, but she never pursued her talent aggressively. Laura was never one to seek the spotlight—her modesty was one of the things Henry fell in love with. When she wasn't painting, she would hop on her old bike and ride down the dirt roads. She especially enjoyed the one lined with flowering myrtle trees in early summer. She biked alone to the local ponds and freshly tilled fields. There was a pasture with a herd of Jersey milking cows, and she would stop there. The cows knew she would show up daily at that specific section of the fence, where she spent a few minutes petting them. She loved animals.

After spending time with the cows, she would head down the road to another field, this one a horse ranch. Horses were one of her favorite animals. If she had any extra apples or carrots, she would pack them into a bag and take them on her rides. She fed the apples and carrots to the horses while patting and scratching their necks. Her favorite was a dapple-gray stallion with a dark-gray body and bright white freckles on his hindquarters. She nicknamed him Apollo, and just being there with him often placed her in a trance-like state.

During their time off, Henry and Jackson would go into the woods that lined the property, hunting for small woodland creatures, which Henry grilled for dinner. This had two benefits: it reduced the amount of money spent on groceries and focused Jackson's energies away from mischief. That summer, they killed seven woodchucks, four turkeys, thirteen rabbits, more than forty frogs, two opossums, a dozen pigeons, one raccoon, and fifty-two squirrels. Quite a catch!

The two also went fishing in the creek, which yielded dozens of fish. Henry liked to BBQ during the warmer months, and the only catch that escaped the fire was the turkeys—they met the oven inside Laura's kitchen that year. Laura ended up making homemade turkey pot pies for everyone, and anything else was used as lunch meat for the kids. The scraps went to Betty and Grumpy, who enjoyed every morsel.

The summer went on as if it were a never-ending camp for kids to discover themselves. All the children grew. It was at least a vacation from their realities, which were not too bad (emotional issues aside—being an orphan was not easy for a child to deal with), and they all bonded. Even a few children who were awaiting the courts to grant custody to their parents and guardians had made brief stays at the

Kennedy House. This ruffled some feathers, particularly with Bobby, and even more so with Jackson.

During that summer, a young couple stopped by a social worker. They had applied to adopt a child. Mrs. Lawrence had fallen in love with Emma from the pictures she'd seen and the stories she'd heard. Emma's curly light-brown hair was in pigtails, and her big brown eyes gave her the appearance of a doll. After a few months of applying and getting approved, they came to pick her up.

All the children were crying except Jackson and Felix.

Once again, Jackson was at the back of the pack with clenched fists. Felix felt intense energy coming from him.

Jackson glared at Felix, still full of resentment, just as he had when Felix first arrived. The real reason Jackson could not stand Felix was that, since Felix's arrival, he had been the catalyst for change. Jackson was receiving less attention from the other children and the Pines. He had just found his spot, and it suited him. When Felix arrived, it disrupted the routine he had become accustomed to.

Jackson then said in a vicious and quiet voice, "Why can't they take you? Your parents didn't want you—they left you at a museum and wanted nothing to do with you!"

Everyone hugged and kissed Emma goodbye. Laura's face was damp from joy instead of sadness, knowing Emma was going home to a good couple who would love her. The Lawrence couple was elated to finally be parents but sad that the children were losing a friend.

As Emma gave a final hug to everyone, the Pines and the children all exited the house before the new family hopped into the car and drove away. Emma knelt in the back seat, waving goodbye from the rear window.

As Felix waved goodbye, he wondered, If this isn't my family, who are these people, and where are my parents? Why didn't they want me?

The Kennedy House felt a little empty for the rest of that summer.

Chapter 5

Bosom Buddies

Summer turned into fall, and that meant another school year. This was a special year for Chance—he would be at school and not with Felix.

Sabrina had taught Felix to nod for "yes" and shake his head for "no," but he still did not use words. The household didn't make a big deal of it, as the children already blabbered and talked back too much for Laura's liking.

"It's time to go to bed."

"No!"

"It's time to get up."

"No!"

"You must eat your veggies."

"No!"

Chance was a blabbermouth and found it difficult to stay quiet. Felix, however, was especially good at listening and followed Chance around like a puppy. The two were inseparable. They ate, slept, bathed, and played together like twins.

The other children adored Felix, even though most of his time was monopolized by Chance. Felix enjoyed helping others. Rose and Orchid dressed him up like a princess and had tea parties with him. Felix never complained. He would carry French's books around when French needed an extra pair of hands—after first getting permission from Chance to borrow him.

Chance loved Felix like a little brother, even though he didn't understand that the word "love" had multiple meanings. Chance used different words to try to describe his feelings—such as "best friend" and "little brother," thinking that love was only between a boy and a girl. Girls were gross to Chance, so the idea of describing his feelings for Felix as love never crossed his mind.

Before the start of the school year, the two boys didn't sleep much. Every time Chance mentioned school, Felix shook his head "no." Chance, like a big brother, comforted him and told him it was only for seven hours and that he would be back home before long. Felix was still distraught.

On the eve of the school year's commencement, exhaustion overtook the boys, and Felix succumbed to sleep, his head drooping as he nodded off. When morning arrived, Chance slipped out of bed to avoid disturbing a sleeping Felix before getting ready for school.

As he finished taking a shower, Felix stood in the doorway with panic etched into his face. Still in his T-shirt and underwear, Felix grabbed Chance's hand and wouldn't let go, making it hard for Chance to get dressed.

The two made their way to breakfast.

Henry noticed Felix wasn't touching his food. "Hey,

Chance, what's going on with Felix? Is he not feeling well?"

Chance, chewing his cereal, glanced over at Henry before swallowing. "He doesn't want me going to school and leaving him behind. He's been squeezing the blood out of my hand ever since I finished taking a shower," Chance said, raising his hand with Felix's still attached.

Henry and Laura tried to console Felix, reassuring him that everything would be fine. But no matter what they said, Felix wasn't willing to accept the reality of the situation. He knocked his food off the table, throwing a tantrum, on the verge of tears. This was the first fit they had ever witnessed from Felix, so when it happened, the Pines and the children were shocked.

Breakfast ended, and everyone finished their food except Felix. He didn't touch a single berry in his bowl when it was replaced. He switched to a tighter grip on Chance's shirt, tugging on it as if he could keep him there.

The children's school lunches were packed and resting on the kitchen counter, all labeled in brown paper bags. Lunch that day consisted of peanut butter and raspberry jam sandwiches, string cheese, an apple, and fifty cents for milk. Laura hurried everyone to get ready to catch the bus, but with Felix still attached to Chance's shirt, it made it difficult for Chance to put on his backpack.

The sun hadn't yet risen, and it was pitch black outside that morning. The inhabitants of the Kennedy House heard the rumbling and saw the bright yellow beams of light from the bus's headlights as it came rolling down the street.

The children walked to the edge of the driveway and lined up. Chance dragged a panicked Felix across the lawn. This didn't make Chance happy, seeing Felix's anxiety, but he knew he had to go.

Laura took hold of Felix's free hand and tore him away from Chance. The shirt now resembled a shirt several sizes larger than the one Chance had put on, stretched out from Felix's tugging.

Felix wept for the first time in his life. The streams rushing down his red cheeks flooded his face like a river's banks bursting. No other time had such intense emotion escaped the young boy; it was as if his soul was being sucked out of him.

Chance boarded the bus, and the door closed. Chance turned around to say goodbye, waving and mouthing the words "don't worry" as the bus sped off.

The fear and sadness on Felix's face quickly turned into fury, and the tears continued to flow. He let out a howling scream. "Noooooooooo!"

This was the first time Felix had spoken, and the word sent a shiver down Laura's spine. Seizing the opportunity to escape, Felix chased after the bus. Unfortunately, he was too small and slow to catch up, and he screamed again, "Noooo!"

Hearing the anguished cry, Henry ran out of the house to see what had happened. Felix was out of breath and sobbing uncontrollably.

"What happened?" Henry asked.

Laura, still in shock, could only stammer the words Felix had spoken.

Henry replied, "He's just being a boy. He'll have to grow up eventually. This is just another stepping stone."

Laura called out to Felix to come back, but he was still in a rage. It was a fight-or-flight situation for Felix, and all he could do was run and hide. He made a sharp turn and sped off toward the backyard. Laura started after him.

But Henry grabbed her arm and said, "Don't worry about

it. Felix is a good boy. He's probably just headed to the back-yard. Let him cool down, and he'll come in when he's hungry. He always shows up around mealtime."

Persuaded by his words, Laura went inside.

After waiting for some time to see if Felix would re-appear, the Pines closed the door and went to the kitchen for a cup of coffee. There were a few berry scones left that hadn't been gobbled up by the children, and the Pines stared at each other in silence as they broke the scones apart and devoured them. As Laura Pines sipped her peach blossom tea, she finally agreed with Henry about Felix needing to grow up. Even though Felix was past the terrible twos, which had been a breeze for the Pines, Laura worried about him being outside alone in the dark. She rubbed the tips of her fingers together nervously.

"Are you okay, Laura?" Henry asked, putting down his coffee.

"I think so. I'm just worried, that's all. I know he needs to grow up, but he's not like other children. He's thought-ful and caring. It's as if he is a little adult with the patience and understanding of a senior when he's dealing with the other children. I wish he could speak so he could tell us what he's thinking, but that would take away from what makes him so special."

Felix made his way to the backyard, paused, and sur-veyed the area while formulating a plan of action. His stom-ach grumbled. Feeling the need to hide, he slipped into the vegetable patch, which was still being harvested. He felt around until he could tell what he was touching, then grabbed a few root vegetables and pocketed them. Still on edge and making sure he wasn't being watched, he headed toward the hothouse. He opened the door and quickly slipped inside without being seen.

The hothouse was dark. To ensure he was unnoticed by the Pines, Felix closed the door behind him. As he turned, his face brushed against a large, delicate flower, which puzzled him. It was something he hadn't expected, causing him to stop and ponder for a moment. He figured it was a flower because a sweet fragrance wafted through his nostrils, but Henry hadn't planted any flowers near the door of the hothouse—at least not that he could remember, and he knew almost every inch of the hothouse.

This was the first time he'd been in the hothouse alone. Henry always supervised the children when they were inside. Unable to see well, Felix got on his hands and knees and crawled to the back corner where three large potted flowering bushes, big enough to hide behind, were located.

As he crawled past the small fishpond filled with koi, he heard bubbling sounds that seemed like a bunch of small voices trying to speak while drowning. Still angry and upset, Felix was determined to find a hiding place. When he reached the three pots in the back of the hothouse, he ducked under the flowers and made his way to the back of the pots before lying on the chilly cement.

Exhausted from the lack of food, the running, and the energy spent from his rage, Felix decided to take a nap. The sun's morning rays illuminated the sky but had yet to crest the mountaintop. Trees and buildings were barely recognizable, as if it were twilight, giving the landscape a crisp, mysterious quality.

When he woke, Felix got back on his hands and knees, retrieved the soiled vegetables from his pockets, and made his way back to the pond where he had heard the strange bubbling sounds. He dipped the vegetables into the water and brushed off the soil, cleaning them as best as he could. He had two medium-sized carrots and a handful of radishes. He nibbled on a carrot while stewing in his anger and frustration. He was alone and didn't like it at all.

At school, Chance found the class exciting for the first hour or so. He enjoyed meeting new people and exploring unfamiliar places; however, once the initial excitement wore off, school became dull, making him feel trapped in a new, foreign prison. Even Chance's teacher noticed the shift in his mood. While the other children played, Chance stared at the clock as if each tick of the second hand dragged on for an eternity.

The other children from the Kennedy House were having a great time reconnecting with classmates they hadn't seen over the summer. They re-established bonds and chatted about everything that had happened during the three summer months. The extra studying over the break ensured that the Kennedy House children wouldn't forget the lessons they had learned the previous year and would even be ahead in more advanced subjects compared to their peers.

Jackson, on the other hand, was sent to the principal's office for skipping math class and hiding in the janitor's closet.

Chance's teacher wasn't sure if he was depressed or ill, but she knew something was off. He completed all his assignments well, and when the class was asked to write the alphabet, he wrote it in cursive, hoping this would make the time pass more quickly. He wondered if having Felix there with him would make school better. He felt lonely without his little brother and knew Felix would be feeling the same way. Chance wondered what Felix was doing. Is Felix missing me as much as I miss him?

When recess arrived, Chance followed the teacher and the rest of the students outside. While the other children interacted with each other, Chance removed himself and found the largest tree to sit under. One of the boldest girls ran up to him and kissed his cheek. He responded by glaring forward with a blank expression, avoiding eye contact. This was unusual since girls generally grossed him out. At the Kennedy House, when girls kissed him on the cheek, his reaction was, "Ewww!" followed by throwing up his arm and saying, "That's not fair!"

Lunchtime was similar to recess for Chance. He took his lunch to the farthest table and ate alone. The only thing that held his attention was the ticking of the clock. After the first hour or so, he had formulated a plan: he would run to the cubbies where his backpack was, bolt straight to the bus, and grab the first seat. This would allow him to be the first person off the bus when it reached its destination. He needed to get home as if his life depended on it—the only problem being there were still several hours until the bus ride back home.

Meanwhile, Felix had a very different experience that day. As the sun crept over the mountaintop, making its way to the waking town, it reflected off the dewy grass and rooftops of Kennedy House, giving the sleeping property a feeling of new life and possibilities.

The Pines were cleaning the house while a moody Felix lay passed out on the hothouse floor.

"I'm going to cut the grass when it warms up and dries off a little later," Henry told Laura.

"It's been almost an hour, and Felix still hasn't come back," she replied. "If you see him, send him in so he can at least eat something. He must be starving by now!"

Felix decided to pretend to be asleep if someone found him. He squinted to make sure no one was around.

Suddenly, the flowers on the bushes all turned toward him. When he realized what was happening, he fell back, hitting his head on the metal and glass wall. What's happening?

The hothouse was empty except for himself, the plants, and the fish. Bees darted in and out of their colony right outside the hothouse. The long pink and yellow flowers bobbed up and down on their own, as if they were chuckling.

Felix shook his head in disbelief. He had never seen anything like this before. Curiously, he reached out cautiously and touched a bunch of flowers. The moment he made contact, hundreds of voices flooded his mind.

What he heard sounded like all the girls from the Kennedy House talking at once, multiplied many times over. Trying to decipher the myriad voices proved to be too overwhelming. Felix was in disbelief. Still touching the flowers, his thoughts seemed to transfer into them. You can talk? Why have I never heard you before?

The whole bush shook with what seemed like giggles. Then hundreds of tiny whispers flowed out. "Aw, he's such a special boy! See, he knows what we're saying!"

The responses rushed back into his mind, and Felix's eyes widened further as endless thoughts spun in his head. The flowers could actually read his mind. No one at Kennedy House had prepared him for this!

He wasn't frightened but rather confused about the world he'd been living in. Was it all a lie? Why hadn't Chance told him about this? Overwhelmed and having not fully digested the tiny amount of food he'd eaten, Felix passed out from exhaustion and shock.

The sudden rumbling of the lawnmower woke Felix. He had been asleep for a while, and the abrupt noise jerked him awake. As the lawnmower moved away into the distance, Felix reached out with his mind toward the flowers, trying to confirm whether he had been dreaming about talking to them.

To ensure he wasn't going crazy, Felix's fingertips cautiously approached the delicate blooms. When he made contact, hundreds of voices flooded back into his mind.

One centralized voice emerged from the core of the bush, like a mother calming her children. This voice silenced all the others.

The bush's voice had a soothing and disarming effect on Felix. "Dearest one, can you calm yourself? I have a few things I need to tell you."

Felix nodded while still touching the plant.

"Now, I need you to clear your mind," the bush said, able to read Felix's vital signs through contact.

Felix nodded again, and the bush continued. "This world isn't as it appears. Humans no longer draw upon the energies of the earth and have become deaf to all that surrounds them—even us."

Felix was silent as he tried to absorb every word the bush had to say.

"You must never tell anyone that you can understand us. You'll be labeled a freak and a threat. You'll be shunned. We're here to help you grow and learn about yourself if you wish to learn, but only in secret."

The two other flowering bushes stretched out their branches and communicated to him in unison. "You aren't like the other children here. You're special and must take care. There are people out there willing to harm you if they find out about you. They would make you disappear. We have even gone into hiding to protect ourselves. We have seen the horrendous atrocities that these humans have committed and continue to commit against our kind around the world. You're in danger; trust no one!"

Felix asked, "Why would they make me disappear?"

The bushes responded, "Even though your elders are sweet, caring humans, and they grew us from seedlings, they cannot comprehend anything greater than themselves. That is why you're a threat to human normality."

At that moment, Henry entered the hothouse to gather his daily bouquet for Laura, causing Felix to contort his body behind the pots to avoid being seen.

After Henry finished his task, Felix returned to speaking with the rest of the plants in the hothouse. He touched them and learned from them: their personalities, how they shared their experiences through their roots, or by intertwining their branches, creating a linked consciousness.

The sun had warmed the hothouse with its golden rays. One of the potted plants with small pink flowers asked Felix, "Isn't the song lovely?"

Felix appeared confused. He hadn't heard any song—what were the flowers talking about? The flowers instructed him to clear his mind and close his eyes to become attuned to his surroundings. After a few moments of meditation, he noticed a chorus of humming and buzzing he had never heard before. The beehive that Henry tended, right outside in the courtyard, came to life with the warmth of the heated air. Slowly, more bees emerged from the hive, making their way into the hothouse through a pipe large enough for their passage. Hundreds of bees swarmed, performing a synchronized ballet while their joyous song about a new day rang out.

"Good morning to you, and you and you,
There is lots of work to do, for me and you, and
you.
We don't have time to waste, the honey's sweetness
can't be replaced.
The queen, our queen, is a dancing queen,
She relies on us to keep the hive pristine.

How are you and you today?
Busy, busy as a bee, we buzz and sway.
We flutter and hover in a choreographed spree,
Creating golden treasures from the blossoms we
see.
We dance and hum, in perfect harmony,
A symphony of wings, our shared melody.
So rise and shine, and greet the new day,
Together we'll work and joyfully play."

The song continued as Felix watched the bees, but they acted as if nothing was unusual. When the bees landed on the flowers to pollinate them, all the buzzing stopped at once.

Felix wondered, Did the flowers tell the bees that I can understand them?

The little yellow workers turned to face Felix. If bees could show shock, they would have. They lifted off and began a slow hover toward Felix. Only the buzzing of their tiny wings could be heard as they surrounded him like a dome.

The bees then started singing a new song.

"He sees, he sees, yes us, the tiny bees,
What an odd little boy is he.
We wonder what he sees,
What if he can understand us, tiny bees?
So, shall we go back being bees,
Or seek refuge among the trees?
Shall we hide or bravely stay,
And face the boy who watches our play?

We'll hum and buzz, in joyful arrays,
As we work through the sunny days.
If he understands our tiny plea,
Perhaps he'll join our hive and be part of our spree."

Felix figured they were assessing him, so he stood still and waited. The bees were trying to figure out his intentions. The bees had never encountered a being who understood what was happening around them, and Felix was filled with anticipation.

Eventually, the bees resumed their work, moving from flower to flower and ensuring their job was done.

Felix stumbled back to the bushes where he had slept. He reached up and touched all three bushes with both hands, asking them to tell him everything they could.

"You have questions?" the three bushes asked.

"Why didn't you try to contact me before today? You had plenty of chances," he asked before they could say anything else.

"You were always with that boy, so we never had an opportunity."

"Does anything else talk?" he inquired.

"Oh, of course. The animals talk too. You must warm them up to the idea so they become receptive to you. Knowing what they like isn't a bad idea either."

The bushes explained that animals were not tactile-based, and Felix would have to learn their languages or find a different way to communicate. After hearing this, he got up, dusted himself off, and made his way back into the house stealthily so the Pines wouldn't notice.

Knowing that Betty, the old orange tabby cat, would be resting on the couch under the afghan, he headed to the parlor. Betty glanced at him as he tried to sneak into the room. She meowed, as she usually did when addressing the children. Concentrating to keep his mind open, he listened for a few moments until he was able to discern what Betty was saying.

She was half-awake and repeating herself as if intoxicated. Betty said, "Be useful; come over and scratch my back and behind my ears."

He complied with Betty's request. Betty had tried to influence the children to pet her in the past but had been unsuccessful 50 percent of the time. She lay back down and closed her eyes, soaking up the sun near the large bay window.

Felix scratched the areas she had indicated, and to his surprise, Betty lifted her head, opened her eyes wide, and meowed in ecstasy. Felix was hitting all the right spots. Her hind end poked upward while her front limbs stretched out as if she were filing her nails on a scratching post.

"Good human. A little stronger and more vigorous scratching would be nice!" Betty purred.

Felix did as he was asked. Betty stared at him curiously. "Do you understand me?" she meowed.

Felix nodded. To confirm this wasn't a fluke, Betty instructed him to sit. Before he could do so, he heard the familiar footsteps of Laura approaching. He quickly scooped Betty up in his arms and hid out of view. Laura poked her head into the room, and Betty remained silent.

When the coast was clear, Betty climbed back into Felix's lap, finding the perfect position and curling into a ball. Once she was comfortable, she started talking to Felix, recounting memories of his first day and moments that had made her laugh. And yes, cats do laugh.

Betty began talking about Chance, and Felix, missing his best friend, started to cry. Caught off guard, Felix didn't notice Henry and Laura peeking through the French doors.

Henry and Laura stood silently, observing what was happening in the room. Even though they couldn't see him clearly, they knew Felix was on the other side hiding, so they decided to give him space. Henry quietly stepped back and gently pulled Laura away, allowing Felix some time to sulk.

Laura was taken aback by Henry's gesture, and a moment of empathy gripped her heart. Henry noticed it in her eyes and embraced her, giving her a passionate kiss—something they hadn't shared in quite a while.

Betty told Felix to cheer up, saying that Chance would be back later in the day, and he stopped crying. Betty then urged him, "Human, go out and have fun. Stop moping around. There's an entire world for you to discover!"

She crawled out of Felix's lap, and he reluctantly got up. He wandered the house until he spotted Grumpy, the fat pug, lying on his side and soaking up the sun.

Grumpy was snoring when Felix reached down and

petted him. Grumpy immediately opened his big, beady eyes and woofed. Felix opened his mind to the dog and understood the stern voice saying, "Human child, go away; I have no time for you and your kind!"

Grumpy was referring to children. He wasn't a fan of high-energy creatures and preferred those that moved slower than a sloth. Felix, always kind to everyone, was angered by the old dog's reaction.

Felix picked up the dog bed and Grumpy's toy lion. Grumpy barked and threw a fit. "Put it back, you evil child! You woke me up, and now you're taking my things away?" Grumpy growled, showing a mouth of missing teeth.

Felix stuck out his tongue in response. He then turned around and marched off, carrying the dog bed and toy lion to the hallway closet so Grumpy couldn't retrieve them. Grumpy ran around the first floor, barking and woofing.

Felix headed upstairs to the boys' bedroom and crawled into bed for a nap. He decided that sleeping the day away was better than moping around until Chance came home from school.

A few hours later, the children arrived home from school. Chance was excited to tell Felix about his day, but his overexcitement caused him to trip over his own feet. He launched himself off the school bus and landed in the shrubs that lined the driveway. Orchid and Rose helped him out and dusted him off before he dashed inside to find Felix.

Chance raced through the house. When he couldn't find Felix on the first floor, he ran to their tree in the backyard but still saw no sign of him. He double-checked all the usual places where they spent time during the day.

"Where's Felix?" he exclaimed.

Laura lovingly looked down at Chance and told him Felix was upstairs sleeping. Before she could say more, Chance bolted out of the kitchen and raced upstairs to where Felix was sound asleep. Betty was curled up under Felix's arm, and when Chance entered the room, her eyes opened.

Chance was taken aback; he had never seen Betty cuddle up under anyone. The only times he had seen her show that much attention were during her occasional attempts to smother the other children with her belly. Betty slipped stealthily from under Felix's arm and exited the room.

Chance climbed onto the bed, settling slightly above Felix. Felix instinctively reached out and grasped Chance, even in his sleep. The two then napped together.

Laura sent French to wake them for dinner, as neither had appeared yet. French came crashing into the room, waking them. When Felix saw Chance, he teared up as if he hadn't seen him in fifty years.

"Hey, you two old folks, get up! It's time to eat!" French shouted, making sure the entire house could hear.

Chance slipped out of bed, holding Felix's hand. "Hey, it's time to eat, and I have lots to tell you!" he said with a grin.

Felix wiped his face with his free hand and followed Chance down to the kitchen table.

As Felix sat, Henry glanced at him. "Are you okay? You disappeared for a long time today! Laura was worried about you!"

Felix nodded in response, but everyone was still buzzing about the first day of school. Chance wasn't paying attention to the school gossip and instead went into detail about his teacher and the girl who kissed him on the playground. Felix was captivated by every word. Chance only paused to breathe when the food was being passed around the table.

"I have a happy announcement for you all," Henry said, clearing his throat and standing up.

Bobby blurted out, "Are you getting us a puppy?"

Without hesitation, Laura dashed that flame of excitement. "Grumpy is still with us, and we won't be getting a puppy until he's no longer breathing."

"Another baby's coming, isn't it?" an irritated Jackson asked with disgust.

Bobby turned to Jackson, and they began hatching a plan to get rid of Grumpy or send him to an early grave. Jackson reminded him that no one would want that mangy, old, drooling poop-maker.

"Hey, cheer up. There are other options for getting rid of that fleabag," Jackson said.

"No," Henry replied, "this is about something we all didn't think would ever happen!"

Chance, this time, yelled out, "We're going to Disneyland?"

"No!"

The children slumped in their chairs in disappointment as Henry laughed and said, "Felix said a word."

All eyes turned to Felix. He felt like he was being examined by the Inquisition.

"What word was it?" Trisha asked.

"No," replied Laura.

"Only 'no'? Well, that's kind of lame," Jackson said under his breath.

"We all have to start somewhere, don't we, Jackson?" Laura said sternly, glaring at him.

The announcement ended, but the children continued to stare at Felix, making him uncomfortable. The attention directed at him to see if he would talk bothered Felix, so he ran out of the dining room as quickly as possible. Chance ran after Felix, knowing exactly where Felix would go if he was feeling bad—the big tree in the backyard where he felt safe and where they spent the most time together.

Allowing the rest of the house to finish their meals, the Pines then ushered the children into the study. Laura covered Chance and Felix's dinner plates with foil so they could eat later without worrying about the older boys stealing their food.

Outside at the tree, after several minutes of convincing Felix that everything was okay, Chance finally got him to follow him back inside. While most children had stuffed toys and blankets to comfort them, Felix had Chance. Chance pulled Felix by the hand, bringing them shoulder to shoulder and walking side by side back to the house, with Felix resting his head on his taller brother's arm.

Back in the kitchen, Laura was at the sink finishing the dishes with Rose. She patted Rose on the back. "You're such a great help. It's getting late, Miss Rose; you should join the others in the study."

Rose bounced from her heels to the balls of her feet before hugging Laura and seeing the two boys come in from outside. Knowing she wouldn't speak to them for the rest of the night, she skipped over and gave them both a hug, wishing them goodnight as she always did.

"You both must be hungry," Laura said, inspecting the pair.

Both boys nodded, and Laura walked over to the oven, pulling out two white plates covered in foil. Their faces mirrored those of hungry puppies waiting all day for their owner to come home and feed them. "Shouldn't you wash your hands?"

The pair scurried down the hall to the bathroom, where

they scrubbed their hands. Laura had taught them to hum "Twinkle, Twinkle, Little Star" to know they had washed well.

After cleaning up, they raced back to the kitchen to gobble up their dinner. If Laura hadn't saved it for them, Theodore would have certainly wolfed down the remaining food. Felix licked his plate clean before Chance grabbed it and set it in the sink.

Felix then followed Chance to the step stool, and the boys finished washing the plates and silverware, with Felix trying to keep his balance on the small step and unable to actually see into the basin.

Once they finished, they noticed a large warm cookie on a plate with a big scoop of melting ice cream and three forks stuck into it. The boys' eyes widened, and grins stretched across their faces.

"Are you going to join me, or am I supposed to eat this whole gooey thing by myself?" Laura asked, grabbing one of the forks.

They rushed over to the counter and devoured the dessert. None of the other kids got dessert (except Rose—a chocolate bonbon—for helping Laura with the dishes). Rose popped it into her mouth without mentioning it to any of the other kids.

Laura spoke clearly and softly to Felix, but loud enough for Chance to hear. "Take your time. There's no rush for you to speak. Just know you're supported and cared for here."

She tussled Felix's hair and rubbed the back of Chance's shoulders before getting up from the counter, leaving them the last few bites of cookie and ice cream.

The boys finished off the rest of the dessert, with Felix dropping the plate and forks into the sink, creating a crashing sound. Felix ran to Laura and hugged her legs, showing his appreciation for the dessert and the kind words.

"I would hug you back, but my hands are wet and covered with soap," she said.

The two boys then ventured to the study, where Henry was helping the other children with their homework. When they arrived, he was reading a story about a boy named Harry who lived in a mystical land with dragons and played an unusual game on broomsticks. This was the children's favorite story that Henry read to them.

By eight-thirty, all the children had finished their homework and had listened to Henry's story.

Laura popped her head into the study, announcing that it was bedtime, but none of the children wanted to go to bed yet. Whines and moans were the only responses. Reluctantly, they all headed upstairs to their warm beds.

Chance and Felix were the last in line to brush their teeth, which was fine with them as it gave them more time to chat. Felix hung on to everything Chance told him, but the comment Jackson made in the hallway always stuck with him. If Chance weren't his big brother, why would Chance and the others treat him so well? His life felt like the families he saw on TV. To Felix, Chance was the big brother he had always wished for, Felix's best friend.

However, the poison Jackson had planted in Felix's mind had him questioning everything he had come to know. Why was everyone so nice to him? Who were his parents, and where were they?

When the two crawled into bed, Chance lay on his back while Felix nestled up to his midsection, resting his head on Chance's stomach and wrapping his arm around Chance's leg like a body pillow. Felix drifted off to sleep, comforted by the soothing sound of Chance's stomach digesting his food, like a calming white noise.

Chapter 6
Letting Go Is Hard

Morning arrived, and things unfolded much like the day before. Felix threw a fit when Chance was about to leave, and Chance felt sad about leaving his best friend behind.

"No!" Felix shouted as the school bus door closed. This time, his "no" wasn't as loud as the day before, but Chance still turned around. It was too late; the bus had already moved on from the front of the Kennedy House to the next pickup.

Instead of running into the bushes, Felix ran into the house. The Pines cleared a path for him as if he were Moses parting the Red Sea. Felix walked straight up to Betty, the orange tabby, scooped her up in his arms, tossed her over his shoulder, and walked off.

Betty started meowing—not in pain but in shock. "Child, if you're going to snatch me up and carry me off, I'd like at least my head to be scratched!"

Felix scratched her head as he marched past Grumpy, who was still mad at him from the day before. Grumpy woofed, but Felix paid him no mind, heading out through the French doors that led to the backyard. He ended up at the hothouse with Betty, closing the door behind them.

"Human, why are we in here? I don't catch mice, if that's what you had in mind."

Felix walked to the back corner where the bushes were. When they reached them, the branches parted to make a path for them. He sat down, laying the tabby on his lap, and pouted while stroking Betty's orange fur.

"Well, that was abrupt! Child, why am I in here with you?"

Felix sat on the cold cement floor; Betty sat up and turned all her attention to him. The dim light leaking from the house into the hothouse allowed Betty to see the now recurring waterworks from Felix's eyes. Felix had shifted from sitting to lying down.

Betty moved closer to Felix and licked his face clean of the tears. Then she nestled into the nook of Felix's body, as he was curled up like a bean. She knew that Felix never responded to her unless she made a request, so she didn't bother to ask what was wrong. Instead, she lay between his arms and stomach, guarding him as if he were one of her kittens.

After a nap lasting half an hour, Felix woke up to find Betty still there. When Betty noticed Felix was no longer sleeping, she head-butted him softly. "Oh, child! I don't do all this babysitting for free. It's time to pay up." She rolled over on her side. "Right there. That is where you need to start rubbing!" With one paw, she pointed to her belly.

Felix satisfied Betty's request, and once she was done being scratched, she got up and made her way to the hothouse door. Felix paused to listen to the same song he'd heard yesterday from the bees. Once the song was finished, he had a brief chat with the flowers. Betty then urged Felix to explore, which seemed like a reasonable idea, so he did as she suggested. He wandered into the front yard, a place rarely visited except for gardening, and hid himself inside the lilac bushes. The bushes advised him to explore the property and get to know the various creatures inhabiting the grounds, so he walked around the front yard and overheard two red squirrels fighting over the nuts they were storing. He also heard birds flying overhead, singing lovely songs as they migrated to warmer climates.

After exploring the front yard, he made his way around the back. The big tree there, with its leaves starting to turn golden yellow, stood out against the reds and oranges that lined the property. The tree spoke slowly, as if a machine was powering down. It turned out it wasn't speaking to Felix but had fallen asleep and was sleep-talking.

Felix continued to the pond filled with fish. He got on his hands and knees and made his way toward the cool water. He felt the difference in air temperature compared to the pond. Ensuring no one was watching him, he saw his face reflected on the water's surface as the koi fish rose to meet him. With their gurgling voices, they said "hi" and "food" repeatedly. A young fish asked him to join them. He thought, I don't want food, so I'll just swim with them.

Felix stripped down to his underwear before plunging into the water. A few months ago, Henry had taught him how to swim. He was the quickest of the children to catch on, surprising Henry with how quickly he learned. This made Henry wonder how odd it was for Felix to be so young and yet so capable.

As Felix plunged into the water, he was surrounded by fish. It was like a spectator sport; the young boy doggie-paddled around the pond, afraid to use the technique Henry had taught him, as he might hit one of the fish.

The koi found it amusing since his technique was drastically different from theirs. The little fish, with its tiny voice, then said, "Go under the water."

Never having done this before, Felix was a little nervous, but he took a deep breath and dived down. Opening his eyes, he saw the horde of fish surrounding him, and they all simultaneously said, "Hi!"

The tiny fish spoke again. "Why are you holding your breath?"

Felix quickly thought it over and decided to blow out the air from his mouth and lungs. Immediately, he choked as if something was stuck in his throat. His lungs burned as they filled with water, and he sank farther into the pond's chilled depths.

"Calm down and breathe!" the tiny fish shouted, not realizing this advice could be dangerous.

Felix, being an obedient child, did as instructed—at least as much as he could. Not understanding he was drowning, his body lurched and cramped as his chest shuttered, making it feel like it was on fire.

Then something unexplainable happened. Felix's lungs slowly transformed into webbed filters, able to extract oxygen from the water. His lungs now functioned like internal gills. He would suck water in through his mouth and then push the oxygen-extracted water out through his nose.

The tiny fish giggled and asked, "Are you okay now?"

Felix nodded in shock.

"Good," the little fish said. "Now follow me."

The fish dived farther down, with Felix following. Normally, Felix was a fast learner, but he found underwater swimming challenging. The little golden-yellow fish's tail moved through the water like silk being dragged, propelling itself forward. The fish slowed down and spent a few minutes teaching Felix how to maneuver his body.

"By the way, my name's Dip," the tiny fish said.

Felix didn't know how to communicate back with Dip, but Dip could read Felix's facial expressions, much like Betty did.

Felix grasped the lesson after a few failed attempts, expending a lot of energy. Once he got the hang of swimming underwater, he swam like a torpedo. Felix enjoyed the new sensation—almost weightless swimming below the surface and the lack of limitations in his movement.

Dip showed him around the pond and introduced him to some of the older fish. Seeing Felix's face full of curiosity and wonder, Dip became more adventurous, showing off. When they reached the murky and muddy areas with stacked rocks, Dip explained why they should avoid those areas, as turtles would eat the little fish if they got too close or started lurking.

Felix didn't like the thought of the little fish getting eaten, and he gestured to Dip, asking where the turtles were. The tiny fish told him where the invaders could normally be found.

Felix spent the next few days removing all the turtles using various tactics. While monitoring his targets, he witnessed a young fish, around the same age as Dip, being bitten in half and devoured by a turtle. Felix watched in horror and was sickened by the sight, while Dip cried out in distress.

The most challenging turtle to remove was a cantankerous old snapping turtle known as Deathmouth. This task required careful planning, so Felix took a few days to study his formidable foe before putting any plan into action. This victory would be hard-fought, requiring significant effort to remove such a massive adversary from the pond.

Felix carried the other turtles across the street and past a ditch to ensure they couldn't return to the pond. He knew he wouldn't have such an easy time with the old turtle.

Deathmouth attempted to bite Felix several times, but Felix was surprisingly agile in the water. He observed Deathmouth's behaviors and habits, noting that staying away from the front of the turtle was the safest approach. The fate of the poor little fish from a few days prior fueled his determination.

Deathmouth's neck was faster than Felix's reflexes, and seeing the turtle snap a branch in half with its jaws kept Felix on high alert. He realized that to defeat such a formidable foe, he needed a different strategy. Normally, Felix would gently pick up the turtles and carry them out, but since this turtle had no intention of leaving and only wanted to inflict harm, Felix decided to adopt a more aggressive approach. He recalled a phrase he had heard on TV, "An eye for an eye," and resolved to apply it to his situation.

Felix grabbed a rock and swam stealthily behind Deathmouth before smashing its leg with the rock. If the turtle was going to snap at his limbs, Felix would retaliate in kind. Surprised and wounded, the turtle's head and limbs retracted into its shell. This defense made it impossible for Felix to grab onto anything, so he couldn't drag the turtle out of the pond. Deathmouth was two-thirds Felix's size, and this massive turtle was no small foe. However, Felix was determined and undeterred by the challenge.

Felix's anger was further fueled by the fact that Chance was away at school and knowing that Dip and the entire fish community were afraid of the huge turtle. These factors provoked him even more, so Felix climbed onto Deathmouth's back and secured himself with his legs. He began bashing the turtle's shell with a pointed rock.

After about twenty-five blows to the top of the shell, a crack appeared, but Felix didn't stop until the hole in the shell was the size of an orange.

A roar came from inside the shell. "Stop attacking me! What do you want?"

Felix hopped off Deathmouth's back, rock still in hand, as Deathmouth extended his head and neck out of the shell cautiously. Once Felix knew the turtle could see him, he pointed toward the nearest shore of the pond. Behind him, the fish community cheered, and the expulsion of the turtles had become a source of entertainment for the koi.

The turtle understood what this meant: he was being exiled from the pond he had ruled over for years. Felix kept his arm outstretched, guiding Deathmouth out of the pond and off the property.

Limping due to his injured foot, Deathmouth struggled to make his way. Felix walked beside him as if he were a well-trained dog, continuing into the woods until their paths diverged. Felix stood at the tree line until Deathmouth was out of sight. The last thing he saw was the turtle's shell disappearing into the undergrowth.

Felix hurried back to the pond, where the fish gathered around him once more. The bright oranges, golds, yellows, reds, and whites of their scales shimmered in the sunlight, creating a moving watercolor effect.

The fish thanked Felix and bestowed a special blessing upon him, naming him the Keeper of the Pond. They followed him around as if he were royalty. Though they tried to converse with Felix, he struggled to keep up with every voice talking over each other. Nevertheless, this wasn't a significant problem, as the fish were not keen on listening to others in any case.

The young fish played tag with Felix, though it was some-what unfair since they were faster in the water and could hide in crevices Felix couldn't reach, leaving him "it" most of the time.

Felix was never bored with the pond's inhabitants; they kept him entertained and distracted from his worries.

Chapter 7
A Day at the Pool

A few days later, Henry was in the kitchen filling the kettle with water to make coffee when he noticed Felix drying off in the grass by the pond. Henry turned off the stove, placed a few plates on the kitchen table, and kept an eye on Felix as he headed out the French doors.

He quietly approached Felix and said, "So you don't need supervision when swimming anymore?"

Felix looked up at Henry sheepishly, as if fearing he might be in trouble, but he slowly shook his head no.

"So, you like the water!" Henry said.

Felix responded with an enthusiastic nod.

"Do you want to go swimming after lunch?"

Since Chance wasn't around and the Pines weren't keeping him busy, Felix was eager for a distraction. He was enjoying the freedom to make his own choices, even though he usually just went along without much thought. The only thing he preferred over swimming or eating was Chance. He was definitely up for both activities, but if not in the pond where would he swim?

Henry scooped up Felix and carried him back into the house. Felix was still wrapped in a towel, with only his feet and gray eyes visible.

Henry finished preparing the meals and set them on the table, along with freshly squeezed orange juice. As Felix ate, Henry told him it was getting too cold to swim outside. Felix didn't understand that freezing water wasn't suitable for swimming, and Henry worried he might end up baby-sitting two sick people if Felix kept that up. Felix didn't mind the water, as Henry had placed several heaters in the pond to prevent it from freezing in the winter.

After they finished their meal, Henry prepared Laura's breakfast plate. When Laura was sick, she preferred English muffins with blackcurrant jam and lemon tea with honey. Henry had already gone into the hothouse that morning to select some of the finest blooms. Today's bouquet featured cabbage roses and bells-of-Ireland.

"Hey, buddy, can you grab Laura's basket from the parlor?" Henry asked.

Felix nodded and dashed off to retrieve a wicker basket full of yarn and cross-stitch projects. It looked as though he might tip over from the weight of the basket with the slightest breeze.

The two made their way up to the Pines' bedroom, where they found Laura still asleep. They placed the food on the side table and the basket on the floor next to the bed.

With the children at school, the house was peaceful and quiet, allowing Laura to rest.

Henry took Felix with him to pick up supplies at the local gardening store. He wanted to buy some bulbs to start in pots for the winter. To involve Felix in the decision-making, he let him choose the flowers for the pots.

Felix examined the bins with pictures of the flowers and pointed to the checkered lily, common hyacinth, Aztec lily, and firepot dahlia. Henry also picked up fertilizer and grass seed for the spring, which was on sale this time of year.

Afterward, they visited the sporting goods store on Main Street, where they bought a blue Speedo with a white stripe for Felix to wear while swimming at the school's pool.

Henry then stopped by the bookstore to pick up a few titles French had requested and some books about King Arthur and the Knights of the Round Table. They got their books and then stopped for ice cream.

"Hey, little buddy, it's getting late, so we'll go swimming tomorrow. Is that okay?" Henry asked.

Felix just licked his cone, unbothered by the delay. Henry sighed and ruffled Felix's hair.

Laura hadn't seen Felix much in the past few days except at mealtimes. Being sick and confined to bed left her bored and struggling with depression. Keeping her mind occupied was a challenge.

Henry wanted to avoid catching the flu, so he slept in the parlor to stay away from the illness.

The next day, after sending the children off to school, Henry kissed Laura on the forehead, trying not to wake her. She opened her eyes, her face lighting up with joy. Felix waved from a safe distance and then headed back downstairs.

"What are you two up to today?" Laura asked, reaching for her tea.

Henry looked at her with a silly grin before taking her temperature. "I'm taking the little fry to the pool today. It looks like your fever is going down; it's a hundred."

"That's good to hear. I'm feeling a little better," she said.

"Now go have fun."

Henry kissed her forehead again before hurrying down-stairs, where Felix was waiting. Henry wore a sweatshirt with an image of a swimmer and the year 2001 printed on it, along with fitted blue jeans. Felix wore an oversized shirt that belonged to Chance and a pair of shorts.

Henry picked up Felix and carried him out the door and into the old Chevy pickup parked in the driveway. Felix scoot-ed to the middle of the bench seat as Henry jumped in and settled into the driver's seat. He placed Felix on his lap, letting him pretend to drive as they headed into town.

As they drove through the streets lined with bright au-tumn leaves, the truck seemed to barrel toward an explod-ing star. The vibrant colors were mesmerizing on this cool autumn day. They saw people raking leaves in their yards or out shopping as they passed through Main Street.

They arrived at the local high school and parked. Henry picked up Felix and placed him on his shoulders. The school was a three-story brick and stone building with a metal roof, and the large trees on the front lawn gave it an Ivy League appearance.

They headed around to the back of the building where a large newer addition bore the sign "Home of the Behe-moths." Henry walked up the steps and opened the double doors. Inside, it was quiet except for the muffled sound of a whistle. They walked down a long hallway lined with pictures of sports teams and glass cases filled with medals and trophies.

As they approached the gymnasium, Henry pointed out his picture and others he recognized from the old photos. He hadn't changed much from the photos except for his added facial hair.

As they reached the double doors at the end of the hallway, an old man rushed toward them. "Oh my God, it's Hammerhead Henry!"

Everyone in the room turned to look.

"Yes, Coach," Henry replied.

Some of the students gathered around.

"Henry, it's so good to see you!" Coach Cramer said, hugging Henry. He then turned to Felix. "Who's the little guy?"

"This is Felix. He's turning three a little later this year. He doesn't say much, but he loves the water. I taught him how to swim over the summer," Henry said.

Coach Cramer grinned widely. He picked up Felix and placed him at the edge of the pool. Felix was accustomed to being picked up and set down, thanks to Matthew treating him like a stuffed animal from time to time.

Henry followed Coach Cramer to the end of the pool, where more children gathered. "If he's your boy, he'll surely be an Olympian!" Coach said to Henry.

Henry didn't correct Coach Cramer about Felix not being his child.

The pool was full of teenagers. Coach Cramer set Felix down before raising his whistle to his mouth and blowing it like a foghorn. Any remaining noise or splashing ceased, and all eyes were on Coach Cramer.

"Attention, everyone, this is Hammerhead Henry. If you don't already know, he was the state champion in 1999, 2000, and 2001. He went on to be a collegiate Division-A champion, swimming in five events. He's honored us with a visit today. He's here to introduce the newest addition to the family, Felix, who will hopefully, one day, live up to his father's achievements and maybe even surpass them!"

Every year, and at every practice, Coach Cramer told tales of the Hammerhead, the most awarded and successful swimmer he'd ever coached. These stories had become legends in the halls of the school, and all the students clapped and cheered. Now that the legend had a face, he was no longer just a myth, as many students had paid more attention to the trophies than the photos on the wall. This grand introduction made Henry blush.

"You ready for a swim?" Coach Cramer asked, a twinkle in his eye.

Felix nodded, as he always did, and Coach Cramer yelled to clear lane one. Felix removed Chance's shirt and shorts and leapt into the water without hesitation.

"Oh, he's a quick one!" Coach Cramer exclaimed.

Wrapping his arm around Henry's shoulders, Coach Cramer chatted with him while they watched Felix swim. Coach noticed a familiarity in Felix's technique. "Geez-oh-Peets, you've got him swimming with your old technique! It took you years to master that, and he's already got the basics down—just needs a little tweaking." Coach Cramer squeezed Henry's shoulders with excitement.

Henry could only respond proudly, "Yeah."

"Does he know how to launch off the board?" Coach Cramer asked.

"Not yet, but he's a really fast learner. Don't you think he's a little young for that?" Henry replied.

Brushing off the concern, Coach Cramer looked around the room and called out, "Eric, Jake, Bryan, and Taylor. Line up and demonstrate how to set and launch."

The four senior boys lined up and showed how to launch off the board. While Felix watched, Henry stripped down to his old Speedo, the same one he wore in college—green and gold, though slightly faded. Coach Cramer beamed as if he were back at one of Henry's meets.

Henry helped Felix out of the pool and onto the board. As Felix observed the boys, he noticed their movements were similar to how Betty, the tabby cat, pounced on birds when hunting outside. This similarity made Felix ponder the connection between the teens and Betty.

He assumed his position on the board and launched himself into the water like Betty pouncing on a bird. Coach and Henry watched in amazement as Felix nailed the dive on his first try. Most of the children were focused on meeting Hammerhead Henry rather than paying attention to Felix.

Coach Cramer clapped. "Well done, Felix, well done!"

The kids responded with cheers, joining their coach.

"It's rare to see such explosive strength in someone so small. What have you been feeding him?" Coach Cramer asked.

Henry was unsure how to explain, so he simply said, "Other than swimming, he just runs around a lot and plays."

Coach Cramer nodded. "Yes, indeed. He's definitely your child. All that power, energy, and focus—he's like you were growing up. That boy is like a shark! No, a black marlin!"

Henry jumped into the pool for a few laps, and they stayed in the water for about thirty minutes. Henry then returned to Coach's side as he instructed different lanes to pick up the pace, stay centered, and occasionally to stop flirting.

"Does it bring back any memories for you, Henry?" Coach Cramer asked.

Henry simply shrugged with a gleeful smile. Hammerhead and Coach then discussed Felix's future while planning out practices and training sessions for him.

After Felix finished swimming, he got out of the pool. The repetitive back and forth of the swimming practice bored him, as there was no one to interact with like when he played in the pond at the Kennedy House.

Coach Cramer gave Henry and Felix a hug goodbye and asked, "Will we see you tomorrow?"

Henry grinned and shrugged. "I think that's up to Felix."

Felix waved to the class and the coach as they headed back toward the double doors and down the hall. They hurried to the truck, their stomachs growling in unison.

Henry was happy to have seen his old coach. It had been almost ten years, and Coach Cramer had been like a father to him. He felt a similar pride for Felix, marveling at his natural abilities.

They reached the truck, and Henry opened the driver's door, sliding Felix inside. Henry turned on the radio to a country music station. Felix wasn't pleased with the station, so he reached out and changed the dial. He settled on a station playing classical music, which started light and airy but soon sped up. The music was energetic, beat-driven, fast-paced, and had a rock ballad feel, featuring electric violins, violas, and other stringed instruments.

Felix bobbed his head to the music, and Henry noticed from the corner of his eye. Seeing Felix enjoy the music was a welcome change from the moody child he'd seen over the past few months. He placed his hand on Felix's head, rubbing it in approval of his goofiness. Little could ruin Henry's day. Both rocked out to the unlikely music as they drove back to the Kennedy House, filled with giggles and humming.

Felix was so absorbed in the music that he didn't notice Chance wasn't home. He was captivated as if under a spell.

Upon arriving at the house, Felix grabbed some fruit from the bowl on the table before disappearing into the hothouse. He quickly made his way to the back corner, cleared his mind, and reached out to communicate with the wise, flowering shrubs. They asked if they could place a thorn crown on his head.

"Why?" he asked.

"We believe you're ready. It's your birthright, though you've been denied it so far. The crown might hurt a little," the shrubs explained. Felix agreed, and the bushes twisted and lengthened their branches around the top of his head. The thorns pierced his scalp in a few spots, and once the skin was breached, a flood of information swirled into Felix's brain. Some of it was understandable, while other parts were coded in messages and images he couldn't decipher. He was also told that the rest of the information would reveal itself when he was ready or in times of great need.

The information included the fact that "only one species could speak to plants the way he did"—the elves. The plants could not detect any specific information about Felix's and assumed he was an elf. The plants communicated through touch, experiences, and stories passed down from one plant to another.

The knowledge the shrubs imparted contradicted what Felix had learned from books and TV specials. The elves were described as pale, pointed-eared, soft-spoken, intelligent, graceful, agile, peaceful, and mystical. In contrast, he had previously heard that elves were small, subservient, and mocked as abnormal.

Felix had not seen these traits in anyone he had met, although a few people in the house had one or two. The shrubs described elves as living gods.

"What happened to the elves?" Felix asked curiously.

"The elves foresaw only destruction for the human world and left for a haven far away from the non-mystical," the bushes explained.

Felix felt sad at the thought of not meeting an elf.

As a final gift, anyone with the ability to speak with plants as Felix did would be able to recognize him.

"Now, child, you have received all we can bestow upon you. Let our wisdom guide you on the right path toward your future. When you need guidance, free your mind and reach into your consciousness, and the Green Guild will help you. If you encounter other guild members, they will recognize you through touch and share a common bond."

Slightly confused, Felix didn't fully understand the concept of elves or what the Green Guild was. New questions flooded his mind, but he thanked the bushes and left. What this talented soon to be three-year-old had gained was more valuable than he realized at the time.

He walked back into the house and sat near Betty, who meowed to greet him before settling back down for her midday nap.

Laura enjoyed listening to the TV while working around the house. It was tuned to the Nat Geo channel, showing an episode about Africa and its big cats.

Felix watched for about five minutes until he saw a lion take down a zebra. The sight didn't sit well with him, and when he saw the gore, his stomach churned. He immediately got up and left the room as quickly as his legs could carry him, heading to the study. The scene reminded him of the poor little fish he had seen Deathmouth tear apart. Once in the study, he crawled into Henry's lap and fell asleep, not knowing how to express his feelings. Henry chuckled as he began to read aloud the story of the zodiac warriors, rubbing Felix's back.

Laura finished her chores and lay on the couch in the parlor, near Grumpy, the pug. Having just recovered from a fever, she was limited in what she could do before becoming tired. As she lay on the sofa, Grumpy slept on her thighs.

When Felix was alone in the house with his thoughts, had an extraordinary ability to focus on a singular goal or idea, devoting his entire being to it. Lately, Felix had shifted his focus from worrying about Chance to swimming, the fish in the pond, and learning about the world.

He remained puzzled by Jackson's comment about his parents not wanting him and being left at a museum. Unable to understand it fully, Felix sometimes stared at the blanket he had arrived with, which lacked a tag or label like the other blankets in the house. When he brought it to Laura, pointing at the mother-of-pearl paillette pieces sewn onto it, Laura didn't grasp what Felix was trying to convey. She explained where the material was harvested from, which only confused Felix further since they were nowhere near the ocean or any large body of water.

Seeing his confusion, Laura pulled up a few videos on the desktop computer and sat Felix on her lap to watch how mother-of-pearl was harvested. This occupied their time until a familiar sound caught Felix's attention: the bus pulling up. He quickly slid off Laura's lap and bolted for the front yard.

When Chance arrived home, the boys reunited with excitement. All other distractions Felix might have had melted away. Chance missed Felix as well, so their separation was always met with a hug upon their reunion.

Earlier that day, Miss Hauser, Chance's teacher, had announced that show and tell would start the next day. Instantly, Chance's hand shot up, asking if he could bring his little brother to class. Miss Hauser agreed, hoping to bring some joy to Chance, who had shown little interest in anything since he started school.

Chance brought a permission slip home for the Pines to sign. Henry and Laura exchanged glances before nodding in agreement. They thought it might do Felix good to see what Chance did all day while he was at school. Laura was eager for some free time to catch up on things she had fallen behind on due to her illness, and she also wanted to show Felix that his world wasn't ending when Chance was away. On the other hand, Henry was looking forward to some time alone with Laura, as it had been a long time since they had been alone together.

The next day, all the children boarded the bus. As the Pines waved goodbye and the bus drove off, Laura instinctively grasped Henry's hand, as if something had been taken from her. Sensing her vulnerability and the void that needed filling, Henry turned to Laura, winked, and then scooped her up in his arms, whisking her up to their bedroom. This brief respite from her constant dread gave Henry the chance he'd been waiting for.

Felix was ecstatic to be going along with Chance. The bus driver instructed them to sit in the front seat, where she could keep a close eye on the youngest of her wards due to Felix's small size. Chance was eager to show Felix everything he'd done and learned, excited to introduce the most important person in his world to his class. As the time approached, he became jittery. Miss Hauser called the class to attention, instructing the children to think about what they wanted to say about their show and tells.

Chance sat in the middle of the class, sharing his chair with Felix. His excitement was palpable, and the teacher noticed his impatience, as if he had to use the restroom and wasn't allowed to. After nine students had done their show and tell, Chance stood up, grabbed Felix's hand, and hurried to the front of the class.

Miss Hauser leaned down and whispered into Chance's ear, "I know you're excited, but I need you to slow down and breathe. You're going to have a heart attack. Okay?"

Chance turned to her and attempted to calm himself. He took a deep breath, feeling his heart slow slightly, and said, "Hi. My show and tell is my little brother, Felix. Things you should know about Felix are... he doesn't talk much, but he's super cool. We're best friends, and we do everything together."

Felix stood there, gazing at Chance.

"We play pirates in our backyard, and we sail the fastest and strongest ship on all seven seas. The ship is red with white racing stripes. What makes Felix super cool is how he knows what to do when we get into sticky situations with pirates. Felix only eats veggies and fruits, so that makes him Mrs. Pine's favorite because she never has to ask him to eat his veggies. I wished one night and asked God to send me a baby brother over and over, and He finally sent me one."

A boy named Landon, sitting at the back of the class, asked, "Is that the same Felix that my older brother said Coach Cramer was raving about the other day?"

Chance appeared dumbstruck and confused, but Felix, who knew who Coach Cramer was, nodded. The whole class buzzed with chatter. Even Miss Hauser had heard about Felix.

The town was passionate about sports and proud of its twenty-six consecutive state championships in swimming. Whenever something related to swimming happened, everyone in town knew about it within hours.

Chance's association with Felix instantly made him the most popular kid in class. This newfound popularity was a welcome surprise for Chance, who found it challenging to make friends. He didn't have much in common with other kids, and his imagination often seemed outlandish. The town prioritized athletic achievement over the arts, enrolling children in sports from a young age and paying little attention to creative pursuits.

Now that the other kids wanted to know all about Felix, Chance found it easier to strike up conversations. The interest continued even after show and tell had ended. Aaron, a thin kid with glasses, asked if Felix was faster than a fish in the water. Chance didn't know the answer. Sarah, another student, inquired if Felix would be going to school next year. Chance shook his head, knowing Felix would only be three.

The questions kept coming, and Chance tried to answer them to the best of his ability. Although he knew Felix could swim, he was unsure of just how good he was. Chance felt hurt that he didn't know his brother's swimming skills when everyone else seemed to. However, he quickly remembered that Felix didn't talk and couldn't explain things to him.

After lunch, Henry went to the elementary school to pick up Felix and take him to the high school for training. Chance recalled Henry mentioning at dinner that he'd taken Felix to the pool. This thought ran through his mind as he sat at his desk, waiting for the bell to ring. If Henry wasn't exaggerating about Felix, then the kids at school might be. This bothered Chance on the bus ride home, where he was still bombarded with questions.

Felix waited at the mailbox for the bus to drop off all the kids. As the bus pulled away, the children stared at Felix. Shy around unfamiliar people, Felix wasn't keen on stepping into the limelight. He grabbed Chance's hand and hurried into the house.

The pair made their way to the boys' bedroom and climbed onto their bed. Chance asked questions that he knew Felix couldn't answer. He reflected on their time together and realized that Felix had only ever nodded, going along with Chance's decisions. This realization made Chance tear up, feeling guilty for never seeking Felix's opinion or even asking.

Seeing that they still had some time before dinner, Felix decided to try to cheer Chance up. He guided Chance downstairs and into the study, where some of the kids were getting an early start on homework. Chance didn't fully understand what was happening but went along with it.

Felix searched for Henry in the study but found him in the laundry room helping Laura. Felix placed Henry's hand in Chance's before leading them back to the study. He stopped in front of the big Edwardian chair, which stood out among the other furniture, and motioned for Henry to sit. Felix then gestured for Henry to pick up Chance, which he did. Chance watched Felix with anticipation.

Felix, usually not very forward with his desires, ran to the built-in bookcase, grabbed a book he knew Chance loved, and lifted it above his head. Henry quickly understood what Felix wanted. He picked up both Felix and the book, and Felix's excitement was evident as he looked like an excited chimp with a banana. He sat Felix next to Chance, and the two cuddled up together. Henry opened the book with his free hand and began reading where he had left off.

Henry's slightly deep and calming voice filled the room. The two boys snuggled up, listening intently to the story. As their imaginations expanded with thoughts of mystical places, Henry tapped them on the arm to signal them to turn the pages. They listened to the story until Laura called them to dinner with an old schoolhouse bell from the 1800s she had picked up at a garage sale years ago. Laura, being soft-spoken and not one to yell, found the bell handy as it could be heard all over the property. It was loud enough to summon Sabrina from the hothouse as well. Everyone moved out of Theodore's way, fearing getting knocked over as he headed for the food. The children's footsteps thundered like a herd of wild buffalo running from a barreling train.

For dinner, Laura made hobo casserole, a quick and easy meal featuring tater tots mixed with refried beans, grilled vegetables, and a layer of cheese on top. The dish was seasoned with Mexican spices and sauce, then baked until golden brown. She also prepared some seasoned chicken breasts on the side for anyone who wanted meat with their meal.

The makeshift family finished every bite—there wasn't a morsel left. Felix stayed behind to help with the dishes, and Chance joined in, giving Rose the night off. Laura and the two boys cheerfully washed up, with Laura humming a lovely tune. With the extra hands, the dishes were done in half the usual time.

Once they finished, Laura noticed that Felix was about to fall asleep while standing.

"I think it's time for bed for this one," she said, catching Chance's attention.

"He was a little tired at dinner," Chance agreed. "It's from all the swimming he's been doing."

Laura placed Felix over her shoulder and carried him up the stairs like a sack of potatoes. She opened the door to the room and walked over to the boys' bed, untucking the covers with her free hand. Once the covers were loosened, she gently laid the now-sleeping Felix into bed.

"Shouldn't we brush our teeth?" Chance asked, turning his attention to her.

"We can let it slide just this once, don't you think?" she replied with a widening grin.

Chance then crawled into the bed where Felix was. A few moments later, he too was sound asleep.

Smiling, Laura leaned over the boys, stroked their heads, and whispered, "Get some rest, my little angels. I hope you have the most wonderful dreams."

Chapter 8

Adventures to Be Had

A month had passed, and little had changed, except for Jackson and Bobby constantly pestering everyone about Felix out of jealousy. They were annoyed by the attention Felix was getting. Trisha occasionally swatted them with rolled-up newspapers, as if they were misbehaving dogs.

Mornings started the same way, with Felix throwing a fit whenever Chance left for school. After his tantrum, he would talk to the plants and animals, seeking the latest information from them and listening to their stories before they went into hibernation.

Felix knew he would be going to the high school later that day as part of the new routine Henry had set up a structured schedule for him. Felix thrived with this routine, though it kept him from seeing Dip, the little koi fish, as often as he'd like to. However, all the training in the pool had paid off, and Felix could now keep pace with the fish in the pond. He would wait for Dip to appear and wave to him.

That morning, Felix stuck his head into the water. Dip had learned that nodding meant yes and shaking his head meant no. So, when Dip asked a question, Felix could respond, even if it was just with a yes or no answer.

After communicating with Dip, Felix left the pond and headed back to the house, where Betty was waiting for him on the back patio. "Human boy, why do you enjoy the water so much?" she meowed, not expecting a reply but simply voicing her thoughts.

Felix, with his hair still dripping wet, sat next to her and listened. Betty, aware of how compliant Felix was and how much he enjoyed stories, instructed him where to scratch and rub while recounting the greatest hunt of her life. She described a "murder spree" of about sixteen mice in seven minutes. She hadn't been hungry; she did it to show her affection for Henry and Laura. She piled the bodies on the kitchen rug where Laura would stand to wash dishes, detailing how she killed them, including the cruelest—a young mouse she batted around until its eyes bulged out.

The final detail did not sit well with Felix, so he quickly went into the house, cutting Betty's story short.

Felix rushed up the stairs to change into his swimsuit, windbreaker pants, and an oversized shirt that Chance had outgrown. Felix thought the shirt had somehow gotten bigger, but he had actually been losing his baby fat. He grabbed his small bag, which contained two of Chance's favorite toys and a towel.

Henry had been waiting at the door for a bit. "I have something special for you, but you'll have to wait!" he said, smiling.

Felix shrugged it off, assuming it was some new swim technique. Henry always got excited about showing him new things.

They climbed into the truck, as usual, with Felix sitting on Henry's lap, listening to their favorite radio station. When they arrived, Felix no longer paid attention to the team photos. Instead, he glided his hands over the trophy cases as he walked down the hallway, admiring the shiny cups and figures on the shelves, draped with countless medals.

They opened the door and were greeted like war heroes. After navigating through the enthusiastic boys and girls clamoring to talk to Henry and Felix, Coach Cramer stood with his chest puffed out and back straight as a pin, waiting next to the edge of the pool. Beside him was a duffel bag in the school colors—light blue and gold—with the large, embroidered words "Black Marlin."

After receiving his hugs, Coach Cramer bent down, picked up the bag, and handed it to Felix. The bag appeared full. Felix hugged Coach Cramer's legs, and Coach Cramer beamed, ruffling Felix's hair. Felix had never seen a bag like this before and thought it might be a pillow, so he squeezed it.

"Aren't you going to open it?" Henry asked.

Felix looked puzzled as Henry took the squishy pillow with handles. Henry unzipped it and began pulling things out, placing them on Felix's lap. The first item was a huge, fluffy towel with the letters "B" and "M" printed on it. Next, there was a small blue tracksuit with "Black Marlin" embroidered in gold, a swimsuit, a pair of swim goggles, and a small package wrapped in blue paper. Felix unwrapped the gift to find an MP3 player filled with the same tunes they rocked out to in the truck, plus a few songs Henry and Laura had enjoyed when they were growing up.

Felix, always thankful for everything he received, gave Henry a big hug. He then ran over to Coach Cramer, repeating his gratitude.

Coach Cramer knelt in front of Felix. "You know, my little black marlin, when you're old enough, you're going to be my next champion."

Coach Cramer turned to Henry. "And your boy thought it was just a stuffed animal." The two men laughed heartily at Felix's reaction to the duffle bag.

Felix held onto all his new belongings, turning his attention to the two men.

After a long day with little instruction, Felix finally grew tired from the endless back and forth across the pool. He wasn't trying to show off, but the spectators couldn't help but be impressed by this young child and his abilities. Felix moved through the water with the grace of a fish, gliding effortlessly as if he had been born in the water. The spectators marveled at his incredible talent at such a young age, analyzing every move he made.

When Felix got out of the pool, Henry was waiting with a huge fluffy towel to dry him off. Felix appreciated things that were soft and plush. During the summer, they sometimes took field trips to local farms to see the baby animals. This is where he gained his appreciation.

A few of the varsity boys came over to chat with Henry and Felix. One of the tall, well-defined boys ruffled Felix's hair and said, "You did great, Little Marlin."

Felix glanced upward, as if expecting instructions, while trying to fix his tousled hair.

"Hey, big guy, it's getting late. Go get changed," Henry said, nodding at Felix to see if he was ready.

Felix took his new bag, walked to the locker room, and changed. He took everything off except the swim goggles, which he perched at his hairline, mimicking what one of the older boys had done.

Henry thought it was amusing to see such a little boy

carrying such a big bag, yet it made him swell with pride. Watching Felix excel at something Henry had so many fond memories of filled him with emotion. Not wanting Felix to struggle any longer, Henry took the bag, slung it over his shoulder, and the two headed home after a lengthy round of goodbyes, ending with another warm hug from Coach Cramer.

When the two arrived home, they put everything away, except for the goggles that still rested on Felix's head. They then went into the kitchen, where Laura was prepping dinner. She was peeling potatoes while four whole chickens marinated in the refrigerator. The marinade smelled delightful, with hints of rosemary, lemon, and cracked pepper. Felix's food was already prepped: grapefruit, melon, and the broccoli was waiting to be steamed.

Henry peeled the potatoes, and Felix handed him new ones once each was finished. The three worked merrily, while Laura hummed a soothing Irish tune that Henry recognized immediately. Laura then cubed the potatoes, oiled two tinfoil pans, and seasoned the potatoes with rosemary, salt, and pepper.

Felix dashed off to the study, grabbed his favorite book, and raced back to the kitchen table, handing it to Henry.

"Oh, is it time for this again? All right," Henry said.

Felix stared up at Henry with anticipation. Henry took the book, opened it to where the bookmark was placed, and began reading. Laura lifted Felix onto her lap, leaning him against her like a girl with her doll. She removed the goggles and set them on the table, stroking Felix's hair as they listened to Henry read page after page. As the scrumptious smells from the kitchen filled the air, story time continued until the other children returned home from school.

When Felix heard the door open, he quickly grabbed the goggles and put them back on his head. He bounced off Laura's lap and raced over to Chance, who was still in the hallway. The two boys hugged enthusiastically until Felix felt Chance's stomach growl. Holding hands, they hurried into the kitchen together.

The chicken was perfectly timed to be done an hour after the children arrived home, giving them enough time to put their things away and wash their hands. Henry pulled out the hot dishes from the oven. Once everything was placed on the counter and the foil removed, Henry carved the birds with precision.

As the children lined up at the kitchen island, Henry called Felix up first to get his food, as a reward for his help with the preparations. Chance stayed at the back of the line while Henry scooped some potatoes onto a plate for Felix. Laura buttered Felix's steamed broccoli and took his plate to the table.

Felix followed the plate, climbing into his chair and waiting for Chance to sit down. After serving Felix, Henry moved on to prepare the remaining plates.

The twins always loved roasted chicken, and this recipe was one of their favorites. They would always get the wings and legs to be alike, even in their eating. The other children didn't mind as long as the food was warm and delicious.

Once Chance reached the table, Felix dived into his meal. If Chance wasn't stuffing his face, he was telling Felix a story. Chance always had a tale to share, regardless of how dull the school day had been.

Tonight, Chance retold a story the teacher had read to them. "It was about a girl who broke into a bear's house and had the nerve to eat everyone's food. In the end, she was caught sleeping in the little bear's bed. I reckon she got five to ten years."

Noticing Felix's goggles, Chance asked, "What are those?" pointing at Felix's head.

Henry, not taking his eyes off his plate, answered, "They're called goggles, and they're made for seeing underwater."

Felix nodded in agreement, though he knew he didn't need them to see underwater.

"Right now, they look like baby horns on Felix's head," Chance said with amazement. Everyone chuckled, with a few kids shaking their heads or rolling their eyes.

The two boys finished their dinner as the other kids chattered about their day at school. After dinner, as was routine, all the children went to the study to either work on homework or listen to Henry read.

With the book in hand, Henry settled into his big, comfortable chair. Chance and Felix stayed behind to help Laura with the cleanup, allowing Rose and Orchid to spend more time together.

Once the dishes were done, the pair joined Henry in the study and climbed onto his lap as he read until bedtime.

Chapter 9

A Wet Wonderland

As fall turned into winter, Felix's days felt emptier without his interactions with the outside plants and animals. While watching a TV show about missing kids, he wondered if he might have been misplaced or lost, and if his parents were trying to find him.

Laura often caught glimpses of Felix wandering around the Kennedy House with Chance's fluffy monster in hand. He would frequently find himself next to Betty, who licked his face and tried to steal the toy from him to get all of his attention.

One day, Henry turned on the TV and saw Harry, Ron, and Hermione from the book he had been reading to them. This caught Felix's attention in a way only Chance could. For the first time, Felix could see faces that matched the images Henry had described. Over the following weeks, Felix watched the Harry Potter movie repeatedly.

At the pool, Felix was distracted by thoughts of the characters from the film. Even after training, he was consumed by the movie and fascinated by the mystical creatures.

He went to the art supply bins, grabbed a binder with paper and colored pencils, and paused the movie to draw the creatures as best as he could. Sometimes it was easy, but other times he struggled to get it right.

Recognizing his budding interest, Laura would set him up at the table while she prepped food, encouraging him to draw different things from a book she kept in the study. Her goal was to build his hand-eye coordination and foster his creativity.

She noticed that Felix enjoyed drawing ancient Greek and Roman beasts more than landscapes or still-life works. She guided him in detail techniques, helping him improve his drawing skills and anatomical accuracy as much as she could.

With Christmas approaching, the children were about to begin their winter break, and Felix's birthday was also coming up. The estate was soon to undergo its yearly holiday transformation. On the last day of school before the break, Henry and Felix left for the day, while Laura went to the garage to retrieve the Christmas decorations.

She pulled down twenty-five rubber containers from the rafters, which included a nine-and-a-half-foot-tall artificial Virginia pine. They preferred a fake tree to cutting one down from nature. The other containers held garlands resembling real cedar branches, and handmade stockings with each child's name finely stitched on them.

Laura's prized decorations were from a local glass-blowing artist. The ornaments were shaped like ornate marbles, inflated like balloons. Some had leopard and giraffe spots, while others featured stripes, polka dots, and swirls in brilliant colors.

These were not your ordinary ornaments; they cost between $85 and $150, depending on the size. The tree topper was a large, three-dimensional heart made from various colors of stained glass, with golden ribbons cascading down. Once decorated, the tree resembled a cone of stacked, colorful lollipops with their sticks cut off. Laura didn't allow the children to help decorate the tree, fearing they might break the ornaments.

After school, the children avoided the formal sitting room, so they hadn't noticed the tree yet. After dinner that evening, Henry finished reading a few chapters of their book, and the children completed their homework before heading to bed.

With Christmas only a few days away, and the excitement in the air, the children found it hard to sleep. Once they finally drifted off, Henry and Laura got out of bed to tackle the remaining decorations.

While Laura finished the parlor, Henry went outside to wrap lights around the cypress trees and retrieved wreaths from the garage. Each wreath, the size of an extra-large pizza, was tied with a large red velvet bow. The wreath above the front door was the largest, made of red glittering velvet poinsettias, with a perfectly crimped bow.

Laura strung garland on the fireplace and banisters, hung the children's stockings on the mantel, and replaced the usual decorations with white and crystal variations, giving the home a regal yet cozy European appearance.

On Christmas Eve, after all the decorating was complete, Henry and Laura wrapped the children's gifts in secret, making sure not to be heard creeping down the stairs. The gifts usually included school supplies, clothing, games, and other items to keep the children occupied. They had been delivered by the mayor a week before the holiday. Local charities in the surrounding towns contributed to gift bins, many of which ended up at the Kennedy House. These offerings were useful to both the children and the Pines. To keep the gifts a surprise, they were always stored in the garage.

When playing in the snow, Bobby and Jackson would annoy most of the children by pelting them with snowballs. The girls would make snow angels, build snowmen, or go sledding down the hill at the back of the property. Trisha and French usually helped Felix, Chance, and Matthew build a snow castle, while Theodore, always pouting, would sit on the porch, wanting to go back inside.

The children had been told that if they came downstairs during the night, Santa would skip the Kennedy House and not bring them anything that year. This threat allowed Henry and Laura to move about the ground floor without interruptions.

The children didn't receive allowances unless they saved their school milk money or collected quarters instead of buying snacks. French helped with a local kid's paper route, and French, Mitch, and Sabrina spent many weekends at the old folks' home reading to the elderly. Many of the elderly residents' children would give them money for snacks from the vending machines. They saved this money throughout the school year, which added up to a tidy sum. This allowed the children to buy Henry and Laura a gift certificate for their favorite restaurant and two tickets for a movie of their choice during one of their date nights.

Christmas morning had arrived, and when Theodore's feet hit the floor with a thud, all the boys woke up, initiating the annual stampede in the boys' room, which in turn woke up the girls. The herd of children raced downstairs to the formal sitting room. As French, the fastest in the house, burst through the double doors, he came to a sudden halt. If Theodore hadn't paused to pilfer candy from his stocking on the banister, he would have crashed into French.

The tree looked as though it had exploded with gifts. Each child had their own color or pattern of wrapping paper. The Pines sat on the couch, sipping hot chocolate with marshmallows floating on top, enjoying the scene as the children darted toward their piles of presents. The beautifully decorated room quickly transformed into a chaotic mess of boxes and wrapping paper.

Chance and Felix discovered they had received a joint gift. Inside the large box were a new tire swing for the backyard tree, a tricorn hat, a bandana, and foam pirate swords. Chance immediately put the bandana on Felix's head and the tricorn hat on himself before jumping up and exclaiming, "Arrrr, Felix, these waters be teeming with Present sharks! We must get to dry land, or all shall be lost!"

Chance grabbed Felix's hand and rushed to the staircase, foam swords in hand. From the stairs, Chance pointed at the sea of debris. "Look! The sharks are monstrous and could swallow you whole!"

Laura laughed and rolled her eyes at Chance's dramatic speech, hiding her amusement behind her cup of hot chocolate.

"I know you're all excited about your presents," Henry said, "but I need the boys to break down the boxes and the girls to collect and fold the wrapping paper. Everything needs to go out to the recycling bin."

The children complied, reluctantly setting their new gifts aside. Once everything was cleaned up and all the gifts put away, the family gathered around the kitchen table to watch the Pines make pancakes. There were fresh fruit, chocolate sauce, powdered sugar, honey butter, and whipped cream, as well as bacon, sausage, and eggs. After the meal, the children cleaned up, giving the Pines some time to rest and open their gifts.

It was a Kennedy House tradition to go to a nearby town to help at the homeless shelter, serving food and handing out old toys. The older children assisted with the food, while the younger ones distributed the toys. Theodore, Bobby, and Jackson were not trusted to be unsupervised, so Henry had them shovel and salt the sidewalks to make them safer for visitors.

After serving lunch at the shelter, they would visit the town's Christmas maze, made from blocks of snow and ice, with a large carved ice sculpture of an angel in the center. Henry also brought sleds for the group to use on a large hill nearby.

While the others sledded, Laura returned home to decorate the desserts and set up the buffet. She had a large ham with pineapple rings and maraschino cherries in the oven. She prepared mashed potatoes, yams with marshmallows and brown sugar, string beans with sliced almonds, succotash, and gravy. For dessert, there were cherry pie, apple pie, pumpkin pie, chocolate pudding, a variety of cookies, fruit tarts, and dozens of cakes decorated like they were from a French patisserie—a talent Laura inherited from her mother.

Laura heard the van pull up, but the front door remained closed. After six minutes of silence, the door finally opened, revealing the children holding bouquets of flowers. Henry had secretly handmade each arrangement over the past two days, and Laura was delighted by the unique and lavish designs.

The formal dining room was set as if the Queen of England were visiting. Navy blue satin drapes were drawn, the crystal chandelier sparkled, and a lace tablecloth draped elegantly over the table, completing the regal look. The family feasted like royalty that night. With no homework to be done, they retired to the study, where Henry read aloud from the book about witches and wizards, and a boy named Neville won his house—the House Cup. Laura joined them with a platter of cookies and a pitcher of milk for everyone during story time.

After their nightly routine, the children slipped into bed with full bellies from the feast. Felix, still awake and excited, decided he needed to go meet Dip, whom he hadn't seen for a while. After waiting fifteen minutes, Felix crept out of bed, careful not to disturb Chance.

Unbeknownst to Felix, Chance was still awake and watched him slip out of the room, down to the ground floor, out the back doors, and into the backyard. Curious but unsure of Felix's intentions, Chance followed him quietly.

When Felix reached the edge of the pond, he stripped down to his underwear and slipped into the water. The pond had not frozen over thanks to the heaters. Chance crept closer to the edge of the water, searching for Felix's head in the darkness. Felix knew where Dip swam during the night, and once he found him, they swam together under the moonlight.

Chance panicked when he hadn't seen Felix's head above the water for a few minutes. Shivering from the cold, he ran around the pond in knee-high snow, desperately searching for Felix, not knowing what to do. His heart raced, and the heat from his skin created wisps of steam that curled into the night sky, while liquid salt streamed down his face.

Unbeknownst to Chance, Felix and Dip were on the

other side of the pond. Chance, not as skilled a swimmer as Felix, leapt into the water in a frantic attempt to find his little brother. He dove under the surface, his panic increasing.

Felix and Dip were playing tag at the far end of the pond, unaware of Chance's distress. As Chance made ripples on the other side, he moved further into the deeper part of the pond, shivering constantly but still diving down and feeling around for Felix. His anxiety grew, and he began to cry as he continued his search with no success. The water's temperature was sapping his strength, but he pushed on, diving deeper and deeper into the pond.

As Chance turned to make his way back to the surface, his arms slipped out of the sleeves of his shirt, transforming it into a nightmarish straitjacket that constricted him in a cruel embrace. Overcome by a mounting panic, he flailed desperately, trying to find the elusive openings of the sleeves, but the cold, dark water distorted his sense of direction and stole his breath away. With every passing second, his chest tightened, each gasp for air grew desperate and feeble then the last. The crushing weight of fear and exhaustion fogged his mind, leaving him helpless and disoriented.

In a final, agonizing bid for freedom, Chance swam blindly, his movements growing slower and more labored as the water around him seemed to close in like a suffocating shroud. But no matter how hard he fought, the surface remained just out of reach, an unattainable reprieve. As his strength finally gave out, his body, now motionless, hovered for a moment in the dark depths, never reaching the floor or the surface of the pond when he was alive.

By the time his lifeless body began its slow, haunting ascent, Chance's struggles were over. His face, once vibrant with life, was now a mask of tragic emptiness. Eyes wide open, they stared unseeing into the void, reflecting a heart-wrenching image of lost hope. He floated face down, drifting eerily like an autumn leaf ensnared by the tangled roots of waterlilies, a ghostly figure forever suspended between life and death. Each ripple on the water's surface seemed to mock the futility of his final, desperate fight, leaving behind only the chilling silence of his tragedy.

Felix and Dip were still playing when a group of older fish swam towards them. The oldest fish, a giant white koi with silver and gray speckles, bubbled air and said in a stern voice, "There's a body in the pond near the lily pads on the other side, and it's not moving."

There was only one area in the entire lake-sized pond where lily pads were still alive. Dip and Felix darted in that direction, followed by the group of elder fish. When they reached the lily pads, Felix swam closer to inspect the body, which was tangled in the roots and stems, obscuring its identity.

Felix grabbed the body by the foot and pulled, swimming toward the shoreline. It took him a while to free the body from the tangled lily tendrils, many of which had broken off. Once he reached the shore, Felix was distressed as he dragged the body up the embankment. He struggled to clear away the debris from the cold body.

As Felix gently removed the last of the debris from around Chance's neck, he was met with the stark, heart-breaking reality of his big brother's face. Collapsing onto Chance's lifeless body, Felix's sobs tore through the silence, each one a raw cry of despair. His face contorted in a grief so profound it seemed to strip away all hope and light. Overcome by a tidal wave of sorrow, he gasped for breath, his tears mingling with snot and saliva that streamed uncontrollably from his anguish.

"No!" Felix's scream shattered the night, a soul-wrenching cry of agony he had never known before. With Chance's head resting in his trembling lap, the inconsolable child held him close, his heart breaking with every ragged breath. The weight of the unrelenting despair pressed down on him, a darkness so suffocating it seemed to swallow all the light from his world.

Death had always been something that lingered close by, a terrifying concept to Felix, a shadowy presence on the periphery of his young life. But now, it had consumed him entirely. In this moment, he felt as though a part of himself had been irrevocably torn away. Chance had been more than a brother, a beacon of joy and laughter, and now, that light was extinguished forever. Felix's entire being ached with the realization that he had lost his closest companion, and with him, a piece of his own heart.

As Felix let out another heartbroken howl, his body went rigid with grief. A blinding pillar of light erupted from his mouth and eyes, shooting up into the serene night sky, an ethereal beacon of his inconsolable pain. He could neither see nor comprehend the spectacle unfolding around him, only the crackling, electric hum that filled his ears and the intense, searing heat radiating from his core. In this moment of overwhelming sorrow, he was lost to the world, consumed by a profound, otherworldly anguish that left him feeling as if he had perished alongside his beloved brother.

Moments later, a gust of wind swept through the area. A hooded figure appeared from the center of the commotion, slowly standing upright in the cratered snow.

Felix, still consumed by his immediate loss and pain, did not notice the arrival. The figure, clad in velvet, rose-colored robes, moved toward the two boys. Kneeling beside them, a long, golden braid of hair peeked out from the hood, and a soft, gloved hand reached out to Felix.

As the hand touched Felix's face, the hooded figure received visions of everything racing through Felix's mind. A teardrop fell from the hood and crystallized before hitting the ground. The figure sifted through Felix's memories, absorbing information and skimming through his life's events.

From within its robes, the figure produced a plush, knitted blanket and gently laid it over Felix. The figure then rose, twirling around as its robes swirled like rose petals before making its way toward the Kennedy House, leaving no footprints.

The door opened silently as the figure gestured with a wave of its hand. It retrieved a ruby-red bag with beaded fringe and lacquered bamboo handles. The figure glided through the house, first to the study to grab a few books. Then it ascended the stairs to the boys' bedroom, where the remaining boys slept. The figure took the blanket that had been at the foot of the bed—the same blanket Felix had been found in. After gently placing it into the bag, the figure also took Felix's teddy bear and Chance's fluffy monster, putting them both into the red bag.

The figure then picked up Felix's swim bag and unexplainedly stuffed it into the small red bag. Miraculously, everything fit, even though the bag seemed far too small to contain all the items.

Next, the figure went to Chance and Felix's dresser drawers, retrieving a few items of clothing. Then, heading to the study, she gathered a handful of books. With a twist of its fingers, a milky-colored mist billowed from beneath the robes, filling the house and spilling out through the windows and doors, which silently opened.

The hooded figure made its way back to Felix on the bank. In one swift motion, it lifted Felix, leaving Chance behind. Felix, still in shock, reached out desperately for Chance, but it was too late—he couldn't reach his brother's body. One of the gloved hands disappeared beneath the robes. With a snap of its fingers, the figure put Felix to sleep, his head resting on the figure's chest. The figure then soared upward, hovering hundreds of feet in the air. The mist continued to envelop the house, spreading over the entire property, the town, and reaching for miles in all directions.

The figure hovered in place, observing as the milky mist covered the land. Once everything was shrouded in mist, the figure snapped its fingers again, transforming the mist into golden, glittering dust that erased all memories of Felix's existence. The dust then vanished, along with the figure and Felix, leaving the Kennedy House emptier and the epicenter of Felix's life lying lifeless in the snow.

The figure held Felix tightly as they soared westward. The rose-colored robes cocooned them as they sped past green forests, snow-capped mountains, and brightly lit cities that glittered like yellow diamonds. They swept past a rocky coastline before heading out to sea. The full moon illuminated the giant swells as they weaved in and out of the mountains of water, traveling thousands of miles in what felt like seconds.

When they reached their destination, the rose-colored cocoon approached a giant wall of wind and water that stretched for miles. The wind pushed back against them, and a hand emerged from the robes. With a swish of the wrist, a small opening appeared in the wall of water, allowing the cocoon to pass through. The opening sealed behind them as the wall of water returned to its previous state in the stormy sea.

As the cocoon passed through the wall, a bright flash occurred. The mysterious figure's robes unwrapped, revealing a woman a little taller than average, who hovered in place with golden-brown eyes peering downward. Despite her full figure, she moved as gracefully as a feather in the wind. She checked on Felix, maintaining the sleep she had placed on him. Floating down from the opening as if gravity didn't affect her, she remained calm.

Suddenly, a deafening, high-pitched screech shattered the silence as two enormous, razor-sharp claws swiped through the air with deadly precision, their lethal intent unmistakable. The woman, her face set in grim determination, traced an urgent pattern in the air with her finger. As she completed the intricate gesture, an ornate red wire cage sprang into existence, enveloping her and Felix in a shimmering, protective barrier. One of the monstrous creatures, its eyes glowing with feral hunger, lunged toward them with murderous speed. But as it neared, the cage erupted in a blinding flare of searing light, sending the beast crashing violently to the ground. Its wings ignited in a blaze of fiery destruction, the creature's agonized shrieks piercing through the chaos. The force of its impact, followed by the horrific thuds and bone-crushing noises, reverberated through the air as it plummeted, dragging the second beast down in a catastrophic tumble. As the dust settled and the silence reclaimed its grip, the woman pressed forward, undeterred by the deadly encounter.

With Felix still under her spell and asleep, she traveled forth, illuminated by the colossal heavenly orb in the night sky named Kalli, whose light resembled a moon hanging in the night sky. Her face was lit by its glow. She struggled to suppress the emotions stirred by the images she had seen in Felix's mind, haunted by the lifeless body of a young boy lying in the snow—a painful reminder of her own past.

She gazed upon a hidden paradise, a realm of enchanting beauty enclosed by majestic mountains. As she descended, she drifted past snow-capped peaks, where fluffy, horned creatures, like whimsical sprites, clustered on the cliffs. Below, the land was a tapestry of shimmering lakes and winding rivers, their surfaces glinting like silver under Kalli's light. The air was alive with the melodic symphony of crickets and frogs, creating a soothing chorus that complemented the serene landscape.

Forests of emerald-green trees stretched as far as the eye could see, their trunks soaring over five hundred feet tall. These ancient giants had roots so massive they seemed to twist and dance beneath the forest floor. Among the roots, delicate winged creatures fluttered, their wings shimmering with iridescent hues, while the largest of the trees supported tiny villages nestled high in their canopies. These villages were connected by intricate rope bridges, swaying gently in the breeze like strands of golden silk.

As she moved further, the landscape transformed into enchanting swamps, where fireflies drifted like floating lanterns over the water. Some of these tiny lights were quickly snatched up by fish with long, agile tongues, their lithe bodies launching out of the water in a graceful ballet. Nearby, villages perched on stilts danced with the reflection of the water, and one extraordinary village floated serenely on an island in the center of a crystalline lake, its homes seemingly suspended in time.

The flowers that adorned the land fluttered and swayed in the breeze, their vibrant petals dancing like confetti in the wind. Some petals, caught by playful gusts, were lifted from their stems and carried aloft, giving a sense of etherealness.

Cradling Felix in a tender embrace, she approached a towering rock formation crowned by a grand, opulent castle. As they drew closer, the castle emerged through a veil of soft, misty clouds. It was a marvel of elegance, with twelve majestic turrets reaching skyward, their ornate glass ceilings glowing warmly from within. The castle's walls shimmered with an otherworldly light, casting an enchanting glow that illuminated the surrounding landscape.

The grounds of the castle were reminiscent of a quaint English cottage garden, meticulously tended with vibrant blooms and lush greenery. Behind the castle, a colossal tree stood like a sentinel, its enormous white bark catching the moonlight and reflecting it with a silvery sheen. At twilight, the tree's leaves took on a mystical gray hue, adding an ancient mystique to the already mystifying setting.

Onward they soared, past the towering spires of the castle, toward an altar nestled beneath a grand stone pavilion. The altar was flanked by two lit braziers, illuminating a large, cradle-like basket in the center. Gently, the woman laid Felix into the basket.

She then retrieved two items from a pouch hidden beneath her robes: a silver flute and a small dagger with a crystal handle. Setting the dagger aside, she raised the flute to her lips and played a hauntingly hypnotic melody while dancing around the altar. She continued her performance until her gaze fell upon something stirring from a castle door.

Her eyes locked onto a small, glowing object emerging from a crack in the door. A bright, orange-sized light scurried frantically toward her. As it neared the altar, it revealed itself to be a spider with a transparent, bulb-shaped vial filled with shimmering liquid instead of an abdomen.

The spider stiffened as it approached the dagger; its hind legs twisted opening the vial's cork. Once the cork was removed, the spider became motionless.

The woman stopped playing and approached the altar. She picked up the dagger and plunged it into the brazier's flames before carefully piercing Felix's large left toe to draw a drop of blood onto the blade. She flicked the blood into the vial and sealed it. Resuming her playing, the spider began to dance as the contents of the vial swirled rapidly. After a few moments, the bright white light transformed into a deep sapphire blue. The woman's rose-colored robes appeared lavender under the shifting light.

Once the vial's contents had fully transformed, the spider's abdomen turned clear again, and the woman's robes returned to their original rosy hue. She had prepared bandages for the wound, which she wrapped around Felix's toe. After tenderly kissing the toe, the wound quickly sealed.

The woman's sultry voice rose in a solemn chant, as if summoning the dragon gods from the watery depths. "Mizu, from the darkest and deepest depths of the oceans, the Bringer of Life, claim your disciple. Teach him and guide him in the ways of thyself. For you are the only one the seas will obey!"

Behind the pavilion, in the middle of the lake, stood a cluster of statues as large as houses. Five dragon statues represented the elements: earth, fire, lightning, water, and wind. The highest statue, wings spread as if in midflight, circled a massive stone pillar. The second statue depicted a dragon descending the pillar. The third reared up against it like a fierce steed; the fourth sat regally at the base; and the fifth was partially submerged, its back and head poking out of the surrounding water.

These statues symbolized the five elemental gods: Jupiter, the god of lightning; Amun, the god of wind; Vulcan, the god of fire; Terra, the goddess of earth; and Mizu, the goddess of water. These deities were believed to have birthed all things, bestowing their powers to other living creatures.

As the woman's chant concluded, the eye socket of the semi-submerged dragon statue glowed a brilliant red. The spider leapt from the altar and scurried toward the statues, bounding from stone to stone across the water until it reached the semi-submerged dragon. Climbing the dragon's neck, the spider inserted itself into the eye socket. The eye glowed brighter, shifting from red to blue, causing the dragon's resting wing to rise and reveal an entryway.

Moments later, the statue's mouth released a thick fog that blanketed the water. As the fog settled, a light shone from the doorway, and a figure emerged. The figure appeared more as an apparition than a physical being, casting a ghostly blue glow as it glided across the water.

Draped in a flowing blue gown resembling a kimono, the figure floated gracefully over to the cradle holding Felix. The woman in rose-colored robes retrieved the bag containing Felix's belongings and placed each item atop the altar. The lady in blue waved her hand over the items, causing them to levitate. She then lifted Felix and cradled him in her arms. The glowing blue figure bowed to the woman in rose before drifting back across the water, followed by Felix's belongings. The woman in rose wiped her eyes and waved goodbye, then gathered her things and vanished from sight.

The statue's wing lowered back into place, and the eye ceased glowing. The spider emerged from the socket, hurriedly making its way down the statue and back across the water to the castle.

Inside, the space was warm, heated by a large brazier hanging high. The walls were adorned with mosaics depicting aquatic scenes and creatures interacting playfully. The floor was covered with nest-shaped beds of hay cradling babies, animals, and eggs.

Before proceeding further, the woman gestured at a cabinet, and its doors swung open. Inside, a liquid mirror undulated as she guided Felix's belongings into it. She then placed Felix into one of the empty nests, surrounded by other children and their various baby animals like puppies, kittens, rabbits, owlets, and others. Some nests held lizards and snakes.

Felix remained still, sleeping through the night.

In the morning, Felix awoke to the sounds of giggling and cooing from other babies playing with their animal companions. Confused and startled by his new surroundings, Felix struggled to remember the events of the previous night.

He cried, seeking refuge in a shadowy corner of the room to avoid the attention of the Blue Lady. Terrified and uncertain, he tried to hide.

When the Blue Lady discovered Felix's absence from the nest, she searched the room thoroughly until she found him behind a column, curled up and sobbing uncontrollably. She gently placed her eerily transparent hand—surprisingly warm to the touch—on his back. Without speaking, she rubbed his back soothingly until his breathing began to steady.

Her lips didn't move, but Felix heard her voice clearly.

"Is something wrong, my child?"

Felix didn't respond; he curled up tighter, consumed by his pain.

"My name is Miko, though some call me the Blue Lady. You're safe here. There's nothing to fear. What's your name?"

Felix didn't answer, so she placed her fingers gently on his temples, peering into his mind. She saw everything that had happened to him as his memories flashed before her. She felt the strong bond between Felix and Chance, and then witnessed the heartbreaking sight of Chance lying lifeless in his arms. When the mist had transformed into golden glitter, Felix was out of reach of it.

Miko gasped and gathered Felix into her embrace, holding him tightly. Unsure how to comfort the distraught boy, she began to sing a soft, soothing melody. Though Felix couldn't understand the words, the song had a calming effect.

Miko continued to sing slowly and gently until Felix, exhausted from crying, finally relaxed in her arms. Once again, Miko asked for his name, but he did not respond. His limited communication skills, primarily restricted to saying "no," left him struggling to express himself, except for his telepathic conversations with plants and the one-way conversations with animals.

Looking up at Miko, Felix saw the kindness and empathy in her eyes. He reached down and picked up some hay, bending the pieces into the shape of an "F" and so forth and then the final letter, "X," spelling out his name.

"Felix," Miko said softly. "Your name is Felix."

Felix gave her his full attention and nodded.

"Do you know when your birthday is?" Miko asked.

Felix bent the hay into the answer: December 29.

Seeing his response, Miko approached an old carving on the wall that shifted slightly each day. Her finger glowed blue as she traced runes on the carving, revealing a new set of characters.

"So, Felix, born December 29. It looks like you have a birthday coming up in two days. Let me be the first to welcome you to Yurden."

Felix looked at Miko, puzzled.

"This is your new home, and it's called Yurden," Miko explained.

Felix's expression shifted from sadness to horror to confusion.

Seeing his distress, Miko quickly addressed it. "It's okay. I'll explain everything. Let's start with this: Yurden was created as a sanctuary for the elves when they could no longer live in the world of humans. The elves also brought along certain humans with unique gifts and creatures that would have been hunted 'til there were none left.

"Yurden is a hidden land, a pocket dimension." Realizing he might not understand, she added, "A pocket dimension is like a secret hiding place that only special people know about, far away from everything else. It's a special place that you will come to call home."

Noticing the other residents of the nursery gathering around, Miko said, "We'll continue this discussion another time."

The morning had just begun, and the children were eager to meet the new arrival.

"His name is Felix, and he doesn't speak at the moment," Miko explained to the children.

The children introduced themselves and their animal companions. Some were still too young to talk and remained in their nests. Felix, though nearly three years old, was more mature and developed than most children his age.

As time went on, the children gradually became better acquainted with one another while being taught by Lady Miko about being Water Weavers. She shared her knowledge through stories and occasional demonstrations of her talents.

One of the older children asked when they would be able to control water like Lady Miko could.

"When you grow up big and strong," she replied. "And only after you attend school. First, you will need to receive your brands. Until then, you won't be able to control water as I do. Even when you can control water, it will still be many years before you master talents such as mine."

A few days after settling in, Felix was still sleeping in Chance's shirt and cuddling with the stuffed animals that Lady Rosalyn had collected for him. He was gradually adjusting to his new surroundings but remained deeply saddened by his loss, crying himself to sleep each night.

In the morning, Lady Miko cradled Felix in her lap and said, "I need to tell you something. I know I haven't explained why you are here. Felix, you are a weaver, and where you came from, they would hunt you down. You would never be safe as long as they knew you existed. This place will protect you, and you're accepted here for who you are. It will be hard for you to adjust, but I'll do my best to make the transition as smooth as possible."

During the day, Lady Miko provided Felix with more information about Yurden, while he spent hours gazing with fascination at the guardian dragon at the entrance to the room. He imagined how excited Chance would have been to see a dragon for the first time—a dream come true for him, but one Felix would never witness. These thoughts did little to lighten his mood.

One day, Lady Miko gathered Felix and a few older children in a circle. Her fingers moved gracefully through the air, weaving as naturally as breathing. A liquid shape materialized in front of the children.

"This is a model of the planet," she said.

A girl pointed at the shape and asked, "Why does it have a hole in the middle? Mater and Kalli don't."

Miko nodded. "That's a great question. Our planet is shaped like a disk and spins like a wheel. One side always faces Mater and Kalli, while the other side remains permanently dark."

As she wove her hand again, the colors of the disk shifted; the water turned blue, and the land green. "Our planet has five continents, but we will focus on Yurden, where we are located."

She pointed out Yurden. "Once, Yurden was a single nation, but after a long and bloody war, it split into three nations: Ioesses, Heedafien, and Ozmare. We are located in Heedafien, near the border of Ozmare."

Miko pointed out each of the nations. After covering the main points, she answered the children's questions until their curiosities were satisfied.

Felix absorbed everything he heard, paying close attention to the explanations, questions, and answers. He remained silent, finding it difficult to express himself.

These lessons occurred once or twice a week, depending on the nursery's schedule.

As the days passed, Felix kept to himself, trying to adapt to his new environment and asking as many questions as he could think of. Even though Felix was trying to adjust, it was a very unpleasant ordeal for him. Lady Miko did her best to cheer him up and managed to do so occasionally.

Felix was not only coping with the death of Chance but also grappling with the thought that his parents had abandoned him and the loss of his friend Dip. These thoughts add-ed to his emotional distress.

During evening story time, which was meant to lull the

children to sleep, Felix was instead kept awake, captivated by every word Lady Miko spoke. He loved listening to her voice, as he no longer had the daily stories Chance or Henry used to tell him. Felix eagerly absorbed all the information Lady Miko shared.

During his first week in this new world, Felix developed a habit of sleepwalking. He would wander, stuffed animal in hand, to the stoic dragon guarding the entrance. The dragon would monitor Felix, retract its teeth, and gently scoop him into its mouth to return him to his nest.

Unfortunately for Sangbi the dragon, Felix didn't stay put. He would get up and make his way back, as if the dragon were a magnet and Felix were a metal ball. After several trips back and forth, the dragon relented and allowed Felix to stay wherever he pleased. Felix found the dragon's wing and crawled underneath it, making his way to its belly.

Being a spirit, Lady Miko never slept. She quietly laughed as she watched the frustrated dragon finally give in to the sleepwalking child under its wing. Eventually, the dragon bonded with Felix, who was unlike any child it had ever encountered.

Time passed, as it always does, and eventually, Felix turned four. He recalled the lessons taught by the shrubs and could hear the voices of the children's animal companions. As he sat in his nest, he relaxed and opened his mind, eavesdropping on the nonhumans' conversations. Felix soon became more popular with the creatures of the shelter than with the other children, as he could understand their conversations and desires.

Chapter 10
Amassing Misfits

As time passed, new babies arrived, and children left once they turned five, moving on from the safety of their nests. From ages five to ten, the children lived in a new home and attended school.

Felix learned many new things during his time in the dragon statue but still had many questions he hadn't asked. The seasons changed, and Felix's birthday was now only three and a half months away. Every Weaver child brought here on their first birthday was paired with their mirrored soul. Felix was behind the other children in this respect and was aware of the ceremony, though he was unsure of the details. He hadn't yet acquired a mirrored soul.

On the morning of his pairing, Lady Miko explained what a mirrored soul was and why he hadn't received one when he first arrived. "Babies are so trusting; they rely on others, so bonds form much more quickly than with older children. They are companions who help guide their partners and comfort them in hardships," she explained. "When you're bonded to one, it will live as you do. It will know what you are thinking and feeling, and you can communicate telepathically."

After breakfast, Felix was told to sit in the middle of the nesting room. Lady Miko explained that they would finally be pairing him, and that he would be able to choose his mirrored soul, but the soul had to choose him as well.

Felix sat in the center of the room where the children played. He felt a little anxious as the wing of the statue lifted, revealing a tall man with pointed ears carrying two stuffed bags and two more strapped to his back and chest.

"Felix, this is Silas," Lady Miko said. "He is the elven caregiver to the orphaned forest children."

Felix thought for a moment, recalling the books Henry had read to him. Elves were depicted as short, peculiar creatures with large eyes, yet Silas was tall with striking features and a kind, thoughtful demeanor. Silas had tanned skin and dark hair, wearing brown and green clothing suited for blending into the forest. Felix realized that what the plants had told him was true, and he was interacting with an elf, which contradicted everything he had been read and seen on TV.

Silas knelt and opened the bags. Out popped some of the cutest and fluffiest animals Felix had ever seen, along with a few less cuddly ones that crawled and slithered out. There were ducklings, kittens, puppies, cubs, owlets, bunnies, turtles, and lizards, among others. More than seventy baby animals emerged, and Felix was to choose one for himself. He had seen other children choose before, and now it was his turn.

Lady Miko watched with no sign of apprehension as the creatures spilled onto the floor. Normally, after the children arrived in Yurden, Silas would appear in the nursery, and whichever baby animal made its way to a child's nest would bond with that child, becoming their mirrored soul.

Unlike the babies, Felix did not have an easy time with it. Opening his mind, he heard a jumble of voices—too many to focus on. He scanned the animals one by one, pointing at each, shaking his head as he eliminated them. After dismissing twenty-three options, he spotted a little black, bushy-tailed animal hiding behind Silas's feet. Felix opened his mind again and listened in, unable to make out the quiet voice. He pointed, and instead of shaking his head, he tilted it with curiosity.

Silas glanced behind his heels and picked up the black fluffball. He inspected it briefly before walking over to Felix and handing him the creature.

Felix's outstretched hands retracted quickly, cradling the animal. After a few moments, he understood what the creature was murmuring repeatedly. He lifted the ball of fluff near his ear and could make out whimpers. The ball shook with nervousness.

"I want to go home. I don't like this place. All these people are going to pull on my tail."

Felix's eyes widened with joy as he lifted the fluffball to his cheek and smelled its fresh, baby scent. Felix blew his warm breath into the fluffball, and it stopped shivering in panic. Silas then walked up to them, touching Felix's forehead. He placed a few fingers into the fluffball, and a green light emitted from his thumbs.

As Silas set his fingers on Felix, he murmured, "Hoo, a guildsman, aye." Then, raising his voice, he declared, "Yer souls are intertwined. Ye're bound tae each other. From this day on, ye'll be as one forevermore."

Silas turned to Felix, who was staring with curiosity. "Ye hae tae name her."

Felix was taken aback. He had never spoken in front of anyone when prompted and had never intended to.

Silas added, "If she disnae get a name, the pact cannae be woven."

Felix's face grew even more panic-stricken as he glanced between Silas and Lady Miko. Seeing the worry in Felix's eyes, Lady Miko came over and sat beside him. She rubbed his back soothingly.

"Don't worry about it, Felix. Just calm down and breathe; you'll be fine. Think of the best name you can." She handed him some hay to shape into letters, as he had done with his own name.

He mustered as much courage as he could and attempted to say the name that came to mind. However, all that came out were garbled stutters, whimpers, and forced breaths.

Lady Miko praised him for trying on his own but suggested he use the hay to spell out the name, and she offered to help him sound it out.

He placed the fluffball in Lady Miko's arms and grabbed the hay. The first letter he bent was L. Lady Miko then demonstrated how to shape his mouth to produce the L sound. After much struggle, Felix managed to produce a soft L sound. The second letter he bent was E. She instructed him to exhale, and Felix complied. The E sound came out unexpectedly when she started tickling him a little. The third letter was N. Felix responded with a short, harsh, and stunted "N."

Lady Miko then asked if there were any more letters. Felix shook his head.

The other children exchanged glances, having never heard Felix speak since his arrival. Some babies in their nests, as well as dragon hatchlings, raised their heads to see what was happening. The rest of the children, visible from the kitchen doorway, watched with curiosity.

Miko repeated the name a few times for Felix. "Len. Her name is Len?"

Felix slowly formed the three-letter word in his mouth, stuttering and pausing several times. "L-l-l-l-l-l-e-e-en." As Felix finally managed to say the name, Silas's glowing thumbs came together, and a Druidic green band with knots appeared, glowing brightly around Len and Felix's foreheads.

"Felix has chosen Len tae be his mirrored soul, and noo the bond is sealed and can only be broke by death. Felix, ye and Len will be connected, but she can choose tae break the link if she wishes. Len might also unwillingly disconnect if she faces trauma. Prolonged disconnection can put a strain on the heart."

The glow faded, and Silas, still kneeling, placed the remaining animal babies back into the bag. With a final glance at Felix, he disappeared into the darkness.

"Aw, Felix, you have a vixen!" Lady Miko exclaimed. Two black, beady eyes and a muzzle peered out from the fluffball.

Felix didn't know what a vixen was, and Lady Miko realized this only now.

"You picked a mirrored soul without knowing what it was?" she asked.

Felix nodded.

She explained that a vixen was a female fox, behaving like a cat but with a dog's personality. She knew to ask only yes-or-no questions to get the quickest answers from him.

In the end, joy was evident in her voice as she said, "You're a very peculiar and sweet person, not like the norm."

Lady Miko deduced that Felix had chosen Len because,

like him, she was scared and needed a friend.

"By the way, you're now linked to Len, and she can understand your thoughts, and you can understand hers. Babies can be matched with their mirrored souls without a name because their hearts and minds are pure, allowing for an almost instantaneous bond. You, on the other hand, have experienced such great sadness, which has hardened your heart in ways that most children have not. This makes you special. Oh, and congratulations on your second word!"

Lady Miko kissed Felix on the forehead and went to check on the other children, allowing Felix and his new companion to bond.

Poking her little head out from her curled-up position, Len spoke to Felix. "You're not going to pull my tail, are you?"

He shook his head slowly and firmly.

Len unwrapped herself and sat up. "Can you speak?"

Felix shrugged.

"Well, since we're in each other's heads, I guess answering these questions will be a lot easier for you from now on."

Felix felt like he had gained something no one could take away from him—something that could never just leave. He spoke to her telepathically but initially resisted reading her thoughts, feeling it might be intrusive. He soon learned that they could block each other from certain thoughts if they wished. This small comfort lifted a weight from his shoulders.

Len walked around her new partner, sniffing him and familiarizing herself with his scent. She learned as much as she could about Felix—his likes, dislikes, and reasons for choosing her. This information helped her lower her guard, becoming more relaxed and affectionate toward him.

Len shared that her parents and siblings had been eaten by a pack of wild dogs. She had been hidden in a hollowed-out tree root, out of reach. It took four days before Silas found her, whimpering, hungry, and crying for the family she had lost.

Felix cried as he listened, his thoughts returning to Chance. He curled back into a fetal position in the nest. Len worried that she had said something wrong.

When she sensed his sadness, she placed her two front paws on his arm and licked his face dry. She begged him not to cry and pushed her way through his arms, moving them away from his face and lying her body between his face and hands. She rested her head on his neck, watching over him as he cried himself to sleep. This shared sense of loss deepened their bond of compassion and understanding for each other.

Len became Felix's guardian and source of security. She understood that he was sensitive to other creatures' pain and internalized it. From that day on, Len never left his side unless absolutely necessary. Over the next several months, the two grew close until it was time for Felix to leave the statue.

Len always offered her advice with love and the best intentions. She encouraged him to practice his letters until he could confidently say them and even form short sentences. He practiced privately, away from the other children, occasionally trying out his new skills on Lady Miko.

By the age of five, Felix was different from the other boys. While most were loud and rowdy, he remained quiet and well-mannered. Len appreciated these refined traits. During the day, she tried to nap because she was up most of the night guarding Felix, and playtime drained her energy.

When they weren't playing, they learned as much as

they could from Lady Miko. The children often asked her to demonstrate how to control water. In one demonstration, she held a goblet full of liquid. After performing a hand gesture, the water flowed out of the goblet, twisting and twining around Miko's fingers and wrist, slipping around each finger as she wiggled them. All the children watched in amazement as the water formed into spheres and then into beetles that crawled down her body and onto the noses of each child. Once the beetles reached their destinations, they burst, splashing the children's faces and making them giggle with delight.

Lady Miko knew she would soon be saying goodbye to Felix.

When dawn broke, the pond was still, laced in fog. The wings of the statue opened, and out stepped Felix, holding Len in his arms. Lady Miko hovered closely behind.

As they reached the edge of the pond, she offered some final words of wisdom. "You two are about to begin your journey. I wish you good luck and all the best on your new adventure. Take care of each other and offer guidance when needed. Remember that you have each other, even when hope seems distant. Both of you will be each other's guiding stars."

She leaned down, kissed Felix on the forehead, and stroked Len's fluffy cheeks. "Now, Len, remember that Felix might defy you and make foolish or irresponsible decisions at times. Don't worry too much about it. He will always come back and apologize for not listening to you. He needs to learn, and you must guide him as best you can."

Lady Miko stood up. "Here they are, Rosalyn," she said.

Felix turned around to see a smiling woman he vaguely remembered and now had a name to match the face.

"Ah, Felix, 'tis been a good while. Ye've surely grown.

This way, if ye please," Lady Rosalyn said, reaching out for Felix's hand. With a flutter of her fingers, Felix's belongings levitated and followed them.

The air was cold, but Rosalyn's hand was warm to the touch. "'Tis been quite a while since ye've been out o' that statue."

Felix glanced up at Lady Rosalyn as they passed the grand stone pavilion where he had been identified as a Water Weaver.

"Felix, this here be Heaven's Gate Castle, one o' the places where ye'll learn to hone yer skills. First, ye'll be sent to the village o' Dennington, where ye'll study the basics o' language, mathematics, etiquette, history, and other matters to become a proper and useful member o' Yurden."

As they walked, Felix took in the sights. One major difference he noticed was the unusually large size of the moon. Summoning all the courage he could muster, and with Lady Miko's prior help in forming words as she had when he spelled Len's name, he stuttered out, "Lady Rosalyn, why is the moon so big compared to the sun?"

"Well, Felix, ye're no longer on Earth. What ye call the moon is known here as Kalli, and it's much larger, for it's bigger than the planetoid we're on. Also, the sun here is called Mater. Mater orbits Kalli, like a mother looking after her child."

Felix was still coming to terms with the fact that he was in a new land and had much to learn.

Heaven's Gate was a grand castle. It featured tall towers, extensive manicured gardens, and a large stream that flowed from the statues into a lake beside the castle, cascading over a cliff to create a magnificent waterfall next to the dragon stables.

Rosalyn and Felix approached a pair of large, green-studded doors. With a graceful flick of her fingers, Rosalyn made the massive doors swing open, and they entered. As they passed the threshold, the doors closed with a dull thud. The walls were adorned with towering marble columns, pedestals with intriguing busts, large tapestries, and grand paintings.

They proceeded down a lavish hall until they reached the foot of a grand staircase. A huge stained-glass window behind the spiraling steps depicted the five dragon gods ruling over all life.

Further down another hallway, the three made a sharp turn and found a door slightly ajar. Rosalyn waved her hand, and the door opened. A single light hung above a small table with an oversized doily. Beside the table were a rocking chair and a modest wooden kitchen chair. On the other side of the room was a split door, the top half open and the bottom closed. Above it, on a small ledge, was a leather-bound book.

Rosalyn waved her arms over the table, and—poof—two beverages appeared in the center. With her other hand, she directed the floating bags to stack themselves against the wall.

Felix approached the large duffel bag and opened it, placing Len on the fluffy towel inside.

"All seems to be in order. Art thou ready, Felix?" Rosalyn asked.

He nodded, though he wasn't entirely sure what he was agreeing to.

"Let us begin, then." She took his wrist and placed a bracelet around it.

Felix picked up one of the cups from the table and drank the deep red liquid, which left a satisfied smirk on his face. The juice stained his top lip, giving him a red mustache.

The bracelet on his wrist had three cords and a purple stone encased in a bronze bezel setting.

"Now, ne'er take this off, Felix. 'Tis for yer safety and access to the castle. No one can remove it from yer wrist but ye yerself, no matter what they might try."

Rosalyn then took out a familiar crystal dagger—the one she had used to prick his big toe when he first arrived. This time, she pricked his finger, collecting blood on the blade and touching it to the purple stone on the bracelet. The stone glowed brightly.

"The bracelet now doth mark ye as its one true owner." Rosalyn placed her belongings on the rocking chair.

Felix put his finger in his mouth to stop the bleeding. Lady Rosalyn walked over to the split door and dragged the still-bloody dagger across the cover of the leather-bound book. With a flick of her finger, a small spark flew out, cauterizing the wound on Felix's finger as he pulled it from his mouth to inspect the cut.

The book's cover transformed instantly. Gold lettering appeared on the spine and cover: Felix Grey, Water Weaver.

Lady Rosalyn, now focused on the book, turned around with a gleeful expression.

After finishing their refreshments, the three headed in the opposite direction, Felix's bags in tow.

Felix noticed a glow emanating from the floor at the end of the hall, growing brighter as they approached. A large golden circle appeared before them, adorned with foreign symbols and images. They stepped into the gilded circle.

Lady Rosalyn said, "Barrel Hall."

The three were engulfed in golden light. As the light faded, they found themselves outside a large stone building—Felix's new home.

Barrel Hall was designated for children who hadn't been

born in Yurden and would stay until age ten unless granted permission otherwise. The inhabitants would study at Dennington School before moving on to Heaven's Gate Castle.

Dennington was an unassuming and modest village with plenty of character. It featured an old school, a post office, a general store, many small homes, and one large manor house. Surrounded by a dense forest, the village was hidden from view.

Half of the manor house was dedicated to boys, while the other half was for girls. The children residing there were lightly managed, having been taught how to act, behave, and what was expected of them while growing up in the statues by the guardians. They knew that just before mealtime, there was a bit of free time, so they engaged in about half an hour of play. This brief period was always the most enjoyable for the residents.

Lady Rosalyn had planned her visit perfectly, aiming to get in and out of the house with minimal distraction or delay.

A little girl sat curled up with a book upstairs at the round windowsill directly above the front door. Her hair was big and bushy, and she wore gold-rimmed glasses with a freckled forehead. She had noticed a large flash of light coming from outside the house, which had distracted her.

Len was the only one of the three who noticed the girl.

Rosalyn led Felix quickly up the stairs and into the boys' dormitory. The room was lined with bunk beds, quite different from the hay nests he had become accustomed to. Next to his new bed was a locker for his belongings.

Felix started to put his things away, but Lady Rosalyn told him to wait. She raised both hands and waved them over Felix and his belongings. A red glow enveloped him and his bags.

"If aught of yours goes missing, all ye need do is call for it. Should someone have taken it, they'll be given a severe—shall we say—smacked bottom for their ill-advised conduct."

Felix hugged her gratefully.

"I wish I had not other matters to attend to," she went on. "I feel as though I'm abandoning ye without spending any good time with ye. Let me see... Ah yes! I nearly forgot. Felix, I ken ye're eager to learn about yer abilities, but ye'll need to wait a bit longer. Unlike the nursery ye've just left, this whole town is protected and sealed. Only the teleportation circle and the charms I've set will work here, and only certain visitors can weave within the barrier. So, no weaving just now. 'Tis to keep everyone out of mischief."

"Oh, how time doth fly. I'm so sorry, but I must be on my way. If ye would be so kind...here's a letter. Please give it to Mrs. Simmons; she's the caretaker of the manor." Lady Rosalyn spun around, and with a puff of smoke, she was gone.

Most of the children were outside playing with their mirrored souls, so after Rosalyn left, Felix pulled Len out of the bag and placed her on his bed. He put his things away in the locker before grabbing his MP3 player and headphones. He curled into a ball, and Len crawled in beside him, keeping a watchful eye until she eventually fell asleep.

Less than an hour after Felix arrived at Barrel Hall, two pairs of small hands began exploring Felix and Len. A young girl petted Len and woke her. It was the same girl who had been at the window upstairs. She was joined by a small spider monkey, who was playing with the headphone cord. Felix woke, startled by this unexpected intrusion.

"Hi, I'm Anastasia, and this is Mr. Nibbles—but everyone just calls him Mr. Nibs. What's your name?"

Felix sat up, trying to stay calm and make eye contact with the girl while attempting to form words. Before he could answer, Anastasia jumped off the bed and began exploring the room.

"So this is what the boys' room is like. I've never been in here before."

Posters and pictures of strong men and women alongside fantastical dragons adorned the walls. Her fingertips glided over a well-preserved poster of a man named Vivi Odin, who was holding out his hands—one with a fireball and the other with lightning shooting from his fingertips.

Felix's gaze swept the room. It was tidy, with some beds adorned with stuffed animals. A few lockers were slightly open, revealing clothing and toys that were haphazardly stored.

Len prodded him telepathically. "It's all right, Felix. You don't need to be so jumpy. Go introduce yourself to her. She seems like a good person."

Felix, still nervous, attempted to tell her his name. After nine agonizing tries, Anastasia reached into her bag and handed him a piece of paper and some graphite, assuming he could write. Her guess was correct, and he wrote down his name.

Anastasia took the paper and exclaimed, "Oh, your name is Felix!" She extended her hand for a shake.

He picked up Len and placed her in front of him as a shield.

"What's her name?" Anastasia asked, reaching for Len.

Felix went back to the paper and wrote down Len's name.

Anastasia cradled Len in her arms and exclaimed, "She's so fluffy and cute!"

Len had no objections to Anastasia—especially since

her hands avoided Len's tail and only went to the back of her ears, where she enjoyed being scratched.

"Not that I'm biased, but I'd have to agree with her. I am quite cute," Len said with a sigh of contentment.

Anastasia was a sweet girl. Her short, plump frame made her glasses seem small on her rosy, freckled face.

As Felix tried his best to speak, Anastasia braided her hair into one long strand. She listened with kind eyes and curiosity. Frustrated, Felix gave up and decided to write everything down instead.

"Do you like to read?" Anastasia asked.

Felix shrugged. He didn't know how to read but enjoyed being read to, since at the Kennedy House, he had only learned the alphabet, basic words, and the fundamentals of addition and subtraction from Henry and Laura.

"I've been reading since I was three," Anastasia stated.

She always carried a satchel with no fewer than three books inside. The weight of the books usually made her walk with a slight wobble. She pulled out the books to show Felix, and once the bag was emptied, Mr. Nibs climbed in to take a nap.

The first book was *The Five Dragon Gods and Their Origins*, the second was *Heaven's Gate Castle's History*, and the third was *Aurora the Beloved*, Anastasia explained as Felix glanced over each book.

"That one's my personal favorite, but you can choose whichever one you like," she said as Felix set the third book down.

The book on dragons captivated him, as Lady Miko used to tell him stories about them. She had described their magnificence and the legendary feats they performed. Felix had enjoyed those epic tales, and since Chance was fascinated with dragons, Felix was, by extension, as well.

Anastasia put the other two books back into her bag, relocating Mr. Nibs to another spot for his nap. She then climbed onto the bed and began reading aloud about the five dragon gods. Felix listened intently while Len fell asleep on his lap as he gently rubbed her back.

As Anastasia read aloud, a group of boys entered the room and noticed them with displeasure. They booed and hissed at Anastasia.

Angered, Felix stood up, grabbed Anastasia by the hand, and lifted Len with his other arm. They marched past the boys, pushing them out of the way with his shoulder and jabbing them with his elbows. Anastasia stepped on their toes, and Mr. Nibs tugged at their hair. They managed to escape before the boys had time to react to their newly acquired aches and pains.

Felix led them as far away as he could. Not yet familiar with the house, he followed his nose to the kitchen, drawn by a sweet aroma wafting through the air. They found a table and climbed onto the chairs with Len and Mr. Nibs.

An older woman stood behind a large butcher block, watching them. "Anastasia, is this the new arrival? The one I received a letter about?" Mrs. Simmons asked while kneading dough for pies.

"Yes, his name is Felix, and that's Len," Anastasia replied, as Mrs. Simmons continued her work.

"Well, you must be hungry after your journey from the castle." Mrs. Simmons walked over with a few apple turnovers, sprinkled with powdered sugar.

Reaching into his pocket for the letter he was supposed to deliver, Felix stuttered out, "Th-thank you."

"There's no need to be nervous, Felix. This is your home now, until you go back to the castle. Oh, another letter from Lady Rosalyn, I see." Mrs. Simmons chuckled in response.

"I don't think he knows how to talk too well yet, but he's been writing answers to the questions I've been asking," Anastasia explained.

"Oh," Mrs. Simmons said, her eyebrows raised. She was a husky woman with curly gray hair and a plump, warm face marked by thick creases. She wore a flour-covered apron over a long-sleeved, green-and-blue-striped dress, slightly unbuttoned at the top to keep cool in the warm kitchen. Mrs. Simmons was the caregiver of the house and its inhabitants.

"So why aren't you two outside having fun like the other children?" she asked.

"I was reading, but a bright flash of light distracted me. I set my book down to see what was happening, and out popped Lady Rosalyn and Felix through the teleportation circle," Anastasia explained.

Mrs. Simmons nodded, as if this was perfectly normal. "Well, if you're going to read, please do so aloud. I'd like to hear a happy story," she said. She then picked up her half-drunk glass of wine as Anastasia resumed reading from where she had left off.

As Felix devoured his turnover, Mrs. Simmons went to the icebox, took out some chicken tenderloins, and placed them in a bowl in front of Len so she could eat as well while listening to the story.

Over the next few days, Felix got to know both Anastasia and Mr. Nibs, the playful monkey. Len was glad Felix was making friends quickly.

For the next few months, Felix rarely talked to the other children, even though some attempted to start a conversation. He had bonded with Anastasia through the time they spent together while she read her books to him. He worked diligently on his speech and learned to read and write. Over time, Felix picked up reading and writing faster than he improved his speech, which remained a struggle. Anastasia had arrived a few months before Felix, and since they spent so much time in the kitchen, Mrs. Simmons decided to request homework from the school, as they would not be attending until the next session. This work was to be completed with her supervision in the kitchen, allowing her to keep an eye on them while she performed her tasks. Secretly, Mrs. Simmons also wanted to refresh her knowledge on a few subjects to stay in touch with her charges.

Mrs. Simmons knew Anastasia was exceptionally bright, but she found Felix to be cunningly brilliant. Over the months, Mrs. Simmons watched Felix solve problems in inventive ways that surpassed his peers. He was creative in everything he did. Anastasia had already achieved a reading level comparable to that of a high school student, but Felix excelled in growing plants and other areas that required wisdom beyond his years. Book smarts were not his strong suit, however.

Between Anastasia's reading sessions, Felix's summer lessons with the Pines, and the extra work from Mrs. Simmons, they became more advanced than most children. By the time the new school year began, Mrs. Simmons had given them enough schoolwork to challenge even an adult.

Under Anastasia's constant tutoring, Felix's reading and speaking skills improved. He became more confident in his speech. Although he didn't speak often, when he did, it was done thoughtfully.

When they started their first year at Dennington School, they found the regular workload boring, as it didn't challenge them. Felix wondered why the older children who didn't live in the manor disappeared halfway through the day.

The next day, they approached their teacher, Mr. Mitchem, and Anastasia asked about testing out of their current year. Mr. Mitchem was skeptical, as this was an unusual request.

Mr. Mitchem was a thin, spindly man with glasses that barely stayed on his face. His hair was perpetually disheveled, as if he had been struck by lightning several times. He seemed to dread any questions directed at him.

As his bony hands rifled through desk drawers crammed with papers, he pulled out two aptitude tests and handed them to Anastasia and Felix. These tests would determine their current level of schooling. They took the tests back to their desks and began immediately.

Anastasia finished first, followed by Felix. All one hundred and thirty-nine questions were either answered or left blank. Anastasia received one mark for a question she had answered with, "I would rather not discuss such morbid things," which was about death.

Felix, on the other hand, missed only a few questions, particularly those on the history of Yurden. He was more interested in plants, animals, and fantastical tales than mundane topics.

Once graded, their scores exceeded the exam's qualification threshold, meaning they were far above their expected level.

"So you two are who Mrs. Simmons was getting all that extra work for?" Mr. Mitchem asked.

They both nodded, and a gleeful expression spread across the thin man's face. A newfound spring appeared in his step, which hadn't been there for years. He returned to his desk and beckoned them to follow him.

"Since you two seem to have ravenous minds, you probably would like to stay ahead of your classmates and finish your lessons as soon as possible," he said, leaning over his cluttered desk.

Anastasia was excited by the prospect and nodded vigorously, but Felix didn't fully understand what Mr. Mitchem was implying.

Anastasia turned to Felix, noticing his lack of response.

"You know what that means, right?" Anastasia asked.

Felix shook his head.

"It means we don't need to stay here as long in school. If we study hard, we can focus all our time on books and spend more time with Mrs. Simmons."

Felix understood, but what Anastasia didn't realize was that if they completed all their schooling, they wouldn't spend as much extra time with Mrs. Simmons. From a brief, one-sided conversation with Lady Rosalyn, Felix had learned that once they finished their classes with satisfactory results, they would be transferred to Heaven's Gate. He dreaded losing another person he had grown attached to. The loss of Chance still haunted him, and despite his new bonds, he continued to sleepwalk nightly, often ending up at the foot of the front door.

"Well, let me get things arranged for both of you today so that tomorrow we can start your higher education. Why don't you both go home and tell Mrs. Simmons the great news?"

Anastasia, without thinking, grabbed Felix's hand and tugged him along. She stopped at their desks to grab her satchel before darting for the doors, with Felix following sluggishly behind.

The pair walked side by side down the cobbled streets, passing a few townsfolk. Anastasia rambled excitedly about how thrilling it was going to be for both of them.

Felix, on the other hand, reached into his bag and pulled out a sandwich wrapped in brown paper. It was toast with jam and custard, sliced in half. He made sure to eat slowly so that if Anastasia asked him a question, she wouldn't mind that he couldn't answer with his mouth full.

As they crossed the stone bridge over a stream, Felix noticed a flower growing in one of the cracks that he had seen earlier that morning. Mid-chew, he stopped in his tracks and stared down at it. It had lovely, pale purple petals with a deep blue center.

Anastasia noticed Felix was no longer beside her and turned around to see where he had gone. She watched in silence as he stuffed the rest of the sandwich into his mouth, dropped to his knees, and touched the flower's leaf.

The flower kept repeating, "I'm strong... I'll survive." Then, noticing Felix's touch, it added, "Please don't harm me."

Felix responded telepathically, "I'm going to take care of you. Don't worry."

He ran back to Anastasia, searching through her satchel for a pencil. Once he found one, he returned to the flower and carefully dug it out of the crack, making sure not to break too many roots. He then scooped some of the soft, damp earth from just past the bridge and wrapped it around the seedling in the brown paper.

The flower asked, "Is this the end for me?"

Without answering, Felix placed the flower into the soil and wrapped the paper around the base of the roots.

"This feels spacious!" the flower responded once its roots were able to spread out. It thanked Felix for saving it from the many feet that passed by daily.

The two finally made their way back to Barrel Hall, where

Anastasia opened the door for Felix and the plant. They found Mrs. Simmons in the kitchen. Before she could ask why they were home so early, Anastasia was already explaining the situation. Mrs. Simmons nodded while sipping her red wine. Acknowledging Felix, she smiled at the flower he was holding.

"Oh, isn't that a beauty?" she said, noticing the brown paper wrapped around the soil and roots. "Are you planning to plant this in the garden?"

Felix nodded.

Mr. Nibs and Len, sensing the pair's return, had been relaxing upstairs on the long hallway rug. When Len got up, Mr. Nibs climbed onto her back for a ride. They hurried downstairs and made their way to the kitchen. Since it was still early, the ladies from town were still helping with the cleaning.

Meanwhile, one of the men from town, Mr. Waxman, was outside tidying up the garden and yard. Mrs. Simmons ushered the group to the front yard, where Mr. Waxman was pulling weeds from the flowerbeds to clear the area for planting.

Mrs. Simmons interrupted his work. "Bennett, dear, would you mind if Felix planted a flower in the flowerbed?"

"I don't see why not," he replied, turning around to face the small group behind him. "Well, who are these two? We're not skipping school, are we?"

Mrs. Simmons responded quickly. "Highly unlikely. These two are not the type to do that." She laughed.

Anastasia chimed in, "This is Felix, and I'm Anastasia. Mr. Mitchem allowed us to leave early since we took a test and both did really well. He said he'd be arranging our schoolwork, so there was no point in us staying in school the full day."

"Well, it seems you have some clever ones on your hands," Mr. Waxman said, smiling at the pair. "Now then, what do you have there?"

Felix stepped forward.

"Oh, my word. Where did you find that?" Mr. Waxman asked.

Before Felix could answer, Anastasia blurted out, "It was in one of the cracks on the bridge."

"This is an elvish flower; they are typically only found in the forest. I'm surprised it was able to grow without help. They grow around trees and attract all types of bees and butterflies. They are called whispering bells. I'll tell you what... why don't you make this planting bed yours? If you find various kinds of flowers you like, you can transplant them here."

Felix glanced at Mrs. Simmons, and she nodded in agreement before he could ask for her permission.

Mr. Waxman instructed Felix to plant the flower next to the wall so it could clasp onto the stones. Felix asked Len to dig a small hole near the wall, and she obliged. Felix placed the flower into the hole and covered the roots with soil.

While Felix was working, Mr. Waxman retrieved his watering can and set it down next to him. Before watering the flower, he took a deep breath and exhaled onto it—something no one noticed.

The tiny flower's roots expanded and grew rapidly. Felix then took the watering can and drizzled cool water over the flower.

"Now, Felix, you'll need to take care of this bed yourself, weeding and watering the plants you put in here," Mr. Waxman said.

Mrs. Simmons interjected, "That shouldn't be a problem. He already helps me with the garden in the back. We should let you get back to your work; we wouldn't want to keep you from your tasks. I know how Jenny gets when you're late getting home." She waved goodbye to Mr. Waxman and ushered the group back into the house.

Anastasia then filled Mrs. Simmons in on the rest of what had happened at school before she began reading to them.

Early the next morning, Felix and Anastasia went to the back garden and sprinkled feed for the chickens. After that, Felix checked on the flowerbed out front to see how the flower was progressing before they headed off to school.

During the night, the plant Felix had planted had grown a good nine inches and had clasped onto the stone wall.

Anastasia set off with a spring in her step, excited about the day ahead. Felix, a little less enthusiastic, kept pace modestly beside her.

Mr. Mitchem had prepared some work for them, which displeased Felix internally. To distract himself, he thought about the chickens running around eating all the bugs climbing on the plants. The hens were plump by any standard.

The children took the work from Mr. Mitchem and headed outside to a stone bench. The air was filled with the scents of freshly cut pine and ripening vegetables and herbs. Anastasia read aloud from her books while Felix listened with interest.

After a few hours of studying, Mr. Mitchem asked them to return to the schoolhouse to take tests on what they had just learned. They had two hours to complete and submit their tests.

While Mr. Mitchem attended to the other students, the schoolhouse buzzed with younger children learning about simple machines, levers, and screws, while the older children studied great writers and their contributions to language and sentence structure.

Felix and Anastasia breezed through their tests, finishing just under forty-five minutes. Anastasia handed her test to Mr. Mitchem, followed by Felix, who smiled as he submitted his.

Mr. Mitchem called Anastasia to the front of the room, where Felix was standing. "Are you sure you don't want to go over your answers and double-check them?"

The two stared at him and shook their heads.

"I see. Well, you can go outside and play if you'd like. I'll let you know how you did."

Instead of playing outside, they decided to explore the bookshelves for anything they hadn't yet read. Finding nothing new, they grabbed a few of their favorite books from previous reads.

After grading Anastasia's test, Mr. Mitchem was in disbelief. He suspected cheating because she hadn't missed a single question.

He then checked Felix's test, which was also perfect but answered differently. Mr. Mitchem wondered how they had managed to get all the questions right in such a short time.

Upon reviewing the tests again, he noted that Anastasia's language was elegantly crafted, reminiscent of poetry he had read in his youth. Felix's responses, in contrast, were blunt and lacked sophistication but were full of enthusiasm.

Mr. Mitchem approached the pair, who were engrossed in their reading. Quietly, he crouched beside them and asked, "Where are the two of you off to today? Anywhere exciting?"

They looked at each other and then held up the books they had not yet started. Anastasia's second book was *Tra-*

ditions of the Tridindal Merfolk, and Felix's was *The Final Voyage to Valinor.*

"Ah, so under the Magna Caeruleum Ignotum and the Exodus of Earth—both fascinating and complex places."

The pair stared at each other and shrugged. Anastasia had unknowingly turned Felix into a bookworm.

"All the extra work Mrs. Simmons gave you, she got from me," Mr. Mitchem said. "That explains why the difficulty kept increasing—it was meant to keep you engaged."

Day after day, they went to school, and before Mr. Mitchem could start roll call, Anastasia asked for all the schoolwork so they could complete it before returning to their reading.

After a few days, he placed all the advanced work on their desks before school started. The stack of books piled up as they had plenty of time to fill each day.

When the year ended, Felix and Anastasia had turned six and were among the brightest children Dennington had ever seen.

Chapter 11
Advancements

Year two was approaching in just three short months, and most of the children from Barrel Hall were tanned from their outdoor activities—not to mention the numerous scrapes and bruises—while Anastasia and Felix had barely seen the midday sun. The only time they glimpsed it was while tending to the garden.

The summer months flew by, and Felix's front garden burst into an explosion of flowers at a rate Mr. Waxman had never seen before.

On rare occasions, Felix and Anastasia ventured to the river that flowed through the town to soak their feet in its cool waters. There, Anastasia read aloud, and Felix braided long blades of grass into various structures. Occasionally, they played in the river under the bridge, catching frogs and newts and identifying each species. Every time Felix went out with Anastasia on their walks, he carried a small bucket and shovel to collect plants for his flowerbed.

Aside from Felix and Anastasia, the other children at Barrel Hall weren't eager to return to school. Anastasia's latest interests were geography and geology. When they visited the bridge, she noticed pebbles in the river, including a green stone with orange crystal flecks, which she placed in her pocket.

Anastasia read aloud about the mineral composition of certain rocks. These interests kept her and Felix ahead of the other children, helping them retain information they had already learned and exposing them to knowledge beyond typical classroom instruction.

Not wanting to be caught off guard and continually guessing what to expect from the pair, Mr. Mitchem prepared himself. The extra work he'd done was met with joy. He had two brilliant students, and it had been a long time since he had been so engaged. Knowing they had a greater array of knowledge than the rest of the students, Mr. Mitchem learned from Mrs. Simmons that the two were still hard at work. So he placed a final exam on their desks with questions that were designed to test even the most knowledgeable adults.

On the first day back at school, Anastasia examined what Mr. Mitchem was pointing to. Noticing Felix already at his seat, untying a stack of papers, she thanked Mr. Mitchem before hurrying to her desk. She quickly untied the string and scanned the documents. Everything covered topics she had learned with Felix over the summer, though some questions were added to challenge them. When they encountered the advanced questions, they exchanged glances. Felix was surprisingly nonchalant, while Anastasia was puzzled, disliking the feeling of being unprepared.

The final assessment took Anastasia a total of two hours and twelve minutes to complete. Although they were allowed to use their books if needed, Anastasia confidently proceeded without any aid.

Felix took a little longer, using the books to verify his answers. However, he remembered most of the information and finished in an additional twenty-six minutes. Their learning speed was comparable to that of college students in medical school.

Mr. Mitchem graded the final exams, and unsurprisingly, they both performed exceptionally well. They absorbed information like sponges.

Mr. Mitchem requested that Lady Roselyn bring as many different books as she could on her visits. The pair devoured the content eagerly.

Mr. Mitchem occasionally stopped by to chat. Once they had completed the requirements to graduate school at age six (instead of the usual age of seventeen), they committed even more to their reading schedule.

They no longer spent the full day at school. Instead, they picked up the weekly selection of books that Lady Roselyn delivered and sometimes attended private lectures on topics chosen by Mr. Mitchem. Occasionally, Anastasia corrected inconsistencies in Mr. Mitchem's work. When this became more frequent, the lectures ceased. Mr. Mitchem realized he could no longer offer the pair any more meaningful tutelage. They were more informed and better-read than he was.

Managing their newfound independence, they visited town and had lengthy discussions with the visiting elves about their ways of life. Anastasia noticed that the elves paid most of their attention to Felix. She wasn't sure if it was because she asked too many questions or if she was getting on their nerves. She often pondered this but soon forgot about it.

Anastasia spent so much time helping Felix with his vocalizations that he made significant improvements in speaking. He occasionally stuttered, but only when he was emotional.

At Barrel Hall, they spent a considerable portion of their day in the kitchen, learning to cook every dish Mrs. Simmons knew. They also enjoyed experimenting with new recipes. The three had grown into a tight-knit family.

Mr. Nibs and Len often played together, as they were well-versed in the trio's daily routine.

One day, Felix asked where Mrs. Simmons's mirrored soul was. Mrs. Simmons teared up and replied, "That's something I'd prefer not to discuss."

Felix, sensing her unease, hugged Mrs. Simmons to comfort her, while Anastasia held her hand tightly before they headed out to the garden.

The vegetables grown earlier that season had overtaken the patch. Mr. Waxman extended the fence to accommodate the new planting beds Felix and Mrs. Simmons had planned for, nearly tripling the size of the patch. There was a surplus of vegetables, so they were sold at the town farmers' market, and a substantial portion was purchased by Heaven's Gate.

They also started a small business making jam, which they sold around Heedafien through a third-party brokered by Lady Roselyn. Anastasia helped as much as she could, writing the labels while the others sorted and cooked the fruit. Since her task was quick and simple, she often found herself reading to the group. They named their line of jams *The Drunken Berry*.

The tidy sum of money they earned allowed Mrs. Simmons to redecorate several rooms in Barrel Hall. She also had a cellar dug for root vegetables and installed racks for her growing wine collection. The extra income enabled them to hire Mr. Waxman and his wife to pick fruits and vegetables when they were too busy in the kitchen.

The money was split three ways. Felix and Anastasia saved a substantial portion of their earnings in the bank but splurged the rest on books, snacks, and occasionally something extra for themselves or a new dress for Mrs. Simmons.

Despite her newfound wealth, Mrs. Simmons remained plain and modest in her public persona.

Mr. Waxman gradually did less work in the front yard as Felix demonstrated an extraordinary gift with plants. The once-small seedling Felix had rescued from the crack in the bridge now covered the entire stone wall that connected the courtyard to the front yard, the front of Barrel Hall, and part of the eastern-facing wall.

The courtyard was filled with various types of foliage and countless flowers, resembling a watercolor painting. Hues of pink, purple, red, white, and yellow swirled together.

Felix's garden was fragrant with herbs and a myriad of floral scents. In his free time, he cleared dead blooms from the garden and collected them in a bucket for composting. As he gathered seeds from the decaying blooms, Anastasia read aloud while Mrs. Simmons relaxed with a glass of wine and kicked off her shoes.

The two ladies sat on metal garden chairs under a cherry tree leading to the road from Barrel Hall. Len also helped with digging and weeding when she could. Mr. Nibs, ever curious, climbed the cherry trees to check on a bird's nest with three baby birds, watching them grow a little each day. The other children's mirrored souls occasionally joined Felix and Anastasia, as they saw them more frequently.

One day, Anastasia and Felix returned to Barrel Hall and headed straight for the kitchen. Mr. Nibs slid down from Anastasia's shoulder to the floor, while Len went over to the stove, where Anastasia had made a sleeping pad from Mrs. Simmons's old striped dress for Mr. Nibs and Len. As usual, Mrs. Simmons was in the kitchen, cooking up a storm and waiting for them to join her.

Felix was lost in thought, contemplating why Lady Miko and Lady Rosalyn could use their powers while no one else in Dennington could.

Noticing Felix's distracted state, Mrs. Simmons asked, "What's on your mind?"

Felix, stuttering slightly, explained, "Well, Lady Miko and Lady Rosalyn can use their powers. Why can't we? Lady Miko said I would be able to control the elements like she does."

Mrs. Simmons took a moment to find the right words. "There are protections placed on this town. Only Lady Rosalyn and the Ancients can use their powers here. This is to protect the people inside, both from each other and from the outside world. Dennington is a haven for people like me."

"What do you mean, people like you?" Anastasia asked.

Mrs. Simmons stopped her work and sighed. "I'm what is known as a Kank."

"What's a Kank?" Anastasia asked, puzzled.

"A Kank is someone with abilities but no way to control them or turn them off," Mrs. Simmons explained. Anastasia's mouth dropped open in surprise.

"It's okay if you haven't read about Kanks. We've been

largely scrubbed from history to keep us safe. Society believes that when a Kank is discovered, Heaven's Gate disposes of them.

"Being a Kank can have disastrous effects if not controlled. Sometimes the weave of power is loose, with imperfections in its tapestry. The universe is an imperfect fabric. This might be graphic, but I'd rather you hear this from me than from someone else. None of the other children know that we are all Kanks living in Dennington, and I trust you both not to reveal this to the other children at Barrel Hall. Sometimes, a Kank's power builds up and doesn't disperse properly, leading to accidents that can injure or kill the weaver and those nearby. Buildings have collapsed from uncontrolled energy waves, killing dozens. Kanks have been isolated from society, and in the past, they were executed on sight if found outside Dennington's protection.

"Lady Rosalyn was tasked with sealing this town, and it has remained hidden for hundreds of years. Any Kanks born are brought here, and if a Kank is found outside the seal, the residents are instructed to execute them by decree of the first High Lord Dragoon. Dennington serves as a counterbalance to the negativity of the outside world, but the stories of Kanks causing disasters and death have left us unseen and forgotten. Lady Rosalyn placed me here to live safely and to lead a normal life. Once you've been branded, your powers become manageable without requiring intense emotions."

"Are you okay?" Felix asked gently.

"Yes, I'm okay," Mrs. Simmons replied, her eyes misty. "I'm incredibly grateful to Lady Rosalyn. Without her, I wouldn't have had the chance to grow up and know my parents, even if only through letters. She has done so much for me. Felix, you asked about my mirrored soul. I had a little blue bird named JJ. When my powers became unstable, I thought of JJ for comfort. Unfortunately, my powers caused him to explode."

The pair consoled her, and after a few minutes, things returned to normal.

Anastasia mouthed to Felix, "Oh my gods!" while glancing down at Len and Mr. Nibs.

Mrs. Simmons resumed kneading bread dough on her butcher block.

Felix, who preferred being read to, asked, "Anastasia, could you read aloud, please?"

"Oh, that would be lovely," Mrs. Simmons interjected, wiping away a few tears.

Felix was momentarily puzzled before asking Mrs. Simmons, "If Lady Rosalyn placed you here when you were a child, why does she appear so young?"

"To be honest, I don't know. She has always looked the same since I was little. I've aged, but she hasn't," Mrs. Simmons explained.

Anastasia had only a few pages left in the book, so she read aloud as requested. The topic of Mrs. Simmons being a Kank was not brought up again in her presence.

A few minutes later, Anastasia finished reading the last few sentences and announced, "The end."

"So when do we get to visit Heaven's Gate Castle?" Anastasia asked.

Mrs. Simmons replied, "When you turn ten—unless your birthday is close to the start of the new school year. In that case, they might let you start a little early. You must also be at a high enough level in your classes, which I don't think will be a problem for either of you."

"I was born on August twenty-third, so I'm in. What about

you, Felix? When were you born?"

"December twenty-ninth," he replied.

"Oh, Mrs. Simmons, do you think they'll let him come?" Anastasia asked. "He'll be nine."

"I don't see why not, if he's as smart as you," Mrs. Simmons responded, turning to Felix and winking.

Felix pretended to read his book. Len jumped onto the bench next to him, resting her head on his lap. He wondered why Anastasia had asked that question right now.

Len reassured him everything would be fine and advised him not to dwell on it.

Life in Yurden kept Felix busy, but not so busy that he could stop thinking about what had happened to his parents, the Pines, and why they hadn't wanted to keep him. The loss of his older brother Chance weighed heavily on him as well.

As Felix and Anastasia's time continued with no formal schooling required, they wrote papers on the books they had read and sent them to Mr. Mitchem for scholarly discussion. This ongoing exchange helped them maintain proper grammar and refine their language skills—a significant benefit for Felix, who was in serious need of both.

Over time, they all grew a little bigger, including Len and Mr. Nibs. Despite all the time spent reading, Felix kept Anastasia more physically active than she would have been on her own, causing her to lean out.

Chapter 12

Heaven's Gate

A few years passed, and not a single book in Dennington had been neglected by the pair. They now relied solely on the shipments from Heaven's Gate that Lady Rosalyn brought with her.

One day, Lady Rosalyn stayed a little longer to discuss with Mrs. Simmons and Mr. Mitchem a petition to allow Anastasia and Felix to attend Heaven's Gate full-time and earlier than scheduled. The three agreed that the pair were bright and responsible enough to undertake this endeavor.

Mr. Mitchem knew it would take some time to get an official response from the headmaster, so he made a special request to Heaven's Gate Castle for more books to lend to the ravenous bookworms while they waited. This personally requested shipment posed no challenge for the pair, and Lady Rosalyn brought crates of books on each of her visits.

Having immense pride in the two, she was entertained by their constant pursuit of knowledge, sometimes including a few classics she enjoyed reading. They polished off everything they got their hands on, absorbing the information from the pages like blood-starved mosquitoes.

Felix and Anastasia had completed more than 1,033 books, including those Lady Rosalyn took from Kennedy House, which they had read several times.

They heard back from the headmaster via Lady Rosalyn. It had been decided that, based on the information gathered, Anastasia and Felix had completed all their required classes before age ten. Additionally, the successful business with Mrs. Simmons showed they could handle responsibility, and the quarterly reports relayed to him indicated that the two had matured enough to manage themselves at Heaven's Gate. However, a few details still needed to be discussed with the staff before a final decision was made.

Lady Rosalyn and Mr. Mitchem met with the group at Barrel Hall to discuss the contents of a letter for Felix and Anastasia. As the letter was read, the headmaster decreed that Anastasia would be living full-time at Heaven's Gate, but Felix's age still posed a question regarding his attendance. Mrs. Simmons clutched the stem of her wine glass tightly. The news settled into Anastasia's mind, and she realized her eagerness had caused Mrs. Simmons's newfound anxiety.

Felix heard the stem of the glass snap, his eyes darting from Mrs. Simmons's hand to her face in shock and concern as the bottom half of the glass shattered on the floor. Mrs. Simmons's flour-covered face revealed streaks of rosy flesh, while wet streams of tears rolled down her cheeks. She wrapped one arm around each of her companions and squeezed them into her bosom. Mr. Nibs narrowly avoided being squashed.

Mr. Mitchem excused himself from the table, noting the

situation. "You three have much to discuss. I'll see myself out."

Lady Rosalyn stayed for a while, ensuring that Mrs. Simmons was okay. Once she was confident that Mrs. Simmons had calmed down, she hugged her gently.

It was late into the evening before Mrs. Simmons regained her composure and told the two to go upstairs and get ready for bed.

The remaining days were bittersweet. They had to decide what to do with the business they had created together. Since both would be stepping away from the workload, they decided to bring in Mr. Waxman and his wife. Mr. Waxman would tend to both gardens Felix had been managing, as well as pest control, with the addition of more chickens. Mrs. Waxman would assist in the kitchen with cooking and jarring the jams. With their business contingency plans arranged and settled, it was decided there would be two funds kept for Felix and Anastasia, allowing them to make purchases as needed.

One evening, Felix left Barrel Hall and went for a stroll alone, with only Len by his side. They walked in silence as Felix contemplated how much he would have cherished sharing his experiences in Yurden with Chance. He would have told him about the special abilities people possessed and especially about the dragons. Felix would have loved to tell Chance about Anastasia and Mrs. Simmons, and how Chance would have adored Len as much as he did.

As he gazed at the sky, Felix remembered lying in the tall grass by the big oak tree with his big brother, holding hands and watching the stars. Chance had often told him stories about their future adventures, including soaring through the sky on broomsticks, like Harry the wizard from the books they loved. Felix longed to tell Chance how much he missed him and would never forget him, but knowing he would never have the chance to do so made his heart ache.

The sky above him now was different, with not an endless number of stars but a single, enormous moon named Kalli, that softly illuminated the landscape. Yurden at night was bathed in twilight; it never grew completely dark. The outlines of objects were always visible, though it was hard to discern their details until one got closer.

Felix thought about the times he had spent on his hands and knees weeding, while Anastasia read and Mrs. Simmons sipped her wine. Len had been by his side, tearing out weeds with her teeth as the chickens foraged for displaced grubs and insects. Felix had a sense that this chapter of his life was ending, and there was nothing he could do to stop it.

The next morning, everyone in Barrel Hall had gathered at the front door, where a piece of parchment was posted. When Anastasia read their names, she jumped for joy and pushed her way through the crowd of children to where Felix was standing, with Mr. Nibs on his shoulder and Len cradled in his arms. She grabbed him by the shoulders. "You made it! We're going to be in school together full-time! Your age wasn't a factor!"

Felix showed enthusiasm to match Anastasia's excitement, relieved that his best friend would be with him at school. However, his excitement soon gave way to uncertainty about what lay ahead.

On their final night together, Mrs. Simmons allowed them to stay up later than usual. She made blueberry crumble and warm milk, and after placing the snacks on the table, asked Anastasia to read one of the happy fairy tales she used to read while they enjoyed their treats.

Instead of a fairy tale, Anastasia chose *Carnis, the King of the Mound,* a story about a black unicorn and its unlikely friends. They sat on the window bench, cushioned by pillows, while Mrs. Simmons wrapped her arms around them and kissed the tops of their heads. Tears welled in her eyes as her heart broke.

After Anastasia finished reading the short story, Mrs. Simmons sent them to bed. They hugged her and wished her goodnight. She could barely bear to see them go and, with a voice choked with emotion, told them to have sweet dreams. This was the only night she wouldn't tuck them in, and her grief was evident, making it increasingly difficult to hide her sadness.

The next morning, Mrs. Simmons prepared a big breakfast, including Felix and Anastasia's favorite dishes. Struggling to hold back tears, she focused on her work but eventually had to excuse herself. She went into the pantry, leaned against the shelves, and cried. After five minutes, she returned to the kitchen, her face tear-free but with lingering redness and sadness.

Felix noticed her grief-stricken expression. He stopped eating his berries, got off his stool, and walked over to Mrs. Simmons. Anastasia was too focused on her waffles to notice. Felix took Mrs. Simmons's hands in his.

"I remember when you were just up to my hip. Now you're all grown up," she said, reminiscing.

Felix wrapped his arms around her waist and pulled her close. "My precious one, thank you," he whispered.

Mrs. Simmons gasped. "You were awake?"

Felix nodded, resting his head on her chest and hearing her heartbeat. She covered her mouth as tears streamed down her face. After a few moments, she accepted the situation, though the tears continued. She kissed him on the forehead and held his cheeks. The entire hall watched them.

"My word, you'll be all right without me! You're all grown up, and I didn't realize it."

Felix looked into her eyes. "We'll be fine. Will you be okay without us?"

Mrs. Simmons took a deep breath. "I'll have to manage somehow without you two. You'll need to visit regularly. Now, get back to your breakfast before the cream melts and soaks the corn cake!"

After breakfast, all the children left the dining hall except for Felix and Anastasia. Mrs. Simmons urged them, "You two need to wash up and get ready. Everyone who is leaving today has parcels on their beds."

A fifth of the children would remain at the manor, while the rest were going into town for a field trip to learn a new skill. The trip included a basket-weaving demonstration, designed to minimize distractions for those leaving and to help the attendees improve their finger flexibility and movement, which would aid them in performing the weaves later at Heaven's Gate.

Before leaving the kitchen, Felix and Anastasia checked in on Mrs. Simmons to make sure she was okay.

"Go on, you two. Otherwise, you'll be late, and we all know how Lady Rosalyn likes to stay on schedule."

The two hurried to the bathrooms to get cleaned up and then raced to their beds, where they found two long, black boxes and a black card. Anastasia glanced at the embossed initials "A.B." on the card and read the letter:

"Welcome, Anastasia. We are excited to have you join Terra House and uphold our colors and values. We're glad you're joining us. See you soon. T.A."

As the other girls scrambled around like hens, Anastasia untied the large black ribbon sealing the boxes. She opened the first box to find deep-green robes, a mint-green tunic, and a pair of tan pants. The second box contained black knee-high boots and a black leather belt.

She dressed promptly, making sure everything was clean and tidy. Then she pulled her hair back into a tight ponytail, securing it with the black ribbon from her box. Gazing into the long mirror, she reminisced about her past, recalling the chubby little girl she used to be.

Now, she was taller, her hair was longer, and she had blossomed into a lovely young lady. Mr. Nibs clapped his hands in approval before being pushed aside by other girls eager to see their own reflections.

Once she finished inspecting her appearance, she strolled down the hallway to the boys' room, with Mr. Nibs perched on her shoulder. The hallway was bustling with children darting in and out of rooms, colliding with her in their excitement. There was no time for apologies; they vanished as quickly as they appeared. She held her breath, anticipating Felix's reaction to her new outfit.

Her hand reached for the doorknob, but just before she could grasp it, a boy dashed out of the room, almost knocking her over.

Felix reached his bed and saw two long black boxes with thick black ribbons on them, ignoring the attached card. The boxes were beautiful, reminiscent of some packages Henry and Laura had given him and the other children on Christmas Day, but these were far more regal in appearance.

He ran his hand along the lid before slowly opening it. Inside the first box were royal-blue robes, a sky-blue tunic, and tan pants. The second box contained black knee-high boots and a black belt.

He dressed slowly, starting with the pants, then the belt, boots, tunic, and finally the robes. The robes were more like a vest with a capelet that barely reached the top of his hamstrings.

Len leapt onto the bed to watch him change into the new garments. "Well, aren't you a dashing young man," she commented.

Felix stood in front of the mirror, appraising himself, just as the door swung open. Anastasia stood there, stunned and speechless, clearly shocked to see him in the blue robes. A frown crossed her face.

Mr. Nibs placed a hand on her head, stroking her hair as if to comfort her.

"What's wrong?" Felix asked, confused by her reaction.

"I never asked you what dragon you were raised in!" Anastasia replied, sounding dejected.

"Why does that matter?" Felix asked, puzzled by her response.

"Your robes are blue, and mine are green. That means we won't be in the same house. How could I have forgotten that?" Anastasia sighed.

"What? So we won't see each other as much?"

"I never saw you in Terra Dragon. Since we've fast-tracked through regular school, we won't be seeing Mrs. Simmons anymore either. I should have realized something was off when you mentioned Lady Miko. I had never heard that name before. The spirit who cared for me was Lady Amara. And now that we've tested out of regular classes, secondary school isn't an option for us anymore. So, we'll be staying at the castle for the entire year."

Felix was not entirely surprised by this news. "Can't we visit Mrs. Simmons at all?"

Anastasia thought for a moment. "I'm not sure, but we can always ask. But Felix, you're a Water Weaver, and I'm an Earth Weaver, so we won't be housed in the same dorms. Our houses are against each other," she hesitated to say.

"What do you mean 'against each other'?"

"Remember the five dragon gods who created Yurden, to ensure 'all which had survived many a millennium' wasn't destroyed? Hildegard's Prediction? Does any of this ring a bell?"

Felix thought for a moment before recalling the prophecy. "'The end of the immortals' reign and the self-imposed exile of the elves.' That's in *The Final Voyage to Valinor.*"

Anastasia explained, "Heaven's Gate Castle separates everyone by their element, and we compete against each other to win accolades. There are twenty-one students from Barrel Hall going to the induction ceremony: six for fire, five for earth, four for lightning, four for wind, and two for water. This doesn't include the children born in Yurden."

She sat on Felix's bed next to Len and tied a bow around Len's neck with the ribbon. "I'll explain more later. We need to head downstairs."

She took Felix's hand and led him out of the room, with Len hopping off the bed and following.

The children and their mirrored souls made their way downstairs to the entrance of the estate. As the children opened the front door, Lady Rosalyn materialized from the portal.

"On time, are ye? I do have a fondness for those who keep to their hours. Now then, children, come forth and line up before me!" Lady Rosalyn commanded.

The children surged out of the house, forming three lines before Lady Rosalyn. The mirrored souls remained inside the manor. The children were so excited they struggled to maintain their composure—except for two.

Lady Rosalyn noticed the gloomy expression on Anastasia's face.

"Now, everyone, take a deep breath. Hold it in. And now, slowly let it out. I know ye're all eager for the day's events, but we must carry ourselves like proper young folk. Before we begin, a few matters to attend to. Anastasia Beazletin and Felix Grey, step forward, if ye please."

The two glanced at each other and then back at Lady Rosalyn with concern. Mr. Nibs and Len reassured them from the doorway that they had done nothing to get into trouble.

As the pair approached Lady Rosalyn, she leaned forward and whispered to Anastasia, "Miss Beazletin, I need ye to show a touch more enthusiasm. This glum look as if the world hath ended won't do at all—especially when ye are so well put together."

"Sorry, Lady Rosalyn," Anastasia replied.

"There's naught to fear. Ye two haven't wasted your time here. Ye finished your primary and secondary schooling ahead of the usual mark. Ye should be proud of your achievements. I know I am." she said, her eyes gleaming.

Frankie Tyler, one of the boys who liked to pick on Anastasia, was dressed in crimson red robes. He made a grotesque face and stuck his tongue out at Anastasia. Lady Rosalyn noticed this from the corner of her eye. With two quick twists of her wrist, she blinked and snatched Frankie's tongue. She pulled it upward, making him yelp in pain. Holding his tongue, she guided him to the front of the group and let go of it. She then placed her hand on the crown of his head, forcing him to face the crowd.

"Well now, Frankie, born on the first of June, the lad who used to speak with a lisp." The crowd gasped and chuckled.

"With a heart-shaped birthmark upon his bottom, no less! Oh, and I nearly forgot—who wet the bed 'til he was seven years old."

She knew this would have the desired effect on the group standing before her.

The entire group erupted into laughter.

"Now, Frankie, pray tell why ye find it necessary to pick on Anastasia, when a touch of humility would serve ye better. And think ye, if your parents were present, would they take pride in your behavior?"

He didn't answer. Instead, he lowered his head in embarrassment and anger.

"If I be correct—and I am—Frankie, ye only passed your classes by cheating on your tests, did ye not?"

Frankie stared at her, stunned. "How do you know?" he asked, horror-stricken.

"I know all there is to know about ye. Now get back in the house! Your invitation be revoked."

He ran off toward the house, crying in fury. With a snap of her fingers and a twist of her wrist, Lady Rosalyn removed Frankie's clothing, and he went running into the house stark naked, his face flushed with tears and shame.

"While ye have dwelt here, we allowed ye to grow and flourish with simple guidance and the freedom to act as ye wished. I might not have intervened save to enchant your belongings. Your deeds, both noble and base, have been weighed. Allow me to share a truth little known: these two toiled harder than any of ye, both in the classroom and out. While ye played, they studied, lent a hand about the house, and even fed ye. If I learn that any of ye cause them the slightest trouble, more than just your backsides will be bruised, and ye'll wish ye had learned to be grateful and keep any destructive thoughts at bay."

She turned to Felix and Anastasia. "Now, for the both of ye, your education shall be solely at the castle."

Anastasia and Felix turned to each other, their gloomy expressions reappearing.

"This again? What seems to be the trouble now?" Lady Rosalyn asked.

"We won't be able to see Mrs. Simmons anymore!" they replied simultaneously.

Lady Rosalyn smirked. "Oh, come now. With your strong work ethic, ye'll have ample chance to visit Mrs. Simmons in your free time. I'm sure she'd like that as well!"

The pair smiled with relief at the good news and headed back into Barrel Hall to retrieve their things.

"There be no time for all that packing. Allow me to do it for ye," Lady Rosalyn said, making a graceful movement with her arms and a flicker of her fingers.

Felix and Anastasia's belongings flew downstairs, folding and stacking themselves into two large trunks, each embossed in gold with their names.

They both had stacks of books that wouldn't fit. Noting the delay in closing the trunks, Lady Rosalyn performed a few more weaves. The books were strapped together with a red cord and shrank in size. The stacks then bounced up and settled on the clothing before the trunks closed.

"Step forward, all, into the circle—save for you two," she said, glancing at Felix and Anastasia. "Why not take a seat?" she added, pointing to the trunks that now rested behind them. The two promptly sat down.

Lady Rosalyn then became blurry for a second, and a second image of herself detached from her original body. The rest of the children blinked out of sight as they entered the circle, followed closely by the second Lady Rosalyn.

"We must tend to their belongings first," she explained.

"Then ye can join the rest."

With a few more waves of her arms and flicks of her fingers, several brown blurs shot out from Barrel Hall. Soon after, the other children's belongings came barreling out of the house and into brown trunks, each embossed with their names as if branded. The mirrored souls floated out of Barrel Hall, drifting off like bubbles into the distance.

Felix watched the creatures as they drifted away. "What's happening with them, Lady Rosalyn?"

"Oh, they're bound for the menagerie to be checked for any unwanted pests. We can't have naught like that coming into the castle," she replied matter-of-factly.

Mrs. Simmons stood next to the front steps, teary-eyed, drying her face with her flour-covered apron, with bits of dough stuck to her cheeks.

The two went to console her.

"Please don't forget about me," Mrs. Simmons said between sobs.

"Oh, good heavens, Mrs. Simmons! Steady yourself!" Lady Rosalyn said. "They shan't forget about ye; I'll see to it."

The pair kissed Mrs. Simmons goodbye and said, "We'll see you soon and will tell you everything we can about Heaven's Gate."

Lady Rosalyn instructed them to mount their trunks as if they were riding a horse. "Hold fast to the straps." Once she confirmed they were secure, with a flick of her wrist, the trunks lifted off and soared upward.

Mrs. Simmons waved mournfully, telling herself she needed a drink once the children were out of sight.

The trunks soared higher and higher until they reached the clouds. Racing through the sky, they could see for miles over the landscape, encountering birds that flew close by. They suddenly veered toward a colossal pillar of rock, rising from the earth and reaching into the sky. Emerging from the thick clouds, a castle appeared to float in the sky, and they made a quick loop around its grounds.

Felix was awestruck. A giant tree stood over a thousand feet tall, several hundred feet thick at the base, with branches stretching more than a mile wide. The clouds swirled around the pillar of stone on which Heaven's Gate Castle sat, darkening the sky.

They landed at the back of the castle.

"Couldn't we have just teleported here like everyone else?" Anastasia asked.

"Ye aren't like everyone else! And I wouldn't have missed the thrill of fear upon your faces for all the world. How could anyone pass that up?" Lady Rosalyn responded with a chuckle. "Most of ye won't be able to fly for at least four years. That was my indulgence. Now, ye'll be late, so make haste. Follow the side of the castle until ye spy a group forming."

Lady Rosalyn guided the trunks into the castle, and Felix and Anastasia hurried around to the front. They passed an unusual part of the structure that was newer and awkwardly positioned. Felix glanced inside as they passed, realizing that was where Len and Mr. Nibs had been taken with the rest of the mirrored souls.

Lady Rosalyn checked to ensure no one was nearby. Once she confirmed the area was clear, she lifted off the ground, spinning upward and weaving signs as she gained altitude. Her robes seemed to transform into a pair of wings. As she ascended, the clouds closed in around the castle, blotting out the light from Mater, their sun. She vanished from sight in a burst of flames.

By the time Anastasia and Felix reached the front of the castle, they were out of breath. Hundreds of students were gathered, with all five elements represented evenly in size;

however, the number of royal blue robes was less than half that of the other houses.

Noticing the disparity in royal blue robes, Felix asked, "Anastasia, why are there so few Water Weavers?" though he already suspected the answer.

She looked at him cautiously, knowing he tended to panic. "It's not because of popularity or anything like that. Water Weavers are rarer by comparison. They are also the most powerful of the Elemental Weavers. Don't you remember what the book said about Water Weavers having a harder time controlling their power? It has something to do with being more emotional by nature."

"What do you mean? They don't do so well?" a now overly concerned Felix asked.

"Let me see," she said, trying to recall what she'd read. "Water is unpredictable and can be hard to control because it's a lot like emotions. It flows in any direction and has the power to shape the earth."

Realizing which book Anastasia was quoting from, he nodded in agreement as he recalled what it had said.

She continued, "Remember manipulating one's element? It was explained that those who are in control of their emotions have an easier time bending the elements to their will. That doesn't mean they have stronger powers; they just get better results. Certain emotions can be distractions, which can hinder a weaver's intentions. Weavers infuse the most stable emotions—serenity and calm—into their weaves, which amplifies the effect. Most Water Weavers are known for being kind souls. I remember there was a side note in the book that I didn't read aloud. It said that being kind-hearted and sometimes fragile can be a disadvantage for Water Weavers in the beginning."

Even though Len wasn't nearby, she knew what he was

thinking. "Felix, listen to me," she said. "I'll help you focus, and we'll make sure you can control your powers. Remember, I'm here for you whenever you're unsure, and I'll strengthen your resolve."

The two clasped hands and made their way to the front, where the rest of the children from Barrel Hall were waiting. Once they joined the mix of colorfully robed students, they noticed something was off. It then hit them: they were surrounded by groups of older students, who were watching the new arrivals with keen interest. The older students, who had been waiting in the front garden, gazed intently at the newcomers.

Suddenly, several temporary teleportation circles flashed into existence, joined by another group of sixty-two students native to Yurden. When the unannounced arrivals materialized, they comically knocked over some of the students who were unaware of the expected routine, causing the older students to burst into laughter.

Anastasia lost her footing when she was abruptly jostled by an incoming student. Felix grabbed her hand, helping her regain her balance and preventing her from falling into the other students nearby.

Chapter 13
Introductions

The front of the castle glowed from the lit braziers, and the crisp scent of autumn hung in the air. A chill mingled among the new students, who shifted uneasily, their eyes darting with anticipation. The older students, gathered in small clusters, watched the newcomers with a mix of curiosity and impatience.

Amid the murmur of hushed conversations, a sudden roar of flames erupted from the two large braziers flanking the grand, studded green doors of the castle. Startled gasps swept through the crowd as the fire danced in the cool night air, casting flickering shadows that seemed to twist and writhe. For a heartbeat, silence enveloped the front garden, a palpable pause before the spectacle.

The heavy doors creaked open, and from the darkness within emerged a figure shrouded in long black robes. His mane of black hair, streaked with threads of gray, was neatly combed back, though a few strands fell in a deliberate arch to the left. His piercing blue eyes, reflecting the fierce glow of the braziers, scanned the assembled students with a gaze that seemed to pierce through time itself. A matching black and gray beard framed his stern face, his short hair impeccably groomed.

As he stepped into the light, his presence seemed to cast an aura of enigmatic authority. The man's voice, deep and resonant with a soothing Irish brogue, cut through the stillness. He spoke with a calm, measured cadence, his words deliberate and imbued with an almost timeless quality.

"Ah, welcome back, students. Ye've braved the turn of summer, and here ye stand. I extend me greetings to our returning scholars and our fine newcomers. For the next thirty-one million, five hundred fifty-six thousand, nine hundred and fifty-two seconds—" He paused, a cheeky grin creeping onto his face. "—ye're part of Heaven's Gate's grand ticking clock."

He brought his hands together in a slow, deliberate motion, tucking them beneath his robes as if he were adjusting the delicate gears of an intricate timepiece. His pale skin gleamed with the light, casting an almost ethereal glow. The stillness of his posture was both commanding and contemplative, as if every movement was measured against an invisible clock.

The students watched in awe, their breaths held in a collective hush.

"For the new arrivals, welcome to Heaven's Gate. As we say around these parts, Ye've got to take the rough with the smooth,' and that's a lesson ye'll learn in spades. I'm the headmaster of this grand old place, and I'm here to set the wheels of your minds spinning. Knowledge be the key that unlocks the door to power, and if ye haven't grasped that yet, ye're in for a bit of a bumpy ride. Each year here will test both your smarts and your grit, and how well ye handle it all will be the measure of your success.

Ye might come from all sorts of backgrounds and places, but remember this: what binds ye is far greater than what sets ye apart. Life's a constantly shifting puzzle, and ye'll need a whole toolkit of cogs and gears to make your way through it, both within these walls and beyond. Just as not every screw fits every clock, so too do different friends play different parts. Ye'll need to tinker and adjust to make your time here truly count."

He took in the sea of curious and slightly befuddled faces, many still working through his metaphorical twists. "The road ahead will challenge ye in ways ye might never have imagined. Keep your wits about ye and heed the advice ye're given; even if the reasons aren't clear at first, they're there to keep ye safe and help ye find your way through the year ahead."

He nodded towards a few students. "Some of ye will rise above the pack, while others might find yerselves wrestling with a fair few challenges, and some might just stay where the hands of the clock have left ye. Conquer even the smallest tasks, and ye might see your name etched in the annals of history. The power to shape your own future is well within your grasp.

Heaven's Gate and its leaders are here to teach, guide, and keep a watchful eye on ye. Only time will tell if we've managed to steer ye right. Your triumphs and missteps will echo through your house, so give it your all and make them proud. Ye might find us a bit stern or distant now and then, but it's not because we don't care. We have every faith in your ability to face whatever comes your way with grit and determination."

He rubbed his hands together, eyes sparkling with a mix of mischief and anticipation. "And now, enough of the chinwag. I'll hand ye over to the heads. Time's slipping through the hourglass, and the sands are running out."

When his speech concluded, the man dissipated as if he were being slowly erased from existence, causing the students to do a double-take.

"He's the one who decided we would stay here full-time at Heaven's Gate," she informed Felix.

The five heads of the houses then made their entrances separately.

The first head of house made a dramatic entrance from an urn of flowering shrubs, which erupted into flames like a volcanic explosion. Several students leapt back in fright.

"It's Professor Pompeii!" a girl cried out.

Stepping out from the heart of the inferno, Professor Pompeii made an entrance both dramatic and flamboyant. He emerged from the flames as though summoned from a forgotten myth. His appearance was a vibrant mix of ancient Greece and wandering gypsy: he wore blood-red silk robes adorned with golden trinkets and a scatter of shimmering gems.

His icy white beard cascaded in meticulously curled ringlets, several of which were adorned with tiny, sparkling baubles. His skin, pale with streaks of yellowing, lent him an air of age and mystery. A golden clasp held his knotted white hair in place atop his head.

With a flourish of his arm, Professor Pompeii addressed the crowd with grand enthusiasm. "Onward!" he exclaimed, his voice rich and vibrant with excitement. "So much to do, my loves, and not a moment to waste!" His speech was delivered with the flair of a grand performance. His eyes danced with a blend of mischief and eagerness as he gestured for the students in crimson robes to follow him.

Captivated, the students followed him eagerly up the

front steps. As they moved, their robes fluttered like flames. The urn's blaze gradually faded, leaving a swirling cloud of smoke and ash that drifted into the night sky.

Once the crimson-clad students had disappeared, an expectant silence enveloped the remaining onlookers. A gentle breeze began to stir, gradually intensifying until it became a vigorous wind. The students' robes billowed and danced in the powerful gusts, creating a mesmerizing display of fluttering fabric.

Searching the skies, the children spotted a cyclone spiraling down from above. The fierce wind blasted several students off their feet, sending them tumbling to the ground with resounding thuds. The cyclone touched down on the front steps of the castle, and from its eye emerged a striking figure.

As the whirlwind dissipated, the robes of the onlookers fluttered wildly in the aftershock. A stunning, statuesque woman stood where the tornado had been. Her long, feathered black hair cascaded around her shoulders like a raven's plume, and she was adorned in layers of iridescent silk that seemed to dance and ripple perpetually, as if caught in an eternal breeze. Her face bore a pleasant expression, though her raised eyebrow and the mole that perched just above it hinted at a touch of haughty amusement.

"Professor Zephyr!" a boy who had been knocked off his feet cried out, struggling to regain his breath.

With a condescending smirk, Professor Zephyr looked down at him. Her voice, laced with a refined haughtiness, drifted over to the children. "One must always be sure of one's footing, non?" she said with a melodious chuckle. "Come along, students, s'il vous plaît!"

The children in white robes, dusting themselves off, quickly regrouped and scurried to her side. Their voices soon faded into the distance as they followed her down the hall, leaving behind the echoes of their hurried footsteps.

Moments after the students had vanished, a profound, echoing rumble emanated from below, compelling those left behind to steady themselves against the trembling earth. Without warning, the ground erupted, parting like the jaws of some ancient beast. From the gaping fissure, an imposing figure emerged. As his powerful form emerged into the light, the chasm sealed behind him, vanishing as abruptly as it had opened. The man's presence was nothing short of awe-inspiring; he was rugged and unkempt.

"Professor Agate!" several students called out as the man, with a bushy beard and a smooth bald head, stepped nearer.

He responded with a deep, resonant laugh, rich with warmth. "Indeed, that is I," he proclaimed.

His robes seemed to be woven from a blend of natural elements, reminiscent of forest undergrowth and earthy textures, lending him a distinctly primal appearance. As he approached the urn, he observed that the flowers had been scorched and were still emitting wisps of smoke.

"It appears Professor Pompeii will need to be spoken to again," he remarked with a sigh tinged with mild exasperation.

He then reached into his pocket and produced a flask, from which he carefully poured a golden liquid over the smoldering remains. Once the smoke dissipated, he opened a pouch and sprinkled its contents into the urn. His hands, as large as a dinner plate, moved with blunted jerks. As he turned back toward the students, a robust flowering plant with delicate yellow blossoms had emerged from the urn.

"This way, children!" he called, prompting the students in emerald, green to follow with much enthusiasm.

Knowing that Felix disliked drawing unwanted attention, Anastasia said, "You need to trust me and follow my instructions, okay? Don't try to learn everything all at once." She hoped this advice would help minimize any negative attention he might receive from the other students, especially since she wouldn't be around to shield him as she had at Barrel Hall.

Before leaving, Anastasia gave Felix a reassuring hug and then hurried off to catch up with the rest of the students in green robes making their way inside.

Once Anastasia was out of sight, Felix felt an immediate sense of isolation. With the number of students dwindling and no longer accompanied by Len or Anastasia, he found himself without the support he had relied on.

Then, a streak of lightning split the sky, followed by a deafening crash and an explosion of light that revealed a tall, imposing figure. The man, dressed in buttercream-colored robes adorned with numerous medals and honors, stood before them. His blond hair was neatly styled, and his strong brow and square jaw. At his side was a sheathed sword. He moved with the precision of a seasoned soldier, each motion deliberate, as if enforcing the principle that order and method were paramount.

"Professor Bolton!" several female students and a few males called out with a mix of admiration and eagerness.

"Enough of that, ja? The rest of you, follow me, bitte," he responded tersely. As he spoke, the students in yellow gathered swiftly and marched with purpose toward him. Moments later, they too disappeared, just as the other groups had.

The smallest of the groups, the Water Weavers, wandered around, anticipating some form of spectacle, but nothing occurred.

Then, an authoritative sound cut through the stillness—

the sharp, rhythmic click of high heels, growing more insistent with every step. Emerging from the doorway where the other groups had disappeared was a diminutive woman who commanded immediate attention. Her presence was intimidating, with a stern, unyielding expression framed by short gray hair. She wore a silver jumpsuit clung tightly beneath flowing robes, and knee-high heeled boots emphasized her formidable stature. Black-tinted glasses concealed her eyes and a large, diamond-encrusted brooch in the shape of a climbing cat adorned her robes.

"I possess no patience for needless theatrics," she barked, her voice cold and commanding, echoing through the corridor with the finality of a prison warden's decree. "Pray, follow me."

The students, disillusioned by the lack of dramatic flourish, fell into line with a sense of resigned compliance. Their earlier excitement ebbed away, replaced by a palpable sense of subservience as they trailed behind her. With a swift, almost imperious gesture, the woman caused the massive green doors slammed shut behind them, sealing them off from the world they had known.

One of the children, voice barely more than a whisper, ventured, "Professor, what's your name?"

"I am Professor Dorothy Madeline Elizabeth Stewart. You shall address me as Professor, Lady Stewart, or Professor Stewart. Nothing else will suffice. Any deviation from this shall be met with strict consequences."

Professor Stewart led them through a series of hallways and passageways until they reached a grand circular room three stories high. Dominating the room was an imposing stained-glass window that depicted a majestic water dragon resting in a serene pond adorned with water lilies.

As Felix glanced down, he noticed that the floor of the

room was covered by a vast pond with unusually large lily pads floating on its surface. At the far end of the room, a small island pedestal supported a grand statue of a seated dragon positioned before the stained-glass window.

"Pray, follow the elder students. They shall guide you through the process," Professor Stewart instructed in a tone that left no room for error, ensuring the new students dared not make a misstep.

The older students gracefully stepped onto the lily pads, carefully making their way to the back of the pond. There, they slipped between the dragon's body and the wing of the statue, revealing a spiral staircase that descended into the depths below.

"Whatever you do, stay away from the water!" one of the boys warned, his voice tinged with urgency. "The lily pads' roots will ensnare you, mummify you, and pull you under to drown. Don't believe me? There's a grim warning etched into the stone under the water to the right. And if that's not enough to scare you, know this: the Water Elemental lurking in the pool is far from forgiving. Last year, three students attempted to breach our dorms and never made it out. They met their end right here."

"What house were they from?" one of the new students asked, their curiosity piqued.

"They were from House Vulcan," the boy replied. "Not that it would have mattered if they crossed the pool. The bracelet is the key. You must stroke the inner wing of the dragon to open the door."

Once inside the statue, a spiral staircase wound downward into the castle's basement. At the bottom, they emerged into a lavish chamber with a dark blue lapis lazuli floor streaked with black veins. Silvery frescoes of water dragons and portraits of past house heads adorned the walls.

A colossal fireplace, grand enough to roast an entire steer, dominated one wall, its imposing structure carved from dark stone with intricate, swirling patterns. Above it, an opulent portrait of a regal woman captured the gaze of anyone who entered. Clad in an exquisite, earthy-toned gown that seemed to shimmer with every hue of the forest, and draped with a gossamer shawl that sparkled subtly, she exuded an aura of unassailable grace. Her long, flowing hair cascaded like a dark river, and a formidable black dragon loomed in the background, adding an aura of mystique and power to her majestic presence.

Flanking the fireplace were two magnificent statues of the Dragon God Mizu, masterfully sculpted from deep blue azurite. The statues were lifelike, their scales intricately detailed, and they faced each other in an eternal, vigilant stance. Before the fireplace, sumptuous couches upholstered in rich fabrics of royal blue and silver, were arranged in pairs. High-backed chairs, upholstered in matching velvet, complemented the seating arrangement. Above, royal-blue banners, emblazoned with silver dragons in intricate patterns, cascaded from the vaulted ceiling, their edges shimmering as they caught the light.

On the far end of the room, an immense window stretched across the entire wall, its crystal-clear glass so flawlessly crafted that it seemed to dissolve the boundary between the interior and the outside world. The window framed a subaquatic vista of a pool area that extended perilously off the cliff face, descending in a cascading waterfall down a sheer stone pillar. At the top, the water surged with untamed vigor. Below the fast-moving current, the water settled into a tranquil pool where it flowed gently, revealing a mesmerizing array of vibrant fish and shimmering aquatic creatures. Their graceful movements cast ripples of light through the serene depths.

"Pardon me!" Lady Stewart's voice boomed, cutting through the room and silencing the children. Even those engrossed in the fascinating sights turned to face her.

"This shall be your home until your graduation. You will encounter challenges that will test you beyond your limits. Despite my earnest efforts to guide you, failure is a distinct possibility, and in the gravest of circumstances, it may even lead to death. I expect you to take this matter with utmost seriousness—let us fervently hope that such a dire fate does not become your reality."

Felix stared out into the water, his expression inscrutable.

She continued, her tone matter-of-fact and detached. "If you should meet your end, make certain you are not beneath the foot of a dragon. I shall not be searching for any spleen lodged betwixt its toes."

"Rule number one: Only those students who are Water Weavers may enter this house. Rule number two: I shall not tolerate any form of filth. If it be necessary, I shall personally ensure that you slumber in dragon manure, whether you desire it or not. This is not a threat—merely inquire of Mr. Grixbee."

She gestured toward a boy at the back of the room, impeccably dressed in a neatly pressed shirt with his hair combed to perfection. No one would have guessed he had been forced to endure such conditions.

"No, it's not a threat, Professor," he said quietly, adding under his breath, "The smell..." He visibly shuddered.

"Rule number three: Do not bring dishonor to this house. Should you do so, the consequences shall be severe. This is a rule I find myself compelled to repeat each year, even to those who have heard it before. You possess extraordinary abilities, yet you are also engaging with one of the most chaotic and perilous elements. It must be controlled and mastered, lest it lead to your destruction."

As she spoke, shock spread across the faces of the first-year students—except Felix. They were not expecting such a stern introduction, especially after the safety and comfort they had experienced until now. Yurden was revealing itself to be a harsh and unyielding place.

"You are all under my charge from this moment henceforth. My duty is to ensure your success. This shall be your new family, and you will either support and protect one another or face the consequences. Your triumph depends upon your cooperation—this is not negotiable. Now, direct your attention to the painting above the fireplace."

The entire group shifted their focus to the painting hanging over the mantle.

"That is the High Lord Dragoon, Lady Aurora Sylvia Tenecia Leon Willow-Grove. She was not merely a leader, but a living embodiment of virtue and nobility. Her very presence radiated purity, an unwavering strength, and an intellect so profound it seemed to brush the divine. Her kindness knew no bounds, and her supernatural strength was matched only by the depth of her compassionate heart.

Lady Aurora's influence transcended the ordinary. She was the last of the High Lords Dragoon, a title that conferred not merely power but an almost sacred duty. Through her unparalleled wisdom and relentless dedication, she wove together the disparate threads of Yurden, crafting it into a unified realm. Heaven's Gate, the pinnacle of her achievements, stands as a testament to her vision and grace.

Her death, wrought by vile greed and an insatiable lust for power, marked a tragic turning point. Since her untimely fall, Yurden has been plagued by instability and disarray.

Lady Aurora's legacy is one of reverence and awe; she is a beacon of what one ought to aspire to be. Her life was a perfect blend of strength and benevolence, a balance that many strive to achieve but few attain.

I share this with you, for I, too, seek to honor her enduring legacy through my own actions. Each day, I endeavor to uphold the values she represented, and I hope you shall find inspiration in her story to guide your own journey here."

The newer students were stunned by the abrupt shift in the Professor's demeanor, a stark contrast to the sternness they had just witnessed moments before.

She then shifted her focus to the group. "Now, upperclassmen, attend to their preparation."

Lady Stewart nodded toward a girl before turning and ascending the spiral staircase, her departure marked by silence.

The younger students, bewildered, exchanged confused glances, unsure of what "attend to their preparation" entailed.

A girl stepped forward, introducing herself as Julie Maxton. She began to explain the layout of the house and the essential rules. For instance, the corridor leading to the dorms featured a staircase that split: the boys were to go to the bottom, and the girls to the top.

The dormitories each contained four beds and were equipped with two tall windows carved directly into the cliffside, reminiscent of arrow slits but slightly larger. Julie explained that Heaven's Gate had once been a fortress before its conversion into a school. Currently, there were forty-three upperclassmen Water Weavers—twenty-five females and eighteen males.

Julie's voice took on an urgent tone. "New students: your belongings are already in your assigned rooms. Your names will be posted on the doors. You don't have much time. Be back in the main room in five minutes!"

The students scrambled in response. Felix moved quickly down the corridor, scanning the names on the doors. He reached halfway down the hall before spotting a parchment labeled "Felix Grey."

Opening the door, Felix found four beds in the room. Len was already lying on one of them, looking relieved to see Felix. Another boy was in the corner bed, someone Felix had not noticed during Lady Stewart's speech. The two boys exchanged a long, silent stare.

Felix would come to be grateful that Lady Rosalyn had ensured he was placed among students who were dedicated to their studies and would understand his peculiarities. As one of only eight children ever sent to Heaven's Gate before the typical age, Felix was already subject to considerable expectations.

Chapter 14
A Boy and His Raven

His new roommate's name was Marcus Erikson, a tall, lanky fifteen-year-old who preferred a quiet environment free from unnecessary noise. With dark brown hair parted down the middle, alabaster skin smudged with charcoal, a mole under the left side of his lower lip, and thick bifocals, Marcus was a stark contrast to the boisterous energy of his surroundings.

This arrangement suited Felix well since he wasn't very talkative, and Len enjoyed observing everything around her. Marcus's constant companion was a raven named Tom.

Marcus finally spoke, breaking the silence. "Ah, you must be special. You got one of the nice trunks. My name's Marcus. Since it's your first day, you need to head back to the common room and leave your fox here."

Felix glanced at Len.

"You'll be fine, Felix! I'll just stay here and keep the bed warm for you," Len chirped.

Felix looked back at Marcus. "Will you watch over her

while I'm gone?"

Marcus shook his head as he put his robes back on. "Unfortunately, I can't attend to her. We all must attend the ceremony. However, Tom will keep her company while we're away."

Felix waved to Len before heading back to the common room.

Len gave a pawing goodbye.

Marcus followed Felix out, adjusting a peculiar hat on his head before closing the door behind him. They made their way back to the common room.

Most of the older students had already left the dorms, except for Julie, who was waiting with the rest of the new students in front of a roaring fire. As the newcomers assembled, the older students emerged, dressed in their full ceremonial garb. Their hats, which covered everything above the tips of their noses, were adorned with eye slits just above the brim for visibility. Each hat was intricately sculpted to resemble various animal features—beaks, fangs, whiskers—adding an air of mystique.

Felix entered the common room alone, uncertain of what to do next.

"What took you so long?" Julie asked. "Oh, wait, you're not with any of the other first-years—never mind." She had noted that Felix was the only first-year not paired with other first-years.

"The branding ceremony will start soon," Julie continued. "Remember what Lady Stewart said. Honor this house and avoid bringing shame upon it."

A girl raised her hand. "What do you mean by branding ceremony?"

Julie explained, "You'll receive a brand that will help you tap into your powers more effectively. This will take place in front of the entire school."

Her audience listened intently as she detailed the process. "All five dorms will converge at the Crystal Sanctum, located at the center of the castle. The older students will enter from two doors on either side of the massive metal doors. "Once all the non-first-years are inside, the smaller doors will lock, and the massive metal doors will begin to reverberate."

Julie then led the first-years toward their gathering point but stopped just before the final corridor. "Remember this, as you'll need to repeat it. When it's your turn, stand in the center of the room and say: "I, [your name], of house Mizu, do present myself before all gathered here, to bear witness to mine induction into this most noble of houses."

She had them practice the verse until they could recite it confidently. "Once you've said this, extend your right arm outward and upward with your sleeve rolled back. "I hope none of you have any phobias... But forget I mentioned that. Let's move out!"

The massive metal doors gleamed as though recently polished, their surface intricately carved with a depiction of the world in its pristine, untouched state.

As the students gathered, Anastasia emerged from her group upon spotting Felix in his blue robes. He quickly moved to the back of the line to avoid drawing attention, slipping in to hug her.

The five older students from each house, who had guided them to this point, now stood before the doors, smiling. "We hope you're ready!" one of them said.

They then turned and knocked three times on the metal doors, one after the other. The five students exited through smaller doors on either side. Once these smaller doors closed and locked, the massive metal doors reverberated and slowly swung open. A resonant vibration filled the air, akin to the sound of a tuning fork combined with a crystal, creating a harmonious tone.

The doors revealed a circular room adorned with tiered seating beneath a jagged crystal canopy. The ceiling was encrusted with countless tiny crystals, droplets, large chunks, and thin strands, sparkling like a starry night sky.

The man in black robes appeared once more, but this time, his presence was amplified by four ethereal images that materialized from the north, east, south, and west, converging in the center. As they joined, he became more solid and distinct. Now, his attire was clearly visible: a high-collared robe adorned with subtle black embroidery. His eyes, dimly glowing near the crowd, seemed to flicker with the faintest streaks of lightning.

He welcomed everyone to the momentous ceremony, his breath forming visible clouds in the cold air as he spoke. Addressing all ninety-eight new students, he directed the sixteen non-human students to take their places with their respective houses. The students complied without question.

The human students, left without an explanation, exchanged puzzled glances. It would later be clarified that humans are uniquely challenged in managing their powers compared to creatures like dwarves, elves, or fairies, who possess an inherent control.

The remaining eighty-two students formed a line against the circular wall. Felix and Anastasia, standing side by side, nervously held hands at the end of the line.

The headmaster, cloaked entirely in black, moved to the center of the crystal canopy and spoke with a commanding presence. "Valerie, would ye care to join us, me old friend?"

As he finished speaking, the room was engulfed in darkness. The crystals embedded in the ceiling and walls began to glow, illuminating the space with an otherworldly light. A shimmering gold clockface emerged from beneath the headmaster, expanding to encompass the entire floor, creating a breathtaking display.

A deep, ancient voice croaked, "If I must."

The younger students scanned the room anxiously, desperately trying to locate the source of the eerie voice. The upperclassmen, however, wore devious grins, eagerly awaiting the spectacle to come.

From the hole in the center of the ceiling, a massive, glowing crystal began its slow descent from a silk strand. The sight was so overwhelming that several students recoiled in terror, some even paralyzed by fear. The crystal, shaped like the abdomen of a colossal spider, elicited gasps and screams from the crowd—the reactions the upperclassmen had anticipated.

Dangling high above the headmaster was Valerie, a towering Cryolite widow spider. His imposing presence cast a shadow over the room.

The headmaster addressed the crowd. "Please step beneath Valerie as the clock hand indicates your turn."

The first boy, short with disheveled brown hair, appeared visibly nauseous. As he stepped forward, his face contorted with terror, he was met by Valerie's eight emerald-green eyes, glowing with a sinister light. The boy slowly rolled up his sleeve, revealing his right arm, but before he could speak, he fainted in front of the entire school. The older students struggled to stifle their laughter, though a few chuckles still escaped into the room.

Professor Pompeii stroked a curl of his beard thoughtfully while Headmaster O'Connor approached the unconscious boy. With a swift zap of electricity from his finger, he revived him.

"Shall we give this another go?" the headmaster asked, his tone unyielding.

With a look of utter resignation, the boy nodded. Rising unsteadily, he recited, "I, Charlie Gerard Jones, of house Vulcan, do present myself before all gathered here, to bear witness to mine induction into this most noble of houses."

As Charlie finished, the clock on the floor turned a deep red, and its hand spun rapidly counterclockwise. Valerie extended his legs, poised like a predator waiting for prey.

Charlie presented his arm once more. Valerie grasped it with his front legs. The spider's abdomen glowed a fiery red as it spun, embroidered an intricate design onto Charlie's forearm. The design crystallized instantly, causing a sharp pinch that made Charlie yelp.

The crystal shattered, leaving a red line with a Celtic knot pattern and a dragon's head on his wrist. Charlie walked away, gazing at his new marking with a mix of awe and discomfort.

One by one, students stepped forward: a girl, another girl, and then a boy. The procession continued for hours.

During the ceremony, three disruptions occurred. Ivan, Savannah, and Margot were identified as Kanks—students with uncontrollable powers.

Ivan was unable to control the wind he had inadvertently summoned, which spiraled into chaos. The violent gale hurled students into the walls as they were caught in his line of sight. Crystals from the canopy shattered, sending deadly shards scattering through the air. Amid the mayhem, the headmaster and professors acted with urgency, their combined powers managing to subdue Ivan before the destruction could escalate further.

Savannah inadvertently unleashed a torrent of water

that surged uncontrollably from her pores, creating a potentially deadly flood that swept some first-year students off their feet and carried them away in its current. The water rose rapidly, threatening everyone in the room. Assessing the situation, Professor Zephyr acted swiftly, warming the air to counter the chill, while Lady Stewart evaporated the water to prevent any further issues that might arise. After Savannah was subdued, the pair then dried the saturated students who had been caught in the flood.

Margot, as she recited her oath, was seized by Valerie. The spider's barbed legs gripped her forearm tightly, causing her to tremble uncontrollably. Valerie's legs twisted in a nightmarish dance, making Margot's eyes cross in terror. Once the branding was completed, Valerie detached his legs, and Margot lurched forward, vomiting molten lava balls with alarming force.

Valerie scrambled up his silk strand to avoid the eruption, but Margot's uncontrollable lava balls hurtled towards the first-year students. Several of the molten projectiles struck the upper-tiered seating, sending potentially deadly splashes of lava into the crowd. Professor Agate intercepted most of the lava balls mid-flight, turning them into large gemstones with gravity manipulation. One ball, however, veered off course, heading straight for a girl near Anastasia and Felix.

The girl was struck by the lava, suffering severe third-degree burns. Her spine-chilling scream pierced the air. Felix threw himself over Anastasia to shield her as the lava sizzled perilously close to their heads. The intense heat and the fear-driven chaos overwhelmed them, their heartbeats pounding in their ears as they huddled together.

Headmaster O'Connor briefly halted time, allowing Professor Agate to retrieve a small, ragged pouch from his pocket like before. The other professors quickly responded to contain the chaos. Professor Pompeii used his abilities to transform most of the lava still liquid oozing out of the walls it struck into rock as he sucked out all the heat from them. Meanwhile, Professor Agate administered an Aeternus Somnus seed (eternal sleep) to Margot, paralyzing her. Her eyes rolled back as she fell to the floor, stiff and motionless.

Professor Agate then lifted her as if she were a piece of wood and placed her beside Ivan and Savannah. After the ceremony, Lady Rosalyn was summoned to escort the three Kanks to Dennington, ensuring their safety among their kind.

Finally, it was Anastasia and Felix's turn, as they were last in line. Anastasia's palms were sweaty and clammy, and Felix wished her good luck as she stepped forward.

Anastasia didn't like spiders. Although she enjoyed learning about them, encountering them in person was another story. Spiders creeped her out, as did anything with more than four limbs, even to the point where the hairs on the back of her neck stood up.

The clock beneath her was green, and every few seconds, its hand whipped past where she had been standing.

With a confident exterior, Anastasia approached and said, "I, Anastasia Louise Beazletin, of house Terra, do present myself before all gathered here, to bear witness to mine induction into this most noble of houses."

Valerie then turned emerald green and stitched the same design onto Anastasia, causing her to cry out, "That bloody well hurt!" She took her place back at the wall, rubbing her forearm.

Finally, it was Felix's turn. He walked skittishly into the middle of the room, keeping his head turned toward Anastasia the entire way. She gave him a thumbs-up.

As Felix glanced up, his eyes widened. He was now face-to-face with a spider his own size. All eight of Valerie's eyes scanned Felix as if searching for the perfect place to strike.

Seeing the raw panic in Felix's eyes, Anastasia silently urged him to steady his breathing from the safety of the wall. Felix, trembling, closed his eyes and drew a deep, shuddering breath before stammering, "I, Felix Grey, of house Mizu, do present myself before all gathered here, to bear witness to mine induction into this most noble of houses."

As soon as "House Mizu" escaped his lips, the clock on the floor erupted into a searing shade of blue, its hands whirling with frantic intensity. Valerie seized Felix's arm, and a torrent of energy that surged from him, coursing through the spider's body as if its limbs were grafted to his skin. The spider's abdomen spun wildly with unprecedented hues of blue, casting an otherworldly glow.

The room fell into a hushed awe. Students whispered in shock, while the heads of houses and staff were riveted by the spectacle unfolding before them. Valerie, seemingly entranced, meticulously wove a gauntlet onto Felix's forearm.

A profound silence enveloped the room as brilliant flashes of blue light sliced through the air. The heads of houses rose to get a clearer view, bracing for any possible crisis. The children closest to Felix, lined against the wall, stood frozen in stunned disbelief.

Valerie's legs moved with feverish speed, spinning silk with an almost frantic precision. As he completed the intricate work, a blinding blue light burst from Felix's arm where the gauntlet had been branded. Felix let out a raw, feral howl of agony as the pinch took hold, and Valerie, now dazed, clambered up the thread to hang from the ceiling. His once-glorious crystal abdomen had dulled, becoming a lifeless, milky gray.

Lady Stewart sprang into action, her face a mask of urgency. She dashed towards Felix, her eyes locked on the gauntlet brand seared onto his arm. The other heads of houses quickly followed, their expressions grim and concerned, forming a tight circle around Felix. The man in black, driven by intense curiosity, joined the encirclement, his gaze never leaving the scene.

Lady Stewart's shock was palpable—she had never encountered anything like this before, nor had any of the staff, including the venerable Professor Pompeii, who had witnessed over two thousand years of history.

A murmur of alarm rippled through the students, escalating into a cacophony of anxious voices. The headmaster, his tone authoritative, instructed the remaining students to return to their houses immediately and await further instructions. The tension in the room was hung like a dense fog, as everyone waited for answers in the midst of the escalating situation.

The entire school buzzed with speculation about the stuttering boy from House Mizu. Anastasia, however, was consumed with worry for Felix, fearing the worst. She lingered a little longer than the other students until Professor Agate sternly ordered her to return to her common room. Although she knew Felix would be the most unsettled by the events, she reluctantly complied.

As the last of the students exited, the heads of the houses paused their examination, equally mystified by the unfolding events.

Once the students had returned to their houses, their imaginations ran wild, concocting increasingly elaborate tales to explain the bizarre occurrence. Jealous whispers circulated—some speculated that Felix had somehow bribed

Valerie to make his design more impressive than theirs, while others bitterly suggested he was of royal lineage. The rumors grew more outrageous by the minute, fueled by envy and the sting of perceived injustice.

Felix, however, was consumed by a profound sense of dread as he felt the weight of countless stares bearing down on him. It was a familiar, uncomfortable attention that brought back unsettling memories of the day Henry had announced his first word at the kitchen table—an event that had left him feeling exposed and vulnerable.

Surrounded by the heads of each house, Felix faced a harrowing ordeal. The professors meticulously examined the brand on his forearm, their scrutiny almost clinical. They twisted and pulled his arm in various directions, draining it of blood and inducing a numb, painful tingle that seemed to crawl down his entire limb.

In a desperate bid for answers, the headmaster levitated up to the ceiling to consult with Valerie, the ancient spider. The headmaster hoped to glean some insights from Valerie, but the spider remained in a comatose state, utterly unresponsive. Valerie had expended all his energy in climbing the silk strand and was now in no condition to provide any explanations. Felix's dread only deepened as he realized that the answers he desperately needed remained frustratingly out of reach.

After about fifteen minutes of being scrutinized like a lab rat, Felix's sense of dread reached a breaking point. Overwhelmed by the relentless examination, he spotted a brief gap in the encircling ring of legs. Adrenaline surged through him, triggering a primal fight-or-flight response. With a frantic jerk, he yanked his limp and numb arm free and sprinted for the door. His sudden, explosive movement took the professors completely off guard. He darted past them with startling speed, driven by sheer panic. His eidetic memory of the school's layout became his lifeline as he navigated the labyrinthine of corridors with fierce determination. Within moments, he was out of the chamber and hurtling down the passageway, the echo of his rapid footsteps a testament to his desperate bid for freedom.

Professor Zephyr bounded toward the double doors with an air of smug amusement, flashing a grin. "Well, Lady Stewart, if I had not seen that telltale blue robes on the boy, I would have sworn he was one of mine by the way he moves. Clearly, he has learned a thing or two about finesse, non?"

Lady Stewart's eyes narrowed as she retorted with icy venom, "Ah, Arevik, let us count ourselves fortunate that he is not. Your students are notorious for running wild under your so-called guidance, often resulting in naught but chaos and disaster."

Professor Zephyr's smirk widened, her tone dripping with condescension. "Jealousy, Lady Stewart? It must be so. If your students weren't so bogged down by your own ineptitude, perhaps one of them could actually become the champion of Heaven's Gate—like I did. Or maybe we would finally see one of your students achieve something noteworthy, a feat that has been elusive since you took over House Mizu. That was, what, when I first started attending classes here? Some people cannot handle ideals that do not fit them. Historically, the Water Weavers were the epitome of strength—until you tarnished their legacy, non?"

Lady Stewart's glare could have frozen fire as she slowly extracted her long silver and black lacquered pipe, exhaling a dense plume of smoke straight into Professor Zephyr's face. Professor Zephyr sneezed and coughed violently, the smoke lingering—a harsh reminder of Lady's Stewart's disdain.

Professor Bolton interjected, cracking his knuckles. "Ladies, as much as I enjoy a good argument, now is not the time for a catfight—unless you are, perhaps, challenging each other to a contest?"

The two professors halted their bickering and stepped back as the headmaster descended from where Valerie hung, having given up on his attempt to extract more information.

"There's no better time than now to check on your students, so it is," the headmaster declared with authority. "They must be all abuzz with speculation—especially your students, Lady Stewart. This peculiar situation offers a grand opportunity for observation. I expect to receive detailed updates on any new developments, mind ye!"

Lady Stewart nodded curtly and swiftly made her way back to her house. The sharp clicking of her heels echoed through the hallway as she departed.

Professor Agate sighed with a chuckle, shook his head, and exited the room. The hanging lights, suspended from chains, swayed slightly with each of his footsteps.

Professor Bolton gave a brief salute and followed suit, only slightly disappointed that Professor Stewart and Professor Zephyr hadn't settled their differences in a more dramatic fashion.

Professor Pompeii responded cheerfully, "Ah, what an exhilarating evening! A mystery to unravel, and I get to witness it all unfold! I swear, my blood is practically boiling with anticipation. Maybe I should cool down a little" He then intertwined his fingers, twiddling them, and left the room in a flourish.

The last to leave, Professor Zephyr moistened the corners of her mouth and bit down on one of her nails as she whirled down the corridor.

The headmaster was left alone in the silence. After a moment of contemplation, he gazed up at the ceiling, as if hoping the answers to his questions might descend and reveal themselves. As he passed through the archway, the massive metal doors closed behind him, sealing the room in total darkness. This newfound attention would undoubtedly unmoor Felix, who was already prone to worry. Yet, this anxiety also drove him to move with a sense of urgency that would prove useful in the challenging situations ahead.

Felix quickly reached the room with the lily pads, his heart pounding with fear. He leapt onto the first pad, scrambled across to the second, and then jumped to the third. As he reached for the fourth, he barely skimmed the water with his boot. Behind him, a menacing mound of water began to rise, forming a shapeless, churning mass that surged toward him, while tendrils of water lilies reached out from the surface in a desperate attempt to ensnare its prey.

Unaware of the looming threats, Felix focused on the path ahead as he crossed the lily pads. He reached the dragon statue, touched its inner wing for reassurance, and then hurriedly descended into the house.

The water elemental, having missed its chance to capture Felix, crashed into the statue before sinking back into the basin, its last futile attempt to seize its prey. Meanwhile, in the main room of the house, the debate about Felix and the bizarre event ceased abruptly. A heavy silence fell over the students as they turned to the base of the stairs, where Felix came hurtling down.

Horrified by the stares, Felix felt an overwhelming dread that he might again become an object of scrutiny. He darted toward the boys' dormitory hallway, a blur of blue. The sight only fueled the students' curiosity, and they began to chase after him.

Felix reached his room, where Marcus was already inside. He slammed the door shut and locked it, bracing himself against it in case the other Water Weavers tried to force their way in.

Marcus glanced up from his reading as Felix grabbed Len off the blanket where she had been lying and swiftly slid under the bed with her, seeking refuge from the outside world.

The hallway was filled with boys, and even a few daring girls who hoped to sneak a glimpse of Felix's arm, crowding outside Felix and Marcus's room.

Marcus answered the door to the persistent pounding and saw the eager crowd. With a smirk, he said, "So, you all want to see Felix? He's currently in a meeting. Please make an appointment, and he'll try to pencil you in as soon as possible. Death might come sooner though." He then closed the door with a maniacal laugh, pushing back the curious students.

Noticing a sliver of blue robe peeking out from under the bed, Marcus realized that Felix wasn't fully hidden. Trying to reassure his new roommate, he said, "You'll be fine. It can't be that bad. You don't know what's coming. If you're going to hide, you might want to pull in your robes. They wouldn't dare try to break down the door!"

Marcus settled on his bed and began reading aloud, just as he had for Tom before Felix's mad dash of an entrance.

After about five minutes, Len cautiously poked her head out and signaled to Felix with her tail that it was safe. Felix emerged, and they crawled out from under the bed, their immediate assumed danger momentarily averted.

"I was wondering when you'd reappear," Marcus said kindly.

Felix didn't respond, staring instead at his right arm.

Len licked it soothingly, trying to alleviate the stinging.

"Give it an hour or so, and the irritation will go away," Marcus reassured him. He walked over to Felix and inspected the remarkable design on his arm. "That's pretty cool. Mine just has this simple pattern." He rolled up his sleeve to reveal his own brand, which, while beautiful, was relatively plain compared to Felix's.

"Why does yours have a second color and mine doesn't?" Felix asked.

"Well, some Weavers can control more than one element. I can wield both Water and Lightning, but Water is always my dominant element, so I'll always be a Water Weaver. You might end up controlling more than one element, too— it's a surprise and often a bit of a headache. I have to admit, though, I like your brand a lot more than mine." Marcus's brand was a straightforward Celtic knot with a dragon's head at the end.

Marcus patted Felix on the back before heading back to his bed and picking up his reading where he had left off.

Feeling less like a freak and wishing everyone had reacted as Marcus had, Felix got off the bed and began exploring his new room. Each bed had a wardrobe next to it, and while they were similar to those at Barrel Hall, they were much nicer. His trunk was placed at the foot of his bed, and a desk stood on the opposite wall, corresponding with the other three beds.

He unpacked the stacks of books from his trunk and placed them on his desk. As he unbound them, the books slowly regained their original size, towering over him and cluttering the desk.

The room was clean and well-kept. Marcus had a penchant for sketching, and the walls were adorned with dragon drawings and what seemed to be the inner workings of machines he had studied. Felix found the images captivating and was intrigued by the easy access to books he had not yet read. If he could muster the courage, he would ask to borrow a few.

Felix enjoyed watching dragons on TV and often imagined adventures with Chance, slaying or taming them together. He wanted to share these thoughts with Marcus but kept them to himself.

He returned to his trunk and pulled out a few rolled-up posters he'd collected at Barrel Hall, including his favorite of Vivi Odin, one of the greatest dragon riders. He had several posters, including one autographed by Vivi himself. He hung them on the wall, a task he had hesitated to do before out of fear they might be damaged by the boys at Barrel Hall.

Len leaped into Felix's arms, and he held her like a baby while listening to Marcus read aloud to Tom. The book was about war tactics and their effectiveness, with detailed descriptions of various situations and how understanding one's surroundings could turn the mundane into a deadly advantage.

After about an hour of reading, Marcus looked up from the page. "Well, roomie, it's almost dinnertime. Want to grab a bite?"

Len, having heard Felix's stomach rumbling, said, "Go ahead and eat. Mine will be arriving soon." She jumped out of Felix's arms.

Moments later, two silver bowls of food and water appeared next to Felix's desk. A feeder descended from the ceiling, delivering Tom's meal. Tom flew from the bed to the perch and began devouring the seeds and dried fruit.

"You don't need to wear your robes," Marcus said. "Just

pants and a shirt will do. I'm assuming you'll want to wear a long-sleeved shirt to hide your brand."

Felix went to his trunk. On top of his packed items were a few brown paper parcels he hadn't seen before. He quickly opened them and found new clothing inside. He grabbed a soft blue tunic and stripped off his wool robes. After putting on the tunic, he dug through the trunk to find his old clothes but had no luck.

"Did you misplace something?" Marcus asked, leaning over.

"My clothing. It's all gone!"

Marcus placed a reassuring hand on Felix's shoulder. "They're all in the brown paper parcels. When Lady Rosalyn enchants you at Barrel Hall, your clothing gets enchanted too. As you grow, your clothes grow with you. If you tear them, they mend themselves. Didn't you ever wonder why you never needed to buy new clothes as you got bigger? When you started attending Heaven's Gate, your clothing transformed into school attire."

Felix suddenly found it hard to breathe. The realization that he no longer had the T-shirt Chance used to wear hit him like a wave. He gasped for air, struggling to regain some composure. Despite having toughened up enough not to cry, the loss hurt deeply. At least he was grateful to still have Chance's fluffy monster.

Felix folded the empty parcels and closed the chest after hanging up his clothing. He went to the trash can to dispose of the wrappers. As soon as the paper touched the bottom, it vanished into thin air.

Before Felix could ask, Marcus said, "All the rubbish bins in Heaven's Gate are enchanted too. Many things here are enchanted to save time for academic study."

Felix was taken aback but intrigued to discover what

else was enchanted. In the meantime, he changed into his new clothes.

"We'd better wait a bit to make sure the rest of the house leaves for the dining hall first, especially given the un-wanted attention you've been getting," Marcus said, peeking out of the room to check if the coast was clear.

After a few minutes, the two hurried down the hallway, straight for the staircase. They made their way across the pond and down a few corridors Felix had yet to explore. They saw the tail end of the Water Weavers making their way to the dining hall.

The pair quietly slipped into the hall as the doors closed behind them. They took a seat in the top row, away from the rest of the house. Marcus used tiny orbs of elec-trified water to divert attention from his roommate.

The Earth Weavers' tables were next to the Water Weav-ers'. As soon as Anastasia spotted Felix, she quickly joined him.

"Hey, Felix, can I sit with you guys?" she asked.

Felix turned to Marcus. "This is Anastasia. Can we make room for her?"

Marcus extended his hand to shake hers. "It's a pleas-ure. My name is Marcus."

"Thanks a bunch; I'm Anastasia Beazletin," she replied, sitting down next to Felix with a plate of food from the Earth Weavers' table.

Professor Agate's head didn't lift from its current angle, but he noticed a pair of feet moving from his section to the Water Weavers'. Less strict than the other professors, he smiled and chuckled a little, guessing it would be Ana-stasia.

Other professors might have insisted that students re-turn to their own sections. Professor Stewart, for example, would have enforced the rules. However, seeing Felix's distress and knowing that Anastasia had been his companion at Barrel Hall, Professor Stewart decided to let it slide. She chose to observe Felix closely, without adding to his stress.

Anastasia asked Felix if she could take a closer look at his brand to see if she might recognize any patterns. Felix, ensuring no one could see what he was doing, cautiously rolled up his sleeve.

The brand was an elaborate design, featuring a dragon coiled tightly around twisted vines. The dragon's sinuous body formed a continuous loop, with its scales meticulously detailed. The vines wove in and out, creating an intricate lattice that bordered the dragon and intertwined with its tail. The entire pattern was embossed in a vivid blue, contrasting sharply against Felix's skin. The gauntlet's border was adorned with sharp, almost runic symbols. Each scale of the dragon and each twist of the vine was so finely etched that the design appeared bespoke, as if crafted by a master artisan.

Anastasia examined the brand with keen interest. She noticed the way the dragon's eyes appeared to follow her, adding an eerie depth to the design. Despite her scrutiny, she couldn't recall any specific lore or symbolism related to the pattern. The gauntlet was undeniably striking, but its significance eluded her. It seemed to be more than just a mark; it was a masterpiece of enchantment.

As she studied the brand, Anastasia couldn't help but notice Felix's growing discomfort. His shoulders were tense, and his eyes darted nervously around the room. His anxiety seemed to intensify with every passing second, as if the scrutiny was only exacerbating his unease.

The bright blue gauntlet remained a beautiful enigma, its intricate details hinting at something deeper and more significant. Anastasia wondered if the gauntlet was tied to an ancient or hidden power, but without further information or context, she couldn't decipher its true meaning.

"Don't worry," Anastasia said, trying to reassure him as she grasped his hand. "After a week, they'll lose interest."

Nevertheless, a group of students remained fixated on Felix—not merely because of the gauntlet but due to an inexplicable fascination. These students were all tall, fair-skinned, and possessed pointed ears. The elven students seemed irresistibly drawn to Felix's presence.

Anastasia had not fully grasped the extent of Felix's unwanted attention when the entire school had gathered in front of the castle. To better understand their fascination, she turned to one of the books she had stowed away: *Encyclopedia of Yurden's Flora and Fauna*. She had bookmarked the sections on dragons, intending to read them to Felix since he was so captivated by them.

She flipped through the pages until she reached the section beginning with the letter E. There, she meticulously scanned each page until she found the chapter titled "Elves." After reviewing the eighteen pages dedicated to elves, she still could not comprehend why they were so fixated on Felix. The book made no mention of elves having a particular interest in humans.

The book detailed that elves were intrigued by several things, with three primary areas of interest:

I. Dragons: The text described how elves and dragons had coexisted harmoniously for millennia, developing amicable relationships.

II. Flora: It expounded on the elves' remarkable ability to communicate with and manipulate plants for various purposes.

III. Sacred Places: The book noted that elves were fervent guardians of sacred locations, willing to sacrifice their lives to protect them.

Anastasia found the information in the *Encyclopedia of Yurden's Flora and Fauna* frustratingly unhelpful. Felix was neither a dragon nor a sacred location; he was simply a person. The book's insights into elves' interests—dragons, flora, and sacred places—didn't seem to explain their intense focus on him. The only potentially relevant detail was the elves' fascination with plants. Felix's talent with flora had been noted by Mr. Waxman, which led Anastasia to wonder if this might be why the elves were so inexplicably drawn to him.

Her frustration mounted as she considered the possibility that there might be something about the gauntlet or Felix's abilities that was eluding her. Did the elves perceive something she could not? How could they know about his unique ability in a way that she didn't?

Shaking her head in exasperation, Anastasia made her way back to her house. She approached a cluster of elves still fixated on Felix and asked, "May I ask you a question?"

"Yes, but make it quick," an elvish girl responded without looking away from Felix.

"Why is there so much attention on Felix?"

The elves continued to gaze at Felix, their responses indirect and evasive.

One of them said, "Isn't he so cute?"

Another, twirling a strand of her hair, added, "I just want to keep him. He's like a doll!"

Even the male elves lingered, their eyes filled with a longing admiration. It seemed that every elf within thirty feet was utterly infatuated with him.

Anastasia's frustration grew as she tried to understand why the elves were so captivated by Felix. The highborn elves' fixation on a person as though he were an object to be possessed struck her as utterly disconnected from reality.

She scrutinized Felix, examining him with a scientific lens. She wondered what specific attributes might be contributing to his allure. Was it his jet-black hair, his striking gray eyes, or perhaps his unusually pale skin? His ears were not pointed, so he clearly wasn't an elf. She couldn't pinpoint what made him so irresistible to them. The absence of answers only heightened her frustration, causing her to fidget restlessly.

Were there no other children with similar traits? What about Felix prompted the elves to react as though they were encountering a rare and irresistible phenomenon, like a fluffy kitten? Being only ten years old herself, she mused that it must be some hormonal influence. She hoped she wouldn't react so irrationally when she reached puberty.

To Anastasia, Felix felt like a little brother, and the unwarranted attention he received was perplexing. After a while, she resigned herself to the idea that Felix must be some sort of elven catnip—an inexplicable and enchanting curiosity for the elves.

Chapter 15
The School Year Begins

Later that night, back in the dining hall, the table was laden with fillets of fish, succulent beef roasts, and an array of dishes, including mashed potatoes and vibrant vegetables. Felix piled his plate high with mashed potatoes and roasted corn seasoned with garlic. Overwhelmed by the constant barrage of questions and the incessant nagging from other children, who were undeterred by the orbs, he decided that stuffing his face would deter them from bothering him—an approach that proved effective.

He contemplated, *I can't eat twenty-four hours a day, so how can I avoid them when I'm not eating?* He considered two strategies: either avoid bathing to repel them with his odor, or simply hide whenever he wasn't in class.

One bold student braved the newly doubled amount of electrified droplets Marcus had conjured to deter intruders, bypassing both Marcus and Anastasia. She approached Felix directly, her gaze fixed on him. As Felix, cheeks puffed with food like a chipmunk, stared back, she opened her mouth to speak. Reacting swiftly, Felix shoved a large spoonful of mashed potatoes into her mouth. This interruption allowed Marcus to deal with the intruder, while Anastasia burst into laughter.

Professor Zephyr, ever observant, witnessed the scene and chuckled, discreetly covering her mouth with a napkin to stifle her amusement. The headmaster noticed as well and could not suppress his smile.

Felix's attention shifted to the main table. Pointing at the man seated in the center, he asked, "Who is that?"

Anastasia replied, clearly perplexed, "That's the headmaster of the school."

Felix raised an eyebrow and, after swallowing his food, clarified, "I know that! What's his name, and why is he the headmaster?"

Anastasia responded, "William Cullen Edward O'Connor, the Lightning Dragoon. He's the only Lightning Dragoon Yurden has had in the last hundred and nineteen years."

Felix frowned. "What do you mean, the last hundred and nineteen years? He doesn't look over forty."

Anastasia was stumped, unable to provide further details as she had not encountered this information in her studies.

Marcus, however, was well-informed. "That information is contained in *The Secrets and Forbidden Abilities of the Dragoons,* which is restricted to students."

Anastasia inquired, "If students aren't allowed to read it, how did you come by this information?"

"Oh, I borrowed it for a week," Marcus replied with a knowing grin. "One of the Dragoon's powers is the ability to slow their aging process. This ability is conferred through a special seal received upon becoming a Dragoon. While there are other, often forbidden methods to halt aging, the

Dragoon's seal is the most recognized."

Marcus continued, "For instance, Professor Pompeii is at least two thousand years old. He's not an elf, but he's very much alive. According to legend, a sorceress cursed him to endure the tedium of eternity after growing tired of his complaints about a mundane existence. As for why O'Connor became headmaster, it was a position he was asked to assume after the previous headmaster retired, leaving the role of head of House Jupiter."

Anastasia interjected, "He can stop aging? How is that even possible?"

Felix, captivated by the new information, glanced between Marcus and Anastasia.

Marcus nodded and explained, "There is the Blade of the Five Elements, forged with the breath of all five Dragon gods. The elf who created the blade imbued it with honor as a gift. When the victor of the Dragoon games is declared, their blood is applied to the sword's sheath, establishing a connection. If the Dragoon falls in battle, the sword no longer recognizes them. When this occurs, the gem in the sheath emits a blinding light, signaling that the Dragoon games must be held for that element. Losing recognition from the sword means losing the benefit of slowed aging, among other advantages."

Intrigued by the Dragoon games, Felix asked Marcus to elaborate.

"Certainly," Marcus began, "when the souls of the five dragons become unsettled, it can lead to frequent natural disasters unless a replacement Dragoon is found. To participate, a challenger must complete specific tasks. One such task involves spinning one of the five crystal pillars using their energy until it glows and floats. The challenger must then call out the Dragoon god's name and recite, 'I invoke the ancient law of trial by contest.' If accepted, the Festival of Fools begins, acknowledging their claim. Challengers have five days to meet the requirements before the festival starts; otherwise, the challenge is void. It's a rushed process to prevent drastic consequences."

Marcus paused, observing Felix and Anastasia as they processed the information.

Felix then asked, "Why is it called the Festival of Fools, and is the only way to earn a title by besting one of the current Dragoons? Who are the other four?"

Marcus replied, "The Festival of Fools is an extremely hazardous event. Many participants suffer severe injuries or disfigurements, and over the millennia, countless individuals have died. Earning the title of Dragoon is no small feat and carries a heavy burden, as it involves channeling significant power to maintain planetary stability. You already know about the Lightning Dragoon and the Fire Dragoon."

Felix looked at Marcus with a puzzled expression.

"Vivi, the one on your posters is the Fire Dragoon," Marcus said. "The Wind Dragoon is Gwen Van Rearen, and the Earth Dragoon is the Dwarven Crown Prince, Highdale— also known as Tremorfist."

"But that's only four!" Anastasia exclaimed.

"The last one doesn't count," Marcus shrugged.

"Why not?" Anastasia asked.

"The position of Water Dragoon is currently vacant," Marcus explained. "The last Water Dragoon was murdered, and since the perpetrator has not been brought to justice, the Water Trial has been locked ever since. The blade is sentient and can detect foul play, which is why there is no Dragoon of Water. The elf who forged the blade imbued it with honor, so if a Dragoon is betrayed, the guilty party must be avenged. The only entity that can reopen a locked Dragoon

Trial is a Black Dragon, and the only Black Dragon in existence is Gideon. He's been moping around for over two hundred years since Lady Aurora's death. The only positive aspect of Gideon is that he can serve as a conduit for any element, so the absence of a Water Dragoon doesn't disrupt the power structure."

Felix asked, "Why would a dragon mope around for two hundred years?"

Marcus shrugged. "All I know is what the books say. Aurora was visited by a Tear of Kalli, which is a black dragon. A Tear of Kalli appears only once every ten thousand years, but one may manifest earlier if something significant occurs. A black dragon is summoned when something calls upon the Spirit of Kalli. When a pure soul is on the brink of destruction or facing a dire situation, Kalli sheds a tear. Aurora became soul-bonded with Gideon. Soul-bonding is similar to what happens with a mirrored soul, but it occurs naturally without a third-party conduit. The problem is that the Tear of Kalli will only appear if there are no other Black Dragons."

Anastasia added, "Pure souls are incredibly rare, and the last known one was Lady Aurora. Her life was profoundly altered, plunging her into despair, which is why Kalli shed a tear for her."

Felix was accustomed to fantastical stories, but he struggled to discern whether this was lore or an elaborate tale. The fictional accounts of a boy named Harry began to blur with his understanding, making him question everything.

Anastasia knew this story by heart, but like Felix, she was captivated by a compelling narrative. Felix nodded enthusiastically, enjoying the story.

The man in black stood silently, observing the room's activity. As everyone engaged in conversation or enjoyed their meals, Headmaster O'Connor floated up to a height of ten feet. He performed a series of hand signs, and with a sweeping motion, he silenced all sound, rendering the students mute. There was no widespread panic, except among the new students who were confused.

Professor Zephyr again covered her mouth with a napkin to hide her laughter. The new students noticed that all the older students had turned to face the headmaster's table. They followed suit, some covering their mouths in bewilderment.

"I'm glad I've got everyone's ear," Headmaster O'Connor began, his voice a warm blend of friendliness and seriousness. "Now, first-year students, don't be getting your knickers in a twist. If you don't know me by now, I'm Headmaster O'Connor. Let me make it as clear as a bell: some of ye are fresh to this land, while others have grown up here. This realm is a tapestry woven with both dazzling marvels and formidable dangers. I can't stress enough the importance of steering clear of the Divide. It was set up to guard us from Ioesess and its many hazards. And for heaven's sake, keep well away from Baba Yaga's forest unless ye're keen to find yourself in a pot of stew!"

"Right, let's keep the hands on the clock moving!" Headmaster O'Connor said. "We've got three Earth Dragons currently residing on the grounds for the time being. They'll be with us until their new digs are sorted, as their lairs in the southwest region of Ozmare were swept away by flooding. Be mindful around them—they're a bit like a clock with a loose spring, prone to emotional ticks and easily set off. Give them as much space as ye can."

"And here's a bit of advice from the old watchmaker: steer clear of their dung piles. Cleaning up after them isn't a walk in the park. If I've got my facts straight, Flora classes are using it for fertilizer, so some of ye might find your-selves elbow-deep in scrubbing to clear away the stench. It's a dirty job, but it's part of keeping the gears turning smoothly."

"Lastly, remember we're here to learn and grow together. No race, creed, belief, or gender is above another. Each of ye has the potential to be the hour hand on a grand clock, tick-ing towards greatness and achieving remarkable feats. Your destiny is in your own hands; no one else can turn that wheel for ye. Keep these words close to your heart."

He raised his hand, releasing their voices from their en-forced silence. "Now, everyone, lift yer cups and repeat after me:

'One to a task is long and weary, but many as one at a task shall never fail nor be dreary. No single key unlocks all; when many are one, locks and shackles will shatter and fall. Together, fear is replaced with courage, hatred is van-quished, and hope is renewed. Let what differs between us not divide but bind us. Hope for a better tomorrow, how-ever distant it may seem, let this not just be a dream. We be-come so much closer with every step we take together, let this unite us forever and ever.'"

As the last words resonated through the hall, a somber mood settled over the room. A few tears fell onto the floor or onto tables. The saying had been one of the late Lady Aurora's, holding deep significance for many present. Lady Aurora had brought immense joy and solace after years of suffering. Her absence was still profoundly felt, even more than two centuries after her passing.

"With that said," Headmaster O'Connor continued, "Each year will bring its own set of trials, much like the hands of a clock tickin' through different hours. Some of ye will find time movin' slower than others, but those who face their challenges head-on will prove their mettle. Each house will put forward a champion, and these five will spar until only one remains, earnin' the title of Champion of Heaven's Gate."

A twinkle of amusement danced in his eye as he noted the smirks and grins of the older students.

"Lastly," Headmaster O'Connor concluded, lifting his gaze, "For yer safety and that of others, steer clear of the pixies. Time here is precious—don't let a single tick go to waste. Now, get back to yer meals and enjoy the rest of yer evenin'!"

Felix had many questions. He asked Anastasia what her head of house was like.

"Well, honestly," she said, "he's exceedingly kind and quite funny. He likes to join in on the fun we have—like a father figure or a big brother. Oh, and he laughs a lot but doesn't say much."

"He kind of looks and sounds like a younger version of Santa Claus," Felix replied.

"Who's Santa Claus?" Anastasia and Marcus looked puzzled. Felix spent the next few minutes explaining who Santa Claus was and what he did.

"Well, from what you've told me, it sounds like Santa Claus is a Lightning Weaver," Marcus said with enthusiasm. "They're the only ones who can teleport that quickly, and this Santa person would have to be extraordinarily wealthy. Although, I haven't seen or read about any deer-like creature that can fly or move at such speeds, but that doesn't mean they couldn't exist. The bit about tiny elves making toys was amusing. I wouldn't go around telling that story, though. If the elves got wind of it, your head might end up on the chopping block. That description would surely offend them. Especially that one." Marcus pointed to one of the older elven female students. "She's frightening!"

"Also, I'm struggling with the mathematics of your story. This Santa person would have to be able to stop time. Only Headmaster O'Connor and a few others are powerful enough to halt time for short periods, and the person in your story would need to stop it for several hours. Headmaster O'Connor couldn't come close to that. The older students occasionally see parts of the Outer Realm on trips. They mentioned something about overpopulation...was more than six billion people. When I did a quick calculation, there are too many people on Earth. Even if he spent only one second at each home, it would still be impossible to complete the task in a single night. That's if the information you provided is accurate. It sounds like a fairy tale to me, but I did like the bit about getting lots of gifts!"

"Isn't there Christmas here?" Felix asked.

Marcus looked at Felix with curiosity. "You've been here for a while. Has anyone ever mentioned Christmas before? I've been to the Outer Realm and heard of Christmas, but there's nothing like that here. The holidays celebrated in Yurden are Satio, Messis, Ortus, Alysum, Honos, and Cupita."

Felix and Anastasia were familiar with the holidays Marcus mentioned from their time in the nursery and Dennington, but neither Anastasia nor Marcus had ever celebrated anything quite like what Felix had described while in Yurden. Felix's curiosity was piqued, as both he and Anastasia had only a limited understanding of these holidays.

"Satio is also known as the Week of Sewing," Marcus explained. "It occurs in the early part of the year, usually celebrated by the elves and fairies, and is recognized and sometimes observed by other races. It's the time when everyone plants trees near forests to help them grow. Next is Messis, a month-long holiday that usually happens twice a year: once in the early part of the second quarter and again in the late third quarter. The timing of Messis depends on what has been planted and when it's harvested.

"In between the two Messis seasons is Ortus. Ortus is when the elves visit the Living Oath Tree, also known as the Elvish Tree. The tree releases fruit, and both partners eat it. The one who is more nurturing will give birth to a child, and that is the holiday of Ortus."

Felix interrupted Marcus with a few questions. "Why are all the holidays related to elves, and how can male elves give birth?"

Before Marcus could respond, Anastasia chimed in, "This world was created by the two elven gods and the five Dragon gods. Since the Dragons don't have a society that interacts in the same way, the elves developed the system of holidays."

Marcus picked up where Anastasia left off. "Yes, males can give birth, but it's exceedingly rare. Generally, it's males in submissive relationships with their female partners who experience this.

"Alysum takes place in the fourth quarter of the year, typically when the nights are longest and the land is at its coldest. This period is chosen for celebration because it marks the time when people would gather closely together. The festival commemorates the departure of the ark from Earth and the establishment of this place as the new home for elves and other endangered creatures. The festivities can last several days, often extending until food supplies begin to dwindle.

"Honos is observed between the third and fourth quarters of the year and honors the Dragon gods, who chose to relinquish their powers for the benefit of all beings. The abilities possessed by every creature here are gifts from the five Dragon gods. During Honos, all races participate in festivals and offer tributes to local shrines dedicated to the dragons.

"Cupita, known as the Long Mourn, occurs after the end of the fourth quarter and before the new year begins. For two weeks, all of Yurden mourns the loss of Lady Aurora. There are no celebrations—only quiet reflection and remembrance. You're fortunate to have such unique memories and experiences that most people here have never known."

Anastasia added, "My earliest memories are from inside the dragon nursery. I'm surprised you arrived here so late. Non-native children are usually brought here by Lady Rosalyn within twenty-four hours of their birth."

"Oh!" was all Felix could say. He thought for a moment before recalling the warning from the three bushes in the hothouse and Lady Miko: he was in danger if discovered, as humans on Earth were unable to comprehend anything beyond their own understanding and would hunt him down.

Not wanting to dwell on that topic, Felix switched to a different one. "When do we get wands?" he asked. "And will we get to try flying on broomsticks soon?"

Marcus and Anastasia laughed.

"Weavers don't use wands. And why in blazes would you need a broom to fly? Brooms are for cleaning floors," Marcus replied bluntly.

Anastasia, although still chuckling, felt a twinge of sympathy. "Marcus, Felix has these books from his world where people called witches and wizards use wands and broomsticks. So, try to be a bit gentler with your answers."

Turning to Felix, she continued, "I didn't realize you thought those books were real. I enjoyed reading them with you, but those stories are fictional. The writing was incredibly vivid, though I wish they were real too."

Felix, feeling disappointed, shifted the conversation once more. "Can you tell me about your day so far?"

"Well, getting into our house is quite different from what you described about yours," Anastasia said. "First, you need to know which wall to approach. Then, you must find the correct stones in the wall and trace the right runes on them. If you choose the wrong stones or write the wrong runes..." She paused for dramatic effect, "may the gods have mercy on your soul. Incorrect actions cause the stones to jet out and bludgeon you to death."

Felix and Marcus stared at her in horror.

"It sounds pretty intense if you get it wrong," Marcus said. "I thought our house's security was severe."

"The stones shift places every day, so you need to remember their textures and color patterns," she continued, pausing to gauge their reactions.

"Just kidding. All we have to do is swipe our bracelets across certain stones. But the part about the stones bludgeoning you is true. Professor Agate demonstrated that with a makeshift scarecrow. Anyway, our house is truly wonderful. It's like a treasure trove that could never be depleted. The walls are smooth, and the ceiling is adorned with crystals of all sizes, with the larger ones serving as lights.

"The main room is dimly lit and warm, with an inviting glow that feels both enchanting and comforting. The walls are wrapped in rich marble, streaked with soft veins of gold, and feature lovely carvings of Earth dragons peacefully resting among the trees. The ceilings are adorned with deep emerald banners, each embroidered with golden dragons that seem to dance in the gentle flicker of the light. Fur throws are draped over plush couches and potted wobble chairs. Beautiful paintings of legendary figures and ancient tales hang on the walls, framed in ornate gold that glimmers in the firelight. Terra House has a quirky, cozy charm, making it the perfect place to curl up with a book."

By the way, how is Len adjusting?" she asked.

"She's disappointed she can't be with me in the dining hall, but she seems to be getting along just fine," Felix replied with a sigh.

The rest of their mealtime was filled with laughter and more questions and answers, as Anastasia and Marcus enjoyed seared white fish fillets smothered in butter and lemon, and red wine-braised beef. They also had steamed and roasted vegetables seasoned with garlic and mixed herbs. For dessert, they indulged in fruit tarts with a shortbread crust and decadent pastry cream infused with either vanilla or cocoa.

After dinner, the new students were instructed to get a good night's sleep, as they would need it.

Anastasia and Felix hugged each other before heading off to their respective houses.

Once back in his room, Felix settled into bed and placed Len on his lap.

"Well, how was dinner? Did you get to see Anastasia?" Len asked, already knowing the answers.

"Yes, she was there," Felix replied. "She updated me on her new house and mostly asked questions about my gauntlet. She also wanted to know how you were adjusting to life at the castle."

After a few moments of being petted and scratched, Len said, "You seem bored. Why don't you read me a book?"

Felix realized he didn't have any new books to read, so he asked Marcus if he could borrow one. Marcus agreed but cautioned Felix that he wasn't yet skilled enough to fully utilize the powers described in the books, so attempting any of the weaves might not be very helpful.

Felix perused the titles and stopped at a dark blue, leather-bound volume titled *Water Memory and Manipulation* by Kenny Gasney. He took the book back to his bed, placed

Len comfortably on his lap, and began to read. Len curled up into a ball, content to listen.

The book explained that, although water is fluid, it has the capacity to remember and absorb information and emotions. When a weaver mastered the manipulation of water, the possibilities became virtually limitless.

He read about various practical applications, such as making it rain on newly planted fields, unclogging drains, saving drowning people, and even temporarily cloning oneself. Each application was detailed with the necessary movements and hand signs required to perform the described feats.

As Felix quickly finished the book, Len glared at him as if her head might explode from the overload of information. "That's a lot to take in!" she said, shaking her head in an attempt to clear it. "You read that way too fast. Slow down next time. I barely understood a third of it," she complained.

Felix grinned at her, knowing her request was futile—he was like a river, always rushing forward. He returned the book to Marcus's desk and noticed that Marcus was fast asleep, with Tom also perched on the footboard, sound asleep.

It was just after eleven. Felix continued to browse through the titles until he found one that piqued his interest: *Element Conjurations and Meditations* by Efrain Casadonte. Not wanting to disturb Marcus, he turned off the lights and read by candlelight, straining to decipher the handwritten cursive words.

Felix silently slipped from his room and down the hall, his footsteps barely a whisper against the polished stone. The common room lay in serene silence, the only sound being the crackling of the fire—a sanctuary untouched by interruptions, questions, or unwanted gazes. The ambiance was transformed by the ethereal glow of jellyfish drifting languidly near the window, their light casting delicate patterns across the walls. Felix inhaled deeply, letting the tranquil scene wash over him. For the first time since his arrival at the castle, he felt a profound sense of peace, as though he had finally discovered a quiet haven amidst the controlled chaos.

He walked over to the window, where a long bench, lined with plush cushions and oversized, hand-embroidered pillows, beckoned with cozy warmth. Settling at one end, nestled comfortably near a smack of gently glowing jellyfish, he prepared to lose himself in his book.

"Element Conjurations and Meditations" instructed the reader to clear their mind and breathe slowly and steadily. Once the mind was quiet, the reader should focus on the element they were trying to conjure. After achieving the first two steps, the reader was then instructed to select a small task or movement for the element.

When the third task was accomplished, the reader was advised to infuse passion into the activity. A Weaver who mastered their emotions could perform precise and intricate tasks with their element.

Felix wanted to test these concepts, so he devised a plan. To avoid waking anyone or being discovered, he decided to head up the spiral stairs to the pool of water where the giant lilies floated. From there, he could see down the long hallway and hear the stone door in the dragon statue if it opened.

Once at the pool, he sat cross-legged on one of the oversized lily pads. The moonlight streaming through the stained-glass window cast its shadow on the water. Felix gazed into the endless darkness of the hallway and cleared his mind once more. He focused on the water beneath him, visualizing a sphere of water floating in front of him. His skin tingled with a cool, comforting sensation, as if relaxation was seeping from his pores.

Next, he had to choose an emotion. The one he related to most was sadness. He recalled Chance lying lifeless in his arms, a memory weighed down by regret. His face, vacant of emotion, and the tears streaming down his face, were powerful. The gauntlet on his arm pulsed with a dim blue light, echoing his pain.

Instinctively, his arms moved as if guided by an unseen force, his fingers dancing as if playing a piano, as described in the book. When he finished, he slowly opened his eyes. Instead of the single droplet of water he had visualized, thousands of droplets floated around him, sparkling in the moonlight like diamonds. Surprised by the multitude, Felix lost his focus, and the droplets crashed back into the pool like rain on wet pavement.

Moments later, Felix tried again, adjusting the level of emotion. This time, a single round droplet formed in front of him. With a mere flicker of his fingers, he made the droplet dart around him in various directions.

Stopping the droplet at eye level, he placed his hand underneath it, rotating his wrist and fanning it with his fingers. A fine mist surrounded the sphere of water and merged with it. He continued until the mass of water was the size of a balloon.

Feeling confident in the basic concepts, he decided to try something more challenging. He closed his eyes and thought of a fond memory. The pleasant recollection guided his hands, making them move swiftly and gracefully as if his fingers were testing the strands of a spider's web.

When he opened his eyes, he saw an aquatic version of Betty, the cat. Though not an exact likeness, the conjured creature swished its tail back and forth before splashing back into the water. Felix tried again, each attempt refining the resemblance. After about ten tries, he succeeded in creating a conjuration that not only walked around him but also leaped onto his shoulder, leaving a damp mark. Content with his progress, Felix let the conjuration dive back into the water.

As Felix looked up from where the cat had vanished, his heart sank. Tiny lights began to flicker and dance in the hallway, drawing closer with each passing moment. Recalling a book Anastasia had read about Yurden's creatures, he realized only a few beings could produce such light, and only one was likely to be found in a castle. The warning from Headmaster O'Connor echoed in his mind: pixies were known to be mischievous and very dangerous.

A surge of urgency propelled Felix off the lily pad and onto the small island where the statue stood. He moved swiftly, closing his eyes concentrating while hatching a plan. His hands danced through the darkness. When he opened them, he saw five thin, lens-shaped objects floating at eye level. He grazed one of the lenses with his finger, and a droplet of blood formed from the cut he had made. His face hardened with intense focus. With a decisive flick of his wrist, the objects hurtled toward the glowing orbs.

The moment the objects struck their targets, high-pitched screeches echoed ominously down the corridor. The lights surged toward him, their movement quickening and intensifying. Realizing the danger, Felix sprinted down the staircase, nearly stumbling over his own feet as the passageway sealed shut behind him. He darted to the fireplace, the warmth a brief solace, and stared at the painting of Lady Aurora. The image seemed oddly familiar, but he couldn't place why.

With his heart still racing, Felix quietly slipped into bed, reflecting on the night's unsettling excitement and the narrow escape from danger.

The next morning, the first-year Water Weavers gathered in the main room, where Lady Stewart awaited their arrival with an air of impatience. She quickly ushered the lingering older students to their classes, leaving only the small group of new students who glanced nervously at each other.

Next to Lady Stewart stood a small table bearing a black satchel the size of a large purse. With a stern and unwavering gaze, she commanded the students to come closer. "Today, my dear students, you shall each be bestowed with a most essential instrument," she proclaimed. Let me be perfectly clear: should you misplace it, your existence within these hallowed halls shall grow exceedingly arduous. You will receive but one of these from us, so I entreat you to treat it with the utmost diligence and care."

One by one, Lady Stewart pulled out identical satchels from the table, handing each student one as they approached. As Felix's turn came, he felt the weight of the group's gaze upon him, their stares heavy and expectant. Even Lady Stewart's scrutiny felt like a physical presence as she peered over her spectacles.

"The item you have received is known as a Bag of Holding," Lady Stewart continued, her voice sharp and uncompromising. "It is capable of holding up to five hundred pounds without imparting any sense of weight. This bag is to be used solely for items pertaining to your studies. Should you attempt to stow away any contraband, it shall expel such items forthwith and envelop you in dark purple ink.

Allow me to be quite clear—under no circumstances should you endeavor to fit yourself or another within it. Such folly has led to grave troubles in times past, and I shall not tolerate any such nonsense!"

As Lady Stewart's words sank in, a boy hesitated, nearly putting his squirrel into the bag.

After receiving his own satchel, Felix placed it over his shoulder and carefully picked up Len, cradling her as if she were a newborn.

"Now, if you would be so kind as to follow me," she said, gesturing with an elegant sweep of her hand. Lady Stewart commanded, leading the students through the castle to their classrooms and training areas. "You may no longer claim ignorance regarding your classes after this tour," she added, her gaze sharp and unwavering.

The group followed her outside to Umquam Dare—the ever-giving lake. Surrounding the lake were bleachers for spectators, and Lady Stewart directed the students to sit.

Lady Stewart strode with purpose to the water's edge. As she stepped onto the lake, the surface held firm beneath her feet, and she stood there as if on solid ground. "Now, as we must commence with the fundamentals," she announced, her voice resonating with intensity, "let's dive into something that will truly stay your attention."

With a fluid grace that belied the complexity of her craft, Lady Stewart began her demonstration. Her hands wove through the air with intricate precision, and a shimmering ball of water rose effortlessly from the lake's depths. "What you see here is a simple conjuration," she said. "But don't be fooled—far more complex feats await."

Her movements were spellbinding. Massive petals of water unfurled around her from the sphere she had conjured, forming an exquisite lotus flower that spun and began to ascend with breathtaking speed. It soared to about fifty feet, its petals expanding and crystallizing into a frosted white with spiral patterns. As the lotus floated gracefully above the water, it broke apart.

Not pausing, Lady Stewart continued her weave. A single petal adhered to her forearm, while the others whirled through the air like razor-sharp blades. With a swift and decisive motion, she summoned a sword-like weapon from the water. The swirling petals returned, hurling towards her with increasing speed. She raised the shield with precise timing, deftly evading the petals. Each clash sent sparkling shards of crystalline dust into the air, creating a dazzling display of speed and finesse.

The spectacle was nothing short of exhilarating, a dramatic fusion of elegance and danger that left the students breathless with awe.

As she finished, Lady Stewart faced the students, who were visibly awestruck. "I understand you may have questions, but we simply do not have time for them at present." she said, her tone dismissive.

The students, including Felix, were left speechless, their mouths agape. Felix, while still in awe, focused on analyzing Lady Stewart's movements. As she explained the fundamentals, his mind drifted back to the previous night's events and what Chance would have thought of the display.

Lady Stewart had the students line up at the lake's edge to practice the techniques she had demonstrated. She watched from a distance as they struggled to conjure even simple droplets of water, no one able to command the water to breach the surface.

She walked up and down the line, her eyes finally resting on Felix, who was sitting with his fingers trailing idly through the water, lost in thought.

"Pray, is there a reason you are not adhering to my instructions?" Lady Stewart asked sharply.

Felix, taken by surprise, stammered, "W-well, the others aren't having any luck getting the water to lift, so..."

Before he could finish, Lady Stewart cut him off. "Everyone else is making an effort."

Felix felt the weight of every eye on him, a sense of ridicule washing over him. Lady Stewart's stern words and the scrutiny of his peers intensified his discomfort, rekindling the dread he'd felt from previous encounters. Trying to adhere to what Anastasia had told him, he tried not to stand out. The frustration bubbled inside him, morphing into anger as Lady Stewart's reprimands grew more relentless. Her words felt like daggers, fueling his rage.

Len's attempts to calm him were drowned out by the storm of emotions raging within him. Felix's skin flushed red with the intensity of his anger. Lady Stewart's taunts only fueled his fury further, and his focus narrowed entirely on her criticisms. In this state of heightened emotion, something inside Felix began to surge uncontrollably.

Felix stared at Lady Stewart with vacant eyes. Inside his mind, a voice seethed with fury: *That vile creature, a whore from the nine hells. How dare she speak to me this way? I will end her.*

Everyone around Felix watched intently, waiting for him to act. Lady Stewart paced back and forth on the surface of the water, demanding compliance. When Felix remained unmoved, she unleashed another barrage of insults.

Felix, no longer in control of his actions, sprang to his feet. His breath came in ragged bursts, so hot it made his chin sweat. His subconscious had taken over, guiding his movements with an eerie, menacing grace.

Lady Stewart looked down at him with scorn. "What a

foolish error; that is not what I demonstrated," she sneered.

The voice inside Felix snarled back, *Oh, you'll see. You will pay for your arrogance.*

Felix's face flushed a deep, violent red. He abandoned his previous attempt and began a new weave with sharp, erratic precision, driven by a seething rage.

Moments later, one of the boys pointed behind Lady Stewart. As she spun around, a colossal, twenty-foot-tall dragon began to emerge from the water. The creature roared to life, its massive wings flapping with a force that drenched everyone in its vicinity, sparing only Felix.

The dragon's fierce gaze locked onto Lady Stewart. It reared its head and let out a terrifying roar, unleashing a torrent of water that blasted Lady Stewart backward, sending her stumbling.

Lady Stewart's eyes widened in shock as she turned to Felix. "Enough!" she commanded, her voice echoing with a force that shook the air.

Despite the intensity of her voice, Felix remained locked in his trance.

Desperate, Lady Stewart shouted to the students, "Run!"

The dragon lunged menacingly at Lady Stewart. She quickly raised the shield strapped to her arm and expertly dodged the dragon's attack. In a swift, fluid motion, she wove a sign that sent a chain of water snaking around the dragon's neck, pulling it toward the surface. The dragon roared in defiance, blasting Lady Stewart with another crushing wave of water.

Despite Lady Stewart's efforts to subdue it, the dragon began to break free from its restraints. Panicking, Len scanned for a solution but found nothing. With no other options, she bit Felix on the hand. The sharp pain jolted him awake, and the dragon's form dissolved back into the water.

As Felix's pupils returned to normal, Lady Stewart approached him with an intense, questioning gaze. She signaled the other students to return to the stands without breaking her stare.

"That shall suffice for today," she said firmly. "There shall be books awaiting you upon your desks upon your return. I expect each of you to practice this with a glass of water in your dormitories. And not a word of this to anyone outside these walls." she added with a steely glance.

Lady Stewart's gaze remained fixed on Felix as the class hurried away. Felix stood up, casting a long, puzzled look at the drenched Lady Stewart. He rubbed the bite mark on his hand.

"Off with you!" Lady Stewart commanded sharply.

Len urged Felix to hurry as they left Lady Stewart at the lake. On their way back, Len recounted the events to Felix, who was in shock and disbelief. Though he had no memory of Len's recounting, he recalled Anastasia's warning to avoid showing off. He picked up Len and carried her back to the castle.

Upon reaching the castle, the students hurried to the pool that led to their house. Felix veered off toward the library, trying to forget the chaos Len had described, but found it impossible. He was unable to believe he had done what she said he did.

The pair discussed among themselves, concluding that Felix must have blacked out and that the events were beyond his control.

Chapter 16
When One Isn't Enough

Lady Stewart retreated to her office after drying off. Following Headmaster O'Connor's earlier instructions, she went to her desk, retrieved a crystal tablet, and began tracing runes on it. Once she completed the runes, a blurry figure appeared, barely visible to the naked eye. She gave it a set of orders, and it swiftly left her chambers once it understood its task.

It was late morning, and Felix wanted to do some research. He had managed to control a single object for a few minutes, and according to Len, he had made significant progress. He hoped to find information on how to control more than one object at a time, as Lady Stewart had demonstrated. He planned to search the library for this information.

As he walked down the corridors, he wondered what Anastasia would do if she were in his place. Unbeknownst to Felix, a blurry entity trailed closely behind him. His emotions often felt out of sync, unlike those of a typical person. According to the books he had been reading, a weaver's power was linked to the intensity of their feelings. Felix had faced an event far beyond what most children his age would normally endure.

Since arriving at Heaven's Gate, Felix had struggled to focus on his tasks. Back in Dennington, he had Len, Anastasia, and Mrs. Simmons to help him stay focused. Now, he had only Len, and although it wasn't her fault, she seemed to be falling short.

As the library doors swung open, Felix and Len were greeted by a magnificent sight. The room was vast, with walls lined with books. Light from the large arched windows made the worn gold lettering on the spines gleam. The ceiling was adorned with heavenly scenes, and the dark wood of the bookcases matched the reading tables. Rows of solitary bookcases stood like soldiers at attention.

Giant chandeliers hung from the ceiling, reflecting the light in a dazzling array of colors. Felix was in awe.

"You'll never be able to get through all these books in your lifetime," Len remarked.

Suddenly, a high-pitched voice broke the silence. "Hello there! Is everything all right? Can I be of any help to you?"

Felix looked up, expecting to see a young woman, but saw nothing. He and Len scanned the room, noting it was too early for students, as the first class had not yet been let out.

Felix noticed an elevated desk on a platform, which appeared to be intended for someone, but it was empty. Instead, a large, bushy fern sat on the desk.

He turned to Len and asked, "Do you think it's a ghost?"

A small figure emerged from within the fern. It stood no taller than ten inches, with long red hair styled in a messy bun. Its outfit, made of petals resembling the flowers outside the castle, was actually its skin.

Hearing the rustling behind him, Felix spun around again. "Ummm... ummm... uhhhh, are you okay?" he asked.

"I'm quite well, thank you! Why do you ask, love?" the creature replied.

"I think someone shrank you," Felix said with concern.

The fairy burst into laughter, her wings extending and fluttering. "Oh, heavens no! You must be new here! I'm Thistle, and I'm a fairy. What's your name, then?" Her grin was wide and infectious.

"They do exist! My name is Felix, and this is Len."

Thistle continued to chuckle as they spoke. "Oh, we do exist, and I'll let you in on a little secret—we're simply marvelous, too! Now, Felix and Len, is there anything you need help finding, or are you a bit lost?"

Felix nodded. "Could you point me in the right direction? I'm looking for books on controlling water," he asked politely.

"Well, isn't this a bit unusual—a young lad seeking out books! I usually see the girls in here during their free time. If you're fond of books and happen to be a Water Weaver, you should meet Marcus. He's a right book lover, too!" she said, clapping her hands joyfully.

"Marcus? Does he have a raven named Tom?" Felix inquired, suspecting it was the same boy.

"Yes, that's him! So you've had the pleasure of meeting him, then."

Felix nodded. "He's my roommate."

"If you're after water-weaving books, just head down the fifth row to the right. You'll find them about halfway down that section. Just wave your bracelet in front of the binding of the books you fancy, and they'll be checked out to you. All water-related books are both waterproof and fire-resistant, mind you!"

The room seemed endless, filled with an overwhelming number of books.

"A young girl about your age was here earlier with her monkey. She was asking for earth-weaving books. Looks like I've got some proactive students this year! I suppose I'll have a bigger workload on my hands!" Thistle said.

"Oh, Anastasia was here?" Felix asked.

"Yes, indeed! For being new, you seem to know everyone already," she replied, a bit surprised. "Most lads your age don't wander in here until their second year. Now I've got two new students who enjoy reading. Anastasia took quite a stack—ten books, if you can believe it! If you need anything at all, just let me know."

Felix thanked her and made his way to the section she indicated. He quickly found a familiar book and an adjacent one, carried them to a table, and began reading. He focused on a chapter about advanced techniques, hoping that mastering one object would lead to better control.

A few minutes into reading, Len interrupted. "So... is there something you'd like to tell me?"

Felix gave her a puzzled look, unsure of what she meant.

"Your emotions... I know you have trouble sleeping and you fake a smile whenever you see Anastasia. And you still miss Chance. I can hear what you're thinking when you're not actively blocking me. I'm here if you need to talk," she said with concern.

Felix shrugged, feeling there was nothing more to explain. He didn't remember anything to say and avoided discussing Chance, as it was still a painful subject.

He turned his attention to the more advanced book he'd picked up, which was typically read by senior students and teachers. The section on duplicating oneself, known as cloning and constructs, captured his full attention. Constructs, devoid of emotions, followed instructions precisely. This could be useful in overcoming some of Felix's limitations.

The book also discussed water memory, a property that allowed water to retain experiences and information. It mentioned that a weaver could absorb this memory or force someone to absorb the water, thus learning the information themselves.

Felix pondered if a clone could retain information and if he could absorb it from a clone if they had just read the book.

Abruptly, he got up from his chair and returned to the water-weaving section. He swiped several books with his bracelet and quickly placed them into his Bag of Holding. As he finished selecting his books, he approached the front, followed by Len. Thistle looked astonished at the twenty-eight books he'd taken, scratching her head in disbelief.

"Well, good luck with all that light reading, then!" Thistle said, waving goodbye.

Len and Felix exited the library. Felix now had a task: to find a place where he could practice his weaves without interruption. He went door to door down the corridor, avoiding classrooms to prevent being caught by a professor. With some luck, he found a boys' restroom missing its door placard.

The distortion that Lady Stewart had summoned was positioned in the corridor, still monitoring Felix as he searched for a private place. Once it detected that he had entered the bathroom, it moved back in the direction of Lady Stewart's chambers.

Inside the restroom, he searched for a way to lock the door but found none. Len watched as Felix found a door wedge, placing it diagonally under the door to block entry unless someone forced it open. Confident he was secure,

Felix opened his bag and spread the books on the sink basins. He skimmed through a few until he found a chapter on advanced weaves.

The chapter titled "Duel-Wielding" was what Felix had been searching for. After much time, difficulty, frustration, and several failed attempts, he had finally learned how to double weave, using one hand for each weave. He started slowly, turning on two sinks and attempting to summon two orbs of water. This proved to be a challenge, draining his energy as he struggled to maintain even two droplets. Splitting his attention between multiple objects was exhausting. Summoning thousands of water droplets was one thing; controlling them individually was another.

His first two successes lasted only about four seconds before becoming unstable and falling apart. Len soon grew exhausted from having to calm Felix down from his frustration. His exhaustion naturally slowed him down, reducing the time he spent throwing tantrums and allowing him to focus more on his weaves.

After a while, Felix knew it must be around lunchtime, so he packed his bag and stashed it in the farthest stall in the row. He locked it from the inside and slid under it to secure his books before cautiously making his way back to the dormitories. He raced down the stairs to his room as quickly and quietly as possible. Success—he found that all the kids were watching two boys play a card game next to the fire.

As soon as he entered his dorm room, Marcus greeted him. "Why, hello. I heard about the lake incident."

"I blacked out," Felix replied, "and I don't know what happened, but I must be on my way. We'll talk later."

Felix exited the room, now even more embarrassed and more cautious than ever. He removed his boots and sprinted down the corridor with such speed that he slid silently across the common room, gliding on his socks. As he did, a huge cheer erupted when one of the boys finally depleted the other's life total. By the time anyone turned around, Felix was already halfway up the stairs and out of sight. He then raced across the lily pads to the dining hall.

As covered platters of food floated into the room, their tops rose, delicious smells enveloped the room and the dishes settled into their designated places. Felix quickly spotted a serving bowl of rice and vegetables. Once it had descended, he snatched it off the table and darted out of the dining hall. He took a deep breath as he passed through a corridor adorned with flowering vines that emitted a soothing fragrance. The sound of birds chirping filled the space with a pleasant melody.

He sped down the long corridors until he reached the boys' lavatory once more. Inside, he wedged the door in place and sat on the floor to catch his breath. After washing his hands, he dug into his food, shoveling it into his mouth and chewing rapidly. The bowl, which could have served at least eight people, was emptied within minutes, and it vanished as soon as the last morsel was gone.

He then pulled out the book *Water Memory and Manipulation* and turned to the page on clone weaving, folding it into the clef of the book without creasing the paper.

Next, he grabbed *Element Conjuration Meditations* and turned to the page on controlling one's emotions. The instructions advised readers to breathe slowly and focus on the feeling itself rather than the memory, allowing them to control their emotions rather than being controlled by them.

Felix focused again on the night Chance had died. This time, he concentrated on the pain and emotion he felt, rather than the cause of the pain. This weave would be even harder than the last. He read that creating a clone was one thing, but maintaining it was another. The amount of energy required to sustain the clone would take its toll on the weaver.

From his readings, Felix estimated that one clone would deplete his energy reserves in about six hours. Based on this educated guess, he turned to the stall, and in high spirits, began weaving.

He swirled his hands and fingers, crisscrossing them until a figure slowly emerged from the toilet. Out of the water rose a clear, humanoid-shaped construct. Felix examined the clone and decided to focus more on its details. After several failed attempts, he finally succeeded, stabilizing the previously unstable detailed parts.

After taking a moment to assess his work, he handed the clone a book and instructed it to read. If it finished quickly, it was to fetch another book. This thought made Felix unbelievably happy. Next, he moved to the right and, with renewed energy, refocused his efforts to conjure a second clone.

This process was even more challenging. Maintaining the first clone while creating a second made him feel a bit dizzy. Once Felix regained his footing and composure, he instructed the second clone to follow the same instructions as the first. Despite feeling slightly lightheaded, he managed to keep his focus. He wondered if he should attempt a third clone. He wasn't tired, and if the second clone consumed some of his energy, leaving him with only three to work with, surely he could handle having just an hour and a half left.

With great excitement, Felix moved to the next stall and focused once more as his hands and fingers danced through the air. A third figure emerged from the bowl, but this time Felix lost his balance, crashing into the wall and falling to the floor. He grabbed the door frame and pulled himself up, fearing he had lost the clones due to his decision. To his surprise, the third clone was still there. Holding onto the door frame, Felix peeked into the second and then the first stalls. All three clones had survived, and he sighed with relief.

Finally, he instructed the third clone to do the same as the first two. Focusing on all three clones, making sure not to break concentration, he stacked the books into three piles on the basins. Hoping his theory was correct, if the clones were able to read all the books, they were to put them back into the bag and leave them in the farthest stall—just as he had done before. Additionally, once he left, they were to replace the stopper to prevent anyone else from entering.

He left with one final instruction: if they finished the books, they were to remove the stopper to avoid suspicion, dissipate into the bowls, and not make a mess. With that said, he exited the restroom and waited outside the door to see if his instructions were being followed. A moment later, Felix heard the piece of wood being lodged under the door. Rising from his crouch, he hurried back to the dining hall.

Lunch was in progress. Before entering, he scanned the room and found Marcus sitting with Anastasia. He briskly walked up to the tiered seating where his friends were, avoiding the attention of the other students.

Anastasia glared at him and said scornfully, "Where have you been? I've been worried sick. Marcus told me about the training incident. Good heavens, Felix, I told you not to draw attention to yourself."

Felix replied sluggishly, "I'm sorry. I didn't mean to."

Anastasia hugged him. "What's done is done. You must be more careful in the future. How in Yurden did you conjure a Water Dragon, anyway? And why are you late to meal-time? You're never late when it comes to food!"

In response to her concern, he said, "I wanted to test a theory, so I went to the library to get some books."

Anastasia was relieved. "That's great news. I'm glad you're spending time in the library. I thought you might be up to some mischief—or worse, in a disciplinary room. You're lucky this isn't dinner; otherwise, you would have been locked out. Students are still coming in from Dennington, so they can't shut the doors."

Marcus interjected, "Well, hopefully, whatever you're researching turns out to be a success. Anastasia and I have been investigating your gauntlet, but so far, nothing has materialized. We've only gone through a few books and have several more to check, but we haven't found any information about it yet."

Felix grabbed a medley of vegetables and devoured them while maintaining focus on the three clones.

A few students, undeterred by the trio's efforts to avoid disturbances, approached them. The three stared at the un-wanted guests with annoyance, but it didn't dissuade the intruders.

Before anyone could speak, Felix grabbed a bowl of gravy and motioned as if he were going to throw it on the intrud-ers. Having second thoughts, they left, returning to their seats.

Marcus laughed. "You're lucky. If you were any year but a first-year, you'd be challenged to a ranked contest. So it seems orientation was a bust for you."

Felix shrugged. "I learned where the classes are, at least. What is a ranked contest?"

Anastasia looked shocked. "How do you not know that? Remember Heaven's Gates' champion? You have to either beat the most students in battle or defeat the person ranked number one in your house, battling it out in the finale against the other houses' champions. If you're ever going to become a dragoon, you might want to pay more attention."

"Oh yes, I thought that didn't happen until we were a bit older," Felix said, pretending he had been paying attention to the conversation.

Not wanting to divert too much mental energy to outside thoughts, Felix noticed that since he had completed the weaves to create the clones, his body temperature was slowly increasing. This led him to drink large quantities of water and juice from pitchers floating about the room that refilled his cup. Maintaining the weaves burned calories at a much faster rate than if he were just creating a temporary one.

"Once you become a second-year at Heaven's Gate, you can be challenged. Felix, if you show exceptional talent in your first year, more senior students will try to put you in your place as soon as they can," Marcus informed him.

"I overheard a few of my housemates say that Cordelia, the princess royal of the sea elves, comes from a long line of female rulers. She's been raised to regard humans, especially males, as filth, and she's exceedingly cruel in the ranked matches against them," an overly concerned Anastasia said.

Marcus added to what Anastasia had said. "You're not far off, but I wouldn't call her cruel. I'd use the word 'evil'; it's like she's possessed by some demon. Felix, be careful, or you might end up as her next trophy if she can defeat you. It's disturbing to see what she does to other students, and the professors let her get away with it because it's during a contest and they are not allowed to interfere unless it's a matter of life or death. She would be first in line to become the Water Dragoon if she could, obtaining it by any means necessary."

During the meal, Marcus pointed out Cordelia at the front of the tiered seating to Felix and Anastasia. "See? She's right there."

Cordelia was scanning the room for her next victim. She noticed Marcus and glared at him, causing him to instantly lower his head and stiffen.

After regaining his composure, Marcus changed the subject. "Well, enough of that. On a brighter note, after lunch you'll both get to pick the courses of study you want. I had the chance to pick mine before the start of the exams last year."

Anastasia was excited by this news. She noticed that Felix wasn't as engaged in the conversation as he usually was, so she assumed he was preoccupied with earlier events.

Every water weaver occasionally glanced back at Felix with curiosity, yet no one outside of House Mizu, except Anastasia, knew what had happened at the lake—a true testament to Lady Stewart's control over her wards.

Marcus and Anastasia watched in amazement as Felix ate as if his stomach were a bottomless pit. He had consumed three bowls—two with fruit and one with vegetables. Each time a bowl was cleared, it was replaced with a new one.

As lunchtime ended, Felix paused for a moment. Knowing he would need to constantly replenish his food intake, he gave Marcus a plate of food and asked him to take it back to the dorms. Before leaving the dining hall, Felix stuffed his pockets with several biscuits. He knew he would have been noticed if he had carried the food out on a plate. The three of them then parted ways and headed back to the dorms.

Lady Stewart had kept an eye on Felix in the dining hall. Seeing the trio leave, she excused herself to retire to her office. It was a circular room with bookcases from floor to ceiling, two large windows at the back, and six marble pillars supporting the ceiling. In the center of the room stood a Louis XIV-style desk and chair, with two additional chairs upholstered in silver fabric facing the desk.

A large snow leopard lay on a silver-threaded cushion with tassels at each corner. The snow leopard's name was Nikolay. He was aloof and easily annoyed by foolish behavior—much like his mirrored soul.

Lady Stewart was sorting through files on her desk when she came across Felix's. She opened the binder and read the information compiled by Lady Rosalyn, Miko, and Mrs. Simmons. The files detailed that Felix was shy, exceptionally intelligent, and had a remarkable work ethic. He always helped the smaller children, even standing up for those who were picked on. Avoiding tasks was not in his nature, according to the report. Lady Stewart concluded that his behavior was likely due to his shyness, which might explain his hesitation during the exercise. However, something didn't quite add up. She eventually settled on the idea that he might be reluctant to outshine his peers.

The only remaining question was how, at his age, he had managed to create such a detailed and substantial construct. The power alone rivaled that of a senior classmate's abilities. It made no sense and seemed impossible for a child his age.

Lady Stewart wondered if the gauntlet was somehow related. Was it the source of his power? Since it was only his second day, she decided to dedicate more time to observing Felix and doing research of her own.

On their way back to the dorm, Marcus and Felix noticed a few elves heading down a hall that didn't lead to the dorms. Curious, they followed at a distance. The elves at Heaven's Gate were of noble or royal birth and usually didn't sleep at the castle unless they had important matters to attend to. The elves called out names of places Felix hadn't heard of, though some were familiar from stories in the books he'd read.

Suddenly, a roar echoed, sending shivers down their spines. Marcus nearly dropped the plate of food he was carrying. Anastasia had snuck up behind them to find out where their dorm was located.

"I almost peed my pants!" Marcus exclaimed, embarrassed. He excused himself from the pair and headed back to the dorm.

"Would you like to hang out for a bit?" Anastasia asked.

Without hesitation, Felix agreed. "Meet me back in the dining hall in ten minutes." He needed to attend to something important first.

Like a bottle rocket, he sprinted down the hall to his secret laboratory to check on the clones. He retrieved a fork from his pocket, using it to push the door stopper out of the way. Once inside, he was surprised to find that six books had been read. He gathered the finished books. After completing his inspection, he instructed one of the clones to replace the stopper after he left.

His next stop was the water weaver's house, where he went straight to his room. Marcus was sitting at his desk drawing and had left the plate of food for Felix on the desk.

"Hey, thanks for the food. Anastasia wants to hang out, so I'll be back later." Felix asked Len to join him, and she did so with pent-up excitement.

The pair quickly exited the room and made their way down the hall, passing some unsuspecting students.

As they approached Anastasia, Len asked about the day's events. Anastasia was happy to see Felix in high spirits, assuming his experiment had been successful, glancing at the titles of the books in his arms.

When they met back at the dining hall, Anastasia had also brought Mr. Nibs. The group went outside to explore the grounds. They checked out the statues where they had been raised. Anastasia led Felix to Hedgar's Pit, a tiered stone pit, where they watched a few Earth Weavers train while Mr. Nibs and Len lay down next to each other for a nap.

Felix sat on the bleachers next to the snoozing pair while Anastasia showed him her progress—which, at this point, wasn't much. She was able to make dirt lift off the ground and form a weak cyclone.

"So, how did I do?" she asked.

"Good, I think," he replied. "I'm not sure what level we're supposed to be at. Can you do anything else?"

Anastasia looked at him with a concentrated expression. "Maybe. I remember something, though not everyone can summon a huge dragon in their first week, like someone I know," she said, giving him a wide-eyed stare.

Her movements were swift and precise. Dirt and small pebbles lifted off the ground, moving closer together and forming a more compact twister. As she placed her hand into the twister, an object appeared in the swirling sand. She gripped the handle, revealing a saber made of sand and pebbles.

"Nice! Well, does it work, Earth Weaver?" he joked.

"There's only one way to find out, oh mighty overachiever," she replied with a laugh.

"Hey, I take after you, you know," Felix retorted.

Len, not fully awake, shook her head.

Back in the pit, Anastasia ran to the side and slashed at the wall. The sword crumbled and fell apart.

"I assume it isn't dense enough. Can you harden it?" Felix asked.

"I might have a book that says something about that. Could you hand me my bag?"

Felix handed her the bag and stood up to watch as she rummaged through it. She found a book titled *A Weaver's Guide to Geology: Its States and Applications, 4th Edition* by Angus Archstone. Flipping through the pages, she found the section on the impact of density on durability. After reading it, she concentrated harder, retracing her movements with a more blade-like motion.

"Don't forget to pour stronger emotion into your weave," Felix called out.

She reformed the blade. When she finished the weave and grabbed the blade's end, it crumbled into dust. She considered that she might be doing something wrong.

Felix noticed her frustration. "Hey, what are you thinking about when you're weaving?"

She replied that she was focused on the book she'd been reading.

"That isn't good enough. It must be meaningful to produce enough power," he said, jumping down from the stands. "Think back to the day you found out both of us were going to Heaven's Gate—the excitement that made you jump up and down. Use that memory. That should work."

She began her weave again, thinking about how accomplished she felt being validated by the adults and accepted by Heaven's Gate for early admission. With the memory in her mind, her heart pounded hard enough for her to feel it in her chest.

The blade reformed—this time with more sand and pebbles accumulating than before. It then shrank, refining itself from a saber to a rapier-sized blade, with the remaining larger pebbles falling to the ground. The blade was less flexible and felt heavier than it should have for its size.

Anastasia charged at the wall again, this time slicing a groove into it. Soon after the wall was gouged, the damage began to heal.

Felix went to inspect the groove. By the time he reached it, he saw it was already three-fourths repaired.

"What's going on with the wall?" he asked, puzzled.

"The wall is self-correcting, so it will never lose its shape or size."

"Oh, that's cool. Our training ground doesn't have anything special like that."

"Felix, didn't you read *The Secrets of Heaven's Gate* by von Dunamar Keigler?"

"No. It was boring, so I left it alone."

"Well, Felix, you would have known that dwarven paragon Lord Hedgar—the Runesplitter—gifted Hedgar's Pit."

Anastasia rummaged through her bag once more. The rapier dissolved into sand and fell to the floor. She pulled out a large, white leather-wrapped book: *The Secrets of Heaven's Gate*. She flipped through the pages until she found the section labeled "Everything One Should Explore When Visiting the Grounds of Heaven's Gate Castle."

"I checked it out for a quick refresher. Here it is: 'The second-high lord dragoon, Julian Nyrie, settled the debts of the king of the Merpeople. In return, the king of the Merpeople created Umquam Dare, the ever-filling lake.' So no matter how much water is taken from the lake, it will never run dry."

"Oh," Felix said, followed by a curious pause. "I didn't know that. Were all the other training grounds gifts too?"

"Yes."

"So there must be several other gifts around the castle," Felix said, biting into a biscuit he had pocketed earlier.

"There are several gifts to the high lord dragoons as

thanks for their deeds. To simplify, every race had abilities unique to them. The Merpeople could do anything with water, just like dwarves with earth. Also, regardless of whether the gift-giver dies or not, the weave they performed is permanent—unlike my sword, which disappears if I don't focus. The book doesn't explain why the weaves that created the gifts are infinite."

To avoid getting caught up in complex topics, Felix shifted focus and asked Anastasia if she wanted to explore the grounds. He wanted to check out some parts of the garden they had noticed while arriving on their trunks.

Len and Mr. Nibs played in the grass as the pair picked flowers for Mrs. Simmons. Felix touched each plant and asked if it was okay to take from them. Anastasia wasn't aware of his communications with the plants, but they all complied and allowed him to make his selection. By the time they finished, they had a bouquet of pinks, purples, and yellows.

The group was unaware if the translucent and almost undetectable entity trailing them, which was still closely monitoring Felix.

Anastasia glanced at Felix and asked, "How are we going to get these to Mrs. Simmons?"

"Let's ask Lady Rosalyn."

"Okay." Anastasia then called out, "Lady Rosalyn!" in jest.

Within seconds, a loud boom sounded, and Lady Rosalyn appeared before them, startling both.

"Aye, Anastasia, do you be needin' somethin'?"

"Oh wow, I didn't think that would work, but yes, we do. We would like to give these to Mrs. Simmons. What's the best way to get them to her?"

Lady Rosalyn winked. "First things first, you can't just

be givin' them to her like that." From within her sleeve, a crimson ribbon emerged and wrapped itself around the base of the flower stems like a glove.

"That's better. Now, there be two ways to accomplish yer task. The first will take a fair bit of time, as ye'll need to find yer head of house and ask for permission. They might not even grant it. Then ye'll have to make yer way back to the castle and head to one of the golden circles. If ye choose that path, ye'll find yerself at Barrell Hall late in the evenin'.

The second option is to have someone take them in yer stead. I know ye both haven't chosen classes for tomorrow yet, so I doubt they'll agree. I'll take care of this task myself. I'll even let her know ye miss her ... and I won't breathe a word about the incident at the lake," she said, casting a glance at Felix.

"Thank you so much," the pair responded gratefully.

"Is there aught else?"

"I think that will be it," Anastasia said.

The bouquet was placed under her robes, and without further delay, Lady Rosalyn shot off out of sight. They sky began to darken as they watched her rocket away.

Anastasia turned to face him. "Felix, what's going on? You've been kind of out of it. It isn't like you to forget specific things or be unable to give a direct answer," Anastasia remarked.

"It's nothing to worry about. I've been concentrating on a task since before lunch," he answered with hesitation.

"Wait... you've been focused on something since before lunch?"

Felix nodded. "Well, it isn't just anything. Thank you for reminding me. I need to check on it."

They collected Mr. Nibs and Len and parted ways to review the list of classes they needed to choose from. Anastasia hurried off as Felix decided to move as covertly as possible, knowing he would need to dodge some of the other children on his way.

As he crossed the lawn, a huge wave crashed over him. Felix collapsed, face-planting into a large tuft of grass. Unfortunately, Len was dropped, whimpering and yowling as her head filled with all the information pouring into Felix's brain.

They lay there in the grass for a few minutes, trying to regain their composure.

"Oh my gods! Felix, are you trying to kill me?" Len yelled once she could see straight again. "How many books was that?" She stared at him as he sat up.

"Eighteen. Are you okay?" he asked with concern.

"Eighteen? Seriously, Eighteen? Are you kidding me? Just warn me before you get another influx like that, okay?" she yelled, standing up and shaking as if drying off.

Felix wobbled to his feet, and with Len in hand, they headed to the unlabeled restroom.

As instructed, the books were placed back into the Bag of Holding along with the six Felix had taken with him. To appease Len, he ordered the clones to dissipate, ensuring no further accidents would occur for the rest of the day.

Felix grabbed the bag, and the duo soon set off for the library.

Thistle was tending to some plants as Felix entered, passing her desk. A few students were wandering through the rows of books, too busy to notice him.

"Good afternoon," he said to Thistle.

"Well, good afternoon to you as well, Felix! Back so soon, are we?" She was surprised, considering he had left with so many books.

"Yes, I'm here to return the books I've already read."

Thistle waited, expecting him to pull out one of the twenty-eight. Instead, he stacked eighteen from his bag onto her desk.

"There's no way you could've read all these books, surely!"

"Well, if you don't believe me, you can quiz me!" he said with a smirk.

Len, now at his feet, glanced up at him, shaking her head. "It's not good to show off, Felix," she scolded.

Thistle stepped back and said, "Okay, but I'm warning you, this won't be easy."

She scanned over all the books on the counter. "Well, I did enjoy this one." With a quick weave of her hands, she pulled out a black book with a gold and silver diamond-lattice pattern. Before turning it around, Felix rattled off the title and author.

"That book is called *The Dark Goddess* by Francesca Maria Medici; it details the years of Aurora the High Dragoon's reign, where she enacted the Treaty of 3993—which was signed by all races to end the warring. It also covers the good work she did, such as eliminating the Temptress and taming the rogue dragons in 3981 and 3982.

"She was also the last known person to have had ownership of the fourth part of each of the five dragon gods' life forces. The book says she reigned fairly and with compassion, protecting plants and animals, as well as the five phoenixes she hand-raised. She also transplanted the Living Oath Tree.

"She was murdered under suspicious circumstances during the uprising at the Divide, and no one knows for sure why. Would you like to know anything else about the book?"

Thistle, astonished and pleased, nodded with approval. "Well, Felix, it seems you've done a fair bit of reading—more than I could ever dream of in such a short time! Wherever did you find the time for it?" She pointed at a lemon-yellow colored book with a few fingernail indentations from people grasping it. "Could you tell me a bit about that book, then?"

Felix inspected it and thought for a moment. "*Fenrir's Kraken* by Mathis Balgoredo. The book is a firsthand account of a creature said to live in Fenrir's Den. No one else has seen it or lived to report back. It's considered by many to be a legend.

"Somewhere in the middle of the chasm lives a monster. Its tentacles are miles long, and it has a beak that, when closing, sounds like huge sheets of iron scraping against each other.

"Its eyes are a dim, glowing purple, and each sucker on its arms is the size of a small home. The author mentions that when he warned people about the creature, they thought he was mad. It's said that anything falling into the hole, if not water, is swallowed and eaten by the creature."

Thistle, momentarily at a loss for words, said with astonishment, "If you'd like, you can check out some more books, you know."

Felix's theory had proven correct. He was able to retain the information his clones had read. "Would you like me to put the books back?" he asked unexpectedly.

"Oh no, if you did that, I wouldn't have a job at all! Feel free to grab more if you fancy. You'll be able to tell which ones you've already read, mind."

Thistle then waved her hands, and the books floated into the air and returned to their places on the shelves.

Felix turned around as the books drifted away and walked down a few rows. This time, the books appeared different. The ones he had checked out now glowed a light blue, and he was the only one who could see it.

"Well, that was impressive—reciting the books without physically reading them yourself," Len said. "I wouldn't have believed it would work."

He didn't respond, instead scratching Len behind the ears while he read the titles of the new books. He selected several more and placed them in his bag. Once he was satisfied with his selection, he left the library with Len in tow. Felix waved goodbye to Thistle, who was busy tending to the plants around the room.

As the pair left, Felix checked the hall in both directions to ensure no one had seen him. He waited until a group of children passed the intersection of the corridors to make sure he wasn't being watched, yet still had not noticed the entity trailing him.

Making his way to the bathroom, he propped the door open and set Len down. While she sat on the floor watching Felix, he placed all the books on the sink basins. This time, he had grabbed fifty-seven books. He opened the three stalls at the end and sighed with relief. Clearing his mind of everything except the task at hand, he focused on the information he had just obtained.

His newfound knowledge affected his actions. His finger movements became quicker and more precise, and his arm movements swifter and more fluid. As he completed his first weave, a figure emerged from the first toilet bowl.

Len thought, I need to avoid this, so she detached from Felix mentally to prevent the dizziness he would feel, allowing her to assess the situation with greater awareness.

For the second weave, Felix propped himself against the door frame to avoid knocking into it, having learned from the previous experience. Another figure emerged. As Felix regained his composure, the first figure stepped out of the farthest stall and went for one of the stacks of books. Moving to the third stall, Felix sat on the floor and began weaving, but midway through, he decided against it. Maintaining the clones required too much energy, and he realized being present was more important.

Len took this opportunity to reconnect, as they had discussed that this would be the maximum limit Felix could realistically handle for now. Felix opened his eyes and nodded before slowly rolling over and sitting up. Len now understood what was going on.

Felix instructed the second clone to read, replace the stopper under the door, and, once done, put the books back into the bag and disperse.

"Unattended weaves are against school rules. Are you sure about this, Felix?" Len asked with concern.

After ensuring everything was secure, he turned to Len and said, "Don't worry, I'll monitor them regularly, just like I did last time," dismissing Len's concerns. He quickly exited the room.

At this rate, it would still take him well over 111 years to read every single book in the library. That thought crossed his mind as he sprinted down the halls and across the water lilies.

Not all Water Weavers had returned to the common room yet. Marcus was lying on one of the couches.

From across the room, Felix could see that Marcus appeared stressed. Not wasting any time, Felix hurried over to him to see what was wrong.

"What's wrong, Marcus? Are you okay?"

"Wow, how can you tell? I feel dreadful; is it that obvious? I wish I were okay, but I spent my whole summer and extra free time reading and learning about being a better Water Weaver. Unfortunately, I neglected my regular studies. If Lady Stewart finds out, it'll be the end of me. Once she knows what you're capable of, she holds you to that standard and never lets you slack off!" He sighed in defeat.

"Would you like some help? I'll help you if you help me," Felix offered.

"And what do you need help with?"

"How to weave and correct my mistakes," Felix said with a serious expression.

"Do you think you're doing it wrong?" Marcus asked.

"I want to make sure I'm performing the movements correctly."

Marcus laughed in shock and responded, "Deal!"

They went to their room, closed the door, and locked it.

"So, what subjects are you worried about, Marcus?" Felix asked, skimming the list of books and classes he would be choosing from.

Despite Marcus's intelligence, his nerves and worries made him feel inadequate.

"Well, it's math. It's never been a favorite of mine. I've done well, but I've had to put in three times the effort to get it right. There are a few other subjects I could use a refresher on to make sure I don't turn into a jellyfish," Marcus explained.

"Well, after dinner, I'll help you. It shouldn't be an issue."

"I guess I'm lucky to have a super nerd as my roommate," Marcus said with some relief as Felix giggled. Marcus then ruffled Felix's hair, and they shook hands.

Leaving Felix to figure out which classes he wanted to take, Marcus returned to his bed and stroked Tom's throat and belly. "You need to select your classes by circling the courses you want to take on the list," he explained, glancing over at Felix. "The books will appear on your desk once you've made your choices."

Dear Student,

Please select the courses you wish to take. If you are only here half the day, you're required to take three courses. If you're here full-time, you're required to take six classes unless otherwise stipulated. Once you have chosen your desired courses, please sign at the bottom.

Abjuration: 100, 101, 102, 103

Alchemy: 100, 101, 102, 103

Artifice: 100, 101, 102, 103

Astrology: 100, 101

Brew: 100, 101, 102, 103

Cultural Anthropology: DW 100, EL 100-103, F 100, G100, M100, W100

Conjuration: 100, 101, 102, 103

Demonology: 100, 101, 102, 103

Diplomacy: 100, 101

Divination: 100, 101, 102, 103

Elemental Control: (Mandatory D100)

Earth: A100, A101, A102, A103

Fire: B100, B101, B102, B103

Lightning: C100, C101, C102, C103

Water: D100, D101, D102, D103

Wind: E100, E101, E102, E103

Enchantments: 100, 101, 102, 103

Evocation: 100, 101, 102, 103

Fauna: 100, 101, 102, 103

Flora: 100, 101, 102, 103

History: 100, 101. 102

Illusionary: 100, 101, 102

Artifacts: 100, 101

Religion: 100, 101, 102

The Art of War: 100, 101, 102
The Outer World: 100, 101
The Planes: Ast100, Air100, Dre100, Ear100, Fir100, Wat100, Mat100,
Ele 100, Eth100, Fey100, Sha100
The Study of Dragons: 100, 101, 102, 103
Transmutation: 100, 101, 102, 103

Sign X_____

While sitting at his desk, Len curled up at Felix's feet as he reviewed the list of classes several times before making his selection. If there was any confusion or information about the courses, he'd ask Marcus for clarification.

Marcus had to get up and leave for the rest of his classes, bidding Felix good luck on choosing his courses.

Holding the paper in his right hand while shoveling food into his mouth with his left, he pondered. This process took multiple hours. Since Felix was attending full time, he would be taking six courses: The Study of Dragons 100, The Art of War 100, Fauna 100, Elemental Control D100, Brew 100, and Astrology 100.

Once Felix signed his name, six books and a satchel appeared on his desk. Each book had a note attached, listing the name of the professor and the room number for the class.

The satchel contained two outfits and several other items. The clothing was made from a stretchy, royal blue fabric with a silver dragon emblem on the sleeves. One outfit was a long-sleeve and pant combination, the other a short-sleeve and shorts combination, along with a pair of black athletic shoes. Other items in the bag included gloves made from a thick, leathery hide, a variety of brushes, an apron, tongs, shears, and an unfamiliar object with unclear applications. To his surprise, the items were bundled for the classes he needed them for. He placed the clothing in his locker and the tools in his bag of holding.

Marcus had just returned from his final class of the day when he walked over to Felix. "Oh, interesting," Marcus said. "Only one of the classes I thought you would pick. Not a bad variety."

Felix nodded in agreement, and they changed into their dinner attire. They then made their way to the dining hall.

The faculty sat at the head table as the next day's activities were announced. By the time the announcements were over, Felix had devoured ten rolls. Platters of food continued to arrive, descending onto the tables. Out of nowhere, a yelp of pain came from the Jupiter House section. A young girl was clutching her hand in agony.

Felix scanned the area to see if anyone would check on the girl. To his surprise, the professors didn't react. The fork she had grabbed was superheated and had burned her hand. The house captain, a girl with two long auburn braids, attended to the injured girl.

Felix looked around once more and spotted five girls laughing and sneering at the younger girl from the Lightning table. The four girls surrounded an older girl with a malicious grin.

Within a few seconds, Felix realized who had caused the superheated fork, but he didn't understand why this girl had targeted the younger one. He felt it was done out of spite. After thinking for a moment, a particular weave came to mind. He stared directly at the girls and performed a continuous series of weaves underneath the table. As a result, the liquid in the girls' cups tilted, splashing them in the face and drenching them. This interrupted their grins and laughter.

The dark berry juice stained their outfits, and the five girls yelled out in anger and disgust. All the houses turned to see what the commotion was about.

The girl with the malicious grin turned red with embarrassment as her smirk disappeared. She stood up and made her way across the room, knocking into classmates until she confronted the Water Weavers' section. Wide-eyed and enraged, she scanned each student while the entire room watched the scene unfold, though the teachers paid little attention.

As she glared, a senior elven boy stood up.

"What seems to be the issue, Renna?" he asked.

"One of your pathetic leaks sprayed my friends and me with our drinks, and that person is going to pay!" she retorted, snarling at him.

"Oh, really? One of us? How are you so sure it was one of us?" he responded with a smirk.

Even more infuriated, she said, "Who else controls liquids other than a water weaver?"

The elven boy's face lit up with satisfaction. "Well, Renna, that's an easy question to answer. Anyone in the room could have done it, since anyone can attune to more than one element. As you know, being born into a certain house doesn't stop you from controlling another element. While it's not wise to neglect mastering your primary element, it is possible. And let's not forget that wind can also push liquids. But I'm sorry, I shouldn't have expected you to figure out something so elementary on your own."

Renna stared at him, grinding her teeth. She realized he was making her look foolish, which made her face turn an even brighter shade of red.

He continued, "It seems to me, Renna, that what you and your friends got was a small portion of what you deserve. Don't you think?"

Renna looked at him in shock. "What in the hells are you talking about?"

"The young girl in the Jupiter section is what I'm talking about," he said.

"Nox, why would I waste my time on a weakling like that?" she snapped back.

"Don't play dumb with me. It's clear when you're lying. I have a theory, though. The young girl bumped into one of your friends, and you were seeking revenge on her," he said confidently.

Nox added, "Oh, wait—I misspoke. It's not a theory. In the corridor, she bumped into Tabatha. The young girl appeared to be in a hurry and apologized. And then there's the fact that since your first year, when you learned that trick with the cutlery, you've been using it non-stop. Shall we say your creativity and originality are so lacking that they've stunted your advancement? Instead of being clever, you rely on a tired trick to seek revenge on people who don't deserve it, just because you're vindictive."

Renna's face became heated and scrunched up.

"I don't know if you accidentally spilled your drinks on yourselves or if the contents were meant to be ejected from the glasses by an unknown force, but let me make myself clear. If you decide to come after anyone in this section, you'll have to deal with me—in a contest."

Renna stepped back, her eyes widening. She knew Nox was one of the most talented students at Heaven's Gate, and no one ever dared to challenge him.

"Now you can go away," Nox suggested.

Renna backed up and returned to House Vulcan's section with her fists clenched. Noticing one of her own housemates laughing at her humiliation, Renna pointed at him and announced, "I challenge you to a contest." The entirety of House Vulcan then vanished from the dining hall.

Marcus and Anastasia turned toward Felix, their expressions a mix of shock and amazement.

"Wasn't that cool?" Marcus asked.

"I guess, if she did what Nox said," Felix replied with a shrug.

"That was odd for her to take out her frustration on her own housemates," Anastasia said, trying to make sense of the situation.

Outside in the Fire Weavers' training pit, Renna faced off against a boy named Jonas. Their battle was a cat-and-mouse affair. Jonas, unable to stop laughing, moved erratically around the pit, making it difficult for Renna to land a hit. This continued until Jonas's stomach hurt from laughing so hard, which leveled the playing field.

The rest of House Vulcan, including Professor Pompeii, was unimpressed by the spectacle. Jonas wasn't taking the situation seriously, and Renna's form and battle IQ were akin to a toddler throwing a tantrum. Even the four girls who had laughed with Renna appeared physically uncomfortable with how she was handling herself.

Renna, unable to keep up and control her emotions, struggled to go on the offensive. When she became winded from chasing Jonas, she fell to her knees.

Taking advantage of the opportunity for further public humiliation, Jonas sent a fireball straight at Renna's rear, causing her to scream in pain as she doused the flame and covered her burned pants.

"Hey Renna, I guess you're a hothead now, since you're just an ass," Jonas taunted.

Renna didn't respond, but as she got to her feet, she sent a vortex of flames toward Jonas, blasting him against an outcropping of stone and knocking him unconscious. She had finally stopped worrying about what people were thinking and focused solely on Jonas.

The professor called the fight, announcing Renna as the winner by knockout, knowing that if he didn't end it, she might do something petty.

Back in the dining hall, the three of them finished their meals, and by the time they were done, it was eight-thirty. Felix still needed to help Marcus, so before leaving, he handed Marcus another plate of food. He then told Marcus he would use the restroom before meeting him back in their dorm room.

"Well, make sure you hurry. The pixies come out around this time," Marcus reminded him.

Anastasia and Felix hugged each other and said good-night.

"Don't worry; I'll hurry," Felix shouted back to Marcus as he started dashing down the corridors toward the unlabeled restroom.

Before he could reach it, he grew dizzy and weak. He had been pushing himself too hard, not knowing how his body would handle the stress and new activities. He lost his balance and fell, sliding into a stone column, which knocked him out cold for a few minutes. When he eventually woke up, his head felt like it was swelling. The pain from hitting the column, combined with his impaired vision and lack of a sense of direction, made things worse. Bracing himself against the wall, he realized his food hadn't been digested enough to restore his lost energy.

As his vision cleared, he saw a dim light bobbing up and down farther down the hall. Unable to identify it, he stood there, waiting to regain his sight. Once his vision returned to normal, he realized what was coming toward him.

"Oh, hells no!" Felix shouted, running in the opposite direction.

He raced through one hall and down another. After crashing into the column, he had gone the wrong way, and the light continued to follow him, keeping pace. Felix made it to the final hallway where the lily pond stood. He didn't break stride, skidding down the hall as he made a sharp turn.

Once at the pool, he leapt from one lily pad to another until he reached the dragon statue. Knowing he couldn't shoot projectiles at the pixies like before, he didn't look back as he swiped his bracelet and descended the spiral staircase. Once he reached the bottom, he knew he was safe.

Felix lurched forward, out of breath, and placed his hands on his knees. The students still in the common room turned to Felix, startled and curious about his state.

Some of the students began to move in on his position almost immediately.

Without a moment's hesitation, he scurried off to his room, where Marcus was waiting. Felix closed the door and leaned against it reflexively.

"Well, aren't we in a state? Were the other students bugging you again?"

Len jumped off the bed and ran over to Felix. She knew what had happened. The linked blackout she had felt had just ended when Marcus arrived. She stood there with her front paws pressed against Felix's thigh.

"Pixies..." Felix managed between gasps.

"Oh, are you okay?" Marcus asked.

"You should lie down for a moment," Len suggested.

Before going to his bed, Felix described the situation while catching his breath. "I saw a bobbing light coming down the hall and just turned and ran. I didn't look back!

They were following me. I could tell because when I turned the corners, I saw the light reflecting off the polished granite and marble walls."

"Well, you're lucky!" Len and Marcus said in unison.

"Where did you see the pixies?" Marcus asked.

"I fell and hit my head, so I don't remember which corridor it was. When I saw them, I just ran in the opposite direction. Then, when I turned a corner, the reflections were unmistakable. I thought I was going in the right direction, but I wasn't."

Felix tried to slow his breathing as Len crawled onto his lap.

"Are you sure you're okay, Felix?" she asked.

"Yes. I'm just happy to be back, and I'm glad you're here!"

She licked his hand. "Promise me you'll be more careful in the future."

"Len, when have you ever had to tell me something twice?"

"Good point. I just feel like I need to remind you from time to time. Now, please try not to go out alone at night."

Felix pressed his teeth into his lower lip, nodding as he scratched Len behind the ears.

Marcus was curious. "Which way did you think you were going?"

"Toward the library," Felix answered without hesitation.

Marcus looked at Felix with a baffled expression. "That's kind of out of the way to use the restroom, and there isn't one near the library. Were you planning to check out a few books or something?" Marcus had never come across the restroom with the missing placard.

Not wanting to go into detail, Felix fibbed. "I thought I might do a little light reading after helping you out."

"You could have borrowed one of my books if you wanted," Marcus replied.

Marcus then grabbed his math book from his desk and sat next to Felix on the bed. Len moved off his lap to avoid being in the way.

The night went on with Felix explaining how to correctly solve a few different equations, and Marcus struggled but gradually got the hang of it. Len, on the other hand, lay there as Felix rubbed her belly. She wasn't much help, but she knew she wouldn't be.

After an hour, the two boys had worked through more than thirty problems on the worksheets. Felix corrected any errors and explained where the calculations had gone awry.

The boys then went to bed, and Len crawled under the covers, snuggling up to Felix. Tom was already passed out, perched on the footboard of Marcus's bed.

An hour and a half later, Felix woke up. No matter how hard he tried, he couldn't fall back asleep. He stared at the ceiling as thoughts raced through his mind.

Not wanting to wake Tom, Marcus, or Len, Felix climbed out of bed, grabbed his boots and robes, and snuck out of the dorm room. He made sure no one was in the common room as he tiptoed through it and up the staircase, guided by the jellyfish bobbing up and down, lighting his way.

As he poked his head out of the entrance to the Water Weavers' house, he found nothing amiss. He leapt from lily pad to lily pad, glancing back to ensure he wasn't being followed. With socks on his feet and boots in hand, he skated down the polished floors, trying not to make a sound.

Corridor after corridor, he checked to make sure he didn't see any floating lights. Guided by the moonlight filtering through the high arches, he made his way to the side door of the castle. Felix knew that if the pixies were out, he would be in danger, so he scanned the ground for any movement.

Fortunately, not even the displaced dragons were active.

Pausing, Felix slipped on his boots before making his way to the lake. Once there, he ensured he wouldn't be disturbed or noticed. He wiped the water off and sat on the bleachers, removed his socks and boots, and hiked his pants up past his knees. Thinking of all the books he had read, he scanned his memory until he recalled reading about walking on water.

Unknown to Felix, the bracelet had alerted Lady Rosalyn and Lady Stewart that there was a student outside the castle. Within moments, Lady Stewart had thrown on a robe and was about to exit her chambers when Lady Rosalyn appeared in a burst of flames, startling her. The two made their way out of the castle to the location indicated by the bracelet. They decided to watch from a distance, staying far enough away so Felix wouldn't notice them.

Once he had a clear thought, Felix stood and weaved his hands and fingers as the book had described. The reflection of Kalli on the surface of the water rippled as the ball of Felix's foot touched the lake. Once both feet were on the surface, he fell to the lake floor. Being close to the shoreline, the water was only a few inches past his ankles.

He stood on the grass, gazing over the dark landscape, and tried again. This time, he cleared his mind of the pixies. A calmness settled over him, and the weaves began anew. Once the weave was completed, he put his first foot down, then his second. He had done it. He was standing on water. He even jumped up and down to ensure he wouldn't sink.

The water had a springy reaction but held his weight. Finding his footing, Felix ran, jumped, skipped, and cartwheeled on the surface, becoming attuned to its characteristics.

After a few minutes, he wove for a second time. Knowing the clones had finished reading what they could before the lights went out, he attempted this new weave.

This time, a clone rose from the water and stood in front of Felix. He instructed it to attack him so he could train and prepare for any upcoming battles or tests. Felix was unaware that the clones shared his knowledge.

The clone followed its task and lunged at him. Felix dodged away. As he continued, the clone's tactics became more unpredictable, since its knowledge was vast and ever-growing. The attacks came one after another. Felix analyzed the patterns and noted that after every fourth failed attack, the clone would switch to a new strategy. Although the fighting techniques weren't based on any specific style, his reflexes and reaction times were a huge help.

Choosing the right moment, Felix sidestepped one of the clone's attacks and tripped it. The clone fell over and melted into the water. After a few seconds, it reformed and resumed the assault.

After a few minutes of watching Felix, Lady Rosalyn turned to Lady Stewart and said, "Well, it appears my reports were quite true. Ye've got a pupil mastering weaves that even the older ones have yet to grasp. Seems to me, ye can handle it from here on out."

She grinned and walked away, careful not to disturb Felix.

Lady Stewart stayed behind for a few more minutes to observe before leaving Felix to his own devices. She concluded that he was not in serious harm and considered fast-tracking his lessons.

Felix made sure no orbs of light were nearby. Using his dexterity and quick thinking, he dodged most of the clone's attacks with its feet or fists. Occasionally, he took a blow but used it to his advantage, becoming accustomed to the pain and improving his reaction time.

After a solid forty minutes, Felix decided to head back inside to get some sleep, feeling a bit sore from the blows. Before reentering the castle, a memory resurfaced out of nowhere. In pain, Felix wept, and his fingers moved instinctively, as if his subconscious were acting out, while his body trembled.

A figure rose from the water in a nearby fountain, undulating as it took on a distinctive shape. Felix recognized it as Chance by the familiar silhouette of his hair and the way it seemed to wave at him. He collapsed onto the construct, wrapping his arms around it, crying and clinging to it as if it were Chance and could hear his words. He sobbed out all the pain he had been holding inside, unable to contain his emotions. It took quite some time before he was able to calm himself.

Unable to hide his immense sadness from Len, she woke up.

On his way back, he saw a cluster of glowing orbs of light moving around the corner of the castle. Thankfully, the orbs were headed away from his path.

When he reached the bottom of the spiral staircase, Marcus, Len, and Tom met him.

"What were you thinking, Felix? Last time you were out, you were chased by pixies and would have died if they had caught you!" Marcus yelled.

Len, equally frustrated, added, "I swear, Felix. If the pixies don't kill you, I will! You had me so worried!"

Tom continued to observe quietly.

Felix tried to apologize. "I'm sorry I worried all of you. I couldn't sleep and was being super careful, so I did some training."

"Where did you go, exactly?" Marcus asked.

"To the lake," Felix replied with great reluctance.

"You went where?" Marcus said in disbelief. "Well, one thing we can say is you've got nerve. Stupid as it was, you've got nerve."

Marcus shook his head. "Now we all need to go to sleep. Shall we?" Marcus gestured toward the dorm.

Chapter 17

Lofty Expectations

In the morning, Felix dressed at a slow pace, still sore from the night before.

Len, still upset with him, sulked among the linens. Although she understood what had been troubling Felix, she decided not to stay mad for too long.

He turned to Len and told her he needed to go to the place he had shown her to retrieve his bag and return some books to the library. Len looked annoyed but agreed. "At least I don't have to worry about the pixies. I'll come with you to make sure you don't get into any trouble. We'd better hurry so you can let me back inside before breakfast."

Felix and Len made their way to the unmarked bathroom, where Felix grabbed his bag of books—though not all sixty-seven—and resurrected the clones in the stalls. They then hurried back to the library. Since Mater was not lighting up the sky yet, they wanted to avoid disturbing Thistle. Not knowing whether she was awake or asleep, they slipped in quietly.

Felix peeked into the fern and saw that Thistle was still asleep, her body wrapped in the fern's tendrils. He pulled the books out of his bag two by two, placing them gently on the desk to avoid disturbing Thistle. Once the last book was down, they left the library without making any noticeable sounds; even the usual click of the door latch was muffled.

A few students had gathered in the common room. Felix darted past them to let Len back in. Once he returned to the room, he saw Marcus trying to get out of bed.

"Good morning," Felix greeted him. He grabbed all six books for his classes, changed into shorts, a short-sleeved shirt, and black sneakers, and said, "I'll see you later," to Marcus and Len, giving Len a gentle stroke on her head before heading out.

Felix's first class was before breakfast. Crossing the pond, he headed to the other side of the castle. He rushed down the corridor to a door made of dark wood with several studs jutting out. He turned the latch and went inside.

Inside, Felix scanned the room, noting several types of armor and paintings. Most of the armor appeared to be of Asian and European origin, though a few pieces were unfamiliar to him.

In the room, several older students were attending class. An older man, appearing to be around fifty years old, sat cross-legged in the center, stretching his head back and forth. Despite his age, he looked robust and sturdy. Bald, with a piece of fabric wrapped around his head covering his eyes, he had scars peeking out from beneath. His face was lean, with high cheekbones and a square jaw. He wore red harem pants and a long vest with blue trim, and he was barefoot. A hooked bamboo stick rested in front of him.

"Good morning, Mr. Grey," the man said, addressing

Felix.

Felix was startled that the man knew who he was without being introduced. His stutter emerged. "G-good morning."

"Don't be so nervous, my boy! Take a seat. I'm Goryeo Jun-Seo, but you can just call me Goryeo," the man said with a friendly nod.

Felix thought, If he's blind, he must be using sound to detect me.

Goryeo continued, "Since the other students have had me before, let me be frank with you, my young protégé. I'm going to push you to your limits and beyond. If you think I'm being hard on you, it's because I am. Whatever drove you to pick this class means there's something inside you that wants to be challenged and tested. All I ask is that you give me your all. Hai, you understand?"

"My expectations of all of you, except for Mr. Grey, have been keeping up with your training. Line up and show me what you've learned. Shall we begin?"

Felix remained seated as the rest of the class formed a line.

"That means you too, Mr. Grey. We must find out what you're capable of."

Felix looked around, unsure, and stood at the back of the line.

Goryeo stood up with the aid of the bamboo stick. Felix was puzzled. How could Goryeo assess the students if he couldn't see?

An older girl with quick movements approached Goryeo, attempting a leg sweep to knock him off balance. Goryeo sidestepped and rapped her on the head with the stick.

"I may be blind, but I knew that was coming. You need to mislead your opponent. Now, who's next?"

The girl returned to her seat. The next student was a

boy who moved in a zigzag pattern, trying to land punches like a boxer. Goryeo dodged, deflected each punch with the stick, and then tripped the boy, ending the fight.

"You're off-balance. Find your center. Next!"

All the students attempted to land blows but failed, each receiving a strike from Goryeo's stick and being given pointers to improve. Felix watched with great interest as each student before him was unsuccessful.

"Ah, Mr. Grey, don't worry. Just do whatever feels natural."

Before approaching Goryeo, Felix slid off his sneakers and walked five feet away from his professor.

"Come now, I'm waiting."

Felix remained in his spot, adopting a wide stance and staring at the old man. Goryeo decided to swipe at Felix with his stick like a rapier. Felix ducked out of the way without moving his feet before the stick could strike him. Failing to land a blow, Goryeo made a wide swing, again missing his target. This time, Felix followed the stick, grabbing it with both hands and pulling it away from Goryeo, who was holding it with one hand. Since the professor had leaned forward to gain some reach, he was off-balance, giving Felix the perfect opportunity to strike.

Felix hooked the end of the cane around Goryeo's neck, trying to pull him down. With cat-like reflexes, Goryeo fell into a split, ducking low enough to unhook his neck and grab the stick back. Felix realized the stick was just a ploy and that he didn't need it.

"Enough. Well done, Mr. Grey. You're the only one who waited for me to make the first move. It's always better to be on the defensive than on the offensive when you're at a disadvantage. You also took away my one advantage. You may take a seat."

Professor Goryeo then paired the students up and demonstrated some basic movements for a refresher course. Many of the older students felt outperformed by the first-year, but they had enough discipline and respect not to voice their grievances.

Felix found the class enjoyable.

Once class was over, Professor Goryeo asked Felix to stay behind for a moment.

"Such wisdom for someone so young. I have a few things I'd like you to have. I'm sure you'll make good use of them."

He walked over to the wall and opened a cupboard. His hands brushed over several knobby wooden ends of scrolls until he found what he was looking for. He then handed Felix two scrolls on advanced hand-to-hand combat techniques and a pair of sais, a Japanese weapon used for stabbing, striking, and disarming opponents.

"Professor, may I ask you a question?"

Goryeo nodded.

"No longer having the use of your eyes, how are you able to figure out what's going on around you?"

"Indeed, that is a wise question. Since losing my sight, I've had to rely on my other senses. I have honed them to such an extent that I can smell things, and as they get closer, the scents become more pungent. I can sense air pressure on my skin as objects approach, which tells me their direction. I also feel vibrations on the ground as things move. When you didn't move, I expected to land my strike on you, but I didn't sense any vibration, since you didn't move your feet. Instead, you ducked. You're clever. Is there anything else?"

Felix bowed, said no, and thanked him before heading to the dining hall.

Goryeo returned the bow and sat down in a meditative position in the middle of the room, where the rays of Mater began to hit his skin.

Professor Jun-Seo's words made Felix reflect on his own level of awareness and how he might better attune to his surroundings.

In the dining hall, Lady Stewart was paying close attention, still calculating how to mold Felix, as he showed more initiative in his studies than she had ever witnessed before from anyone.

During this period, the trio knew they were being observed by certain curious groups and were unaware of the ever-watchful eyes of the staff. They continued their discussion about Felix's gauntlet and his poor decision-making skills. Eventually, they decided to put aside their speculations about the gauntlet and focus on the pressing issue: why Felix was making such risky decisions and putting himself in danger.

Felix tried to explain that he couldn't sleep and felt that training in water weaving was a better use of his time.

Not wanting to dwell on Felix's mistakes, Anastasia changed the subject. She asked to see Felix's classes to see if any were the same as hers.

She pulled out a scrap of paper with a list jotted on it. "Felix, these are the classes I chose," she said, showing him the list.

Felix saw disappointment on Anastasia's face as he responded to her queries. "I'm taking mandatory Elemental Control A100 with Professor Agate," she continued. "Like my first class, I know you won't be in that one either. My next period is Cultural Anthropology with Professor Balderk. Are you taking that?" she asked, holding her breath.

Felix shook his head, dreading her response.

"What about fourth period? Flora 100?"

Again, Felix shook his head.

A bit more desperate, Anastasia asked, "You must have chosen the outer world with Professor Elaine Pillman!"

Felix shuddered and continued to shake his head.

"Let me guess. You took the Study of Dragons?"

With an elated expression, Felix nodded. "It's taught by Professor Varus Sainnodel."

Anastasia's head hit the table. "I should have known. My other two classes that aren't required are Fauna with Professor Bethrynna Holimion."

"Oh, I picked that one!" Felix exclaimed.

With momentary relief, Anastasia sighed. "My final class is Magical Artifacts with Professor Oskar Emberforge."

Felix shook his head.

While eating, Marcus described their teachers to them, and the pair listened attentively. The meal was full of laughter and questions about what they should expect.

After finishing, Anastasia excused herself. "I need to go to the library, so I'll catch you both later."

The two boys waved as she hurried off.

After Felix finished his meal, he made his way back to the library to grab more books related to his classes, hoping to run into Anastasia to check on her.

When he arrived, he paused to survey the massive room. The number of books he'd had the clones absorb seemed a bit excessive, but he shrugged it off and grabbed several more. Returning to the unmarked bathroom, he continued with his usual method. This time, he gave the clones both the class books and the scrolls, instructing them to be cautious with the scrolls since he wasn't sure if they were as durable as the books. His weaving skills were improving with all this repetition.

Felix's next class was with Lady Stewart. Once again, she took the students out to the lake to work on their gestures and finger-weaving abilities. Most of the children kept their distance from Felix, wary of what he might do.

Lady Stewart corrected each student on their mistakes and offered guidance on how to improve their weaves, keeping a watchful eye on Felix. She noticed that he kept dropping the weave whenever he felt observed, trying to conceal his actions from the others.

"Mr. Grey, pray accompany me, if you would be so kind." Lady Stewart commanded, already walking on the water. "Sir, I expect naught but perfection from your esteemed self. Step forth into the limelight you so oft shy away from," she said, quickening her pace. "I am well aware that you possess the ability to walk upon water; thus, the mere conjuration of a water ball is but a trifling feat for one of your caliber."

Felix stiffened with dread—how did she know he could walk on water? He hadn't even disclosed this to Marcus or Anastasia.

"I wish to be most explicit with you, dear sir," she said, her tone strict but encouraging. "I am yet to uncover the full extent of your potential, but what you have thus far revealed intimates that it far exceeds your tender years. I entreat you to exert yourself in your studies and strive to attain the utmost of your capabilities, for you owe this to yourself. Undertaking six classes this term is no trifling endeavor, particularly with any extracurricular pursuits you may engage in. I hold steadfast faith that you shall restore greatness to this house. My lofty standards shall not falter; expect no special treatment."

Felix thought, Is this what Marcus warned me about?

Lady Stewart then turned to check on the other students, who were still struggling to correct their forms and manage their emotions, causing them further anxiety.

Unaware that Felix had already weaved the series of

hand gestures to join her on the lake, she nearly collided with him as he quickly dodged out of the way.

"Well, is this not most intriguing? You are far stealthier than I had previously perceived," she said, her tone a mix of astonishment and approval. "I must confess, I had not even perceived your presence. Now, let us put your hand-eye coordination to the test, shall we?" She continued, pulling out what looked like two sword-shaped letter openers from her pocket. She tossed one to Felix, and with a snap of her fingers, it transformed into a rapier.

The blade spun end over end as it descended, and Felix caught it in midair by the hilt. He stepped back, adjusted his stance, and swung the blade through the air to test its feel and handling.

"Well... I trust you are prepared," Lady Stewart remarked before charging at Felix. She moved swiftly, slicing through the air.

Felix sidestepped her attacks and parried with his blade, deflecting hers.

For the next few minutes, Lady Stewart pressed her attack without relenting.

Felix decided to watch her closely and analyze her movements, staying on the defensive. He deflected her attacks and waited for her next move.

The other students lost interest in their task and noticed this. Lady Stewart, seeing their lack of focus, conjured a wave of water with a weave from her free hand and doused them, shouting at them to get back to work.

"Come now, Felix, you cannot remain on the defensive for all eternity!" she urged with a hint of impatience.

Felix had never faced a formal swordfight before—his experience was confined to playful duels with foam swords alongside Chance, where the stakes were nothing more than bragging rights. Now, under Lady Stewart's watchful eye, the stakes were much higher. The intensity of their duel was palpable, with Felix struggling to match her lightning-fast, precise strikes. Each swing of her blade seemed to cut through the air with effortless grace, leaving him scrambling to keep up.

He darted and weaved, his heart pounding as he narrowly avoided each of her powerful thrusts. The sounds of their blades clashing rang out sharply, reverberating across the lake's still surface. Felix's mind raced, his body moving on instinct as he tried to anticipate her next move. He could feel the weight of the rapier in his hand, its balance shifting with each defensive maneuver.

After several minutes of intense evasion, Felix took a deep breath, forcing himself to focus. He recalled the techniques Lady Stewart had demonstrated earlier and decided to seize the initiative. With newfound determination, he launched a counterattack, employing four of her own techniques with a blend of urgency and precision.

Lady Stewart's reaction was immediate and fluid. Her blade moved with practiced ease, effortlessly deflecting each of his strikes. The duel shifted into a rhythm of rapid exchanges. Her coaching interspersed the clash of steel with sharp, instructive commands, guiding Felix's actions and forcing him to adapt on the fly.

Felix's mind sharpened with each parry and riposte. The challenge demanded that he think quickly and adjust his tactics in real time. His sweat mingled with the lake's mist, creating a stark contrast against the calm waters below. As the fight continued, Felix's movements grew more confident and calculated, his earlier hesitation replaced by a fierce determination.

Lady Stewart's eyes gleamed with a mix of approval

and challenge as she observed his progress. The duel, now a dynamic dance of swordplay and strategy, tested Felix's problem-solving skills like never before. With each piece of feedback she provided, he adapted his approach, rapidly applying her lessons. His rapid improvement and growing proficiency under her guidance were testament to his ability to learn and thrive under pressure.

After another ten minutes of fencing on the lake, she without a warning stopped and congratulated Felix. "Until the morrow, Mr. Grey. You are well acquainted with the less I imparted to the class, and I must say, you wield a sword with commendable skill. We shall refine your techniques on another day. If it pleases you, prepare yourself for your next class."

Felix handed back the rapier and bowed his head. The rapier once again shrank back to the size of a letter opener with a snap of her fingers.

He exited the lake, making his way back to the castle. As he passed the other students, he heard a boo or two, but they were bowled over by a blast of water from Lady Stewart.

Chapter 18
Fitting In

Felix's next class was Fauna 100, taught by Professor Bethrynna Holimion. Len trotted alongside Felix in full gallop as they headed to the menagerie—a large indoor/outdoor space on the castle's outer wall. Inside the archway, lush green spaces sprawled, housing an array of fascinating creatures. Unlike a traditional zoo where animals are confined, the menagerie allowed its inhabitants the freedom to roam.

Among the curiosities was a peculiar creature with stringy hair and massive horns, lounging on a bed of hay. Nearby, a cat-like beast with giant, flapping ears surveyed the surroundings. Felix marveled at the sight of creatures he had never imagined, all seemingly at peace in their environment.

To his right sat Professor Holimion, a thin and elegant woman with tan skin, golden-brown eyes, and caramel-colored hair. Her thick brows gave her a wolf-like appearance. She wore a long yellow dress with oversized pockets that bulged with various items, and her hair was adorned with wheat and strawflowers.

Rising from a wooden stool, she approached Felix with a graceful stride. "Well, who might you be?" she asked.

Startled, Felix stumbled over his own feet, his attention divided between the intriguing creatures and the elegant professor.

With gentle grace, Professor Holimion helped Felix to his feet by grasping him under the arms. As she touched him, her ears twitched in reaction. "Are you alright? I hope I didn't startle you."

Felix brushed off his clothes and managed a sheepish smile. "Just a little," he admitted. "I'm Felix. What's your name?" He extended his hand.

"Bethrynna," she replied, shaking his hand. A cool sensation passed between them, and she noted that his ears weren't pointed.

"Wait a minute, you're a green guildsman? No, that can't be..." Her confusion was evident.

Felix's face reflected his own confusion. "What is a green guildsman?" he asked. I have heard the term before, but no one has explained exactly what it is.

"It is a being deeply connected to nature, far beyond what humans can naturally achieve," Bethrynna explained with gentle curiosity. "Green guildsmen are typically born as Elves or Fairies, but others can attain this title through many years of dedication and a profound commitment to studying, nurturing, and becoming one with the flora. I find it quite intriguing that you're neither an Elf nor a Fairy and still so young. How did you come to possess such knowledge and affinity with nature to earn the title? It makes you quite the mystery."

Before Felix could respond, Bethrynna shifted topics.

"Do you know anything about the Sphaera Elatio?" she asked.

Felix shook his head. "No, I don't."

"Well, it's a good thing you're in my class then—or did you wander in by mistake?" she inquired with a slight smirk.

"I'm definitely in your class. Lady Stewart let me out early, and I wanted to see the animals while I had the chance, without a lot of distractions," Felix explained.

As they continued their conversation, Len slipped away from Felix and settled beside the large, stringy-haired creature.

Bethrynna crouched to Felix's level and began explaining the various animals one by one. Felix, curious, asked why the animals weren't caged.

"All the animals are domesticated and at ease here," she replied. "They don't feel the need to leave, and there's no need to restrain them. They consider this place their home, where they receive plenty of food and attention. The gate is always open if they ever want to leave, but they prefer to stay."

When the other students arrived, they eagerly interacted with the creatures, and even Len enjoyed some well-deserved belly rubs and ear scratches.

Professor Holimion retrieved a handful of nuts and berries from her bulging pockets and handed some to Felix for feeding the animals. She looked at him with a maternal warmth, noticing that he had a similar effect on her as he did with the younger elves, though not as pronounced.

"We're running out of time. Class is about to start, so please find a seat," she instructed.

One by one, the students settled on the ground. Unlike Felix's first two classes, this one was overflowing with students.

Anastasia spotted Felix and quickly made her way to him, having saved a spot for her. "It's nice to have some

271

normal time with you," she said, hugging him warmly.

Unbeknownst to Anastasia, Mr. Nibs had scampered over to Bethrynna and jumped into her lap. "Oh, could this be? Yes, it is... oh, you. My word, I haven't seen you in ages!" She cradled him affectionately. "Now, who is this little devil's partner in crime?"

Anastasia stiffened, worried she might be in trouble. "He's mine, Professor. I'm sorry for his behavior," she said, wincing.

"Oh, there's absolutely no need to apologize," Bethrynna said, her eyes lighting up with affection. "I found this little gem when he was orphaned and took him under my wing before passing him to Sylas. I was so reluctant to part with him—he was just too precious. How could I resist? Even now, he's as endearing as ever, radiating that same irresistible charm. I can't help but feel a bit sentimental seeing him now; he truly is a little bundle of joy."

"I'm so delighted to hear you've been caring for him," Bethrynna said warmly, her voice filled with genuine affection as she watched Mr. Nibs return to Anastasia with a contented laugh. "It's clear he's truly happy."

She then smiled softly and continued, "Now that we've settled in, let's begin our lesson. For introductions, I'm Professor Bethrynna Holimion, but please, call me Beth or Professor—whichever feels more comfortable for you. I'm looking forward to getting to know all of you."

Out of respect, the students chose to call her Professor.

"Let's get started, shall we?" she continued. "Marigold, come here."

A large, horned beast rose, revealing a slumbering Len underneath.

"Anyone but Mr. Grey—since you're already familiar with this—could you please tell me what this is?"

Anastasia stood up, eager to be called upon.

Bethrynna, slightly taken aback by Anastasia's promptness, said with a hint of surprise, "That was quick! Please, tell us your name."

"Professor, my name is Anastasia," she began with poised elegance. "The creature you see is known as a Bedgetti, often affectionately called a meadow cloud. Elves and Bedgetti have coexisted harmoniously for millennia, particularly among the elves who dwell in the grasslands. While Bedgetti do not consume grass, they are renowned for feeding on weeds and brambles, which facilitates the harvesting of crops for the elves. The elves shear the Bedgetti and tend to them with great care. The wool harvested from these creatures is renowned for its magical properties: it warms the wearer when cold and cools them when hot."

She sat back down.

"Everyone, please give Miss Anastasia a round of applause. You must have read the textbook from cover to cover. I might have to ask trickier questions from now on. If not I don't think I'll have a job for much longer after today," she said with a chuckle.

The classroom buzzed with excitement as the students eagerly petted and played with Marigold. It was a hands-on class that offered practical experience with the creatures. As the session drew to a close, Anastasia and Felix parted ways, both pleased with the extra time they had spent together.

During the class, a few students from other houses gathered around Anastasia, clearly impressed by her extensive knowledge. They introduced themselves and spent the remainder of the session clustered together, forging new friendships. The lively interaction made it clear that no one wanted to leave.

Bethrynna Holimion was undoubtedly one of the most popular professors at Heaven's Gate, her warm and engaging teaching style leaving a lasting impression on her students.

On his way to his fourth class, Felix was ecstatic. For their safety, mirrored souls weren't allowed to accompany students to *The Study of Dragons*.

The class was in the dragon stables on the side of the cliff. Leaving Len in the dorm room, he made his way down a dark hallway with no windows. The walls were ice cold, with half-circular grooves in them with a fish scale pattern. The path murky being only lit by dim lanterns.

Once he reached the end of the hallway he found a large metal door with two reptilian hands holding glowing red orbs. He could hear children at the other end of the hall approaching. Felix pushed open one of the doors just enough to squeeze in before closing it.

The room was bright and airy, a stark contrast to the dim passageway that led him there. Arched ceilings gave the space an expansive feel, and openings in the outer wall revealed nothing but the vast, empty sky. Stone staircases on either side led to other levels, and further down, Felix could see dragons basking in the sunlight, comfortably settled in what appeared to be stalls. This place was known in Yurden as the Dragon's Perch, and the castle had 120 such openings. Midway down the level sat a large pavilion, where pews with small desktops attached formed a horseshoe around a large table.

Felix took a seat at the far end of a row and observed a tall man with his back turned, studying scrolls. The man was slender, reminiscent of Henry, with raven-black hair pulled back into a bun. Several piercings adorned his long, pointed ears. When he turned around, Felix noticed two large scars on his face, resembling claw marks—one running diagonally from his left brow to his cheek, and the other extending from his chin in the same direction. His skin was the color of cream, and his sapphire-colored eyes conveyed a kind yet battle-hardened demeanor.

Dressed in a brown leather vest and tan linen pants, he wore two shoulder holsters with pouches under his biceps. His boots had slots for various tools—some held small knives, while others contained long darts.

As more students filed into the room, Felix tried to blend in, pulling up his hood and slouching in his seat. The class went silent when Professor Sainnodel, the tall man, grabbed a stack of papers from his desk and began handing them out. The quiz, titled "General Traits of Dragons Based on Their Elements," had five sections with five questions each. Students were instructed to place the completed quizzes face-down on the desk.

The first section featured pictures of dragon wings. Felix was excited, having read extensively about them and studied the illustrations Marcus had drawn. He eagerly filled in his answers with a quill. A note on the quiz indicated that not every dragon fit the general descriptions.

Section One: Characteristics of Wing Edges, this section details the distinctive features of dragon wings, categorized by elemental types. Fire dragon wings are marked by the presence of holes. Wind dragon wings exhibit a structure akin to corsets. Earth dragon wing edges appear ripped or torn, while lightning dragon wings are characterized by pointed edges resembling unfinished barbs. Water dragon wings display slackness similar to a sail that is not pulled taut.

Section Two: Scale Description, in this section, the focus is on the scales of each elemental dragon. Fire dragons possess serrated scales with pronounced ridges. Wind dragons' scales are speckled and layered, resembling the pages of a book. Earth dragons' scales have a bark-like texture and are brittle in nature. Lightning dragons are identified by crowned and spiked scales. Water dragon scales are typically teardrop-shaped and exhibit reflective properties.

Section Three: Tail Characteristics, the third section examines the tails of dragons. Fire dragons feature spiked tails. Wind dragons' tails are adorned with hooked barbs. Earth dragons have tails resembling mauls, while lightning dragons possess forked tails. Water dragons are distinguished by tails with fins.

Section Four: Number of Toes, this section asks to specify the number of toes on each type of dragon. Fire dragons have four toes. Wind dragons have three toes. Earth dragons possess five toes. Lightning dragons also have three toes, while water dragons have four toes but can actually just have fins or flippers.

Section Five: Dragon Egg Features, the final section asks one to please describe the characteristics of dragon eggs. Fire dragon eggs are covered with scales resembling armor. Wind dragon eggs resemble oval-shaped cabbages. Earth dragon eggs appear as clusters of pebbles, making them the most challenging to identify. Lightning dragon eggs exhibit jagged vein patterns. Water dragon eggs are characterized by a jelly-like consistency and may be partially or fully translucent.

Felix completed his quiz swiftly, a feat that would have impressed Anastasia. Varus Sainnodel, having stopped reading his book, leaned forward and snatched the quiz off the table as soon as Felix placed it down.

Felix turned to leave but was halted by Professor Sainnodel's voice. "Where do you think you're going?"

Felix, nerves getting the better of him, stuttered, "M-my desk."

With a deep, rich voice, Professor Sainnodel scanned the quiz and said, "It seems you know your dragons, Mr. Grey."

Felix's gaze flitted between the floor and the quiz in Professor Sainnodel's hand. The professor slid a book across the desk to Felix. "You might enjoy this." The title read *The Lords of the Sky* by Freya Crescent.

Once all the quizzes had been submitted, Professor Varus Sainnodel addressed the class with a measured, yet pointed tone.

"My name is Varus Sainnodel," he began, "but you may refer to me simply as Professor. It appears some of you are well-versed in dragon lore, while others—well, let's just say there's room for growth. I expect those lagging behind to catch up swiftly. We're here to delve into the anatomy and characteristics of dragons, their habits, and their social codes. Dragons are not only proud and noble but also fiercely intelligent. They have little patience for disrespect and an alarming propensity for consuming the disrespectful."

With that, he proceeded to lay out the foundational knowledge on dragons for those less acquainted with the subject. As the class drew to a close, Felix received his quiz back, marked with "Exceeded Expectations." Satisfied with his performance, Felix looked forward with enthusiasm to the next day's lesson.

For a brief moment, Felix reminisced about how much brighter the day would have been if Chance had been there with him. He rested his head against the cold stone wall, gently holding the book Professor Sainnodel had given him. A few tears trickled down his cheeks, but they were more reflective than sorrowful. Even though Jackson had said his parents didn't want him, he knew Chance had. If only his big brother could have shared in this joy, it would have made the day truly perfect. Felix resolved then and there:

he would excel in The Study of Dragons, determined to make Chance proud and honor their shared dreams.

As he made his way to the dining hall, he heard shouting between a fire student and a wind student. Before Felix could reach the scene, a boy's voice rang out, "I challenge you to a contest!"

In an instant, both House Amun and House Vulcan were teleported to the arena known as Gradus ad Victoriam: the Steps to Victory. There, Professors Pompeii and Zephyr led the cheering for their respective house representatives.

In the arena, Ryland Turner from House Amun and Bernard Andros from House Vulcan were locked in combat.

Felix continued to the dining hall, unsure of what had transpired. It was unusually empty compared to its usual bustling state. Anastasia and Marcus were already waiting for him.

"It will be a quiet lunch today," Marcus remarked, a note of relief in his voice.

Chapter 19

Heartbreak

Felix headed to his next class, Brew 100, with Professor Morgana Gills. He decided it was best for Len to stay in the dorm; he knew that if she were linked to him during the class, any mishap would result in a scolding, something he wished to avoid.

The class was located on the third story of the castle. Felix trudged through the dimly lit corridors, his footsteps echoing against the cold, stone walls. He reached an oblong, spiral staircase of worn, gray stone, its railing smooth and polished by countless hands that had ascended.

Upon reaching the third floor, he moved down a shadowy corridor where the white stone walls seemed to absorb rather than reflect light. The hallway was lined with sunken glass cases, each displaying eerie and macabre collections. Some cases held the skeletal remains of fantastical beasts, their bones arranged in grotesque poses, while others contained mysterious crystals and vials filled with dark powders and eerie, iridescent liquids of dubious origin. As Felix ventured deeper, the displays grew increasingly bizarre and unsettling, their contents hinting at the dark and arcane.

Felix opened a heavy, creaking door to a dimly lit room. The ceiling was draped with vials of glowing liquids in neon hues, their eerie light casting unsettling shadows that danced across the walls. The room was filled with a faint, pulsating glow that revealed only fleeting glimpses of its contents.

Once the class began, students gathered around a short woman who hummed cheerfully as she darted back and forth from different cupboards, grabbing various items.

"There we go!" Professor Gills exclaimed, pouring the final ingredient into the bubbling cauldron she had been working on before the students had even arrived in class. A light purple gas began to waft from it, filling the room with an aromatic mist. Without any warning, the entire class erupted into uncontrollable fits of laughter.

One student, nearly doubled over with mirth, managed to gasp, "Professor, what is this?"

Still chuckling, Professor Gills replied with a twinkle in her eye, "Aye, it's laughin' gas, of course! Just a wee potion to remind ye that the best part o' potion-making is the laughter that bubbles up when things go right."

As the door creaked open, the gas spilled into the hallway, causing nearby students to collapse in fits of laughter. Professor Gills, her laughter ringing like a mischievous cackle, pulled them into the room by their legs. "Looks like our potion's got a bit of a morbid twist—turns out laughter really is the best medicine, but it might be just a wee bit too potent! Who'd have thought a bit o' gas could have ye all laughin' so hard ye'd nearly forget to breathe? It's good to know that in the realm o' potion-making, we can always rely on humor to keep things... lifelessly entertainin'!"

Standing at just four and a half feet tall, Professor Gills

had a sturdy, compact build. Her auburn hair was a frizzy halo around her face, dotted with cheerful freckles. She wore a bright red romper under a black leather apron, long black rubber gloves, and knee-high boots reminiscent of those worn by fishermen.

After several moments, as the laughter subsided and the room regained its composure, she beamed at the students. "And that, me dear pupils, was yer introduction to Brew 100." She apologized to the students who had been affected outside the classroom and instructed them to inform their professors if they were late; she would handle any fallout. "Remember, potion-making isn't just about mixin' ingredients; it's about stirrin' up a bit o' fun along the way. Now, who's ready to dive into somethin' a wee bit less... gaseous?" she said with a hearty laugh and a wink.

The students then began researching various brews, trying to identify their contents based on the listed properties and the effects they caused. Felix worked methodically and completed the assignment before class ended. He decided not to submit it, fearing it might draw unwanted attention, especially since he knew nearly all the answers—thanks to Anastasia's readings and his own botanical knowledge. Meanwhile, the rest of the class struggled, collaborating to answer the questions.

With his homework completed, Felix folded it and tucked it into his pocket, returning to the book Professor Sainnodel had lent him. Meanwhile, Professor Gills reorganized her cupboard with what seemed to be obsessive precision. She then asked the students to choose between learning about vanishing acid or nocto elimitous (limitless night), and to tally their decisions on the board. Felix chose nocto elimitous, though most of the class opted for vanishing acid.

After class, Felix descended to the ground floor and took

his time admiring the stained-glass windows depicting various scenes. His final class of the day, Astrology 100, with Professor Hinata Botan Yamatai, was held in the Orrery Room, located in one of the tallest spires of the castle.

Felix opened the curved door and ascended the tower into a circular room. A petite woman in a kimono, her elaborate hairdo meticulously arranged, greeted him with a gentle bow and spoke in a hushed tone, "Welcome. I am Professor Yamatai."

Felix returned the bow and introduced himself quietly.

"Ah, Felix-san, let us begin your journey," she said, guiding him to a thick tatami mat. "Please lie down here," she continued, gesturing toward the U-shaped head cradle designed for stability. "This will help you remain comfortable and steady."

The room contained twenty students, all seemingly asleep. The scent of yuzu and agarwood filled the air. Professor Yamatai whispered to Felix, asking him to lie down.

She placed his bag beside him and placed three fingers on his forehead. Her eyes rolled back, revealing only the whites, as she spoke, "You are of the star Alnilam."

As she finished, her eyes rolled back into place, and she glanced at Felix with a lazy smirk. She then retrieved a four-pointed onyx star from an embroidered silk bag and pressed it against his forehead. Instructing him to close his eyes, she prepared him for a unique experience.

Once Felix complied, he felt a sensation of being anchored to the spot as his consciousness slingshot out of his body into the vastness of space. He was both confused and awestruck as he soared past planets and stars. He approached a massive blue light, and as his eyes adjusted to its blinding brilliance, he was enveloped in its radiant glow.

Felix's consciousness began to vibrate, and his eyes

rolled back in his head. Images of unfamiliar people and places flashed before him. One vivid scene featured a figure cloaked in black walking down a path, followed by a figure in red. Without warning, the red figure lunged forward, and the black figure vanished in a what seemed like inky whisps. The red figure continued to grow larger and larger until only he could see red.

A profound sense of dread and sadness overwhelmed Felix, echoing the heartbreak he had felt when he lost Chance.

As the other students awoke from their astral walks, Felix lay motionless on the mat, tears streaming down his face. His entire body felt like it was on fire, with sweat pouring from his pores. When he finally returned to his body, he grabbed his bag and fled, not stopping until he reached the unmarked bathroom. He slammed the door shut behind him, and tears mingled with snot as they streamed down his face. The intense heat made him feel like he was burning alive.

Desperate for relief, Felix stripped down to his underwear and turned on the cold water, soaking himself. The water did not ease this discomfort.

His thoughts raced back to Jackson's words about his parents rejecting him, adding to the turmoil of his current predicament. Overwhelmed by these emotions, Felix curled up on the cold, tiled floor, feeling as though he was being roasted alive from within.

Meanwhile, Len, lying on Felix's bed, was thrashing about and yipping in distress. Marcus, returning from his final class, noticed Len's condition. Unable to understand Len's yips, Marcus turned to Tom, who explained that Len was in this state because Felix was in danger.

Marcus carefully lifted Len off the bed, with Tom perched on his shoulder. As they hurried through the corridors,

Tom flew behind them. Panicked, Marcus hurriedly darted down one random corridor after another, desperately hoping one would lead him to Felix's location. Len's pain seemed to escalate as they got nearer to where Felix was located.

In the hallway near the library, Len fainted. Tom flew to an unmarked door and tapped it with his beak. From behind the door came the sound of wailing. Marcus noticed the door was jammed with a wedge. He used a water-weaving sign to seep water underneath the door and then froze it, pushing the wedge free.

Inside, Marcus saw Felix in a terrible state, soaked and steaming. Without hesitation, he gathered Felix in his arms, feeling the intense heat radiating from him. Though Marcus was tall and thin, better suited for reading than lifting, he tried to pick up Felix unsuccessfully.

Marcus turned on the sinks and used water-weaving to channel the water from the faucets to where Felix lay. As the water pooled, it formed a large block of ice. He instructed Tom to find Lady Stewart and take her to the infirmary.

Marcus placed Felix's belongings—and the unconscious Len—on the block of ice before pushing it out the door and down the corridor.

Some students, curious, watched the enormous block of ice being maneuvered through the hallways, though they had no idea who or what was on it.

Navigating a five-hundred-pound block of ice was challenging, but Marcus managed to reach the infirmary. His hands were numb from the cold, and he breathed warm air into them to restore feeling.

The nurse, Sybil Leeks, reacted immediately to the commotion. "Help me get him onto a bed," she instructed Marcus. Noticing Felix's fever, she asked if Marcus could cover him with snow or ice, as her Earth Weaver skills were ineffective in this situation.

Meanwhile, Tom flew to Lady Stewart's office, pecking on the door with his beak. When she opened it with a wave of her fingers, she was confronted by the squawking bird that flew straight to her desk. After a failed attempt at direct communication, Nikolay, Lady Stewart's Mirrored Soul a snow leopard, stepped in to translate. Upon hearing the news, Lady Stewart sprang from her chair, knocking it over, grabbed her bag, and hurried to the infirmary, her cape trailing behind her. Nikolay exhaled and resumed his nap.

Lady Stewart burst into the infirmary, her eyes scanning the scene. "Sybil, what transpired?" she asked.

"I'm not sure," Sybil replied. "I've tried everything to bring down his fever, but nothing seems to work. Even subzero temperatures aren't helping."

Marcus explained, "Miss Leeks had me use snow and ice, but there's nothing more I can do. Len was acting strangely, so I knew something was wrong. She led me to Felix, who I found in the bathroom, soaking wet and burning up."

"Marcus, pray tell, do you know where Felix was prior to this?" Lady Stewart inquired, seeking any clues.

"Yes, his last class was Astrology 100," Marcus replied.

Lady Stewart swiftly weaved two signs, conjuring two watery copies of Nikolay. One leopard headed to Professor Yamatai's classroom, and the other went to the headmaster's office.

Turning to Marcus, Lady Stewart said, "Thank you for your assistance; however, you are no longer required. I beseech you to convey to the Earth Weaver from the dining hall what has transpired, but do ensure that she remains in her place."

Marcus followed the instructions given to him. Professor

Yamatai and Headmaster O'Connor soon arrived at the infirmary.

Leeks, Professor Stewart, Professor Yamatai, and Headmaster O'Connor inspected Felix.

"Hinata, he was in yer class last. Can ye shed a bit o' light on the events leadin' up to this?" Headmaster O'Connor inquired.

Yamatai, speaking softly and with a bow, said, "He awoke from his astral walk and fled the room in distress. I am afraid I do not know more."

"Sybil, I trust ye've turned every cog and cranked every wheel in yer efforts to break this fever?" Headmaster O'Connor inquired.

"Yes, Headmaster. Everything," Sybil responded, her hands clasped on her chest.

"Well, if the clock hasn't ticked down on the physical causes, then it must be a matter of the mind. Sybil, would ye be so kind as to fetch the bottle of Dormien Mortem?"

Miss Leeks ran to the cabinet and retrieved the bottle, which was shaped like an eyeball—the glass was orange, and the stopper was black. She handed it to the headmaster, who squeezed two drops into his mouth. He swished the liquid around and then spat it out.

"Ah, yes, time hasn't been too kind, has it?"

He then tilted Felix's head back while holding his chin up. Grabbing the tube of the stopper, he pulled on it, lengthening it like taffy, and then fed it through Felix's nostril, squeezing more of the black liquid out.

Felix's body lay still, though his temperature was still rapidly rising.

Headmaster O'Connor let out a long, heavy sigh, as if the weight of hours had pressed upon him. "This isn't workin', Lady Rosalyn. We could use yer help."

Through an open window in the infirmary, a bolt of fire streaked in and exploded on the ground, revealing Lady Rosalyn.

She locked her eyes on Felix's limp body. "What be the matter?" she asked, her hands began to fidget.

"It seems there's somethin' out of sorts in his mind, like a gear in a clock that's slipped off its shaft, and it's causin' this fit," the headmaster explained, his brogue thick with concern.

Lady Stewart, unsure of what to do, found her silver pipe and began smoking it. Orange smoke mingled with the scents of tangerine, honey, and jasmine, calming her nerves.

Lady Rosalyn placed her fingertips on Felix's temples. Soon, confusing images began flooding in. She felt a profound dread and tormenting sadness from within Felix. Connected to his mind, she saw images of Chance and the red and black figures, playing on a loop and repeating endlessly.

Lady Rosalyn pulled away from Felix's thoughts, tears welling up as she continued to feel his pain and sadness. "It be his brother, along with two others I dinna know," she said, her voice trembling'. "I beheld a dreadful sight the night I went to fetch him—a lad named Chance lay dead in his lap. I'm not certain I can rid him of this memory; it's etched deep within him. It mayhap be better to lock it away, so it doesna keep comin' back."

"Rosalyn, do what you can, if you please," Lady Stewart urged.

Lady Rosalyn began weaving a complex series of gestures, and with a dramatic flourish, the snow and ice evaporated into the air. She spun gracefully, her movements a blur of shimmering light. As she twirled, runes emerged from her figure—each one striking a different part of Felix:

one on his forehead, one on each palm, and two more on the soles of his feet. Another rune landed on his stomach, and the final one hovered over his heart.

She chanted in an ancient tongue—Draconic—its resonance filling the room with an eerie, haunting melody. As her spinning grew faster and faster, the runes from his hands, feet, and stomach began to swirl around his heart in a mesmerizing dance. When Lady Rosalyn finally came to a halt, the runes converged on Felix's forehead, glowing with an intense, fiery red light.

The runes melted away, their essence traveling up Felix's nose and through his tear ducts, ears, and mouth. As they reached the core of the memory, Felix's eyes snapped open, glowing a fierce red before fading to their natural hue. A liquid barrier formed, encasing the memories of Chance and burying them deep within his mind. The entire process felt like it stretched on for hours, the tension palpable in the stillness that followed.

Sybil, feeling Felix's forehead after Rosalyn finished the sealing ritual, said, "His temperature has begun to recede."

Miss Leeks, Headmaster O'Connor, Professor Yamatai, and Lady Stewart all thanked Lady Rosalyn.

"No thanks be needed. Please, take care o' that lad! He's too young to be carryin' so much pain inside him. He needs all the care and affection he can get."

With that, a teary-eyed Rosalyn vanished into smoke.

Turning to Lady Stewart, Headmaster O'Connor said, "Dorothy, I trust ye can take it from here. Come now, Professor Yamatai, I reckon a spot o' tea is well deserved."

Both the headmaster and Professor Yamatai left the infirmary as Lady Stewart peered down at Felix, realizing that more needed to be done. She wove her hands together and dried him off before helping Sybil place him in a bed with clean, dry linens. She then tucked him in, with Len resting between his arm and torso. Lady Stewart then went to the Earth Weavers' house entrance to summon Anastasia, wanting to personally inform her that Felix was no longer in danger.

Anastasia latched onto Lady Stewart's torso and thanked her repeatedly.

Caught off guard, Lady Stewart didn't know how to respond, but eventually, she held Anastasia in her arms and stroked her head, saying, "Don't worry, he'll be fine."

After Anastasia apologized to Lady Stewart for her lack of self-control, she excused herself to return to the Earth Weaver's house.

Left alone, Lady Stewart shook her head, contemplating how these children might be the end of her. She mulled over Lady Rosalyn's comment that Felix would need all the care and affection he could get. Realizing she wasn't the nurturing type, she decided to let others take the lead.

Once back at House Mizu, Lady Stewart briefed Marcus on the situation, urging him to keep it confidential from the other Water Weavers. After congratulating him on his improved math score—acknowledging his recent quiz performance—she assigned him a new task.

"I require you and that young lady from House Terra to tend to Felix as if he were your own brother. Can you fulfill this charge?" she asked, her tone both serious and caring.

Marcus thanked her, noting that if not for Felix, he would be failing math, and he was happy to oblige. Lady Stewart left the room with a clearer understanding of Felix's situation.

The next morning, Anastasia and Marcus woke early to check on Felix, who was sluggishly getting dressed. Without hesitation, Anastasia leapt on Felix. "I was so frightened!

How are you feeling? How's Len doing, by the way?"

Felix looked down at her. "She's super tired. We should take her back to the dorms."

Anastasia continued, "Lady Stewart informed all your professors that you wouldn't be attending classes today. The only professor who sent work was Gills. All your other professors said you were ahead of the class. Professor Holimion said I could fill you in on anything you miss, even if I don't attend class." Anastasia's cheeks flushed red, and Marcus and Felix laughed.

"It's because you're a know-it-all," the boys said in unison.

"Well, someone has to be the smart one in this group of dummies," Anastasia replied.

Felix made his way to the dorms and gently laid Len down on his bed to recover. Still feeling unwell, he decided to skip class and instead visit Dennington to see Mrs. Simmons.

"Tell Mrs. Simmons I miss her," Anastasia said, her voice tinged with nostalgia. "And take it easy—try not to exert yourself too much. I'll see you when you get back, hopefully around lunchtime with the other students."

They hugged, their embrace holding a bittersweet sense of parting, and then went their separate ways. Marcus escorted Felix to the golden circle.

"Now, all you have to do is say the place you want to go, and it will take you there," Marcus explained.

Felix hugged Marcus tightly, gratitude evident in his eyes. "Barrell Hall," he said softly.

A brilliant light enveloped him. The light flashed and then vanished, leaving him standing before a familiar stone house.

Dressed in his blue robes, Felix stood in front of the great house, feeling a wave of warmth and relief wash over him. He took in the beloved sight, the very place where so many cherished memories had been made. He pushed open the red door and walked to the back of the home, where the familiar sounds and comforting smells wrapped around him like an old, cherished blanket.

Poking his head into the kitchen, he announced quietly, "Hello?"

Mrs. Simmons didn't notice him immediately.

"Good morning!" he called out, his voice rising with urgency after realizing he hadn't been noticed.

Miss Simmons, who was rolling out dough for pies— she was always baking—was startled when she saw Felix. The rolling pin in her left hand flew backward, breaking a windowpane as she rushed to him, wrapping her arms around him and crying with joy.

"Lindsey, I need to leave," she called out. "I'll be back later. Please finish the baking and have the window repaired."

She then released Felix, finished the rest of her glass of red wine, removed her apron, and took Felix's hand, heading to town. She asked why Anastasia wasn't with him. Felix tried to explain as best as he could, though his explanation was vague.

Spending a few hours catching up, they walked by the river. Felix told her about the teachers and the castle, showing her his gauntlet privately, fearful of her reaction. To his surprise, Mrs. Simmons simply admired it, saying she'd never seen anything like it and showing no further curiosity.

They stopped at a café Mrs. Simmons had invested in, where they had a turnover and a glass of lemonade. Felix was proud of her decision, as she had wanted to find a use for her extra income beyond buying wine.

A few hours later, he strolled to the schoolhouse alone, greeted Mr. Mitchem, and chatted briefly before heading back to Barrell Hall. Mrs. Simmons hugged and kissed him good-bye, thanked him for the visit, and asked him to bring Anastasia next time. She handed him a parcel filled with sweets for Anastasia, Marcus, and himself to share while reading together.

As the light from the circle overtook him, he waved good-bye.

Felix returned to the castle, feeling rejuvenated from his visit. With some time before lunch, he headed to the library to return the books he had finished. Thistle greeted him with a wave and a cheerful hello, her surprise evident when she noticed Len was not with him.

"Thistle, could you point me toward the section on Heaven's Gate?"

"Oh, do ye want the history, the architecture, or perhaps somethin' else entirely?"

Felix thought for a moment. "Everything, please."

Surprised, Thistle directed him to the second level. "It's all there in the first six sections on the right side of the ladder. Are ye sure ye want everything? That includes visits from heads of state, school policies, and even guidelines for choosin' qualified staff members."

Felix shrugged. "I might as well learn all of it. Thanks."

Before he could turn around, Thistle added, "Then that will include the next five sections after the ones I've already pointed out."

Felix ascended the spiral staircase to the second level, grabbing books without paying attention to their titles. He swiped his bracelet over each book before stuffing them into his bag. By the time he finished, he had packed a total of ninety-seven books.

Thistle remained silent as he cleared five full shelves. He left the library and slipped into the bathroom, barring entry for anyone else. Once inside, he created only two clones, stacking the books on every sink basin. Knowing this would be a multi-day task, he didn't want to overexert himself. After leaving the restroom, he hurried to the dorms.

Felix bounded down the halls with a spring in his step, despite feeling worn out and sore. As he closed the door to his room, he noticed Len was still asleep. Felix climbed onto his bed and curled up behind Len, cradling her in his arms.

Len woke up and asked, "What happened, Felix?"

Felix wasn't sure how to answer, so he simply said, "I don't know."

With her eyes still closed, her head lifted toward his. "I'm so tired. I'm going to take a nap now. I'm glad you're okay," she said softly before her head settled back onto the bed.

Felix softly stroked her head to the base of her tail, climbed off the bed, and covered her with the blanket that was folded at the end of the bed. He slipped out of the room unnoticed and made his way to the dining hall, carrying the book titled *The Lords of the Skies*.

In the dining hall, food arrived just as he opened the book. He grabbed some potato cakes with chunks of vegetables and munched on them as he read. The book engrossed him.

He had just finished his fourth cake when he suddenly found himself transported to a place he hadn't expected to be. It was a noisy arena filled with blue and red-robed students. Caught off guard with a fifth cake in his hand, Felix looked around, feeling as if he had been transported to another world.

Across the arena, Professor Pompeii's voice rang out with a grand flair, "Students, isn't this simply a magnificent sight? Brace yourselves, for our eyes are about to feast upon a spectacle of unparalleled drama! Now, Renna and

Nox, when this handkerchief graces the ground, the battle of your lives shall commence!"

Professor Pompeii's arm went up into the air, and he released the lace-hemmed cloth. Lady Stewart sat next to Felix, staring intently at the center of the pit. "I expect to see you in class on the morrow," she said, her gaze fixed firmly upon the arena. "This is your first contest. Were I in your position, I would be paying close attention."

As the fabric landed, Renna charged forward and wove a sign. Her fists burst into flames as she attempted to strike Nox. In response, he dodged the attack and wove a sign of his own.

Seconds later, it began to rain, soaking everything in the immediate area. Lady Stewart reached under her robes and retrieved a large umbrella. She opened it and shielded both herself and Felix.

In the pit, Renna's flames were in danger of being extinguished by the rain. Knowing this, she wove again, spreading the flames across her body. As the rain continued, steam began to build around her.

Nox kept his distance and began another weave, summoning a downpour that quickly began to fill the pit with water. He then wove a sign that enabled him to stand atop the rising tide, skillfully toying with Renna and keeping her from getting close enough to land a blow in the eight-foot-deep pit.

After several failed attempts to strike Nox, Renna became frustrated. With great speed, she wove another sign, plunging both hands into the water until it began to boil. She hoped this would make it harder for Nox to stay afloat and would remove some of the water that had collected, making it easier for her to move.

Nox watched her closely, assessing her responses and

trying to discern her patterns in response to his actions.

Soon, the pit was so full of steam that visibility was lost, fueling more cheers and chants. The excessive noise irritated Felix and Lady Stewart. Unable to focus, Felix closed his book and watched the match with greater intent.

Each time Renna intensified her attack, Nox countered with even more rain, never making an offensive move toward her. The rain continued to fill the pit, making it increasingly difficult for Renna to move as the water crept up inch by inch. When the boiling didn't have the desired effect, she created a vortex of fire around herself, hoping it would prove more effective.

Nox's face took on a devilish appearance as he wove another sign. His hands flickered through the air, turning the rain into sleet. As the two weaves clashed, the vortex of fire developed holes, removing some of the water from the pit but turning it into vapor. This vapor crystallized in the frigid air from Nox's new weave and fell back down, continuing to fill the pit with water.

Meanwhile, Nox remained smug.

An unimpressed with Renna's performance, Lady Stewart pulled out her pipe. "I trust you shall not take offense."

Felix didn't respond. The air was now cold with wisps of orange-colored vapor and sweet fragrances. Suddenly, the sleet began to pelt Renna.

As it struck her, she screamed in pain and yelled, "I'm going to kill you!"

Nox's devilish grin widened. The water was now cold and well past Renna's knees. Shivering, she decided to try warming it up. She wove another sign and placed her hands into the water again.

Nox had laid his trap, and she walked right into it. He wove a sign as quickly as he could and placed his hands on top of the water. As Renna's hands were mid-forearm deep, Nox's hands froze the water instantly, turning the entire pit into a solid block of ice. Renna was immobilized, unable to move her hands, fingers, or legs.

The Fire Weavers were outraged and booed, while everyone from House Mizu cheered and laughed.

But the fight wasn't over yet.

Lady Stewart applauded by tapping her knee as Nox walked over to Renna and sat down in front of her. From under his robes, he pulled out a pair of royal blue leather gloves and held them up.

Nox, being someone who never resorted to speaking as though he were of royal birth in front of his classmates, decided to forgo that courtesy. "Now, dear Renna, I shall impart a lesson that you ought to have assimilated long ago; yet, for reasons inexplicable, your failure to advance in the most fundamental aspects of human development has rendered you tragically stunted," Nox taunted, his voice dripping with disdain.

Red-faced with fury, Renna shot back, "Piss off."

Nox responded by slapping her across the face with his gloves, the sound echoing through the arena. "That's no way to address your better, you insolent fool."

Renna's eyes blazed with anger. "When I get out of this, you're going to pay for this," she spat, her voice trembling with fury.

Nox struck her again with the gloves, his expression unmoved. "To issue threats against me is an act of profound folly, my misguided vassal. Do you concede?" he demanded, his tone cold and uncompromising.

Fueled by spite and stubbornness, Renna refused to give in, even as the gloves continued to hit her with unrelenting force. Nox turned to the Water Weavers, his voice dripping with scorn. "I am wholly incapable of either vanquishing the folly that resides within her or eradicating the visage of unseemliness that mars her countenance!"

The Fire Weavers seethed with rage, their anger barely contained, while Professor Pompeii watched with a satisfied grin, pleased that Nox had used gloves instead of his bare hands, considering it a mark of true sportsmanship.

As Renna's anger thickened the air, Nox sighed theatrically and began weaving a new spell. Water poured from the pipes, flooding the pit. Soon, rats began to emerge from the deluge, their tiny, panicked squeaks filling the arena.

Renna's eyes widened in terror as the rats swarmed closer. Desperation edged her voice as she screamed, "I yield! I yield!"

Nox's laughter was cold and merciless. "Pray tell, was that truly so arduous?" he taunted, stepping closer with a triumphant smirk. "Perhaps on the next occasion, you might engage in a more judicious consideration of your thoughts."

As the water continued to rise, Nox reveled in Renna's defeat, while the Fire Weavers' fury reached a boiling point. The Water Weavers, however, cheered for their champion, their cheers blending with the satisfied applause of Professor Pompeii.

He left the pit, and the Water Weavers celebrated as they carried him back to the castle. Renna was left in the pit with the rats, and Nox refused to free her. The Fire Weavers had to melt the ice to release her.

As they walked back to the castle, Lady Stewart listened to Professor Pompeii retelling the battle with grand flourishes and heroics. Felix thought she did this to indulge him, as she would never spend time on such nonsense herself.

Marcus joined Felix at the back of the group as they entered the dining hall.

"Wasn't that hilarious, Felix?" Marcus couldn't stop chuckling.

Felix shrugged, thinking about how Renna had been humiliated and how Nox had toyed with her in a masterful display of misdirection. This fascinated Felix.

Anastasia soon joined the group and asked how the match had turned out. Marcus recounted the event in detail, sharing his thoughts and opinions along the way. Anastasia agreed with Marcus that Renna had been dreadful and deserved the humiliation.

"What sparked the match?" she asked.

Marcus explained, "Nox had caught Renna spitting into a younger girl's hair. As punishment, Nox wove a sign that sent the spit flying back into Renna's own face."

Marcus admired Nox greatly: he was outgoing, charismatic, dashing, and immensely popular. With his dark blond hair and hazel eyes that seemed to peer into one's soul, Nox had a captivating presence.

"He's so cool with everyone and never acts superior until now," Marcus confessed, his admiration evident.

The meal continued with everyone discussing their day. Felix shared Mrs. Simmons's invitation to visit and organized the distribution of the parcel among the group.

After the meal, Felix headed back to the dorms to check on Len. He found Tom keeping her company. Len was awake, well-rested, and had even finished her food.

Felix picked her up, placed her on his chest, and began reading. Then it occurred to him: why was Tom still in the room? In fact, he had never seen Tom outside of it.

Len, communicating telepathically, answered, "Tom

doesn't do well in large groups. It's a sort of phobia."

Felix asked Len to see if Tom would like to join them. Tom squawked and flew over to Felix's side. This was one of the rare times Felix read aloud, specifically to include Tom.

Marcus had a few things he had to finish before he could go back to the dorms to get some shut eye.

The following morning, Felix attended class as planned. The professors were surprised by his commitment, given the severity of his recent illness.

In Lady Stewart's class, she pulled Felix aside once again for a sparring session. Felix felt more confident than before, prompting Lady Stewart to push him even further.

Felix excelled in his dragon studies, impressing his professor daily with his extensive knowledge and dedication—often exceeding the requirements. This strong work ethic carried over into all his classes. Even in astrology, where there had been concerns about his mental stability, he remained focused and untroubled. It was evident that Lady Rosalyn's intervention was effectively restraining his troubling memories.

As weeks turned into months, Marcus, Anastasia, and Felix settled into their routines, becoming like siblings. Marcus took on the role of the protective older brother, Anastasia became the nurturing younger sister, and Felix was the baby of the group. Despite the care he received from the others, Felix remained vigilant about their well-being as well.

Since the suppression of his memories, Felix had stopped sleepwalking, ceased having nightmares, and no longer experienced troubling thoughts. His demeanor had improved significantly. Len was relieved by his newfound mental stability, although she was unaware of the specifics of what had transpired. Both Marcus and Anastasia also noticed a dramatic change in Felix's new carefree outlook.

As time passed, Lady Stewart became stricter and less sympathetic with her students, although she remained flexible with Felix, as Lady Rosalyn had requested. She increased the pressure on those she knew could manage it. Observing a change in Felix's demeanor, she decreed that he was not to be disturbed—a command most students followed, especially those under her supervision. The specter she had summoned to monitor Felix was still in use but much less frequently, as things had quieted down and Felix had become even reclusive due to his intense focus on his studies.

Chapter 20
A Spirited Farewell

Autumn arrived, drawing closer to Halloween back on Earth, yet Felix had yet to see a single piece of candy. This struck him as odd, since he had never encountered candy since arriving in Yurden—though he had enjoyed other desserts. The green leaves had transformed into a spectacular array of reds, yellows, and oranges, as if the forests were ablaze. The scent of spices filled the school, and the air had grown crisp. Just as with Christmas, Felix explained Halloween to Marcus and Anastasia, who both thought it was a fantastic idea. To Felix's surprise, Marcus revealed that Yurden had its own tradition linked to Halloween, known as Wraith's Eve.

As the crisp autumn morning unfolded, Marcus, Anastasia, and Felix gathered for breakfast in the dining hall, the conversation inevitably shifting towards the upcoming ritual. Marcus, with his customary air of scholarly authority, began to elucidate the details of the night's activities.

"Classes will be suspended for the next two days to allow

us to prepare for the summoning ritual," Marcus began. "Each of us will be provided with five candles and a pouch of soil sourced from a graveyard. The purpose of this ritual is to summon one of the restless spirits that linger in Yurden and we assist it in finding peace."

Anastasia, her curiosity piqued, inquired, "How exactly are we to carry out this ritual?"

Marcus took a moment to consider his response, ensuring clarity. "At precisely eight o'clock tonight, we will proceed to any part of the castle grounds. There, we will create a pentagram using the soil provided. Each point of the pentagram will be marked by placing and lighting one of the candles."

Anastasia's brow furrowed slightly as she raised a concern. "But what about the pixies? Won't they be out and about?"

Marcus nodded, anticipating her concern. "Pixies indeed will be out and about, but they are repelled by soil that originates from consecrated or hallowed ground. Therefore, the graveyard soil we're using should suffice to keep them at bay."

Still intrigued, Anastasia pressed further. "If the soil is effective in repelling unwanted entities, why don't we simply use hallowed soil around the castle permanently?"

Marcus adjusted his glasses thoughtfully before responding. "The effectiveness of hallowed soil diminishes after approximately twenty-four hours. Beyond that timeframe, it loses its potency and reverts to a mundane state. Hence, while it is useful for temporary applications, it's not practical for long-term use around the castle."

Anastasia fell silent, deep in thought.

Marcus continued, "The fear of being lured or trapped by the soil makes pixies avoid it like the plague. The souls that constitute the pixies are deeply corrupted and have an aversion to leaving this plane of existence. I hope that clarifies your concerns, Anastasia."

He fixed Anastasia with a pointed look, signaling that he intended to finish his explanation without further interruptions. "Each participant must recite the following chant as part of the summoning ritual:

'**Sorrow and sadness, sadness and sorrow—**
To each their own burden, no more to borrow.
I offer thee solace from grief's dark embrace,
Come forth with no malice, no shadow to trace.

From the veil of despair, rise into the light,
With compassion and warmth, banish the night.
In this sacred circle, where energies blend,
Find peace and completion, as old sorrows mend.

The whispers of darkness, the echoes of woe,
Are soothed by this beacon, let the lost spirit go.
With the light of these candles, both gentle and
bright,
Guide the restless to rest in the calm of the night.

May the soil of the graveyard, with hallowed intent,
Seal the bonds of the past, where lost souls are sent.
By the power of this ritual, let the barriers fall,
Embrace the release, as peace answers the call.'

As their conversation continued, a wave of information from his clones hit Felix. He braced himself on the table, only to have his face plunge into a bowl of cucumber, onions, and cherry tomatoes dressed with lemon-olive oil, salt, and pepper.

Anastasia and Marcus turned to Felix, thinking he was joking or simply bored with the conversation. Marcus lifted Felix's head out of the salad, revealing a piece of cucumber stuck to his forehead. Anastasia noticed that Felix's eyes had rolled back. Trying to stay discreet, they shook Felix to help him regain consciousness.

Anastasia peeled the cucumber from his forehead. "Are you all right? Do we need to take you to the infirmary?" she asked, her tone betraying her concern.

Felix was grateful that Lady Stewart had not noticed the incident, as she was absorbed in her meal.

Felix whispered to Anastasia to calm down, not wanting to draw attention to their group. "This happens to me from time to time. It's nothing to worry about."

Relieved Anastasia popped the piece of salad into her mouth nonchalantly.

"Marcus neglected to address the origin of the tradition established by Seer Menaphillea and her spouse, Lord Demetrius Trapani. The genesis of this practice is rooted in a profound personal tragedy. Menaphillea's siblings met a gruesome fate, their souls becoming ensnared at the location of their demise. Tormented by their restless spirits throughout her life, Menaphillea was driven to seek their liberation. In a bid to provide them solace, she utilized soil taken from their graves to affect their release."

Anastasia was taken aback, knowing Felix wasn't usually interested in history.

Marcus was equally surprised. "When did you find all that out?" he asked.

Felix shrugged. "It just hit me a moment ago."

"Are you telling us that information just comes to you out of nowhere?" Anastasia asked.

Felix shook his head. "I think it has to do with my gaunt-let." He knew this wasn't an honest answer but didn't want to make his friends feel left out.

"Well, Mr. Genius, do you have any more wisdom to be-stow upon us humble peasants?" Marcus asked with a grin.

"Probably not, unless you're interested in school rules and policies—things that are quite boring. Even I wish I didn't know them."

Changing the subject, Anastasia asked, "Do you want to meet up for the ritual and support each other?"

Felix nodded.

"I don't see why not," Marcus agreed.

As the day of the ritual gradually approached, the three spent most of their free time in the library, searching for any information that could assist them. In the days lead-ing up to the ritual, Felix and Anastasia visited Mrs. Sim-mons, spending time with her and sharing stories or any information she wanted to know. This visit allowed the pair to relax and feel at ease, even though they weren't asked, as they resumed doing chores around Barrel Hall, just as they had when they lived there. The time spent with Mrs. Simmons became cherished memories that the three of them would always treasure.

On the day of the ritual, after dinner, they all went to their dorms to change. Felix and Anastasia had received their magus hats: Marcus's hat's features were of a rat, Anastasia's a rabbit, and Felix's resembled a lizard.

As agreed, they met at the Crystal Sanctum. The three approached the door and knocked on the metal. The door creaked open and then closed behind them. Inside, the crys-tals glimmered like millions of stars in the night sky. Valerie, still in a state of hibernation since the branding ceremony, showed little sign of improvement.

They set up the ritual by placing soil into three inter-locking pentagrams, Anastasia had read that locking them together would make the summoning more reliable. Among the soil, there was a curious, tiny piece of soiled gold fabric that no one had noticed. Anastasia quickly wove a spell, causing fifteen clay candlesticks to rise. She then retrieved a Dragoni Respiratie Pepe (dragons breath pepper) from her bag, chewed it, and took a deep breath. When she exhaled, her mouth became a flamethrower, lighting each candle.

Marcus and Felix exchanged impressed glances and applauded her impressive trick.

"How did you do that?" Felix asked.

A bit prideful, Anastasia replied, "It just came to me. If you had taken Flora 100, you'd know."

Marcus's laughter echoed eerily as the three stepped into their pentagrams, their voices rising in a dark chant. The room quaked with an unsettling energy, but no spirits manifested. As the chant continued, the candle flames flick-ered to an unnatural blue, and the soil pentagrams blazed with a blinding white light. The crystals embedded in the walls pulsed rhythmically, amplifying the raw power they were conjuring.

Suddenly, two glistening gray eyes emerged from be-neath Felix's hat, their cold gleam matching the intensity of his gauntlet. The trembling ceased abruptly, the crystals dimmed, and a thick mist began to coil around them, shroud-ing the room in an ominous fog. Out of this mist, three spec-tral forms materialized, standing before each of them. The figures were draped in long, tattered robes that looked as if they had been worn for centuries. The once-white fabric, now a moldy gray, hung in ragged strips, its former elegance betrayed by the decay of time. The golden mosaic patterns were barely discernible, swallowed by grime and ruin.

As the spirits lifted their heads, Anastasia's breath caught in her throat. Their eyes were hollow voids, empty black sockets staring into nothingness. The three female spirits spoke in a chilling, unified whisper, their voices reverberating with otherworldly resonance. "Thou hast summoned us and loosed our chains. We weep not for our end, but souls in pains. Our duty calls us forth anew, to lead thee through the murk and dew. Dread not the quest, though shadows creep, for our loom lies in eternal sleep. Should it remain in disrepair, this realm shall fray and cease to fare. One among thee shall hold the flame, within thyself, the path to claim. Attend our words and take thy cue, the fate of all now rests with you."

Marcus and Anastasia exchanged frightened glances, but Felix stood unmoved as the spirits' gaze fixed upon him, their ethereal forms converging. "Thou, young one, must restore what once was whole. The gauntlet doth hold the key, so it is declared. This charge we lay upon thee, with trust unbroken."

The spirits shifted and merged into an even more grotesquely morbid figure. Her presence bathed the room in a haunting glow. With a swift, deliberate motion, she seized Felix's wrist, where the gauntlet glinted ominously. In a voice that was terrifying, she spoke an ancient incantation, each word profound and dripping with arcane resonance, a power that seemed to shake the very air. As her chant gradually waned, her form began to waver and dissolve, breaking apart into the three grotesque spirits from whence she had come. The room, now dimmed and shadowed, was left in eerie silence, the weight of her command lingering in the air.

"Thy task is thus decreed." The apparitions intoned as they receded into the mist. The pentagrams dissolved, leaving behind an eerie silence.

Anastasia and Marcus gazed at Felix, their faces etched with shock and disbelief.

Breaking the heavy silence, Anastasia spoke with a determined calm, "I'll clean up this mess." With a graceful flick of her fingers, she summoned the scattered soil and deftly returned it to the bags, which soon brimmed once more with the reclaimed earth.

"Wait, I recognize who they are," Marcus said.

Felix looked at him with eager curiosity, waiting for an explanation. Just then, a sharp pinch made him yelp. He glanced down and saw a spool of golden thread inside his gauntlet.

"Follow me," Marcus said. "I think I can solve this riddle."

Marcus led them to the library and dashed to the back of the room. He grabbed a large book from a stand, which was open to a random page, and found the chapter entitled "The Sisters of the Loom."

Marcus read aloud from the historical account: "These three sisters wield dominion over the fate of every being in Oblitus Regnum. Each was compelled to forsake vanity and desire. Their once-beautiful forms became disfigured and repellent, leaving only withered, mummified husks. Their eyes were removed to ensure they could not be perceived as lacking. Their existence was to be one of eternal seclusion, devoted to the care of the Loom of Divinity. However, they were slain in the same year that Lady Aurora was murdered, and the loom was consequently destroyed."

"If Felix has to find this place and fix it, that's insane," Anastasia exclaimed, outraged.

"Well, at least we know where the loom was," Marcus said.

She grasped his arm. "Where is that, Marcus?"

"It's in the Gorgon's Wood," Marcus skittishly answered.

"Felix, you can't go there!" Anastasia implored. "That's a death sentence. The Gorgons will turn you to stone. That's why it's called the Jardin Des Ames Perdues."

"Huh? What's that?" Felix asked, having never heard the term before.

"It means the Garden of Lost Souls. Hundreds of people have entered, and none have returned. So put that thought out of your mind."

Thistle had overheard what sounded like a disagreement and came to investigate. They assured her it was merely a healthy debate.

"Well, be that as it may, it's late, and you three need to finish your task. There's still the waltz," Thistle reminded them.

None of the three were eager to participate in the waltz, but Anastasia and Felix, having never seen it before, were curious.

They proceeded to the newly created teleportation circle outside the front of the castle, set up specifically for this tradition. The circle transported them to Yasma's Farewell, where the Necropolis of Asuma was located. The small town was nestled on the mountainside. Instead of traditional tombstones, a series of crypts were carved into the mountain, and pine trees had been planted in memory of each body entombed there.

The three trekked up the mountainside and settled under the branches of an ancient tree, watching from a distance.

At the heart of the gathering, a sinister black candle, sculpted like a scorpion's tail, cast a flickering, malevolent light across the students. They paired off—boys with girls, girls with girls, and boys with boys. Each student approached the scorpion candle, lighting their own from its dark flame. As the fire touched their candles, their robes transformed into elongated, ghostly gray versions of their former garments. Their hats twisted into eerie masks, and the girls' attire was completed with flowing veils. With candle in hand, they ventured into the encroaching darkness of the woods, spreading out like spectral phantoms.

From the depths of the crypts, ominous figures emerged, cloaked in black and bearing charred, ancient instruments. One figure raised a bow to the strings of an instrument, and an ethereal, haunting melody began to weave through the air. Other violins, violas, cellos, a harp, and a bass joined in a ghostly symphony, their mournful strains melding into a bewitching harmony. As the music swelled, the students, cloaked in shadow, glided in a haunting, synchronized dance beneath the moonlit canopy of the forest.

"Isn't it beautiful?" Anastasia said.

Marcus nodded without meaning to.

As the students danced, the pine trees released a shimmering vapor, and the candle flames burned with a green hue. Dusted in this vapor, the students rose into the air, continuing their dance without breaking step. The contracted spirits joined the students in their frivolity. Floating like spirits themselves, the students waltzed together until the last candle went out.

As the night came to an end, the students descended back to the ground. When they touched the earth, the conclusion was initiated, and the spirits crossed over, exploding into red sparks. These sparks twisted and spiraled like coiled vines, weaving their way toward Kalli.

Suddenly, Felix's gauntlet began to pain him, but he kept it to himself. The source of his discomfort was the spool, as a thread wound itself around his wrist.

Once all the students had landed, their clothing reverted to their normal attire.

The three then made their way back to the other students, hoping no one had noticed their absence from the festivities. As they entered the golden circle, they returned to Heaven's Gate. A somber mood enveloped the castle, and all the students went to bed, exhausted from the continuous dancing and the focus required for such an event.

Over the next month, Felix's pain became less manageable. Len remained baffled by the spool. Classes continued as usual, with students challenging each other as the contests intensified. Whenever they had the chance, Anastasia and Felix visited Mrs. Simmons on their days off.

Classes remained a source of enjoyment for the pair, approached with genuine enthusiasm rather than mere necessity. However, Lady Stewart continued to present a formidable challenge for Felix. The professors, impressed and often astonished by the pair's preparation and skill, acknowledged their efforts with approval. The duo consistently outshone their peers, leaving a mark of distinction that left some of the faculty quite flabbergasted.

As fall came to an end and the days grew colder, people began spending more time together indoors. Felix managed the self-imposed extra workload with ease. He had already read all the textbooks for his current classes and had moved on to those for courses he hadn't yet signed up for. He quickly absorbed every topic that interested him, making side notes and then delving into the library to read every book related to the subject. Recently, due to the constant pain in his arm, he focused on literature about the loom and the three sisters.

Chapter 21
The Gorgon's Wood

Winter had arrived, and the landscape was quiet and still. The vibrant flowers that once adorned the castle grounds had vanished, and the fiery trees that once stretched as far as the eye could see were now bare. The school continued its progression, with an increasing number and frequency of contests. The mood within the castle had shifted; restlessness was growing among the inhabitants.

As winter deepened, students were tasked with giving gifts to orphaned children, both local and many in Ozmare. Anastasia created a collection of bookmarks, crafting crystals of various colors into long, thin shards reminiscent of stained glass. Marcus drew images of animals, while Felix donated his collection of books from Kennedy House about a boy named Harry, hoping to bring joy to other children as he had experienced. The gifts were gathered and distributed by townspeople from nearby communities.

Winter break approached swiftly, and the children from outside the realm were given the choice to stay in Westshore—a picturesque city on the river to the south—or Tinker Town, a settlement located in the north near the mountains. Upon turning sixteen, they would have the option to travel to Earth. The locations in the Outer Realm were chosen for their cultural and historical significance, offering enriching experiences; however, the group did not spend any time learning about those locations.

A week before their departure for vacation, the three sat beneath the pavilion outside. Marcus informed Anastasia and Felix about both destinations. Anastasia preferred Westshore, drawn by its warmer climate and proximity to the sea. Felix claimed interest in Tinker Town to explore its machinery and gizmos, though his true motivation was to get closer to Gorgon's Wood.

Marcus cast the deciding vote. Despite his fondness for warmer weather, he chose Tinker Town, eager to observe and understand the mechanisms and inventions. He delighted in seeing how things functioned and were crafted.

Lady Stewart decided that since it was their winter break, she did not need to have Felix tailed.

When they departed for Tinker Town, they packed their bags of holding and left via a teleportation circle. Upon arriving at the town's gates, Felix winced as the spool on his wrist pulsed and pinched more painfully than usual.

"Is everything all right?" Marcus inquired.

"I think I stubbed my toe," Felix fibbed.

Mr. Nibs, disliking the cold, sought refuge under Anastasia's robes, while Len reveled in the snow, rolling about joyfully. Her coat had thickened, and the tips of her fur had turned shades of gray. Tom perched on Marcus's shoulder, his feathers puffed to trap a pocket of air.

"I think it would be best if Marcus gives us the general layout of the town," Anastasia suggested, handing him a piece of paper and a pencil.

Taking the paper and pencil, Marcus began to sketch out the locations they had discussed. After a few mins of sketching, "I believe that covers all the key places. If there's anything else, let me know," he handed the paper back to her.

They were to stay in a large inn in the village. On their first day, they explored local shops and marveled at the sights. They encountered a realistic merry-go-round with spinning automatons, which fascinated Marcus especially. He had spent countless hours imagining the inner workings of such mechanisms that had to be inside.

The food was hearty and comforting, with warm stews and soups prevalent during the winter months. Despite the quiet season, the town exuded charm. On a whim, they joined some students from Heaven's Gate who were mingling with locals, building snow forts, and engaging in snowball fights. Anastasia, surprisingly accurate with her throws, even managed to hit a few children in the face.

Len was the only one among the mirrored souls who wanted to continue playing in the snow, helping younger children dig tunnels, while Mr. Nibs and Tom kept each other company inside the inn.

The following day, Marcus visited the esteemed inventor Dr. C. Caceres. He had made a habit of visiting the doctor during each stay in Tinker Town, and they had become friends, collaborating on various inventions and projects.

Anastasia decided to explore the mines to the north of town, hoping they hadn't been frozen over. She aimed to unearth gems and minerals she had read about and to gain practical knowledge ahead of her class.

Felix wandered into the shops filled with strange trinkets and devices he had never seen before and discovered a pair of spectacles designed for viewing the sky, particularly for glancing up at Mater. He pondered their potential uses for a moment before deciding to buy them along with a knife that had a grooved green handle, among other items. As he bent the frames to adjust their direction toward the ground, the store clerk looked on in confusion. He thanked the clerk and swiftly moved on.

He picked up a set of small tools he thought Anastasia might enjoy and a book on theoretical flying machines that he believed Marcus would appreciate. Felix also purchased two loaves of bread from a bakery: one was an olive loaf with chunks of onion, and the other was a dessert loaf with berries and a glaze.

After dinner, the group gathered by the fireplace in the lobby, spending the evening together before bedtime. Len, aware of Felix's secretive mission, felt uneasy about the task he was about to undertake. She sympathized with his struggles and wished for his ordeal with the spool to come to a swift end.

Felix reassured her of his determination to complete his task. "Len, I know you would only hinder me if you came along. But I need you to remain linked to me at all times, so you can inform the others if anything happens."

Felix then wrote a letter addressed to Marcus and Anastasia, apologizing for the deception regarding his choice of Tinker Town. He explained that revealing the true reason would have led them to stopping him from pursuing his goal, which was crucial for relieving him of his pain—something he had surprisingly kept hidden from them.

He slipped out of the room while Marcus was asleep. The journey to the woods would take two days on foot, but since the woods were downhill from the town, Felix planned to use a well-traveled road shown on the map that passed near Gorgon's Wood. Once outside of the town gates he started putting his plan into action. Instead of walking, he performed an intricate weave with his fingers and hands. As the weave completed, the snow compacted beneath his boots, transforming them into skis. He let gravity pull him down the hill.

At first, Felix coasted steadily, but as the slope plunged into a steep descent, he was soon racing downhill at a breakneck pace. The distance to Gorgon's Wood stretched over forty miles, yet he was confident there would be a road marker signaling its entrance. The wind howled like a furious beast, slashing against his face as he hurtled down the mountainside.

Tinker Town, perched high on the mountain's base, seemed like a distant memory as Gorgon's Wood loomed far below. The road, a treacherous jumble of bumps and craters, threw Felix into the air with each violent jolt. Each bounce sent shockwaves of adrenaline through him, transforming the descent into a thrilling, nerve-wracking ordeal. His robes flapped wildly behind him, a chaotic blur of fabric in the gale.

"Can you feel that?" he asked as his skis touched down.

"I'd prefer to keep all four paws on the ground, but if you enjoy the sensation of flight, go ahead—just don't hurt yourself before reaching the wood," Len replied.

Slicing through the air at speeds surpassing fifty miles per hour, Felix battled against time itself. The ground raced by in a dizzying blur, and as his heart pounded in his chest, the road marker suddenly emerged through the swirling snowflakes.

With no way to slow down or stop, Felix pointed his skis to collide with a mound of fluffy snow, the impact sending a cascade of powder flying into the air. He was thrown from his feet, tumbling through the snow before coming to a jarring halt. Dazed, he pulled himself out of the frosty crater he had created, his heart still racing. As he brushed the snow from his robes, he took in the extent of the damage—a gaping, uneven hole stretching far beyond the mound's center.

"Ugh!" he groaned.

"Well, that's one way to stop, I suppose. Didn't I say to be careful?" Len chided.

"I'm fine; the wind just got knocked out of me, but nothing serious. I've made it to the entrance of the wood."

"Felix, please be careful!" Len's voice trembled with urgent worry. "You know how I worry! You're aware of what happens if one of those creatures makes eye contact with you! Please, don't take any risks!"

"I know, Len. I'll be as cautious as I can."

At the marker, Felix saw a statue of a crying woman holding her child, with a warning at its base: "Death to whoever enters these woods." He examined the statue under the night sky, then proceeded with extreme caution towards the tree line, trudging through the snow. Once he ensured there was no immediate movement, he put on his new spectacles and entered, noting that the snow cover in the woods was much lighter than outside.

Without a clear plan, he scampered to the first tree and peered around it, ensuring the area was clear before moving to the next tree. This pattern of stopping, checking, and moving continued as he advanced.

The unsettling silence deepened the eerie emptiness of the woods. As Felix trudged forward, his breath visible in the cold air, he soon encountered the first statue: a grotesque stone figure of a man, forever frozen in a contorted expression of abject terror. The eyes, hollow and unseeing, seemed to follow him as he moved. With every step, the sight of another petrified figure came into view—each one more horrifying than the last. The woods became a macabre gallery, filled with an increasing number of statues: people and creatures alike, their forms twisted and frozen in their final moments of anguish. The sight was chilling, a haunting reminder of the terrible fate that awaited those who ventured inside.

"Felix, that place is dreadful! How could you possibly convince me to let you go?" Len's voice quivered, her eyes wide with fear.

"You can worry all you want," Felix said tersely, his voice edged with urgency. "But please, don't distract me. I need to stay focused."

"I'm serious, Felix! You have no idea what those creatures are capable of. If something happens to you..."

Felix's face was set in grim determination, though he felt a shiver of unease. "I appreciate your concern, but I can't afford any distractions. I've still got nearly three miles to cover, and every second counts."

With that, Felix forced himself to press on, his mind racing. Knowing the Gorgons' long, sharp claws would be a serious threat, he summoned a clone to scout ahead, its presence a small but crucial reassurance in his adventure.

Felix broke off a piece of olive loaf, chewing thoughtfully while he watched his clone advance cautiously through the treacherous landscape. The terrain before him was like a battleground littered with the remnants of past conflicts. Felix could hear himself chewing the bread in the eerie silence, heightening his sense of unease. He planned to act only when it was undeniably safe, hoping that the harsh winter might have driven the Gorgons into hiding.

As he ventured deeper into the wood, Felix felt a profound sadness settling over him—a heavy, chilling weight that was hard to separate from the cold that permeated the air.

He maneuvered through the forest with careful precision, darting from one tree to another in a desperate bid for cover. The woods around him felt like a war zone, every shadow hiding a potentially deadly threat. His heart pounded as he kept his eyes on the clone's progress through the dense undergrowth.

Suddenly, a dark shape lunged from the left, and Felix's breath caught in his throat. A swift, brutal strike severed the clone's arm, the limb shattering upon impact with the ground. The clone, undeterred, quickly regenerated its lost appendage and assumed a defensive stance.

Felix's pulse raced as he thought "Is that what I think it is?" His gaze was steely with determination, bracing himself for the imminent confrontation that awaited him in the heart of the wood.

He could almost hear Len's urgent voice in his head, *Stay alert!* The shadow emerging from the darkness was unmistakably a Gorgon. Its serpentine body coiled menacingly, golden eyes gleaming like molten metal in the darkness. Its hair, a writhing mass of glowing, scaled snakes, swayed rhythmically as though dancing in an unseen current.

Felix knew he had to strike from a distance to avoid detection. As the Gorgon advanced on his clone, Felix closed his eyes, his senses merging with those of the clone. A menacing hiss pierced the silence. Felix willed one of the clone's arms to transform into a razor-sharp ice blade and ordered it to strike.

The Gorgon's reflexes were lightning-fast. It twisted away, narrowly evading the blade. Felix's heart pounded as he pressed the attack, but he knew he couldn't sustain this for long. The noise and chaos would draw more Gorgons, increasing the danger exponentially.

In a desperate bid to control the situation, Felix withdrew his first clone, ensuring that the Gorgon's attention remained away from his own position. He swiftly conjured a second clone, its arms now sharpened into lethal ice blades, and sent it creeping silently toward the fray.

The first clone engaged the Gorgon, drawing the creature closer. Felix's heart raced as he commanded the clone to seize the Gorgon in a bear hug, holding it in place. The Gorgon lunged, intent on attacking, but found itself ensnared. Its serpentine hair lashed out, snapping and hissing, freezing to the clone's scalp as the clone completely hardened into ice. The feet of the clone seeped into the frozen ground, making it unable to be moved.

The Gorgon, trapped and writhing in the frozen embrace of the clone, was vulnerable, but Felix's second clone was already charging from behind, ready to exploit the moment. The tension in the air was palpable as the battle unfolded, each movement a deadly dance of strategy and survival.

The Gorgon, a monstrous figure, thrashed against the icy grip that held it captive. Its serpentine body writhed and contorted, but the first clone, a cold, emotionless replica of Felix, held firm. With a sickening crunch of ice, the second clone lunged forward, its blades glinting in the dim light. It drove the blades deep into the Gorgon's chest, a grotesque sound echoing through the frigid air. The Gorgon's blood, a thick, dark liquid, splattered across the ice, staining it a sinister crimson. Its body slumped forward, a lifeless heap.

Felix, his eyes cold and calculating, watched the scene unfold. To ensure the creature was truly dead, he issued a final command. The second clone, with a chilling efficiency, raised its blade and delivered a final blow to the Gorgon's neck. The head fell to the ground and rolled to a stop, its vacant eyes staring up at the sky. A chilling silence fell over the scene, broken only by the soft drip of blood onto the frozen ground.

"That was a masterstroke of cunning, no doubt, but don't let your guard down. Danger lurks in every shadow!" Len congratulated him.

Felix's lips curled into a defiant smirk. "You underestimate me at your own peril. I might be young, but my mind is sharp—sharper than you give me credit for."

Len's voice was laced with skepticism, the weight of his words heavy with unspoken fears. "You're still just a child. It's only natural to question your abilities. Even the bravest of souls falter."

Felix's gaze hardened, a fire igniting in his eyes. "I'm on the cusp of ten. My resolve is stronger than you think. But fine, if doubt is what fuels your vigilance, then I'll accept it. For now."

The Gorgon's blood, a thick, viscous liquid, reeked of rotten eggs, filling the air with a nauseating stench. Felix, his face contorted in disgust, cautiously approached the corpse, rummaging through his bag. He pulled out a sleek, black ink pen, one Marcus had used for sketching. After several dry heaves from the overpowering odor, he stepped closer to the creature.

With a quick, practiced motion, he scooped out the Gorgon's eyes, their milky orbs glistening with a sinister light. Using the green handled knife he bought, he carefully removed each snake head from the creature's head, the scales slithering and hissing as they came free. Felix had read that Gorgon eyes, when baked in volcanic dust, turned into powerful stones used for fortune-telling. These gems were highly sought after, their value could make a banker blush.

The poison from the snake venom glands was used in a brew to cure blindness—and it came with an immense price tag. Once everything was collected and sorted, Felix was off again, with the clones leading the way.

"Can you please let me know when you're about to do something gross? I'd like to disconnect from witnessing that experience," Len said.

"Deal," Felix said.

The woods were dark, with patches of light breaking through the eerie canopy. After a while, a path came into view, and the ground gave way to a stone-laid road covered in snow, along with even more unfortunate souls who had been caught off guard.

As the clones approached the walkway, two more shadows emerged. Felix watched from behind the trunk of a large pine. Trying to make no sound, he moved into the greenery, instructing the clone to keep them distracted.

Felix, hidden among the low-hanging branches, climbed the pine. His gloved hands could still feel the ridges of the tree's bark. Once he reached a vantage point high above the ground, he peered out, his breath misting in the frigid air. Securing himself with his legs, he freed his arms. He then removed his gloves, rubbing them together and blowing warm air onto them before he began to weave a series of intricate commands. Through the spectacles, he watched as the snow on the ground began to stir, clustering into jagged, menacing spikes.

The Gorgons' hisses, a chilling symphony of malice, filled the air as they slithered over the sharpened ground. Though the spikes inflicted pain, it was not enough to deter the creatures.

"I'd disconnect if I were you!" Felix warned.

With a graceful yet menacing flick of his wrists, Felix's

fingers danced through the air, conducting a symphony of destruction. The jagged snow around him shuddered and groaned, responding to his silent command. In an instant, the frozen shards elongated, transforming into six-foot-long spikes of glittering ice. They rose from the ground with a sound like shattering glass, surrounding the Gorgons and the clones in a deadly cage of crystalline pikes.

The air grew thick with tension as the icy prison tightened, corralling its victims into an ever-shrinking space. Felix's water clones, perfect liquid copies of himself, moved with inhuman fluidity. They slithered through a narrow gaps in the icy barrier, their forms rippling and reforming as they escaped the trap meant for their pursuers.

Time seemed to slow as Felix's eyes narrowed, a cold fury burning within them. With a twist of his hands, as if crushing an invisible throat, he commanded the spikes to turn inward. The ice responded with brutal efficiency, lengthening once more with a sound like tearing flesh.

The Gorgons' eyes widened in horror as the frozen lances pierced their scaly hides. Razor-sharp tips burst through their chests in a spray of dark, viscous blood. The crimson liquid steamed as it hit the snow, melting small craters in the white expanse.

Their blood-curdling screams tore through the silent forest, a haunting requiem that echoed off the trees and reverberated through thick chilly air. The agonized wails spoke of pain, of rage, and of the terrifying realization of their own mortality.

Felix sat motionless, his face an expressionless mask as he watched the last vestiges of life drain from his enemies. The forest fell silent once more, save for the soft patter of blood dripping onto freshly fallen snow, painting a gruesome masterpiece.

Not one to let anything go to waste, Felix had the clones retrieve their heads and bring them to him under the branches of the pine. After carving out their eyes and lopping off their snakeheads, he sent the clones to scout ahead once more.

Felix knew he had wasted too much time, and morning would arrive in the next couple of hours. He needed to complete this task before the rays of Mater shone on the woods.

As the clones made their way down the path, Felix hid behind the columns that once lit the way, leaving him exposed. But the glasses had been effective so far. He encountered a few more Gorgons; this time, he didn't stop to remove their eyes and snakeheads—he just put them in his bag of holding.

He continued his approach to his destination when his foot hit a patch of ice. Felix skidded to a stop at the edge of the gap between the crumbling pillar and the decaying stone wall, his breath coming in ragged gasps. A chilling hissing cut through the air, making his skin crawl. Through his special spectacles, he saw them—Gorgons advancing from the rear with a murderous drive, their serpentine eyes gleaming with malevolence.

He didn't waste a moment. With his heart hammering in his chest, Felix sprinted up the ancient stairs, his feet pounding against the weathered steps. Fallen trees and stone blocks acted as if to bar his way. He barely avoided a painful tumble, his focus solely on the overgrown courtyard ahead, its twisted vegetation and crumbling buildings a maze of peril.

As Felix darted through the wreckage, the snap of a brittle branch underfoot sent shadows swarming around him. Panic surged as the Gorgons' hisses grew louder, their presence a creeping terror. In his frenzied zigzag escape, Felix's foot caught on a gnarled root, sending him sprawling face-first into the snow and dirt. The ground slammed into him, the impact forcing the breath from his lungs. Shards of glass from his now broken spectacles embedded into his brow, blood oozing and trickling down his face.

Before he could fully recover, his water clone appeared, a spectral figure of shimmering liquid. It yanked him upright just as one of the Gorgons lunged, its clawed hand slicing through the clone's form with a sickening splatter of water and mist. The Gorgon's talon-like claws, severed an arm from the clone, leaving a splattered trail of liquid.

Felix and the clone continued to hurry, though Felix's limp slowed them down. Blood now oozed onto Felix's eyelids, making it hard for him to see. They made it to the keep and slammed the door shut behind them while the second clone fought off the other Gorgons, trying to keep them at bay.

The locking mechanism was broken, so there was no way to secure the door. They braced their bodies against it, struggling to keep it closed as dozens of Gorgons outside pressed against it. The door groaned in protest as it creaked open just a fraction, before slamming shut with a thunderous crash. The relentless force of the Gorgons' assault pressed against it, the sheer weight of their serpentine bodies straining the ancient wood. Felix and the clone braced their backs and legs against the door, their muscles screaming with exertion. The violent shudder of the door under the Gorgons' assault was nearly overpowering, but their desperate efforts gained them a fragile advantage.

Inside the keep, the rotted wood was a flimsy barrier. The Gorgons' razor-sharp nails punctured through with malicious ease, their claws slicing at Felix and the clone with chilling precision. Each scratch was a brutal reminder of their proximity to death, the claws carving bloody streaks across the splintered wood.

With urgency etched on his face, Felix's fingers began to weave wildly as he shouted instructions to his clone still outside the keep. The clone responded with eerie precision, gaining mass through Felix's new weave. It positioned itself squarely in the middle of the doors, engulfing some of the Gorgons in its body. Felix's fingers moved in a frantic dance, tracing intricate arcane patterns in the air. As he completed the weave, the clone's form solidified into a block of ice, its crystalline structure sealing the gap with a hiss of crackling energy. The ice bonded immediately with the door and the deep grooves in the floor, forming a shimmering barrier adorned with writhing Gorgons attached to it. The now-locked door held firm against the encroaching horrors.

The lower structure was surprisingly intact, though the doors were in a state of decay. Felix knew he had to reach the top. As he ascended the stairs, the spool on his wrist pulsed with a relentless intensity, momentarily incapacitating him. He staggered upward, each step a struggle, until he reached the fifth floor. There, half of the south wall was missing, leaving him vulnerable to the stormy elements outside.

Looking down, Felix saw the Gorgons gathering at the base of the keep, their grotesque forms pressing against the doors and weakened walls. The vibrations from their assault caused loose blocks of stone overhead to tumble, narrowly missing Felix. One massive stone crashed near him, creating a gaping hole. Felix unable to avoid the newly formed crater fell through it, falling toward the fourth floor. In a desperate move, he seized an iron brazier, its cold metal biting into his palms, and barely managed to prevent himself from plummeting to the fourth floor.

Blood obscured his vision as he tried to see where the

ledge ended. Through the crimson haze, he spotted what seemed to be a pile of moldy straw. Swinging toward it, he hoped it was stable. Miraculously, it turned out to be solid ground. Had he not caught himself. He would have snapped the bones in both his legs, as the distance between each level was about fifteen feet. Wiping the blood from his brow to see better, Felix scrambled back to his feet and made his way to the fifth floor.

As he approached a pile of splintered, warped, and charred wood, a searing pain radiated from his forearm, as if something was trying to burst through his skin. He pushed up his sleeve and rubbed his arm, desperate for relief. To his astonishment, he knocked the spool free. It gleamed with a brilliant luster, and the thread began to unravel. One thread, then two, three, four, five, into hundreds—an endless cascade of threads burst forth, wrapping around the tattered wood and repairing it.

The wood floated upward, rearranging itself into its original form—a loom wrapped in threads like a mummy. The threads wove the loom back to its former glory. Once restored, the spool threaded it with astonishing speed before vanishing into the ether. From the newly resurrected loom, threads surged upward from the top of the keep, spreading out rapidly.

Below, the relentless assault of the Gorgons finally breached the door, causing it to collapse. The creatures poured into the keep, making their way toward the stairs with terrifying speed.

But the threads moved faster. They shot out like lightning, ensnaring the Gorgons and wrapping them in tight, shimmering cocoons. Three of the ensnared Gorgons were lifted upward into the keep. The cocooned creatures squirmed within their prisons as the loom continued its weaving. The sacs glowed a brilliant yellow before unraveling to reveal three exact replicas of the spirits who had originally tasked Felix back at the castle. This time, their old, tattered clothing was replaced with pure white robes adorned with intricate blue and gold mosaic embroidery.

The three once-spectral figures faced Felix with their hollow eye sockets and bowed in solemn reverence. They set to work on the loom, their voices blending into a haunting melody as they drew back the large beater. Felix peered over the edge of the floor's gaping hole and saw what resembled giant butterfly cocoons. The Gorgons, once thrashing violently, had fallen still.

A deep rumble shook the ground as threads streamed from the loom, wrapping around massive chunks of rock and rubble. The threads lifted and reassembled the debris like pieces of a colossal puzzle, filling in the gaps with the precision of an embroidery artist. The keep, once decayed and broken, was being restored to its former grandeur.

Countless golden threads burst forth from the keep doors, enveloping the zombified figures once more. As the threads unraveled, the figures transformed into shining knights clad in armor that gleamed like mirrors, their flesh restored. The transformation was complete, the keep was an epicenter of what was occurring.

The three ladies spoke in unison, their voices echoing through the chamber with a chilling urgency: "We thank thee, worthy knight of steadfast will, for slaying dread and clearing paths ahead; thy valor's song shall echo, strong and still, a testament to all the risks thou'lt tread. So let us raise our voices high in cheer to thee, dear Felix, our champion here! You must go. Go now!"

Felix's heart pounded as he sprinted down the stairs, his legs moving with desperate speed. The ancient doors flew open before him, and he burst into the courtyard. Behind him, the loom's threads continued their relentless work, weaving a tapestry of restoration. The once-decrepit walls mended themselves as if by sorcery, and the overgrowth in the courtyard vanished, replaced by pristine evergreen gardens. What had been a forsaken ruin now stood as a freshly constructed marvel, the grandeur of its restored state gleaming under Kalli's light.

This was not the only change Felix had triggered. Unbeknownst to him, he had also lit a spire to the south. As he exited the keep, knights surrounded him, forming a circle ready to lead him out of the woods.

Once the restoration was complete, the threads disappeared, but the three women continued to weave on the loom. As their song rang out, the Loom of Divinity's threads reached up into the sky and disappeared. Although Felix could no longer see the golden threads, he glimpsed a faint glitter, suggesting they were still there, hidden from view.

The sky brightened, and the landscape became clearer as Felix and his escort made their way down the stone road. The once-toppled pillars now stood upright, shiny as if newly waxed, and lanterns lit the shaded pathway, guiding the group. A few Gorgons that hadn't converged on the keep approached them, but when they glared into the knights' shining armor, they turned to stone.

Felix noticed that the stone statues in the woods were now gone. He wondered where they had gone and lamented the fact that the Gorgons had turned to stone, wishing he could have collected more eyes and snakeheads.

Before moving on, the lead knight drew his sword, ablaze with radiant light, and struck a Gorgon statue. The blade sliced through the stone, pulverizing it into a cloud of quartz-like dust that drifted away like mist.

After an hour or so, they reached the edge of the woods. The formation of knights opened, and Felix stepped out. He walked back past the statue of mother and child, then turned around as the knights returned to the Loom of Divinity.

Now the challenging part lay ahead: Felix had to walk up-hill for over forty miles, a slow and arduous trek, as Mater began to brightened the sky. Tired and hungry, Felix rummaged through his bag and found a piece of berry loaf. With the daylight improving just enough to see the road, he pressed onward.

Back in Tinker Town, Marcus woke to find a bed that hadn't been slept in. Scanning the area, he discovered the note Felix had left for them. He quickly put on some clothes and rushed to Anastasia's room. Marcus pounded on the door until a sleepy-eyed girl answered.

"Marcus, what's the matter?" she asked drowsily.

"He went to the Wood!" Marcus's voice trembled with terror.

Anastasia gasped, "He did what?"

"We have no time to waste. Get dressed. We're going to see Dr. Caceres."

Anastasia hurriedly dressed in warm clothing, and they raced across town to the doctor's house. They knocked frantically on the door until they heard from behind it, "Are you in need of something?"

"Dr. Caceres, we need your help," Marcus pleaded.

"What, pray tell, is the matter?" Dr. Caceres asked as he slowly opened the door.

"Our friend Felix went to the Gorgons' Wood last night," Anastasia said, frightened.

"Let me get the horse hitched to the sleigh. Let's just hope he stayed on the road. There are things far worse than Gorgons that prowl the snow at night."

Marcus helped Dr. Caceres hook up the sleigh, and they were off. The automaton horse, powered by a small boiler, trotted steadily. The two men sat in the front, with Anastasia in the back.

"Search under your bench. There should be a blanket there to keep warm," the doctor told her.

Dr. Caceres explained that he could only have made it halfway there, as it was a great distance to walk in the dark and the snow. This did little to ease their anxiety.

After two hours, a figure appeared on the road, approaching them.

Marcus squinted. "It can't be."

"What is it?" Dr. Caceres asked.

"It's Felix, but he's headed this way." Marcus stood and shouted, "Felix!"

The doctor slowed the sleigh as they approached, and the pair jumped off before it could come to a complete stop.

"Are you out of your mind? Do you have any idea what could have happened to you if you had ventured into those woods? Marcus's voice thundered with a mixture of fury and relief. He grabbed Felix by the shoulders, his grip tight and unyielding. "Thank the gods you came to your senses before it was too late!"

Anastasia, her face streaked with tears, threw her arms around Felix in a desperate, trembling embrace. Her sobs were choked with fear and anguish as she clung to him, her relief palpable.

Felix looked at Marcus, his voice barely a whisper. "But I did go in."

Marcus's eyes widened in disbelief. "What? You actually went in? Then that explains the bleeding?"

Anastasia's voice rose to a frantic shriek. "What do you mean, bleeding? Let me see!" She tore through her bag with frantic urgency, pulling out a handkerchief and dabbing at the blood with trembling hands, her eyes filled with a mix of anger and concern.

"Let's go back to town. I'll explain on the way," Felix said softly.

They climbed back into the sleigh, and Marcus introduced Felix to the doctor.

"So you're the famous Mr. Grey I've heard so much about," Dr. Caceres said.

Felix shrugged, "Nice to meet you too," he said softly.

Unable to turn the sleigh around at their current location, Dr. Caceres said, "We need to reach a point where the road widens so I can turn the sleigh around."

"One moment." Before anyone could react, Felix stood, closed his eyes, and moved his hands in a sweeping motion. The snow beneath them turned to a disk of ice and rotated 180 degrees, pointing them back toward town.

Dr. Caceres was astonished by Felix's ingenuity. "Well, aren't we full of surprises, young man?"

"We're going to miss breakfast at the inn," Marcus pointed out as his stomach rumbled.

Felix nodded in agreement and pulled out the remaining loaves from his bag.

"Well, he was more prepared than we were," the doctor said with a chuckle.

As they ate, Felix explained what had transpired. Anastasia squeezed Felix's hand as he detailed his encounters with the Gorgons, though he omitted the specifics about the snakeheads and eye harvesting. Marcus was impressed, and the doctor was intrigued.

When they reached the gates to Tinker Town, they found the entire town had gathered. As they pulled up, they could hear why. Off in the distance, a bright spire was lit up like a beacon.

"Dragoons' Septum is lit," Dr. Caceres said, staring in awe.

Marcus, Anastasia, and Felix had only encountered the subject vaguely through dusty old texts and fragmented passages in their books.

Marcus turned to the doctor. "What does it mean?"

Dr. Caceres replied, "When the crystal spire is lit, it means the throne is ready to be ascended."

As he finished speaking, a fast-moving shadow passed overhead.

Marcus shook his head in irritation when he realized what had cast the shadow. Felix and Anastasia stared up in amazement as a majestic creature soared above them.

"Remember the bastard who refuses to allow another Water Dragoon to be crowned? Behold Gideon the Monotonous," Marcus said with agitation.

The dragon was headed toward the Dragoons' Septum.

The three then parted ways with the doctor and went to the inn. Abandoned by both staff and guests who had gone to see the new attraction, breakfast had been left to go cold. Marcus grabbed a basket with a few pieces of cornbread and filled it with fruits and other pastries. With his free hand, he took a jug of spiced apple cider.

Back in their room, they sat on the beds to discuss what had happened. Tom, Len, and Mr. Nibs greeted them.

Len was happy to see Felix. "I see you kept your promise," she said, nuzzling up to him.

Felix went into detail about his adventure, captivating his audience. He even shared what he had collected during his journey. Marcus was impressed, while Anastasia was grossed out but understood Felix's thought process.

Now that Felix's covert mission was complete, Anasta-

sia and Marcus learned that he had not been hiding anything else from them. Both felt a deep sense of dread that
Felix had concealed the pain in his arm, which had been
there since the night of Wraith's Eve. If they hadn't been
so opposed to him taking on the task, he could have shared
his burden with them, and they could have worked together to accomplish it.

Felix explained that he would never put either of them
in harm's way.

Anastasia had planned the remaining days for the trio.
The boys were fine with having the rest of the trip organized, and Felix even suggested adding a few extra activities
to the agenda, which Anastasia accepted.

To ensure he wasn't planning anything dangerous, she
asked him what he wanted to do. "I want to collect some volcanic dust so I can bake the Gorgons and snakes eyes," he
explained.

Marcus interjected, mentioning that Dr. Caceres had
some volcanic dust in his storehouse, so they could retrieve
some from there. Felix also wanted to visit the apothecary
to sell some of the snakeheads before jotting something down
on a small piece of paper and putting it into his pocket.

As they ate, Felix continued to talk about his adventure
while Marcus sketched a few things Felix described. Anastasia checked Felix for any other injuries, and she found
claw marks on his back.

While reaching for a piece of cornbread, Felix noticed
that the spool had been replaced by a golden needle, which
was a gift from the Sisters of the Loom.

Anastasia asked, "What is going on with your wrist,
Felix?"

Marcus got off the other bed to take a closer look. "I didn't
see this before; it doesn't hurt like the spool did, so I'm fine

with it."

Marcus laughed. "Well, it seems that no matter what you do, Felix, Anastasia's warnings about drawing attention will never cease."

Felix huffed. "Well, no one besides us and Dr. Caceres knows about what happened. So let's keep it quiet."

Felix wasn't as hungry as the others, having eaten the most during the sleigh ride. While the others ate, he discreetly reached into his bag of holding, pulled out the eyes of the Gorgons, and placed them into a leather pouch. He also put the snakes' eyes into a vial. He avoided looking directly at the eyes but could feel their heat, which sizzled his skin upon contact.

The others soon finished their breakfast and wanted to head into town. It was a warm enough day that Tom and Mr. Nibs joined them. They made their way to the doctor's house and asked for some volcanic dust. With no objections, they were given a small pouch full.

Next, they visited a few stores. Anastasia wanted to pick up some items for her class and even found a strange wine contraption she thought would make a novel gift for Mrs. Simmons.

Felix bought a few loaves of bread in assorted flavors for snacks, and as a bonus, he grabbed bungle berry jam and some Cracher De Feu (fire spitter) butter.

At a craft store, Marcus picked up more charcoal pencils for sketching. They spent quite a while browsing, and Felix's stomach growled.

"Can we get something to eat?" Felix asked.

There was a pub down the way that Marcus had mentioned earlier, known for its roast quail with radish and mint sauce, so they decided to go there. On Marcus's recommendation, Anastasia had the quail, and Felix opted for the cabbage soup.

After lunch, they all wanted to do some reading back at the inn. Each grabbed books from their rooms and reconvened in the lounge by the large fireplace.

It wasn't long before they were interrupted by a few students asking about Dragoons' Septum. Trying to avoid getting involved, they ignored the questions and returned to their reading.

The afternoon passed quickly as they read and sipped on ginger and lemon tea. Tom was perched on the high-backed chair where Marcus sat, Mr. Nibs slept on the otto-man attached to Anastasia's foot, and Len lay next to Felix on the hearth. Felix would occasionally pause in his reading to chat with Len about wild ideas he had. Len, however, wasn't having any of it, responding sarcastically and saying she should already be dead from the stress he was causing her.

The following morning, the group ventured into the apothecary, seeking to sell the snakeheads. As they stepped inside, they were greeted by an array of glass bottles and vials lining the walls, each filled with dull and murky liquids and powders. The large windows were obscured by curtains drawn halfway, allowing only a sliver of light to filter through, casting the room in a faint, enigmatic gloom. The air was thick with the faint scent of herbs and chemicals, adding to the room's brooding atmosphere.

After a few moments of browsing, an elderly man poked his head through a doorway. "May I help you?"

Felix spoke up, "How much would it cost for Oculus Conspectus Serum?"

The man gave them a weary look. "Oh, I don't think the three of you could ever afford—"

"Sir, that isn't what my friend asked," Marcus interjected.

The man was taken aback. "It's over two thousand clovers."

"Well," Felix said, "from my reading, the Oculus Conspectus Serum is made from a quarter of the total Gorgon's snakes venom glands. So you could make upwards of eight thousand clovers from just one snake head."

The elderly man looked puzzled.

"How many clovers do you have?" Felix bluntly asked.

"Excuse me?" The apothecary's demeanor shifted to one of guarded curiosity, clearly caught off guard.

Felix reached into his bag and pulled out one of the snakeheads, the gold and brown scales glinting ominously.

"Where did you get your hands on one of those?" the apothecary asked, his voice laced with a hint of greed.

"Doesn't matter, sir. If you're not interested, I'll take my business elsewhere," Felix said, trying to pressure him for a quicker response.

The apothecary's eyes narrowed, his interest piqued. "How much do you want for it?"

"I think four thousand clovers would be fair, considering you'll make a profit of four thousand yourself," Felix replied.

The elderly man's eyes sparkled with avarice. "Four thousand, you say?" He quickly excused himself, his movements abrupt as he dashed to fetch his coat, hat, and gloves. "Please, follow me." He led them down the street with an eager, almost hurried pace, towards a large stone building.

"It's the bank, Felix," Marcus said with a smile.

Anastasia laughed. "Felix has an account. He knows it's a bank."

Marcus was surprised by her comment. "We have a co-owned business. I'll explain everything later."

The elderly man held the door open for them, and they entered the bank. He asked to see the snakehead again, and

Felix handed it over. The man examined it carefully, his mouth cracked open in a grin that revealed his discolored, horse-like teeth. "The venom glands are engorged."

He handed the snakehead back and approached the teller. "I would like to withdraw from my account, please," he said to the young woman behind the counter.

"I'll be happy to assist, Mr. Vitus. How much will you be withdrawing today?" she asked.

"Four thousand clovers," he responded.

"Right away." The woman went into the back, and a few minutes later, she returned with four sacks in her hands. "Here you go, Mr. Vitus. Four thousand clovers. Is there anything else I can assist you with?"

"No, thank you. You've been extremely helpful."

The man took the sacks and handed them to Felix, who, in turn, gave the snakehead to the elderly man.

"Miss, could you please deposit this into my account?" Felix asked the cashier, handing her a small piece of paper he had written on earlier in the room they were renting.

"Right away, Mr. Grey." The cashier disappeared into the back room and returned shortly with a receipt for his deposit and the current balance of his account.

"Thank you, ma'am." Felix turned to Mr. Vitus.

The elderly man extended his hand, and Felix shook it, concluding their business.

Before the man could leave the bank, Felix pulled out a bundle of beheaded snakeheads from his bag. "Let me know if you'd like to purchase more in the future."

Anastasia and Marcus wore ever-widening smiles, while the man's jaw dropped in stunned amazement. "My word, how many do you have?" he asked, his voice trembling slightly.

"Well, as of now, one hundred forty-three more."

The old man's eyes grew impossibly wide, his gaze fixed on Felix with a look of intense longing and incredulity.

"If you need to reach me, just inquire at Heaven's Gate," Felix said, as the three of them walked out of the bank and headed back to the inn.

Once inside the inn, Anastasia's eyes twinkled with excitement as she presented Felix with a small, carefully wrapped gift. "Happy birthday, Felix!" she said, her voice warm with affection.

Felix beamed at her, wrapping her in a heartfelt hug. "Thank you so much!" he replied, his voice brimming with gratitude. He gently unwrapped the gift, revealing a delicate silver pin shaped like a dragon, with a small turquoise set into its eye. Anastasia had mined the turquoise herself and had it set into this beautiful pin by a jeweler just for him.

As evening fell, Marcus took them to a charming restaurant. Felix, in a mood of joyous generosity, insisted on treating them to dessert. Their laughter and conversation filled the air, making the meal a celebration of friendship rather than a birthday. As a surprise of his own, he pulled out of his bag the toolkit for examining rocks that he had bought for Anastasia, along with the book on theoretical machines that could in theory fly for Marcus.

The next day, they decided to try something new. Anastasia and Felix, under Marcus's guidance, began their not-so-successful art careers.

Though their stay in Tinker Town was brief, it was filled with excitement and heartwarming moments. As they prepared to leave for Heaven's Gate the next morning, they carried with them the fond memories of a winter wonderland experience, their hearts warmed by the joy of their shared time together.

As they stepped into the teleportation circle, the scene before them unfolded like a frozen picture. The castle stood in the distance, its majestic towers and battlements obscured by a thick blanket of snow and ice, as if a blizzard had laid siege to it.

Professor Pompeii and a handful of older students worked furiously on the castle roofs, their breath visible in the frigid air as they battled the encroaching frost. Their efforts to melt the ice and snow seemed almost futile against the relentless winter.

Amid the chaos, a careless student stumbled, inadvertently knocking loose a massive ten-foot-tall icicle. The enormous shard of ice glinted menacingly in the pale light as it began its deadly descent toward them.

Felix's instincts flared. With a swift, fluid motion, he threw himself in front of his friends as a shield. His hands moved with blinding speed, weaving through the air as if orchestrating a symphony. In a heartbeat, his elemental prowess shattered the icicle into a flurry of glittering fragments, the icy shards exploding into dust just inches from his chest.

Marcus was astonished. "Felix, that was incredible. I've never seen anyone move like that."

"Thanks, Felix. I would have been dead if you hadn't stepped in," Anastasia added, hugging him in gratitude.

"We should get unpacked," Felix said nonchalantly.

Anastasia went off in the direction of her house, while the boys strolled down the halls, discussing their classes. Felix checked with Marcus to see if he needed any more help.

Marcus declined, saying, "I don't think there's anything more you can teach me unless you plan on covering a different subject."

As they rounded the corner to the lily pond, Marcus asked,

"So, what are you going to do with all that money?"

Felix thought for a moment and replied, "I have a few ideas, but nothing is set in stone yet."

In the common room, the students were discussing the crystal spire, which was now glowing. Marcus and Felix had little interest in joining the discussion—they preferred to avoid large groups and had already talked about it with Dr. Caceres in Tinker Town. So, they retired to their room until dinnertime.

When they reappeared, the student body had gathered to hear Headmaster O'Connor's announcements.

"Ah, me dear students," O'Connor began, his voice warm and melodious, "Ah, what a grand moment in time to be alive, wouldn't ye agree? I trust ye've all had a splendid winter holiday and that the gifts brought ye plenty of joy.

Now, as ye've no doubt heard, the spire's all lit up like a beacon in the twilight. We're still waitin' to hear who's ascended the throne, but I reckon we'll find out soon enough.

I've a few end-of-year announcements to make. We're jumpin' straight into the semifinals for your house championships, so may good fortune favor ye as ye navigate these pivotal moments in yer battles and exams!"

With that, he settled back into his seat, and the room buzzed with renewed chatter as everyone went back to finishing their meals.

Chapter 22
Final Exams

Spring was now on their doorstep. Everyone was busy with classwork, and Felix had torn through over a thousand books, impressing Thistle with his extensive knowledge and diligence to detail.

In his free time, Felix visited the dragon stables with a metal contraption he had found hanging in Professor Gil's classroom. He took the vials of Gorgon eyes and poured them into a bag of volcanic dust, coating them thoroughly. Once each eye was coated with a thick layer of dust, he placed them in the trap-like device.

He positioned the contraption on a bracket over the fire and worked the large bellows, pumping them to increase the temperature. The red-hot embers in the forge brightened, and flames roared around the device.

When he heard the crackling sound, Felix slowed his fanning of the flames, allowing the contents to cool down at a controlled pace, a technique he had learned from one of his books. This process took several hours, but when he finally opened the trap, he discovered golden orbs that sparkled like miniature versions of Mater.

Felix picked up one of the orbs and held it up to the light. As he rolled it in his fingers, he noticed tiny veins of gold within it. Satisfied with his work, he cleaned up the mess, putting everything back in its place. He then secured all the gems in the bag that had once held the volcanic dust, ensuring they were safe.

Between the income from his business in Dennington and the sales of Gorgon venom, Felix was amassing quite a fortune. The gems alone were enough to allow anyone to retire in comfort, so he kept them in a lockbox at the bank back in Dennington.

With the changing of the seasons, Len and Mr. Nibs shed their undercoats. Len was proud of Felix and his accomplishments, while Mr. Nibs didn't care much for Anastasia's academic performance—he just wanted to ensure she was having as much fun as possible.

The snow began to melt, and flowers pushed up through the remnants of winter, painting the landscape with fresh colors. Lady Stewart had trained Felix into a skilled swordsman, and now she could no longer smoke her pipe during their fencing matches. Felix's footwork, taught by Professor Goryeo, had become graceful and unique, while his hand-to-hand combat skills were rapidly improving.

Even on their days off, Anastasia and Felix engaged in mock battles, evaluating each other's skills. Anastasia's tactics kept her opponents at a distance—she either altered the ground to make it difficult for them to traverse or sent projectiles their way. Felix aimed to use as few weaves as possible in combat, relying more on physical attacks.

On the rare occasions Marcus joined their skill-testing sessions, Felix and Anastasia were surprised by his proficiency in battle strategy. He had a knack for unsettling opponents, introducing unexpected elements to his tactics that expanded his range of options.

In Fauna 100, Anastasia and Felix made friends with all the animals and received top marks; it was more of a hobby for them than a class. Felix even sold a few of his snakeheads to Professor Gills.

In Study of Dragons, Felix was unmatched. Ever since he had lived in the statue with Lady Miko, who had shown him his first water weave, and had cuddled with Sangbi, the dragon in the nursery when he first arrived in Yurden, his fascination with dragons had only grown stronger. His eagerness to learn everything he could about them never waned.

In Professor Yamatai's class, Felix continued to receive visions of figures in various colors and states of clarity. These visions elicited emotional reactions, though he struggled to understand their meaning. The constant presence of a black figure brought him both happiness and sadness.

Not recognizing the visions or the people in them, Felix's assignments involved interpreting what he thought they might represent or mean. Professor Yamatai's class had become less about education and more about self-analysis, which turned Felix off.

Felix rarely saw Professor Agate except in the dining hall. Anastasia explained that Professor Agate was a cheerful recluse who avoided leaving the castle. He felt uneasy without the protection of the castle walls, venturing outside only when absolutely necessary.

Occasionally at night, Felix would find Professor Bolton chasing pixies through the corridors, zapping them before placing them in jars. Professor Bolton never noticed Felix moving to and from the unmarked restroom with his stacks of books. One evening, as shadows deepened in the castle corridors, Felix witnessed Professor Bolton slipping away furtively. Heart pounding, Felix spun on his heel and stumbled upon a cluster of pixies shimmering in the dim light just meters from where he stood. Panic surged through him, and he bolted down the corridor, barely avoiding a collision with two older students who were creeping through the castle for reasons unknown to him.

Felix cast a frantic glance back as he sprinted past them, their eyes widening in surprise before they resumed their covert mission, unaware of what Felix was running from. The flickering orbs of light began to converge on the students, merging with them like spectral tendrils of doom. The students had no time to react to the intruders. He noticed something very peculiar; neither of them had their bracelets on, the ones Lady Rosalyn had given to every student.

Suddenly, the students' bodies began to convulse, moving with a jerky, unnatural rhythm as if manipulated by malevolent puppeteers. Echoes of maniacal laughter reverberated through the hallway, and their eyes blazed with an eerie blue glow. Felix, heart racing, pressed himself against a nearby column, watching in horror as the possessed students crashed into objects and walls with reckless abandon, their movements erratic and disjointed, like marionettes cut from their strings.

He trailed them silently, the sound of their bodies hitting the floor echoing like slabs of meat being dropped onto a butcher's block. Each thud reverberated ominously as they staggered toward an outer wall. The possessed students scrambled over a covered parapet, their movements erratic and violent, limbs flailing as if they were the residents of a mad house.

As they slid down to the ground below, Felix caught a glimpse of their faces—contorted in anguish, eyes wide with terror, yet unseeing, as though they were trapped in a waking nightmare. The air was thick with the sound of their desperate gasps and the hollow laughter of the unseen puppeteers, mocking their plight. He felt an icy grip of dread tighten around his heart; these were not just students anymore, but unwilling vessels of chaos, spiraling further into the abyss with each jerky movement, each chaotic crash.

Felix, adrenaline surging, followed their descent with carefully, ducking behind every available cover to remain unseen. Every instinct within him screamed to flee, yet a deep-rooted curiosity, intertwined with a sense of dread, compelled him to continue shadowing the nightmarish spectacle unfolding before him.

Felix felt an undeniable pull to witness the horror, to understand the twisted fate that had befallen the students. Each thud and crash resonated within him, a chilling reminder of their plight. The eerie laughter echoed in his ears, and with every frantic movement of the possessed, he felt the weight of his own helplessness pressing down, urging him forward into the abyss.

The pair continued their unsteady gait around the castle's exterior. They crashed into each other with unsettling regularity as they approached a stone bridge. One student lost their footing and slipped into the stream that cascaded from the dragon statues, eventually vanishing over the edge of the waterfall. The other student, unfazed, continued toward the edge.

Felix tracked the student who had plunged into the stream, following their disjointed path as they floated downstream. The water, illuminated by a sickly, flickering light, seemed to ripple with malevolent intent. Meanwhile, the remaining student made their way to the edge of the pillar. They leaned forward and were swallowed by darkness.

Felix's pulse raced as he sprinted forward, his breaths coming in ragged gasps. In the distance below him, he heard screams—haunting and filled with raw terror. He watched in horror as a spectral light detached from the falling student, transforming into a grotesque, writhing glowing orb. The student's scream was ghastly, a piercing wail that seemed to tear through the very fabric of night, sending icy shivers coursing down Felix's spine.

Shortly after, a second scream erupted from the direction of the waterfall, its thunderous echoes bouncing off the stone pillar. The orbs, now acutely aware of Felix's presence, coalesced into a sinister swarm and began their ascent up the pillar, their malevolent glow intensifying as they locked onto him.

Desperation clawed at Felix as he dashed back towards the castle, the orbs of light in relentless pursuit, their eerie giggles like the whispers of vengeful spirits. He dashed through the winding corridors, his heart racing in tandem with his pounding footsteps. The faint, chilling laughter echoed behind him.

Reaching the pool, Felix leaped from lily pad to lily pad with frantic urgency, his every motion a desperate bid for survival. The dragon loomed ahead, a dark and imposing silhouette against the night sky. He swiped his bracelet and descended the spiral staircase, the sound of his footsteps a frantic clatter in the otherwise oppressive silence. As he reached the bottom, he collapsed against the stone wall, his breath wheezing.

Felix, breathless, leaned forward with his hands on his knees. The students still in the common room turned to him, startled and curious about his disheveled state.

Without a moment's notice, Felix scurried off to his room, where Marcus was waiting. Felix closed the door and leaned against it, catching his breath.

Len jumped off the bed and ran to Felix, knowing what he had experienced. Their mental link had put her in a state of fear. She stood with her front paws pressed against Felix's thighs.

Marcus sat up in bed, concerned, as he stared at Felix.

"Pixies..." Felix gasped, his voice trembling.

"Oh, are you okay?" Marcus asked.

"You should lie down for a moment," Len said softly, her voice filled with worry.

Felix staggered toward the bed, but his breath came in ragged bursts as he struggled to recount the horror. "They're dead!"

"Who's dead?" Marcus demanded, gripping Felix's shoulder with a mix of urgency and disbelief.

"I saw them fall off the edge," Felix stammered, with fear in his eyes. "I saw those bobbing lights coming down the hall, and I just turned and ran! They were following me. I could see their lights flickering off the walls as I turned each corner."

His voice broke, the weight of guilt pressing down on him as he relived the terrifying chase.

"Just breathe!" Len and Marcus said in unison, one in his head, the other aloud.

"We need to tell Lady Stewart. Where did you see the pixies?" Marcus asked, already sending Tom to fetch Lady Stewart.

A few minutes later, Lady Stewart entered the room. "What is going on?" She stared at the pair.

Felix explained the situation in great detail, with Lady Stewart and Marcus listening intently.

"What hue adorned their robes?" Lady Stewart inquired.

"Red," Felix replied.

Lady Stewart checked on Felix to ensure he was physically okay and advised him to rest for the evening. She instructed Marcus to keep an eye on him and to alert her if anything else occurred. Then, she made her way to the headmaster's office to relay to him the situation.

Normally, Lady Rosalyn would have been able to save the students, but the bracelets had been removed.

"Are you sure you're okay, Felix?" Marcus asked, his concern not waning.

Felix bit his lower lip and nodded, scratching Len behind the ears.

Marcus decided that Felix needed a distraction to take his mind off the recent events. He asked Felix to tutor him in math, believing it would be beneficial.

The incident left a somber mood over the school. The memory of the students' deaths lingered, casting a cautious shadow over everyone.

The students were in high spirits as House Amun declared their champion, Rabi Shu. Rabi was the complete opposite of their head of house, with a stern appearance and a calculated demeanor.

House Jupiter also appointed their champion: Darrin Quigley. Darrin was well-liked by his housemates, tall, and the apple of many girls' eyes. His popularity stemmed from his playful nature and knack for making people laugh.

House Vulcan, House Terra, and House Mizu had yet to appoint their champions, though clear frontrunners were emerging in each house.

In the coming days, exam results were expected to be posted, determining the classes for the next year—provided they didn't fail any of the current ones. Anastasia realized that Felix would choose his classes regardless of her input. For the next year, she had selected Cultural Anthropology

EL101 and FR100, Elemental Control E101, Fauna 101, Flora 101, and Magical Artifacts 101.

Felix decided to make a few changes. Disappointed with astrology, he opted not to continue in that field. His second-year classes would include Artifice 100, Art of War 101, Brew 101, Elemental Control D101, Fauna 101, and The Study of Dragons 101.

During a break, Felix and Anastasia compared their classes. Both were pleased to have stayed with Fauna 101. Anastasia suspected Felix would drop astrology, especially after the incident that had sent him to the infirmary with a fever.

At the start of the next week, the entire school, except for the graduating year, gathered in the auditorium. The excitement about the spire had gradually subsided, as no one had claimed the throne. Residents reported that Gideon was circling the spire daily, as if waiting for something to happen.

Felix recalled Anastasia's words: "People forget about things if you don't make waves." Most students had left Felix alone about his gauntlet and his conjuration of the water dragon. Things had finally settled down for him. His nerves had eased, and he now felt more relaxed. His stuttering rarely reared its head.

Before making final decisions on their classes, students were required to be assessed for a secondary element. Children under fifteen could not trigger or obtain another element unless they were of a different species, such as elves unless extraordinary circumstances occurred. Regardless of age, each student had to be assessed in the gazophylacium muneror.

The chamber was a semicircular grotto, with five pedestals along the walls, each representing one of the five elements. The pedestals were adorned with metal and crystal spiders resembling Valerie. In the center of the room stood a massive black leather book, bound and held shut by spider legs. The spider, metallic and black obsidian in color, seemed to hold the book off the ground with its abdomen touching the floor.

Upperclassmen who entered the chamber emerged with looks of disappointment. They had been assessed, but no trace of another element was found.

Anastasia explained to Felix that while some students in the past had gained more than two elements, it was exceptionally rare to obtain all five. Typically, the recipient was grateful, she explained, but had not heard Marcus's opinion on the matter.

As Marcus entered the gazophylacium muneror, the metal sliding door closed behind him.

Anastasia turned to Felix, prompting him to consider something he might not have thought of on his own. "Everyone is born with one of the five elements: earth, fire, lightning, water, or wind. If you have the capability to manipulate a second element, it will never be as strong as the dominant element you were born with. Even if you acquire a third or fourth element, your original element will always be stronger. And even though some weavers don't have to worry about their elements waning, that's like one in ten million."

When Marcus emerged from the chamber, he had a relieved expression. He was pleased not to have acquired a third element, as the idea of wielding another element had stressed him out. He returned to his seat, visibly relieved.

Anastasia entered the chamber with apprehension but emerged with a face full of questions, looking as though she were lost in thought.

Felix stepped into the room, and the heavy metal door closed behind him. As Felix approached each pedestal, the abdomens of the spiders flickered with distinct colors. He interacted only with the water pedestal, assuming it would be harmless. Instead of flickering, it glowed with a brilliant sparkle, and the eyes of the statue lit up. Its legs then bent as if bowing to Felix.

He then moved to the central pedestal, which flickered with a purple hue. Not wanting to inspect anything further, he quickly left the gazophylacium muneror.

Lady Stewart watched Felix return to his seat.

"What's on your mind, Felix?" Anastasia asked.

Felix scratched his head. "What's supposed to happen in there? And what's the middle pedestal for?"

Overhearing Felix's confusion, Marcus explained, "If you can control another element, the spider representing that element is supposed to flicker the corresponding color. I'm assuming you went to the water element?"

Felix nodded. "It bowed."

"Yes, they do that if you control that element. The middle pedestal is different—it bestows the Lunaire."

"What's the Lunaire?"

"If you had read *Aurora the Beloved*, you'd know," Anastasia replied. "But since you wanted me to read the book on dragons, here's the scoop: Lunaire is the ability to draw power from Kalli and Mater. It's said that the wielder of the Lunaire can tap into the power of the external star system."

Felix's confusion deepened, and the words he had been about to say slipped away. Anastasia and Marcus tried to muffle their laughter, teasing Felix gently.

Lady Stewart kept a watchful eye on the three, ensuring no other colors were appearing in Felix's gauntlet.

To get their attention, she took a deep breath from her

pipe and blew a cloud of vapor at them, catching them off guard.

The trio turned to see Lady Stewart's finger pointing in the direction they needed to face. Marcus and Felix understood this as a signal to settle down, so they straightened up.

An hour later, the final student completed their assessment in the gazophylacium muneror. Only twenty-two students that year were gifted with the ability to wield another element. Before the students dispersed, an announcement was made.

Headmaster O'Connor stepped onto the auditorium floor. "Me dear students, I offer me heartfelt congratulations to each of ye who've been blessed with newfound power. This gift comes with its own burdens, mind ye, but remember, every moment ye spend growin' enriches yer time here. Time, me young ones, is a fleeting and fickle companion—its end can be as unpredictable as the weather. Cherish every precious second and use 'em wisely. Now, off ye go."

"Thank heavens I don't have to change my classes just because of another required subject," Marcus said with relief.

Anastasia hesitated before asking, "So you didn't want another element because it would mean more classwork?"

"Yes and no. It's more about wanting to choose my own courses. I don't want my time here dictated by additional requirements. You and Felix are unusual cases, and you'll end up with more classes than anyone by the time you're done. The average student starts here full-time at fifteen, meaning they already have completed fifteen classes. By graduation, they'll have taken another eighteen classes, totaling thirty-three.

"In your cases, you will have completed forty-eight out

of the one hundred twelve classes offered. Essentially, you will have been enrolled in more than a third of the classes."

"That is a lot of classes. Can we test out of some of them?" Felix asked, feeling like there were a few he had read that didn't seem necessary. Anastasia loved learning but understood that it was somewhat unfair.

The auditorium was dismissed, and the trio decided to go to the library to find something to read before dinner.

"Hey, Felix, there was something I wanted to tell you but didn't get a chance to before—our conversation was interrupted by the headmaster. Only two weavers have ever possessed the Lunaire: the First High Lord Dragoon and Lady Aurora, the Last High Lord Dragoon," Marcus said as they headed toward the library.

Chapter 23
True Power

The remaining ten days were full of contests, and even the declared champions of their houses had been challenged for their titles. The day before the grand finale, Cordelia was announced champion of the Water Weavers.

Basking in all her glory, she caught sight of something that infuriated her. Out of the packed stands, she saw *him*. After her last battle, Marcus didn't praise her win. Instead, he was lost in the book he was reading, ignoring the entire spectacle.

A booming call into the stands tore Marcus and Felix away from their books. "I challenge Marcus Erikson to a contest!"

An expression of terror swept across his face, and Felix stared at Marcus, knowing he was helpless to do a thing about it.

Marcus closed his book and gulped, trying to calm his nerves. He'd never participated in a contest before and hoped he would never have to.

The entire house turned to Marcus. Students could be heard saying, "Oh, he's dead."

Marcus placed his book into his bag of holding and stood up, shaking in terror. Felix grabbed hold of his hand, wishing him good luck, trying somehow to boost his confidence. In return, Marcus squeezed his hand in utter fear.

"Hurry the hell up, maggot!" Cordelia taunted.

His legs were failing him on his way down from the back of the stands to the water, visualizing his death playing out in front of him. Hesitatingly, he weaved the sign that allowed him to walk on water.

Lady Stewart approached him and gave him words of encouragement, wishing him good luck in her distant, cold manner before raising a long, silver whistle to her lips.

Felix watched on as if everything was happening in slow motion. Lady Stewart blew her whistle, and a sharp ringing sound streaked through the air, commencing the battle.

Being a seasoned fighter, Cordelia struck first with a quick weave, and water slashed Marcus's cheek. He tried to dodge it, but she drew first blood. "Let us see how much this pathetic excuse for a man can bleed."

Being petrified, Marcus's attacks were far too slow and far too weak to break or stop her offense. Each time she landed a blow, she belittled Marcus repeatedly, toying with him and injuring him as she went along with the verbal abuse.

Felix's demeanor changed. His body retched in response, his hands clenched into fists, and a feeling of hatred brewed deep within as he watched his friend being humiliated and beaten.

After about three minutes, Marcus fell on the water, trying to say, "I concede."

As soon as he started forming the words, Cordelia sent

a geyser of water at his face, stopping him from being able to speak. It knocked the wind out of him and pushed him back. Everyone heard the groans and screams of pain coming from Marcus. As this continued, her taunts became even more degrading.

Felix's temperature soared, turning his skin clammy as beads of sweat streamed down his forehead. His breathing became erratic, and just as he tried to grasp the situation, the voice within him seized control.

In a blur of motion, faster than Cordelia could react, Felix wove a decisive sign. From the depths of the lake, a monstrous arm erupted, it swung itself toward Cordelia. The arm clasped around her head with crushing power, slamming her face into the water with relentless ferocity.

As the tumultuous splash resonated, Marcus, caught in the chaos, managed to choke out, "I concede," before collapsing into unconsciousness.

Felix rose from his seat, his robes slipping away to reveal a gauntlet glowing with a fierce, otherworldly light. He descended the bleachers with a zombie-like shuffle, bumping into startled students who recoiled from his un-blinking gaze. His expression was a cold, emotionless mask as he focused intently on Cordelia, his hands moving in a rapid, synchronized dance of signs.

Lady Stewart and Cordelia were frantically searching for the source of the monstrous arm.

"Who the fuck did that?" Cordelia roared, her clothes drenched and her posture hunched in fury.

They both watched as Felix trudged toward the lake from the bleachers, each step deliberate and ominous. Lady Stewart inhaled sharply, her eyes locking onto the blazing gauntlet.

"You little bastard!" Cordelia shouted. "I don't care if you're a first-year; you're going to pay for that in blood."

With a fierce charge, Cordelia lunged at Felix, only to be intercepted by Lady Stewart. "One cannot engage in combat with a mere first-year, Cordelia."

But Cordelia was undeterred. She sidestepped Lady Stewart, her stance shifting to a predatory crouch, ready to confront her new target.

As if summoned by the tension, Felix's water clone surged into existence in front of Lady Stewart. Simultaneously, a second clone emerged and lifted Marcus from the ground, his unconscious form held like a sleeping child.

The clone's voice, chilling and malevolent, sliced through the tension like a blade. "I challenge Cordelia to a contest," it declared, its tone dripping with a sinister edge that sent a shiver through the air.

Lady Stewart's eyes widened in horror as she watched Felix advance, his gaze fixed and unnervingly unblinking, directed straight at Cordelia.

"Thou art but a first-year, thou—" Lady Stewart started, her voice filled with authority, but the clone's voice interrupted her with chilling calm.

"I invoke Edict Twelve of the Third Year of the Reign of High Dragoon Lord Lady Aurora," it intoned, each word dripping with hostile intent. "This decree grants any student the right to absolve Heaven's Gate of responsibility for their actions."

Lady Stewart's face went pale, her usual stoic demeanor shattered by disbelief. The realization that Felix was knowledgeable enough to wield such an edict left her stunned. "Felix, I hereby forbid it," she commanded, her voice strained with urgency.

The entranced Felix moved toward the water with an eerie, almost mechanical grace. His steps were unnaturally smooth, as if the malevolent entity controlling him was fine-tuning every movement.

The clone's voice echoed again, dripping with disdain. "You deny me? What a thought. Know your place!"

The malevolent force within Felix had complete access to every fragment of his knowledge. Felix's body was a vessel, and he was powerless to resist the dark will seizing control.

Lady Stewart watched in horror, her mind racing as she grappled with the gravity of the situation. Her face was a mask of determination and worry as she tried to piece together a strategy to counter with a rebuttal.

Cordelia stood as though time itself had forsaken her, like an ancient vampiress starved for centuries, her eyes hollow. "I'm going to rip your head off, you little shit."

The clone's mocking laughter echoed across the water. "If only you could," it taunted, its voice dripping with scorn Felix advanced toward it, which stood poised at the water's edge.

The clone carrying Marcus moved with purposeful strides toward the infirmary, while the malevolent presence within Felix continued its dark dance. Felix stepped onto the water, his movements deliberate and menacing, hands weaving together with a sinister grace.

Lady Stewart's voice trembled as she pleaded with Felix, her words urgent and laced with fear. "Cease this at once! Cordelia shall show no mercy for thine actions."

Without breaking stride, the clone turned its cold gaze toward Lady Stewart. "Your concern is noted, but I insist you leave the water."

Cordelia, poised for attack, ushered Lady Stewart to the shore, her eyes fixed on Felix with lethal intent. As the clone mirrored Felix's intricate gestures, the air grew thick with tension. Suddenly, the weave ceased, and the lake erupted in a dazzling array of duplicates—hundreds of Felixes rising in perfect formation, their figures encircling the lake.

A collective gasp rose from the crowd, a wave of astonishment crashing over them as they beheld the sheer multitude of clones Felix had conjured.

The clone's voice, calm and decisive, intoned, "Paragon Hexadon's Prison."

The onlookers were transfixed, their breath caught in their throats.

Lady Stewart's eyes widened in disbelief. "How can this be? Such a weave surpasses anything a youth of his years should be capable of. He is not even an Earth Weaver." Her gaze shifted from Felix to Cordelia, her concern shifting to Cordelia.

Each clone's arms were bent at unnatural angles, interlocking with those of their counterparts, forming an impenetrable barrier. Their stance broadened, their limbs intertwining to create a solid wall. Felix's hands remained in constant motion as a colossal harp of water surged from the lake, its shape solidifying into an eerie, featureless woman with a gaping mouth.

The harp—known as an orator—rose from the depths. Its arms, contorted as though broken, reached out to pluck its strings.

Lady Stewart's bewilderment grew. "Pray, why summon an orator?" she murmured, her confusion mingling with concern for Cordelia.

The original clone, now integrated into the barrier, signaled Lady Stewart to act. With urgency, she shouted, "Cordelia, refrain from touching the barrier wall!" Her voice was piercing as she blew into a long, silver whistle, the sound echoing ominously.

Felix completed a third intricate weave, conjuring a shimmering sphere of water. As he stepped to the side, bullets of water intended for him went whizzing by his head. He pressed it to his forehead, embedding a memory within, before hurling it toward the orator. The sphere struck the harp, dissolving into its watery form.

Without delay, the orator began to sing. The haunting melody that filled the air was one Felix had often listened to on his MP3 player, a chilling reminder of the power he wielded. The orator's fingers danced over the strings, its song weaving a spellbinding, otherworldly number.

Cordelia stood poised, her fingers dancing through the air, weaving intricate signs with a fluid grace. Streams of water shot from her hands like a barrage of shimmering, liquid bullets. Felix, agile and resolute, spun through the chaos, his movements a blur as he sidestepped each attack with precision. The water bullets collided with the barrier around the lake, evaporating into mist with hissing bursts.

In a swift, almost balletic motion, Felix launched himself across the surface of the water, his feet barely skimming the fluid beneath him. His body angled sharply, evading the relentless stream of water bolts with a mix of calculated finesse and raw instinct. Each bolt streaked past him, leaving trails of crackling energy in the air, as Felix maneuvered with breathtaking speed, his focus unwavering amidst the chaos Cordelia was unleashing.

As Felix charged forward, Cordelia's eyes glinted with determination. With a commanding gesture, she summoned a towering wall of jagged ice spikes, a formidable barricade of frozen fury designed to halt his advance. Felix's right foot splashed down onto the water, his knee bent. He wove a sign, then propelled himself off the surface, soaring high into the air.

In a breathtaking display of acrobatics, Felix flew over the ice wall, his body twisting end over end like a missile aimed with deadly precision. Just as he was about to crash down upon her, Cordelia's sharp gaze caught the flash of his descent. Reacting swiftly, she tumbled aside, narrowly escaping the force of his attack.

Felix's descent changed abruptly as he plunged into the water with a splash. His lungs shifted and adapted, granting him the ability to breathe underwater. The haunting melody of the harp echoed through the lake.

Below the surface, Felix's eyes locked onto Cordelia's shadow moving across the water. With callous motion, he wove another intricate sign. In response, enormous, swirling arms erupted from the lake, their massive forms crashing through the water with a thunderous roar. They swiped through the air with terrifying power.

Cordelia leaped to avoid the first arm, but a second reached out, seizing her leg in a vice-like grip. The arm twisted violently, hurling her through the air. She smashed against the barrier with a resounding thud, her robes smoking as if the barrier was able to disintegrate anything that touched it.

The once elegant girl now appeared as if she'd been hit by a tree in a tornado. Her refined appearance was gone, replaced by a wild disarray. Her clothes torn, soaked and scorched, her entire form battered. Blood drizzled from her scalp. The blood dripped past her brow, making her even more enraged. It was like she'd never seen herself bleed before.

Cordelia's gaze locked onto the turbulent surface of the water, her eyes narrowing as she traced the shadowy form of Felix beneath the surface. With urgent, unrefined movements, her hands flew through the air, weaving complex signs. The water responded with a violent whirl, the arms dissipating into a spiraling vortex centered on Felix.

The whirlpool deepened and roared as it pulled away the water that once concealed Felix. As the surface cleared, Felix was exposed, the swirling waters now a churning maelstrom. The water, deprived of its former purpose, surged over the barrier in a dramatic, cascading flood. The torrent drenched everyone nearby, a deluge of chaos and force.

House Mizu watched in stunned silence, their faces reflecting a mix of awe and disbelief. Outside the barrier, Lady Stewart paced frenetically, her expression etched with horror as she witnessed the unfolding spectacle. The once-controlled environment had turned into a scene of elemental upheaval, each moment sending shivers up the spectators spines.

Cordelia stood atop the water resolute. She conjured a series of razor-sharp ice javelins, their edges glinting as they sliced through the air. With a fierce throw, she sent them hurtling toward Felix, each one a deadly projectile.

Felix, however, dove into the side of the whirlpool, he evaded the javelins as their mass was swept away by the water, their intended target slipping through their icy grasp.

As the whirlpool's turbulence settled, Felix emerged from the water with a predatory posture, rising slowly like a tiger preparing to strike. His face twisted into a maniacal grin, as he lunged forward, a relentless force of nature.

Cordelia's expression was a storm of fury, her face contorted with rage as she hurled a torrent of vicious curses at him. The scene was charged with raw hatred, each moment a clash of elemental power and fierce emotion.

They charged at each other, their movements a blur of focused aggression. Cordelia's hands blazed with raw energy as two shimmering blades materialized around her, slicing through the air with the precision of a praying mantis. Her body surged forward. A smug grin curling on her lips, though her movements grew increasingly erratic and desperate.

Just as they were about to clash, Felix made a sudden, unexpected dive into the water. He slipped beneath the surface, gliding like a shadow through the depths. With a burst of speed, he maneuvered behind her, his presence concealed in the water's embrace.

From his submerged vantage point, Felix launched a counterattack. As Cordelia released a barrage of water bullets towards where she thought he was, Felix mirrored the attack from behind, sending his own water projectiles with deadly accuracy. Cordelia, caught off guard, whipped around to face him, but the moment her gaze met his, the water bullets struck her with unrelenting force. The impact hit her head-on, knocking her off balance and smearing her once-confident expression with shock and pain.

They tore through her, and she screamed in pain. Chunks of flesh were now missing from the sides of her arms, legs, and face, and thin streams of blood splashed the top of the lake.

Felix rose from the water once more. This time, a voice came forth that wasn't his own, taunting and ridiculing her.

Before she could get up, he finished another weave, capturing her in a sphere of water swirling at blinding speed. It sent her flying at the wall like a projectile.

Seeing the state of how things were progressing, Lady Stewart tried to call off the match, but she was unable to break the barrier. The water continued to splash out from the barrier through the gaps, sounding like thunder.

Everything Lady Stewart tried had failed. Out of desperation she turned to all the students and told them to run to the castle. It was no longer safe for them. She called out to Julie to get the headmaster.

Julie ran back to the castle as fast as she could to retrieve him.

Meanwhile, the voice coming out of Felix became nastier and more vicious.

Lady Stewart saw where this was going. Felix was going to kill Cordelia.

From outside the barrier she weaved her hand signs, trying to protect Cordelia from his wrath, stalling for the headmaster to aid her.

Becoming frustrated with Lady Stewart's foils, a dark aura formed around Felix, growing as the hate thickened the air.

Julie barged into Headmaster O'Connor's office. She found him tinkering with a clock floating in one of the clouds in his chambers. Out of breath, she tried to explain what was going on.

"Gather up all the Water Weavers in your house and don't be leavin'!" That said, he blinked out of the room, only leaving a brief trail of yellow electrified current in the air.

Within a matter of seconds, he was at the lake and standing next to Lady Stewart. "Not a moment to spare. How'd this come to pass?" he asked.

Lady Stewart gasped. "Marcus was subjected to torture, and Felix assailed from the stands. Something provoked him, though I am entirely uncertain as to what."

The headmaster stopped himself from moving forward, noticing what was before him. "This is beyond me, Lady Stewart. I need ye to listen closely to every word I'm about to say. If he can raise this barrier at just ten years old, there's no tellin' what he might be capable of."

He weaved his hands together. "In a moment, I'm goin' to take over. I need ye to head to my office and fetch the glass cylinder with the red tassel danglein' from the bottom. Bring it to me, will ye?"

As his hand stopped weaving, the golden lines of a teleportation circle emerged. "This teleportation circle will get ye to our location. Off with ye now!"

Headmaster O'Connor's hands weaved again. This time he slowed down time, making everything inside the barrier move much slower. He knew trying to stop time was pointless, since it would only last for a limited period. Slowing it down, however, would allow him to control it for a longer duration.

As his fingers twisted and fluttered for a third time, he placed both hands above the barrier, blinking its contents and him out of sight, landing them in the sea, far north of the continent of Yurden.

On the dark side of the disk, isolated from the world and its commotion, Headmaster O'Connor stood with palpable tension. His fingers smoked at their tips, as though they had been seared by an intense, invisible heat. The barrier, once a shield, came crashing down into the water with a resounding splash. Time seemed to have slowed, yet the aura continued to shift and evolve at a bewildering pace. The sky above was an impenetrable void, save for the relentless sound of massive swells pounding against the barrier. Below, the dark waters were alive with the eerie glow of bioluminescent creatures drifting through the abyss.

Within the barrier, the water twisted and coalesced around Felix, growing in mass with each passing moment. The sea roiled with tumultuous energy as the aura seeped out from the barrier, churning the waters into towering swells that surged like mountains, creating a ferocious squall.

"Lady Rosalyn, I could use yer help!" Headmaster O'Connor's voice cut through the chaos, urgent and commanding.

In the distance, a flare of light pierced the oppressive darkness, streaking across the sky. It arced downward, trailing a fiery path like a falling star. When it exploded in a burst of brilliance, Lady Rosalyn materialized, suspended in the air beside O'Connor.

"Headmaster, what's the meaning of this here?"

With his hand still above the barrier as if to stabilize it, he replied, "This here's the Paragon Hexadon's Prison barrier, made by that wee lad of ten, and I need ye to help me take it down."

She peered into the barrier, not able to see Felix, but she sensed him. She spotted Cordelia's lifeless body lying on the surface of the water.

"Nay... it didn't work." Rosalyn glanced from side to side, trying to analyze what had gone wrong.

The headmaster clued her in as much as he could about what had happened, from what he was told by Julie and Lady Stewart. "Cordelia took on Marcus with such fierce aggression, and that's what set off his reaction?"

"Headmaster, I found him holdin' the most important person in the world to him, dead in his arms. He must care for Marcus deeply. He was protectin' him! Fear of loss must be what drives him." Lady Rosalyn teared up. She knew the rage Felix felt inside all too well, and it made her cry uncontrollably.

"Lady Rosalyn, get a grip, will ye? We need yer help, and we need it now. If we don't put a stop to this, Cordelia's a goner," Headmaster O'Connor urged, his voice laced with the urgency of the situation.

Rosalyn glided back from the barrier, her movements a fluid ballet of grace and precision. Her elegant arms wove intricate patterns through the air, each gesture glowing with an intense, molten light as if her palms were forged from liquid fire. As she pressed her hands against the barrier, flames erupted around it, engulfing the surface in a roaring blaze. Yet, despite the inferno, the barrier remained unscathed, its surface unblemished.

With a focused gaze, Rosalyn scanned the barrier for any sign of weakness. Her fingertips ignited like torches, and she began tracing glowing runes in the air. Each rune floated momentarily before she forcefully struck it with the heel of her palm, sending it hurtling towards the barrier. She repeated this process until the entire outer surface of the barrier was adorned with colossal runes, a tapestry of arcane symbols shimmering against the dark backdrop.

Rosalyn's attempts to breach the barrier were relentless. She unleashed a series of powerful attacks, each one more desperate than the last. Despite her formidable prowess, the barrier stood resilient, unaffected by her assault. Frustration etched across her face, she muttered, "As powerful as I be, there's no way I can break this barrier. My powers were sealed away to protect us all."

Meanwhile in Headmaster O'Connor's office, Lady Stewart located the cylinder floating out of reach. Even if she jumped, she would never even graze the tassel.

"Why on earth would he even trouble himself?" she mumbled, shaking her head.

She searched around and saw a pitcher of water. Weaving her hands, the water came floating out of the pitcher and moved toward the cylinder. It smothered the cylinder and brought it to her.

She slid it into her bag and blitzed out the door. As she made her way through the castle, she caused a stir. Not a single person had ever seen Lady Stewart in such a hurry, and gossip ensued.

Lady Stewart made it back to the lake and ran into the

circle, and in a flash of light beamed forth from the circle, she joined Lady Roselyn and Headmaster O'Connor.

Lady Rosalyn and O'Connor greeted her. "Let's the three of us try one more thing before we pull out me trump card!" he said. "We mustn't hurt either of them. Form a triangle 'round the perimeter and blast it with all ye've got."

Once in position, Lady Rosalyn encased it with her super-heated white flames. Headmaster O'Connor brought forth an endless stream of lightning bolts, zapping the barrier. Lady Stewart joined in, bashing it with giant ice boulders. As the ice hit the super-heated flames. Huge steam explosions burst at the barrier, but the barrier didn't budge.

Headmaster O'Connor's initial weave to slow down time was wearing off, and he could tell. The water that had formed around Felix had now taken shape; it was in the form of a dragon. Its enormous size unsettled them as a spine-tingling sensation ran down Lady Stewart's neck. They gathered again to regroup.

Lady Stewart noticed the form the entity had taken was one of the dragon gods. "Oh Mizu, he is transforming into the goddess. But how is this possible?" She stared at the watery construct.

"If we don't hurry, we're all doomed. That's only the first stage—it ain't in solid form yet." Lady Rosalyn said.

"Lady Stewart, bring it over to me, will ye?" the headmaster said, his arm outstretched.

Lady Stewart put her hand in her bag and retrieved the cylinder. Inside was a piece of parchment rolled up with a black, wax seal.

Lady Rosalyn gasped. "Please don't do it, Headmaster! I can't go back!" Tears ran down her water-logged face.

All three were soaked to the bone as the storm that surrounded them was immense and still growing. Not knowing what Lady Rosalyn was referring to, Lady Stewart glanced back at the cylinder.

"Rosalyn, you've changed. I can see it, and the fact that you don't want to go back means you won't."

O'Connor grabbed Lady Roselyn's limp hand, trying to instill in her the faith he had. "You've learned to love and care again. The vengeance you sought has been replaced by love. I believe in ye. Now ye must believe in yerself; those two children need ye. If ye can't find it within yerself, then all is lost."

Turning to Lady Stewart, he added, "I need ye to grab Cordelia and take her back once the barrier's down."

The savage beating Cordelia took left her body without any noticeable movement. It just lay on the water, vaguely twitching. The loss of blood was alarming.

He turned back to Lady Rosalyn, smashing the cylinder, cutting a finger on a shard as it broke apart. He then grabbed the scroll and broke the seal, running his bloody finger across the parchment. As his blood seeped into the parchment, the brooch on his robes as well as the writing on the scroll glowed.

"Lady Rosalyn, in accord with this bindin' contract, I'm freein' ye from yer confinement. I humbly ask ye to take up the mantle of the Crimson Terror once more." he said, cleaving the scroll clean in two.

Lady Stewart had always believed the Crimson Terror to be nothing more than a fairy tale meant to keep children in line. Now, with her mouth hanging open and her gaze slowly shifting toward Lady Rosalyn, the horrifying stories from her childhood came rushing back, flooding her memory with a chilling realization.

As the contract was torn asunder, Lady Rosalyn's body was lifted skyward, as though an invisible force had gripped her chest and was pulling her upward. A blinding shock-wave of light erupted from her, sweeping away everything in its vicinity.

Before their eyes, Lady Rosalyn's appearance began to dissolve like wax melting under intense heat. The once-matronly and angelic figure transformed into a seductive and deadly temptress. Her figure, previously voluptuous, became statuesque, her sun-kissed tan morphing into an ethereal, porcelain white. Her long, golden hair unraveled into a cascade of fierce, fiery auburn curls, radiating an almost supernatural brilliance.

Her eyes, once warm and kind, now glowed with a demonic, blood-red intensity. Black tears streamed down her flawless face, each drop a mark of her newfound power, which seemed to pulse with an otherworldly force.

Draped in a blood-red gown that fluttered and flickered like living flames, she fixed her gaze on the headmaster with a commanding presence. "Strike the barrier with all your might!" she instructed, her voice a potent blend of authority and menace. "You'll know when to do it."

Lady Rosalyn pivoted toward the barrier, her eyes blazing with determination. "I'm comin'!" she shouted, her voice slicing through the chaos.

Headmaster O'Connor's gaze remained unwavering as he commanded, "Lady Stewart, I'm countin' on ye now."

The mass of water enveloping Felix began to roil and churn. Lady Rosalyn's face was a mask of anguish as she murmured, "Forgive me, please." her voice tight with emotion. Her eyes locked onto Felix, and with a fierce cry, she bellowed, "Solvo!"

In an instant, her gown cocooned her in a spiraling vortex of fabric. It expanded rapidly, growing into a colossal presence that loomed over both the headmaster and Lady

Stewart. As the immense mass of the gown unraveled, it revealed a sight of unimaginable terror.

Lady Stewart staggered back, her heart pounding as childhood nightmares materialized before her. A gargantuan two-headed dragon emerged, its serpentine necks stretching menacingly, wings unfurling to span over three hundred feet. The dragon's scales, a deep crimson echoing Lady Rosalyn's dress, gleamed ominously. Razor-sharp claws and black, spiraled horns adorned its fearsome heads. The air was thick with a nauseating stench, reminiscent of freshly slaughtered meat.

The dragon's heads reared back, unleashing two ear-splitting roars that shook the very air. With a sudden, violent thrust, the heads lunged forward, spewing black flames that engulfed the barrier in a searing blaze. The dragon's wings beat with thunderous force as it circled the barrier, scorching it with relentless fury.

Headmaster O'Connor, his expression grim, recognized the critical moment. With a swift and fluid motion, his hands danced through the air, weaving a complex pattern. Lightning bolts erupted from the heavens, crashing down upon the barrier with a cataclysmic roar. The barrier cracked with a deafening explosion, fragments raining down as it began to crumble.

The deafening sound of the barrier shattering echoed through the air.

The Crimson Terror's tail lashed out with a final sweep, delivering a crushing blow to the barrier. The once-impenetrable shield now bore a gaping hole, as if a crack in an egg had formed at the water line, wide enough for a person to slip through. As the black flames dissipated into the void, the dragon roared and plunged through the breach, engaging the water dragon in a fierce aerial assault that drew his attention and bought Lady Stewart precious moments.

With the barrier's collapse now exposed, Headmaster O'Connor's eyes narrowed in focus. Streams of crackling electrical currents leapt from his fingertips, creating a shimmering shield to protect Lady Stewart's path as she sprinted toward the unconscious Cordelia.

Freed from the barrier's temporal constraints, O'Connor unleashed a relentless barrage of lightning bolts, his aim precise and unyielding. Each bolt struck with thunderous force, striking at the water dragon encasing Felix, its thrashing tail to keep it from harming either Lady Stewart or the unconscious girl. A colossal bolt cleaved through the tail with a blinding flash, severing it with an explosive burst. Yet, in a matter of seconds, the tail reformed, regenerating with a sinister swiftness.

As the dragon's tail writhed and twisted, O'Connor's lightning continued to cut through the chaos, a desperate battle against the ever-regenerating menace.

The dragon construct that surrounded Felix crouched low, its massive frame tensed like a cornered beast. With a guttural roar, it opened its jaws wide, unleashing a razor-sharp surge of water that sliced through the air and cleaved into the shoulder of the Crimson Terror—formerly Lady Rosalyn.

The Crimson Terror's heads reared back in fury, then spewed a blistering inferno that engulfed the water dragon. Flames roared and crackled, filling the air with searing heat. The momentary distraction gave Lady Stewart the precious seconds she needed.

Summoning all her strength, Lady Stewart conjured a majestic construct of a giant manta ray. The ethereal creature surged into existence, its vast wings spreading gracefully. With a powerful sweep, the manta ray whisked Lady

Stewart and the unconscious Cordelia away from the chaos, propelling them toward the safety of the golden circle.

The manta ray glided through the turmoil, leaving behind a shimmering trail as it carried them.

"Head back to the castle and put everything on lockdown!" O'Connor bellowed, his voice rough but urgent, as Lady Stewart cradled the unconscious Cordelia. "I don't know what's comin', but if somethin' happens to me, I'm countin' on ye to steer the school. And remember this before ye go: don't forget to have a bit of fun now and then. Your seriousness can be a bit much at times!"

He thrust the brooch into her hand, its surface shimmering with latent power. "This gives you control of Heaven's Gate!" he said urgently, his eyes blazing with intensity. Lady Stewart, clutching the brooch, stepped into the glowing circle with Cordelia cradled in her arms.

Once back on castle ground she summoned the staff to the headmaster's study. Inside Heaven's Gate, the dragon riders from the soon-to-be-graduating class were assembling in the auditorium, for their daily ride. Meanwhile, the staff raced to the headmaster's chambers, their movements swift and coordinated. Lady Stewart dispatched an urgent alert through the crystal network, warning all of Yurden to take shelter and brace for impending catastrophe.

With authority, Lady Stewart addressed the gathered staff, her voice commanding and resolute. "Prepare yourselves for an imminent assault and ensure the safety of our students." Recognizing the brooch, they bowed their heads in acknowledgment, murmuring, "Yes, Headmaster."

"Professor Sainnodel," she intoned with unwavering authority, "you are to ready the fleet at once—arrange them in omega formation."

"Omega formation? Are you serious?" he replied, eyes

widening in shock.

Lady Stewart's piercing gaze remained fixed on him, her silence conveying the gravity of the situation.

"Yes, Headmaster." He hurried off, making his way to the auditorium to lead the graduating class.

"Professor Agate, might I inquire if Gaia remains operational?"

The burly professor's eyes gleamed with excitement. "She certainly is!"

"Don your golem and take your station at the base of the pillar," she commanded.

Agate lumbered away, his heavy footsteps resonating down the corridor as he moved with newfound urgency.

"Professor Zephyr, kindly assist the Dragon Riders and ensure they are blessed with favorable winds."

Zephyr gave a resolute nod before heading swiftly to the stables.

"Professor Pompeii, might you summon the efreeti to lend their aid?"

Pompeii's lips curled into a wicked grin. "How delicious," he murmured, his form erupting into flames as he sped toward the Fire Plane.

"Professor Bolton, I require your Ark Dome to envelop the pillar and extend over Baba Yaga's Wood. Please await the appearance of the ice before proceeding."

Bolton nodded sharply. "Ja, Headmaster." He turned on his heels, vanishing in a blur of motion.

Lady Stewart returned to her office, where a stone pedestal held a large, floating crystal. Within it, images of the pillar, the castle, and the immense tree behind the castle swirled. She placed her palms against the orb, which instantly frosted over. Chanting in guttural Elvish, she infused the orb with magic. Once she received confirmation that the students were secure and the Dragon Riders were in formation, she pushed the orb downward.

As she did, colossal shards of ice erupted from the pillar, encasing it in a massive sphere of jagged, crystalline spikes. The immense structure gleamed ominously, a formidable fortress against the encroaching threat.

The confrontation between Rosalyn and the water dragon escalated into a tempest of chaos. The sky pit black with an ominous presence, and the storm roared with unrelenting fury. Lightning from Headmaster O'Connor blazed through the darkness, a stark beacon in the squall.

With the barrier now a fractured memory, Headmaster O'Connor navigated its shattered remnants. Felix's dragon construct had transformed into a formidable behemoth, now sprouting massive, menacing wings. As the dragon lifted from the water's surface, it unleashed a colossal rogue wave towards Lady Rosalyn.

With a swift ascent, Rosalyn evaded the watery assault. Meanwhile, sensing imminent danger, O'Connor wove an intricate weave. Lightning crackled violently around him, converging into a serpentine form of jagged electrical energy. A massive electric snake encased him, its intensity crackling with raw power.

O'Connor directed the serpent to slither across the tumultuous water, climbing a towering wave with ferocious speed. He launched himself at Felix, but his strike fell agonizingly short, and the dragon construct's tail slammed the snake backward with brutal force.

Each roar from the dragon reverberated through the storm, sending monstrous tidal waves crashing in all directions.

In a dramatic transformation, Lady Rosalyn reverted to her Fatal Temptress guise, her presence a blazing inferno amidst the chaos. "William, I'll force him down to the surface. You must bind him!" she commanded, her voice cutting through the storm.

As she ascended to a commanding height, her powers coalesced into a fiery tempest. Her gown, now a living flame, billowed with fierce intensity. Rosalyn's hands wove intricate patterns, and six fiery ribbons shot forth like whips, snapping at the dragon and drawing its fury away from O'Connor.

The battle raged on, the storm's rage a reflection of the chaos below. The elemental forces clashed, as Rosalyn's flames and O'Connor's lightning fought to contain the monstrous threat.

The Northern Coast of Yurden was engulfed in a relentless downpour, thunder crashing like a celestial war drum, though the sky remained dark and devoid of lightning.

Above this chaotic maelstrom, Lady Rosalyn danced through the tempest, her fiery presence a blazing beacon. She maneuvered with deadly grace, her ribbons of flame snapping like whips against the monstrous dragon formed around Felix. Each lash of fire against the dragon's scaly hide sent clouds of steam swirling into the storm, keeping the beast disoriented and off balance as Lady Rosalyn circled relentlessly.

The dragon roared, its every roar sending shockwaves that churned the waters beneath. Forced back to the surface, it struggled fiercely, attempting to shake off its tormentor. In a bold move, Headmaster O'Connor, in the colossal snake of lightning, shot up from underneath the water, which began coiling around the dragon, its electric tendrils constricting the beast with unyielding force.

Inside the serpentine coils, the entity fought against its confines, thrashing wildly and biting at the lightning snake in a desperate search for the headmaster hidden within its electric coils. The storm raged on, the tension palpable as the battle of wills continued amidst the roiling waters and unending thunder.

As the entity's focus shifted, Lady Rosalyn descended. Her ribbons of fire, now extended to their full, fearsome length, wrapped around the dragon, encasing it like a crimson shroud. The dragon construct roared in frustration, its scales steaming as it writhed under the relentless bindings.

The storm intensified in response, dark clouds roiling and churning so vast it stretched far above Yurden. The waters below erupted into a monstrous typhoon, its spiraling fury sent ways to the coastline. The tempest seemed to feed on the entity's growing rage, churning the sea into a violent maelstrom.

Lady Rosalyn, undeterred by the chaos, ascended with purpose. She maneuvered herself towards the dragon's head, where Felix's body lay, her movements precise and commanding against the backdrop of the swirling storm.

Lady Rosalyn traced an intricate sigil with her right hand, her long, black nails piercing the dragon's head with fierce precision. A milky-white liquid seeped from her touch, snaking its way through the watery barrier around Felix and reaching his head.

Desperation drove Lady Rosalyn to perform a final, desperate weave. She erased Felix's memories of Marcus's battle and Chance, obliterating the source of the entity's power. With the entity's focus shattered, its form disintegrated in a cataclysmic burst of energy.

The dragon's roar shattered the chaos, its fury igniting an explosion. The entity's form erupted in a violent burst, scattering its essence across the vast expanse. Lady Rosalyn was hurled into the sky, while Headmaster O'Connor was propelled toward Syornge.

Felix was expelled from the construct, tumbling through a torrent of viscous water towards Yurden. As the dragon's control over the typhoons waned, the tempestuous weather calmed, leaving the skies and waters tranquil.

The mass of water carrying Felix arced over the mountains, Heedafein, and the Divide, before crashing down into the sand.

Regaining their bearings, Headmaster O'Connor and Lady Rosalyn met amidst the remnants of the battle. The added powers that once bolstered her now lay dormant, and she found herself unable to sense Felix or the other children. Their frantic search yielded no sign of Felix—he had vanished.

Epilogue

Back at the school, waves of gossip circulated among the students and staff. Anastasia planned on squeezing Marcus for any information she could get out of him, only to learn that he was whisked to the infirmary, unconscious. Deciphering what she'd gathered from the other students, she concluded that something similar to the event at the lake must have happened—but much worse.

In another part of the world ...

The blob of goo containing Felix, launched hundreds of miles through the sky, plummeted to the earth with a thunderous impact. The goo burst apart upon landing, splattering violently like blood from a gunshot wound. This explosive force jolted Felix awake.

Disoriented and with his vision blurred by the remnants of the liquid, he struggled to free himself from the thick, jelly-like substance. As he fought his way through, he gradually felt the wind on his fingertips. He thrashed his arm back and forth to create a channel, allowing himself to breathe.

With a growing gap, he maneuvered his other arm into the space, prying it open until he could slip his head and shoulders through. As his head emerged from the goo, a noxious smell hit his nostrils, causing him to recoil in disgust.

His eyes widened in horror as he took in the view: an endless expanse of sand stretched for miles in every direction. Valleys between the dunes were filled with large pools of bubbling acid, emitting putrid fumes. Felix's eyes, now fully opened, revealed the stark and terrifying reality of the toxic wasteland surrounding him.

Where was he? And where were his friends?

To be continued ...

ABOUT THE AUTHOR

Ian Hart is a globe-trotter and creative soul whose journey through life has been shaped by a rich tapestry of experiences and influences. Born into a family that prioritized sports, Ian initially found himself navigating a world of athletic competition. However, the encouragement of an inspiring art teacher ignited his passion for self-expression, allowing his imagination to flourish.

A massive influence on Ian's artistic sensibilities is Memoirs of a Geisha, a work that deepened his appreciation for the beauty and complexity of Asian culture. He also draws inspiration from the captivating narratives of the Final Fantasy video game series, along with the epic tales found in fantasy movies and vibrant anime. His love for games like Magic: The Gathering and Dungeons & Dragons has enabled him to weave intricate narratives and character-driven adventures.

Having lived abroad and immersed himself in diverse cultures, Ian embraces the richness of art and philosophy that transcends borders. Now, as a writer and artist, he invites readers into his imaginative worlds, where every page is a portal to adventure, self-discovery, and the magic of the everyday. With a heart that beats for creativity and a mind that thrives on exploration, Ian Hart is on a mission to inspire others to embrace their own stories.

www.ingramcontent.com/pod-product-compliance
Lightning Source LLC
Chambersburg PA
CBHW070753280626
47162CB00016B/212